# THE MORELS

# THE MORELS

## Christopher Hacker

**SOHO**

Published by
Soho Press, Inc.
853 Broadway
New York, NY 10003

Library of Congress Cataloging-in-Publication Data

Hacker, Christopher, 1972–
The Morels / Christopher Hacker.
p. cm.
ISBN 978-1-61695-243-3 (alk. paper)
eISBN: 978-1-61695-244-0
1. Families—New York (State)—New York—Fiction. 2. Influence (Literary, artistic, etc.)—Fiction. 3. Family secrets—Fiction. 4. Domestic fiction. 5. Psychological fiction. I. Title.
PS3608.A248M67 2013
813'.6—dc23     2012036639

Interior design by Janine Agro, Soho Press, Inc.

Printed in the United States of America

10 9 8 7 6 5 4 3 2 1

*For Joanna, and for Mom: Every writer should be so lucky.*

# THE MORELS

# 1

# ARTHOUSE

THE EDITOR I WAS TO fire worked out of his one bedroom in Herald Square. He'd been the lowest bidder on our project by far, his single stipulation that we meet him no more than once a week and he be allowed the other six to work undisturbed, a stipulation we'd had to accept — he was the only editor we could afford — until an old classmate of the director's volunteered to cut the film for free. The director told me about it that morning over eggs and coffee at the Galaxy Diner. The inconvenience of starting over, he explained, would be minor compared with the inconvenience of filing for Chapter 11.

It was 1999. The last Checker cab in the city had just been retired. All over, people were stockpiling canned peas, just in case. I was seven years out of college, lived at home with my mother, worked for free by day, and by night swept stray popcorn and condom wrappers from the back rows of the arthouse on Houston.

One always got the sense upon entering the editor's apartment that he was being caught unawares. He answered the door in thick glasses, pillowcase imprint on his cheek. He had a bachelor's tendency toward strewn clothing and empty beer bottles. It was clear he slept in the living room: gathering the bedding from the sofa like a doghoused husband, he'd make a spot for us while he went about his morning ablutions — and we, waiting with our coffee and script notes, were privy to each splash and fart and groan—emerging with Coke bottles shed for bloodshot contacts, ready, as he put it, for business. The bedroom was where the "baby" slept. The windows went magically dim whenever the sun appeared, giving the place with its blinking lights the cool phosphorescence of a command center. A rack of industrial-strength video recorders stood in a corner. Three monitors displayed the frozen grimaces of our actors, time-code numbers in letterboxed margins. The room was decked out in charcoal acoustic tiling, and against the far wall was an opulent leather couch—to impress the clients, he'd said on our first meeting as we sat smoothing our hands across it. Glass coffee table. Brushed-steel coasters. The editor came in and took up the cockpit chair in front of the monitors. The director opened his binder, and they set to work.

It was a white-trash retelling of *Hamlet*. A young man returns to his trailer park from a stint at reform school to find his junk-yard-king father murdered and his widowed mother shacked up with his uncle, the tractor salesman. The dialogue was funny and hillbilly absurd and conjured a vivid world that by sheer force of will seemed already to exist. The writer-director was a recent NYU grad from Sri Lanka. His father, a Sinhalese tobacco magnate, was reputedly the third-richest man in South Asia. The movie we were making was his graduation present.

Editing seemed mostly about fixing the many blunders of production: underexposed footage lightened, boom mics cropped, flubbed lines trimmed. The problem of the day involved a Winnebago crash, which appeared in these monitors about as perilous as the backcountry amblings of a retiree couple. Something to do with poor camera placement. The editor tried speeding up the footage. I normally enjoyed our weekly sessions here. The couch was like the backseat of a chauffeured Bentley; I took careless pleasure being the passenger on this three-hour journey, allowing the two of them up front to bicker over outframes and cutaways. But today was a car-sick three hours. Their bickering, usually playful, had turned ugly. "Decreasing the frame rate won't work," the director said.

"It looks better."

"It looks slapstick."

"Well, I can't cut what I don't have."

"The word you're looking for is *talent*."

This was my cue. "Let's take a break," I suggested. "Get some lunch, talk things over."

I should have been straightforward. I should have sat him down before he'd even gone into the bathroom to put in his contacts. But I had never fired anyone. How was this supposed to go? While we waited at the fourteenth-floor elevators, arms folded, mingling with our brass reflections, I tried to think of a good segue. *And speaking of awkward silences.* The panel indicated that the left bank was stopped on three and the right bank was on its way down, pausing at each and every floor along the way. Some homeschooled brat, probably, pressing all the buttons before jumping off.

There was an open door at the end of the hall. Someone was walking back and forth inside an apartment. A brass luggage cart was parked outside, hung with fresh dry cleaning. At a certain point the person (I could see now that it was a man) took the clothes off the hanger and disappeared back inside, then came back out and wheeled the cart in our direction. "Sorry," he said. "I'd use the service elevator, but the gentleman with the key doesn't work on weekdays."

He thumbed the DOWN button—already lit—then turned to puzzle me over for a moment before testing out my name, like a question. He reached out and gave me his hand, which was firm and damp, and I shook it, trying not to let it show that I had absolutely no idea who he was.

This is a problem, one I've had as long as I can remember, and often gets me into trouble. In eighth-grade shop class I lost the tip of my left index finger to the jigsaw, and it was only as I was leaving that the teacher discovered the stains coming through my front pocket and the tissue soaked in blood. At precisely the moments I should be calling for assistance (*I'm sorry, how do I know you?*),

I freeze up and am forced to fake my way through. He said his name, but I didn't catch it. I nodded. "Been a while."

"Fourteen years," he said. I asked him what he was up to, only half listening to his answer because I was suddenly aware that I had not introduced my colleagues. He said something about being out in the wilds of Queens since I'd seen him last and that he was now a husband and, if I could believe it — he could hardly believe it himself sometimes — a father. Fourteen years? I tried counting backward. Certainly it put him out of college range. High school?

He was a head taller than me, at least, and I'm not short. He wasn't handsome: eyes sunken, ears jutting out like pouted lips, brows joined. The backs of his hands were covered with hair. He was a hairy man. I could see this in the rash on his neck; it was skin that needed frequent shaving. The only place hair was not persisting, it seemed, was along his receding hairline. It was a face that hadn't reached its ideal age yet, I thought, like seeing a grandparent in an old Super 8 and finding the familiar face strange in its youth, improbable. And like someone a generation or two older, he had a gravity about him. He was tall without managing to stoop. Though his nose was large, it gave his face dignity. He had on chinos and a windbreaker, loafers with white socks. It was the outfit of someone who was stumped by words like *phat* and *fo' shizzle* and who, if you took him out to a bar, would complain the music was too loud, and couldn't we just go someplace where we could all sit down? None of this, to say the least, rang a bell.

I turned to Sri Lanka and the editor now, but they had been done with this conversation before it began, striking up their argument again as if this man standing before me were invisible; and indeed to them he was. The movie business is an exclusive club, and to us insiders the rest of you are pitiable wastes of our time. If you were to say that we're all just arrogant pricks, that you hate the movies and wouldn't want anything to do with the business of it, what we hear is: *I'm jealous.* Just observe the way we move into your quiet neighborhood with our cube trucks and honey-wagons, like the Holy Roman Army, even the lowliest of us with our headsets barking orders at you to cross the street: *Don't you see we're filming here?*

The man had pulled out his wallet, apologizing he didn't have a more recent picture ("Boxed up," he explained) and was showing me a snapshot that had obviously been cropped with scissors to fit in the little plastic photo sleeve. It showed a dark-haired green-eyed beauty holding a child—a boy, if the blue overalls were any indication—old enough to be sitting up and young enough to be held neatly in his mother's lap and for the mother to have her chin on his head. The photo sleeve was worn almost opaque, and pocket debris had been stuck inside long enough to have formed bumps around the larger particles. I ran my thumb across it. Like Braille, or an oyster forming its pearl. I handed the photo back and asked their names. He was older than me, by a couple of years. I couldn't think of anyone with whom I had been friends back then who hadn't been my own age. I knew only one married couple, newlyweds—they'd done it on a dare—and was friends with no parents.

What was I up to these days, he wondered, putting away his wallet. I told him about my career in film (here I introduced Sri Lanka and the editor), leaving out mention of my moonlight occupation at the movie theater. I offered an anecdote about production and its misadventures: the night of the Winnebago stunt. The punch line had me picking the short straw and suck-siphoning gasoline from a grip truck because New Jersey gas stations close early on Sundays. Who knew! It was a well-honed bit, one that usually had people in stitches and got that glow of envy going in their eyes. But my friend here was curiously unimpressed. Not that he didn't listen politely and chuckle on cue, but there was something in the quality of his listening that made my own words sound in my ears like a child trying to impress the family dinner guest. He told me it all seemed very exciting, and although his tone wasn't exactly condescending, it was clear that he was saying this only because he could sense I wanted to hear it.

I turned the subject back his way, in part as a stall tactic—Sri

Lanka and the editor were making noises about the stairs, and I had no desire for the lunchtime conversation these fourteen flights would lead us to—but also because the new mystery of who this man was exactly had taken root. He told me he was teaching, or rather would be teaching as soon as the new semester began, at the university uptown. He went on to explain in an offhand way, almost dismissively, that he'd written a book.

Sri Lanka broke in, looking at our guest for the first time. "So what's up with the elevators?"

"The right one's out of order," he said. As if to corroborate, the alarm began clanging.

The editor walked over to the stairway exit. Sri Lanka followed and on the threshold shot me a look that said, *Now.*

I apologized and shook the man's hand again. I wished him luck, a wish he returned with an ironic smile. Was it really so obvious?

On the jog down, Sri Lanka aborted our mission. The timing was all off, he whispered, and so was the power dynamic. We would have to wait until next week to fire the editor. I didn't get it but whispered back that I agreed wholeheartedly. We called it a day after lunch at a deli with upscale steam tables and plastic-utensil seating, which left me with some time to kill before my shift.

At Tower Records I gave over a solid hour to the various listening stations. Under the greasy clamp of those headphones, eyes closed, I tried to lose myself to the music. Instead, I pictured my long-lost friend's odd face. It *was* familiar. But from where? With thirty minutes to spare before my shift, I stopped in at Shakespeare Books.

He'd mentioned the title in the course of our chat, and at lunch I scribbled it down on a napkin. I approached a kid in pajama bottoms, staff tag around his neck, and handed him the napkin. I had been expecting a blank stare, but was led without hesitation to an island display in the middle of the store. Judging by the assured path he traced through the maze of shelves, this was not an uncommon request. He disappeared and left me to sort through the paperbacks on display. The sign overhead designated them as STAFF RECOMMENDED.

I found the book, partially hidden by a new translation of Borges's *Collected Fictions*. Literature? I had been expecting something more, I don't know, academic: philosophy, some proof disproving some other proof. I picked it up. It was a slim volume entitled *Goldmine/Landmine*. On the cover, in bold, was the name:

Arthur Morel.

My job at the theater wasn't the worst thing in the world. There was a kind of glee to our aisle frolic around the emptied auditorium, screen blank, lights up. A perverse pleasure taking in our janitorial duty. Impatient for our rightful place on the red carpet, we ushers spent our downtime debating which actors might play parts in our unsold scripts, dateless schoolgirls planning outfits to the junior prom.

I took my fifteen in the cement break pit with a cup of root beer and a bag of popcorn, then made my way to the ticket booth with Arthur's slim book for the rest of what I hoped would be a slow evening. From behind the bulletproof face of the theater, the booth contained an earplugged rush of silence. The flutter of money being counted, the pebble clatter of change in the pan — these were the only sounds inside. An entire marching band on parade down the street would register as a polite and twinkling spectacle — and, if you were reading a book, not even that. When the shadow of a customer would darken your page, you'd flip on the thin otherworldly chatter of the squawk box. "Two adults," they'd say, as though they were announcing themselves to you generically, in the third person. The machine would clunk up two tickets that you'd slide through the change pan. It was a welcome isolation from the crowd control the other positions required. You relaxed into a crouch on your stool until your butt got sore, just in time for the manager to come count you out.

To my frustration, however, it was not a slow night. Everyone was here to see the new Almodóvar, which had probably just been nominated for something because until now the screen it flickered on played to a virtually empty theater. I read the dedication page four times before giving in to the demands of the throng. It would just have to wait. The late show got out at 11:17. After closing, and if I walked briskly enough, I could make it through my front door by midnight.

Home, I stripped off my tie and had a seat at the upright piano parked under my bedroom window, a mid-century Baldwin that hadn't been tuned since before I left for college. It was a sad old horse. Its uneven keys had the look of nicotine-stained fingernails. The mahogany veneer was splintering off in places; along the side that faced the bare radiator pipe, its finish was blistering like a ripe sunburn. I switched on the small gooseneck lamp on the stand and got out Arthur's book. According to the preliminary pages, it had appeared in hardcover a year prior. There was no author photo, and the About-the-Author, which I was hoping might offer a clue, was not helpful. "Arthur Morel lives in New York City with his wife and son." On the back were several blurbs. Russell Banks and Martin Amis both effused about this debut talent. The *New Yorker*: ". . . an astonishing feat of language." The *New York Times Book Review*: ". . . unflinching eye for difficult truths; one trembles to think where that eye will turn next."

*Astonishing. Unflinching.* I formed a silent chord with my right hand, bringing each key down slowly, to the bump of the key bed.

It seemed that Arthur hadn't changed a bit.

# 2

# A P P L A U S E

AM FIFTEEN—FOR A CHILD PRODIGY, something of a late bloomer. It's Saturday. I am standing on the platform at Christopher Street Station waiting for the Uptown local. This is the age of the brass token, before the hipster renaissance in Brooklyn and Queens, before If You See Something Say Something. You might encounter any number of things on the platform in those days. This morning: a blood-soaked sock and a paper cup filled with quarters, on the cup's side scrawled TAKE ONE I DAIR YOU. As I wait for the train, I try to imagine the scenario in which these two props intersected. The head and rear cars are usually empty at this hour, and I have been warned against boarding either. Safety in numbers, which will be made pointedly clear later that same year when a kid not that much older than myself will enter and sit down beside me in a cleared-out car. He will put a knife to my groin and demand twenty dollars, and after I hand him a wallet with only a few singles in it, he will punch me in the face and take off at the next stop through the ding-dong closing doors.

I board somewhere toward the middle and find a seat. Between my knees, my cello in its pleather case, on my lap my pleather valise. It is a forty-five-minute ride, time enough for music-theory homework— coordinating bouts of scribbling to the periodic moment of stillness at a station. Each stop accumulates and rotates out passengers, and once we pass 86th Street it's mostly us, instrument cases between our legs, working out difficult fingerings on an arm or a knee. A curious look from a paint-splattered construction worker, from a Hispanic mother with a bag of groceries. The subways shriek and buck, dying with a shudder between stations. Sitting in the dark is like floating, the scraping squeal of a passing train a flicker of blue sparks against the scratched windows. Then it wakes and drags itself along to the next stop.

From the exit at 116th and Broadway it's a six-block walk. We fan out, trudging our instruments past the gated Ivy League community, the dozen or so of us on a dozen separate journeys up this hill; after all, it's not as though we're friends. We recognize one another: co-principals in a chamber ensemble or the person whose ear-training homework you might once have copied from. We nod, say hey — once a week isn't enough to learn names. This isn't summer camp; there are no blood-sworn bonds. We dress differently here, in our holiday best, button-down collars, black lace-up shoes, as though we are attending the presence of God.

The conservatory occupies two square blocks, and during the week it is home to grown-ups from around the world who possess the dedication to roam its hallowed halls but not the connections to get them into Julliard, our city rival; Juilliard students will tell you it is merely skill they lack. Either way, on Saturdays the place is ours. In its arched ceilings and marble staircases is the grandeur of a Gothic boarding school. I try always to arrive at least an hour before my first class: winter months I am encumbered with up to twenty pounds of stuff, and the lockers along the southern corridor are only for the college students; if I don't want to be stuck carting this load from class to class, I'll need to find someplace to stow it.

On the second and third floors, a hive of windowless chambers. The plum carpeting, threadbare and pocked with cigarette burns, gives off the salty reek of an old overcoat. It's a ghostly cacophony here — looped phrases of familiar pieces, muffled arpeggios, down the hall a teenage mezzo calling *me! me! me! me! me!* A declaration of self among all this disembodied noise. I am looking for an empty room. The place is packed. I should have come earlier; today is, after all, Competition Day.

The first Saturday in March, same weekend as the Oscars, it is the public face to all the private striving that goes on behind these closed doors. The Concerto Competition is juried by six members of the senior faculty and chaired by Mr. Strasser, conductor of our top-tier symphony. Auditions are held on the same stage on which the winner will perform. To win is to become a celebrity, implicitly declared the school's finest musician, and debut as featured soloist in the Spring Concert, a sold-out audience of parents and professionals looking for the latest talent.

My cello teacher harbored no ambitions for me in this arena, but for three years my piano teacher has urged me to learn a concerto; until now I've refused. I already knew I wasn't the school's finest player; I didn't need a panel of judges confirming it publicly. But this fall, the fall of my sophomore year, I have been learning Liszt's *Totentanz*, a showy one-movement fantasia for piano and orchestra. I picked it up one afternoon after hearing it on the radio. It's too hard for me; getting my performance to tempo is like trying to push a stalled truck uphill, and I have yet to run through the piece from memory without having to stop and retrace my steps; undoubtedly, I will lose the competition, but commanding that dark whirlwind, an entire battalion of players in support, with a packed house bearing witness to my greatness: it is an image too tempting not to pursue.

I find an empty room with a piano on its last legs. Its candle board has been scarred by several generations of frustrated hands, its keys drummed on so often and continuously that there are divots in the ivory, some worn through to the wooden key block. I take off my coat and pace the room. My audition is at ten forty-five. I have some time yet. After a vertiginous, heart-pounding run through the piece, I head off to visit my piano teacher, making sure on my way out to set my coat conspicuously on the piano bench and open several scores on the stand so that anyone peering in will have the impression of my imminent return. It will be necessary, however, to visit my stuff frequently, today of all days, or I might come back to find it in a pile in the hall.

On my way from the room I pass a kid I've gotten to know this semester—gangly, hands swinging at his sides—lost in thought.

Arthur, I say as our paths cross.

Hey, Arthur says. You go yet?

Not yet. You?

Heading down now.

Earlier that year up in the conservatory library. Trying to find a willing accomplice from whom to copy ear-training homework. Class in an hour. Arthur, set up at a table alone. In front of him a spread of pages. I asked him what he was doing.

Writing, he said.

I examined the pages, which were peppered with eraser debris. A handwritten score to some sort of chamber piece, at least a dozen parts, all marked out in a careful, childlike hand.

Composing? But you're at the library. You need a piano, don't you?

I have absolute pitch, he said, so no. I don't need a piano. Besides, it's so noisy down there I can hardly think.

Ear training must be a piece of cake for you then.

You could say that.

Got the homework handy, by any chance?

After my encounter with Arthur in the library, I began noticing him around. He played violin, though I only knew this from the case he toted and the callus on his neck; if we'd shared billing in any of the monthly group recitals, I wasn't aware. He rode the subway, too, and on the few mornings I'd seen him, he was already aboard, which I assumed meant he lived on Staten Island: the subway line terminated at Battery Park, where the ferry docked on the Manhattan side. He was, like me here, something of a loner, which led me to think of him as an only child of divorced parents. On a nice day,

I'd see him on the front steps or during the winter cross-legged in the hallway, reading some old paperback. When looking for a free room, I'd occasionally stumble in on someone I knew in the throes of a particularly passionate phrase; practice is a private activity, and having someone witness it an odd sort of embarrassment, not unlike walking in on someone, pants down, in a bathroom stall. I had never walked in on Mr. Too Good for a Piano.

This semester I'd signed up for a late-afternoon elective: Compositional Technique. Something about that image of the young composer in the library, laboring over his handcrafted score; it was impressive, and around here—among an entire schoolful of child musicians who were younger and more advanced than me—I longed to be someone impressive. Maybe this would help. I could cultivate a scarf, a pencil behind the ear. There were fewer than a dozen of us in this class, including Arthur.

Every week our teacher brought under his arm a small stack of records. After selecting one and placing it onto the turntable, he turned up the volume so high that the pops between tracks could be felt as thuds in the rib cage: a drumbeat to usher in the agony of the Postwar Era. He called these listening sessions *ear calisthenics*. We were stretching our ears, he said. Listening to each piece at full volume was intended to wake us up. Tonality's a drug, he shouted over the music, that lulls you into a complacent stupor! Each piece was a new shock to the system. Each had the quality of spectacle.

Ligeti: the white-knuckle dissonance of a horror movie.

Xenakis: musical instruments performing roadwork construction.

Penderecki: the chaos of an emergency room after a nuclear blast.

Arthur was the only one here who seemed genuinely engaged, who didn't wince through the pieces or laugh at the more over-the-top pratfalls of sound, who didn't look every week as though he'd signed up for the wrong class. Arthur listened rapt, eyes closed, flaring his nostrils as though he were trying to pick up the music's scent. His face recorded the subtlest changes in tone—now hopeful, now restless, now burning with rage! — and through his expressions it seemed clear he got the music in a way that the rest of us did not. Although I thought he was a brownnosing phony, another part of me believed in his understanding enough to take cues for what I should be hearing in these impenetrable walls of sound.

We were given writing assignments that came out less like music than the solution to a puzzle: *Compose a piano étude that will pose a significant challenge to the performer — with only four notes.* If one half of the class was spent at the turntable, the other half was spent around the class upright, the teacher sight-reading our pieces unless we decided to volunteer. As a result of the tight constraints, everyone's assignments sounded interchangeably similar. After one was performed, Arthur was often first to comment, often in the form of a question: *Is that phrase even possible on the clarinet? Won't that be lost if you give it to the viola?* Questions addressed to the student but seemed meant for the teacher. This confusion often provoked a standoff, a kind of stumped silence that grew hostile and that the teacher finally had to break by rephrasing Arthur's question to all of us: *Well? Who can tell me if this note is playable on a B-flat clarinet?* I imagined that the teacher found Arthur as irritating as the rest of us did. When Arthur spoke, we gave each other looks. *What is this guy's problem?*

On my morning subway ride uptown the week before the Concerto Competition, I was jolted awake by Arthur, suddenly beside me. Well, he said, what did *you* think about it? As if resuming some conversation momentarily interrupted. How long had he been here? Had he come over from another seat, or had he been sitting here all along?

I assumed he was referring to the recording we had listened to the week prior, one of the more outrageous experiments from the sixties.

A bootleg tape of the performance:

Under the surf-like ambient noise, a man's voice murmuring,

the creaking of someone walking around on a stage, an incoherent shout, a lull into which comes some coughing, the audience shifting in their seats — then piano sounds, pounding note clusters (fists on keys?), followed by the tinkling refrain of a familiar piece (Schubert?) — pause — a tremendous clap! (the piano's lid being dropped) — the reverberations of piano strings — then a shuffle, grunting, some creaking, several gasps (the audience), shouts (*Hey! What!*) — and a thunderous *crash* that overloads the microphone. Stop tape.

The teacher passed around an oversize mimeographed "score" afterward, which was merely a sheet of paper with a list of instructions:

Recite the Declaration of Independence;

Play "incredulously";

Picture Dresden after the bombing;

Perform the first piece that comes to mind;

Roll the piano off the stage.

Interestingly, those students who had been quick to guffaw at the slightest musical provocation sat stony; the score passing hands might as well have been a crime-scene photo. It was Arthur who laughed. At the sound of the piano crashing, he whooped with laughter. He laughed for so long that he got out of breath and had to wipe his eyes. It was the sound of someone coming unhinged. And when the score came around to him, it sent him on another peal. Even our teacher looked concerned.

But sitting beside me now, he tried to explain. The guy pushed the piano off the stage! I mean, come on: *boom!* The audience, jumping out of the seats? *Watch it, this guy's nuts!* And the stage manager: *You fool, do you have any idea how much that Bösendorfer is worth?* The performer: *But it was in the score!* The composer: *I meant* offstage, *not off* the *stage!* Can't you just picture it?

The problem was, I *could* picture it: the growing alarm, the performer's pounding fists, the incoherent bits of schoolboy lessons. You don't know how far this guy is going to go. Someone whispers, *We should get out of here.* Something dangerous about his prowl about the stage. You yourself want to leave—your nape hairs are tingling—but you're fighting with your impulse not to be rude. And then he's rolling that piano toward the edge, toward you, and you're thinking all the way up to the moment it topples off: He's bluffing. He won't do it. And as loud as the recording seemed, to be there in person for the crash, two thousand pounds of hardwood and iron? And not just any hunk of furniture: a piano, the very embodiment of grace. To see it toppled like that. It must have been ghastly, like watching an elephant felled.

Exactly! Arthur said. Great art should be dangerous. It should make the hairs on the back of your neck stand up! We neuter music the way we listen to it, culturing it up. It's polite chitchat, it's the required two encores, then off for cocktails where a string quartet plays quote 'classics' end quote in the background. Next time you're at a recital look around at your neighbor. Reading the program, dozing off, anything but actually listening! There but not really there. He's wondering how many more movements before he can clap, how many minutes before intermission. Biding time between breaks in the music. This is what's become of the art we practice: an excuse to be seen, a cultural equivalent to eating your spinach. Now, put that same man in the audience of that piano recital we listened to last week and woo-boy! You can bet he's going to sit up and listen.

Since our introduction at the library, my interactions with Arthur had been marginal, brief. This kind of talk was new.

Odd thing I noticed: Arthur's hands were dirty. Green-black under the nails, grime in the crevices of his fingers. And although his clothes seemed fresh enough—hair fluffy from a morning washing—he gave off the sharp whiff of cat pee. He spoke as though he weren't used to speaking his thoughts out loud. And in the strange paradox of the very shy, he had a candor that bordered on rude.

But is it worth listening to, I said. That's the question. I'd rather be asleep through a Brahms piano sonata than awake for a piano being rolled off the stage. I mean, what is that? It's nothing.

What's the purpose of music?

You're asking me?

I'm asking you to think about it. To edify? To please?

To cause a shiver of pleasure.

To cause an emotional response, right. To evoke a mood. Nobody's arguing that this piece is in the same league as a Brahms sonata, as quote 'good' end quote. You give people a choice of recital fare, and they choose Brahms, no question. But which program in the end will fulfill these most basic of musical goals? The one you end up sleeping through or the one that causes you to nearly wet your pants as you run blindly for the exit?

Things I find out about Arthur on our ride up: parents not divorced, not living on Staten Island. I was also technically wrong about his being an only child—he had two older half siblings, his father's by another marriage.

Where did he go to school, I wondered.

No school, he said. The plus side of eccentric parents. He chuckled. The homeschool advantage, you might call it.

So your parents are your teachers?

Not really.

I emerged with Arthur from the station into the crisp light of a New York winter morning feeling as though we had sorted out something essential on this ride, untangled some mystery about music, about our futures. Arthur's violin case, held by its side handle, swung in time to his step. He had a bounding gait that sprung from the balls of his sneakered feet and left me scrambling to keep up, cello's wide hip thumping my side, a reluctant partner in a three-legged race.

Don't you need to take the Regents, I asked. Or, I don't know, a diploma?

For what?

You're not planning on going to college?

You mean conservatory? Do you think they care about SAT scores or whether I failed biology? Have you seen the guys who take over our practice rooms at the end of the day? Half of them don't speak a word of English. The only thing the admissions committee cares about? He holds out his violin case and shakes it. Many of the serious string players carried their instruments around in fancy bulletproof luggage. Not Arthur. Arthur's case was standard issue: violin shaped, leatherette coming up in places. The kind of case that makes you think *machine gun*.

Besides, he says, once I win this competition, I'll be a shoo-in for wherever.

What are you playing?

Haven't decided yet.

But the competition's next week!

I leave my piano teacher's room feeling short of breath and make the long slow march to the auditorium with five minutes to spare. Although I managed to get through the piece for my teacher without stopping, however timidly, I am not confident that I'll be able to repeat the success up there in front of the judges. Many instructors have canceled class today, and in the hallways there is a feeling of celebration. It must be the surplus adrenaline in the air. On the tongue the taste of ozone and Band-Aids.

The back doors to the auditorium are open. I take a seat in the last row, in the shadow of the overhang. Some are picnicking, others napping or fingering their instruments. To one side of me is Diane Flagello's studio, her half-dozen students leaning in for a whispered pep talk. To the other side of me a girl with a shock of red hair is on the brink of hyperventilating. Her mother is rubbing her back and offering her a juice box. Onstage, a violinist works his way through a Mozart violin concerto. His playing is polite, respectable; you could take it home to meet your parents. I have left my score with my teacher as a way of insisting that I've memorized this piece, as a way perhaps of persuading myself into a certain degree of courage, but I see right away what a foolish move this is. I feel naked without my score. Others are clutching theirs like prayer books, eyes closed, moving their lips while rocking back and forth in their seats. I consider going back for it but am stopped by the sound of my name being stage-whispered.

It's a girl in my teacher's studio whose name I forget. She scoots into an empty seat beside me and says, Have you gone yet? Oh, I can tell you haven't. She's a year younger than me, chubby, Chinese American. You look nervous, she says. So am I. Look at my hands, they're actually shaking. And damp—feel.

Two years ago, this girl and I kissed. That's the wrong word. *Made out* is what we did. I was thirteen. We were, for some reason, in an empty classroom on the top floor. It was late afternoon, and most everyone had cleared the building. She asked me to be her audience while she played through a recital program she was due to perform the following afternoon at her church. Something like that. She played it through, and afterward we sat together, improvising clunky duets at the classroom upright. The dust-glittery light through the window went amber, and then it went violet, and then we were sitting in the dark. And as the quality of light changed, so did the atmosphere. The notion of this person next to me as a member of the opposite sex hit me like a revelation. We stopped talking. I turned, slowly, so as not to break whatever this absence of light had cast, and found the wide outline of her upturned face. She was chewing mint gum, and I tasted that contradiction—warm tongue and cool mint—for hours afterward.

We stumbled out into the empty corridor bleary eyed, holding each other's damp hands, parting ways in the company of the security guard at the front door. There existed now a pleasant tension between us, a play of eye contact and little smiles whenever we happened to be in each other's presence.

But she is currently doing little for my nerves; what small degree of focus I gathered on the walk down from my teacher's room has scattered. She is telling me a story about something-or-other involving people I don't know. I fight the urge to stick my fingers in my ears. *Please,* I want to tell her, *shut the hell up!*

The jury sits some rows up on the right. I can make out each member's frosty head: they are the only ones here who look at ease, bored even. They're running late, three people behind. I should be ascending the stage at this moment, nodding to the accompanist, feeling the stage lights sunburn my neck and the backs of my hands, uncertain as I scoot my bench in and adjust its height whether I will remember the opening chords.

The violinist onstage is wrapping up the rondo when I see Arthur in the aisle up front, violin under his arm, tightening his bow. He is executing a stiff-legged rocking side to side, on his face an expression of stern concentration. When his eyes are in my line of sight, I offer a little wave.

Who's that, my studio mate asks. Pei-Yee: that's her name! She tells people to call her Peggy. This little triumph of memory gives my confidence a momentary lift. There is a smattering of applause as the violinist finishes and climbs down to put his instrument away.

Arthur says something to the jury chair, Mr. Strasser, and then takes the stage.

He gets his note from the piano and, holding his instrument like a ukulele, strums it into tune. Some players will obsess over tuning their instruments, drawing on each string and testing it against the harmonics of the adjacent string as though performing a laboratory experiment, like a tuned instrument might help with tone deafness. But for Arthur, it's a few pinches at the pegs and a curt nod to the accompanist, who then begins.

Arthur tucks his instrument into the crook of his neck and raises his bow.

Composition was my last class of the day, and afterward I usually hung back, letting Arthur go ahead of me to spare myself the annoyance of an hour-long journey with the class know-it-all. But on the day of our morning subway chat, I made a point of following him out so that we could continue our discussion.

Applause is the kiss of death, Arthur said. They might as well be saying, *I didn't hear a note you played*. You can feel it in your hands. Bring them together, *bam-bam-bam*, until they're numb. Numb: key word. It's a white noise that replaces the noise the performer makes, like they're erasing what they've just heard. Numbing their ears, numbing their minds. God forbid they let the experience linger. It might—gasp!—actually have an effect on them. And they wouldn't want that. This is supposed to be a nice, quote 'evening out.' Wouldn't want to spoil things.

But who are you imagining, I said. I think you underestimate people's desire to be moved. This audience of yours, they're caricatures. What about me? I mean, I'm in the audience. Our composition teacher's in the audience. We're listening to your performance and are moved. And so we clap. It's the only response available to us to show our appreciation.

My point is about politeness. It's the death of art. You may be applauding out of genuine appreciation, but the guy next to you, maybe he didn't particularly care for me, but he doesn't want to appear rude, so he applauds, and by adding his applause to yours, he's devalued it, canceled it out.

Then what would you have me do?

It's not about what I'd have you do, it's what I'd have your *neighbor* do. It wasn't always like this. Think of Gluck, what the reception at the premiere of *Iphigenia* must have been like. These people were *barbarians*. I don't even think they had seats back then. The guy behind you slopping his mead onto your shoulder, fistfights, if you had to piss you did it in the corner. Do you think they clapped *politely* if they didn't particularly like what they heard?

You're thinking of Elizabethan theater. Gluck was Vienna, the Enlightenment. Your average Hans didn't go to the opera. It was strictly the powdered-wig crowd.

Then Monteverdi, *Orpheus*, if you want Elizabethan times. Fine, or a more recent example, *Le Sacre du Printemps.*

May 1913. Théâtre des Champs-Élysées in Paris. Stravinsky's savage rhythms and Nijinsky's flat-footed rendition of the pagan rites of rural Russia provoke catcalls from the audience. Fellow composer in attendance Camille Saint-Saëns storms out. Supporters shout for the catcallers to sit down, and the catcallers tell the supporters to shut the hell up, and soon enough a punch is thrown, followed by an aisle brawl. The scene, astonishingly, degenerates into a full-scale riot. Stravinsky slips out the back door just as the Paris police are arriving to restore order.

That's real, Arthur said. That's honest. A standing ovation from that crowd would be something to be proud of. But these days, a standing ovation is meaningless. It's gotten so an ovation is expected of any performance that doesn't go horribly awry. How absurd is that? Go see *Sacre* at the City Ballet today, and I guarantee you five out of five performances get a standing ovation. Why? Have the performances gotten that much better? Or the music itself? Has our intrepid composition teacher given a private ear stretching to each audience member so she can appreciate Stravinsky better? Hardly. They're standing and clapping because it's expected. You say it's all one big dare game with modern music, that composers are alienating their audiences at a time when we should be cultivating them, but this code of manners, this politeness, is smothering art, and composers are just trying to fight for their survival. That's why we're pushing pianos off stages, why we prefer the riot to the ovation. The riot has become the ovation of the twentieth century. At least it's honest.

You're telling me that if you win this competition, when you get up there on that stage and perform, you don't want people to clap?

I want people to be honest. Anyway, they'd be clapping for my performance, not for Mozart.

What about your cadenza, I ask. (That moment in a concerto where the orchestra stops playing, and the soloist, freed from the baton's constraints — freed even from the composer's constraints — is given space to let loose, to show his stuff. It's an open hole in the score, to be filled by the performer. Way back when, it had been an improvised flourish less than a minute long, though throughout the ages this practice has devolved into lengthy, shameless displays of virtuosity. Rarely improvised anymore, these spots that composers once left blank have been filled in by transcriptions of legacy performances — Paganini, Heifetz, Kreisler — included in modern editions; and, although marked "optional" most often they were performed verbatim.)

I said, I assume you're not planning on performing one of those store-bought cadenzas, are you?

I wasn't planning to, he said. No.

So you're telling me that when writing your own cadenza, you're going to go for the *riot* and not the *ovation*?

Maybe I should, he said.

Mozart's Concerto for Violin and Orchestra, K271a. Odd choice for someone counting on winning this competition. Of the dozen violinists on the roster, half are playing Mozart violin concertos. Arthur is one of three this year auditioning with the Seventh; and both of the others study in the same studio with Arthur. He isn't exactly making himself heard with his choice of repertoire.

But the moment Arthur's bow touches string, it is clear why he's chosen the piece all the other violinists are playing: he's encouraging comparison. The difference is so clear, so sharp, as to surprise one into a new awareness about the nature of greatness. Arthur's control is astonishing. His *pianissimos* a throaty whisper, his *fortissimos* a roar. His sound is a personality all to itself, a presence that seems to hover somewhere between the top of his head and the grand, twinkling chandelier. Whereas with the previous player each gesture was a reminder of a technique perfectly mastered, Arthur's playing is somehow beyond technique and manages that contradictory illusion of making the impossible seem effortless. It is as though Arthur is displaying some essential mystery of music's unalterable truth, a truth the other player's fastidious attention to technique all but obscured.

Holy moly, Pei-Yee whispers, crouched in her seat, this guy's good!

By the end of the first movement, there isn't a single person in that concert hall not held rapt by his sound. If I am any measure of what the rest of the contestants are feeling right then, Arthur won to a collective capitulation.

When he is done, there is a moment of awestruck silence. I'm thinking of the end of *Close Encounters of the Third Kind*, when the mother ship lands and everyone watches this perfect glowing being emerge, ending once and for all any doubts any of them still might have had. That is who we have in our midst. Or maybe it's just the opposite. Maybe before us is the only real native of a land in which the rest of us — including the judges — are aliens. The only one among us who can speak the language fluently.

I tell Pei-Yee that I have to use the bathroom (Wait, I think you're next!) and go to my practice room and gather my things. My mother is surprised to see me home so early but is glad for the extra hand and enlists me in helping her with dinner.

And dare I ask how the contest went?

The best man won, I say. Unfortunately, that man turned out not to be me.

The previous year mourned the fluke loss of the ASO's entire cello section: six of its most advanced players to graduation, the principal to our more prestigious Midtown rival, and Mischa — who'd been doubling his shot at a college scholarship as his school's star forward on the basketball court — to a broken forefinger, out for the season. This has meant a begrudging promotion of most of our rank from the intermediate orchestra, at least until the school could recruit some better cellists. I used to sit in the back row and fake my way through silently, timing my bow movements with the fellows in front of me. Here, in the advanced orchestra, this strategy has failed.

Mr. Strasser was a ferocious little man who refused to suffer our inferior cello section quietly. Hold it! He'd call, then turning to address the empty seats in the auditorium: Is there a *veterinarian* in the house? Hello? Quick, we have a *dying moose* over here! To each of us in turn he'd point. From your entrance, if you'd be so kind. Rooting out each foul note with the tip of his baton.

Darling, your sound. How shall I put it? Your sound could give my deaf grandmother a stroke. And she's been *dead thirty years*!

In retrospect, I see that his cruelties were not baseless; on the contrary, they were particularly effective in whipping me into shape. For the first time I began practicing my part, and with better discipline than I practiced the piano. I worked over tricky passages until I had them down, memorized even, careful to keep my fingering consistent, bowings as marked. Anything to avoid the humiliation of being called out to saw away in front of a roomful of glaring musicians. I began listening to my fellow cellists and picking out the lightest touch of the baton in our direction. By the night of the Spring Concert we are actually carrying our weight, more or less. Gone is the sneer on Mr. Strasser's face when looking in our direction. We have improved. We have passed his test. All right darlings, he says to us by way of pep talk. Put on your best underwear and play like that next Saturday and we'll have a show!

Those weeks following Arthur's win the whole school seems to wake to his presence. In the cafeteria I watch the sight of Arthur silence each table he passes, one by one. And after he is out of earshot, a topic change, *sotto voce*:

Where's a bully when you need one?

The Ensemble Contemporain commissioned him to write an encore, I heard.

If you ask me, Nacoki was robbed — did you hear his Sibelius? It's like ten times harder than that Mozart.

And the Seventh? What were the judges thinking? Didn't we do the Seventh last year?

That was the Fifth. Three years ago.

I often come across him in the hall now, engaged in some intense discussion with a member of the faculty. In music history, our teacher, who'd always given the impression that no musical achievement more recent than a century old was worth talking about, invokes Arthur's name to illustrate the degree of the teenage Chopin's prodigy as students nod their heads: *Oh, you mean that good.* I'm jealous, sure — jealous of his change in status, jealous of his effortlessness. How I struggled! With my lack of skill, with my lack of discipline. Arthur lacked for nothing I could see.

The Annual Spring Concert is an all-day affair. In the morning the kiddie orchestra performs in the smaller recital hall, followed by a matinee program on the main stage, courtesy of the intermediate orchestra. Classes have ended; it's a day for good-byes. The main event comes in the evening with the advanced orchestra, Mr. Strasser at the helm. It's referred to as the "Concerto Concert," although a full-length program has been prepared: three pieces, with an intermission after the first two.

To start, an overture.

*Fidelio,* Mr. Strasser says, addressing the audience after taking the podium, Beethoven's only opera, was a failure in his lifetime. This was a student concert, after all, and even in the breaks between applause there was time for a teachable moment. Past the glare of stage lights I can see that this concert is better than well attended. It is packed. Although the mezzanine is dark—the only light comes from stray glints off the chandelier—it is alive with movement. It is rumored that scouts from CMA are in attendance, as well as several poachers from Juilliard. Zubin Mehta's granddaughter is a student here, so I'm imagining that the grandfather is here too. Mr. Strasser looks dashing in his white bow tie and tails. He continues. During its short first run, he says, the score went through several revisions, and Beethoven wrote no fewer than five versions of the overture. In time, each has become part of the standard repertoire. Except this one. The "Characteristic Overture in C" was published posthumously. Beethoven considered it too insubstantial to open such a big opera, and indeed it is shorter and more lighthearted than its four brethren and remains mostly an academic curiosity. So, as we find ourselves seated here tonight *in academia* and as we are *curious*, let us draw back the curtain and behold!

With a flourish of his baton, we begin.

An oddly extravagant introduction for such a simple piece, as if he is trying to make excuses to the audience for its simplicity. Sometimes, there's a discrepancy between how straightforward something sounds and how difficult it is to play. The hardest part of this piece for the cellos, the breve sixteenth notes, requires a light, steady bouncing of the bow coordinated with some fancy fingerwork. To get it right involves a metronome and many hours of painstaking work. To get nine other cellists sounding as one, and to have that section interlocking with the others, entail the coordinated efforts of several dozen players and weeks of rehearsal. And yet our passage should breeze by all but unnoticed – if Mr. Strasser has managed to get our balance right, the listener should only really be conscious of the few bell-like notes of the French horn, rounded out by the timpani, the strings a blurred picket fence seen from a moving car. If the listener is more than marginally aware of us, then we have failed. And perhaps this is our unsung heroism as skilled performers and the sacrifice great composers ask of us: to execute a difficult passage without drawing attention to the passage or to ourselves. It is something Arthur's argument hadn't taken into account: that sometimes not noticing is precisely the point. Does every piece and every performance have to hit one over the head? Isn't there any room for subtlety? Couldn't an evening at the symphony be, god forbid, pleasant?

As the final notes give way to applause, Mr. Strasser looks over at us – at me, it seems – and winks. Our playing has pleased him. For the past three years here, I've felt like an impostor, faking my way through lessons and rehearsals, but tonight, in this thrift-store tux smelling of camphor and mildew, in this seat in the school's most advanced orchestra, I feel like a star.

Squinting out into the audience, I think: Arthur is wrong. Of the faces I see, not a single one is asleep or bored or even reading the program. All eyes are on us. The clapping, that burst of sound Arthur described as "white noise," may have numbed a few hands to make, but its effect is anything but a canceling out: it's a sound that enlarges us and fills our hearts.

There is some nervous excitement tonight about performing this concerto because in spite of it being the headline event, it is in fact the piece we have rehearsed the least. Mr. Strasser had bigger fish to fry than Arthur's concerto. The Dvořák we were planning to play after the intermission was a beast and required most of our attention; the Mozart was easy, in a key that facilitated everyone's being in tune—lots of open strings, the brass and woodwind parts describing natural overtones—so that the thing could almost play itself. Mr. Strasser said that as long as we tuned our instruments carefully from the oboe, we would be fine.

In rehearsals, we would always save the Mozart for last. Not a member of the orchestra, Arthur would arrive onstage as per Mr. Strasser's instructions with fifteen minutes left on the clock, and after unpacking his instrument, he'd ride with us through entrances two, maybe three times at most, and then we'd call it a day. We had only played the piece through in its entirety once, earlier today, and although it had gone without a hitch, there was nonetheless something precarious about our performance, at least in my case, each phrase coming to my fingers just in the nick of time.

*Doubtful*, Mr. Strasser says now, addressing the audience, is the word you'll find printed in your programs next to this concerto of Mozart's, as it is considered by most scholars to be a fake. Penned in the last century by a violinist-cum-composer with a flair for pastiche. It is, like the Beethoven, performed only as a curiosity. It is not included in recordings of the complete violin concertos. The place it is most often heard, fittingly enough, is in the audition hall, learned by young violinists who, like the concerto itself, hope to be taken for the real article. It is ironic, however, that our winner, who turns out to be as real as Mozart himself at the same age—virtuoso violinist, accomplished composer—should be offering up this particular piece of apocrypha for us. Well, I think we can all safely assume that this piece, through young Arthur Morel, has never sounded more genuine than it's going to sound this evening.

Applause and the thunder of our feet rumbling the floorboards bring Arthur from the wings to take his place beside Mr. Strasser.

They shake hands.

Arthur is, somewhat scandalously, not wearing a tux. He has on khaki pants and a brown corduroy sports jacket. He's not even wearing a tie. If Mr. Strasser is shocked, he hides it well. There is a stir of eye contact and smirks through the body of the orchestra, cut off by Mr. Strasser's swift turn and raised baton.

I set my instrument in its perch between my knees and, touching my bow to a string dusty with rosin, wait for my cue.

Arthur looks relaxed, more at ease I think than I've ever seen him, and if I hadn't recently come to know that stern inward scowl that was his usual expression (absent now), I would have had no reason to be unsettled.

It is interesting to note that what was unforgettable about Arthur's performance — the cadenza — nobody could recall him ever playing. In rehearsals he skipped it. Even in dress rehearsal when it came time for his solo, he just drew his bow across the open strings and announced he was saving up for tonight. *Saving up?* And what about the audition — I tried to remember. Coming out of that performance had been like waking from a pleasurable dream, foggy and spent: What cadenza had he played then? Had it been his own? If it was remarkable, it was no less remarkable than any of the other notes he'd played. Had he skipped one entirely? This seems unlikely, for it would have been a noticeable omission to at least one of the roomful of listeners. It seems more likely that he performed whatever stock cadenza had been included with the score. Neither was it a question I could ask Arthur myself, as this performance brought about his immediate expulsion from school and marked the last time I would see him for more than a decade.

Coming at the end of the first movement, the cadenza is preceded by a solid ten minutes of performance, and I can't imagine this auditorium ever having been filled with a richer, more vibrant music. Our playing is charged, excited. We bring Arthur to the moment of his solo with the lightest, most graceful touch. Mozart's impostor would have approved. And then:

A pause, the breath before the aria:

I am looking at Mr. Strasser, who produces a wadded handkerchief to swab his glistening head. His eyes are cast upward, the faraway gaze of attentive listening.

And then he frowns, mirroring a leap of panic that I myself suddenly feel — the silence has gone on a beat too long. He turns just as I hear a shout from the audience and something onstage that sounds (I can't be hearing this right) like a loud, wet fart.

In a nearby row someone exclaims, Oh my!

Arthur had been in my direct line of sight, but now he is lost to the craning heads of my fellow cellists in front of me. A ripple of voices from the audience erupts into a full-throated roar. I look down at the front row and understand from each grimace, the muscle reflex of revulsion, even as the savory cabbage stink hits me: Arthur has opted for the riot.

Pei-Yee, who had a front-and-center mezzanine seat for the spectacle, reported to me later: He just tucked his violin under his arm and turned. It was so fast. You almost would have missed it if you weren't paying attention. He just turned and dropped his pants and oh — my — God! It was the craziest thing I've ever seen. He squatted, right there on that stage — and took the biggest, grossest shit!

# 3

# BLACKOUT

"**IT'S HALF THE SIZE OF** the place we moved from," Arthur said, opening and closing doors around the apartment, as if to show just how small.

"And where was that again?"

"Jamaica Queens. Metal detectors at school were the final straw for Penelope. Will put up a fight against the move, but not much of one. I think he's thrilled, secretly, but doesn't want to show it. Maybe he feels his happiness would be a retroactive condemnation of his old friends — or of us. Who knows? Yesterday we went to a parent-teacher conference at the new place. 'Magnet school,' quote-unquote, that's what they call it — I suppose, because the parents cling to the place for dear life. All of us in this meeting, parents and teachers and administrators, could barely contain our gratitude for one another. The handshaking never stopped."

It might seem like I'm pulling a bit of authorial misdirection here for the sake of narrative suspense by not immediately recognizing Arthur Morel. From the moment he said my name, the moment he took my hand. How could it be otherwise? He'd have been unforgettable! It's true. He was unforgettable. I was haunted by that act of his for some time afterward, all the more so for our passionate talk those weeks prior, which seemed to have provoked him into it somehow, and in this way made me feel complicit. In fact, his performance was so powerful, so seared into my memory, that my brain refused to reconcile this man — proud wallet snapshot of wife and child, breezing through his new two bedroom in Herald Square like some sunny realtor — with that brilliant but obviously troubled boy I had known those years ago. Even as we toured the apartment, I trailed in utter disbelief at the seemingly ordinary family man he'd since become.

Arthur opened a bedroom door. The apartment layout was similar to the editor's apartment down the hall. But there, this room housed the editing equipment. Here it housed Arthur's kid. There was something familiar — not just in the structural echo of the space I spent my day, but in the spiritual echo of the one in which I spent my childhood. It was an only child's room. Where unfashionable interests were allowed to flourish, safe from the withering glare of sibling disapproval. Outgrown toys, unembarrassed to be sitting next to current ones: Spawn action figures and a stuffed Barney doll sharing floorspace with a Super Soaker and a glittery pair of silver shoes. Above the bed was a poster of a blurry flying saucer with the caption THE TRUTH IS OUT THERE. Looking around I see other *X-Files* memorabilia: trading cards and comic books and bedding. Arthur: in charge of another human being — with his own room and a preference for campy television. Amazing! Maybe the shock had as much to do with me: it meant that I was an adult, when most days I still felt more like the occupant of this room.

I was led down a short corridor, past several framed photos and a wicker hamper. "Bathroom," he said, pointing to a door opposite the hamper, "and this one is ours." There was no room like this at the editor's apartment. We didn't dwell, but from what I saw, it struck me as consistent with their adultness. Matching furniture, scathed from the recent move — veneers chipped, drawer faces crooked — gauzy curtains, a side table with a clock radio and a little dish for spare change.

We ended our tour out on the patio. Here a few unopened boxes remained.

I said, "I'm surprised you didn't think of homeschooling Will."

"These days they call it *unschooling*. For one, there was just way too much paperwork involved. Lesson plans, certificates in postgraduate pedagogy. And for another, I'm against it. Penelope pushed for a while, using me as some kind of rhetorical point. 'Look how you turned out,' she says. I keep telling her that I barely made it out alive. She thinks I'm kidding! You get the control, as a parent, but at the cost of social isolation. It's a lonely enough business not having siblings. I didn't want to make it worse by denying him nine-to-five camaraderie or the opportunity to get away from his parents for several hours a day."

"Camaraderie? From what I remember, it was mostly keeping your head down so you didn't get the shit beat out of you. When the chips were down, your 'comrades' ran the other way. Not that anyone would blame them — or you. And I'm not talking Bed-Stuy here. This was down on Grove Street, in the heart of lovely Greenwich Village!"

"Well, you can tell Penelope all about it."

Arthur stood with his hands in his pockets, looking out over the rooftops.

I said, "I bought your book."

"Oh no." He turned. "Well?"

"I went into the bookstore right after we ran into each other, and it's been sitting in my bookshelf ever since, wedged between Sartre and Henry Miller."

"Good company."

"Other books I haven't read."

"It's a strange experience," Arthur said, "writing a book. For months you're inside of it, this piece of mental architecture, and it seems to be very important, the most important thing in the world, in fact — every living thought you have comes filtered through the windows of this place. And then it's finished, you step outside it, back into the world. It becomes public property. You walk past it occasionally and think, *What was so important about this place?* Well, maybe you can let me know once you've read it." The spiel sounded disingenuous somehow, as though he had said this very thing before in an interview on NPR.

Okay, I was jealous. It used to be that I was in awe of others' success; not these days. I was too impatient for it myself. Here's the truth: I had started reading the book (how could I not?), but put it down almost immediately. It was just too good. The way it drew you in from the first paragraph with a tidal force. Each page layered with everyday objects refracted to appear startling and fresh, each observation a reminder of how much in life went by unobserved. Each sentence a jewel, not a preposition out of place. It wasn't fair that the guy who was the musical prodigy also got to be the guy who could write this well.

I said, "So what happened to you that night?"

"That night."

"Of the Spring Concert! One day we're having a — what seemed to me — purely theoretical discussion about cadenzas, and the next you've got your pants around your ankles in front of hundreds of parents!"

Arthur sighed like he was relieved to have someone finally, after fourteen long years, ask him about this. "Well," he said. He gazed at me for a while as though only now taking in who I was, as though my question had prompted his memory of where he knew me from, and not the other way around.

"I remember feeling just—tremendous afterward, just afterward, even as I could feel people's shock coming at me. I couldn't really see anything, you can never see anything up there because of the stage lights, but that sense that something, something big, had just happened, and that I had caused it to happen, was palpable. It was an amazing feeling. But then it occurred to me I didn't have an exit planned. I may have doubted that I could pull it off, so to speak, so I never visualized an after. I remember the need to solve the immediate problems. I had my own feces all over me, and I had to find a place to wash up. I pulled up my pants and just traced my way back down the aisle between the first and second violins, the way I'd come. I went back to the dressing room, used the little water closet there to clean up as best I could. And then I went about the ordinary business of putting my violin away. I took my time, loosened the bow, secured it in place inside the case's lid, used my cloth to wipe the rosin from under the bridge, and set my violin inside, closed it up, snapped the latches, and when I looked up there was what's his name." Arthur pauses, frowning. "Odd. What was his name?"

"The conductor?"

"He was out of breath, forming any number of questions on his lips, none of them coming, and I could hear the slow stampede of the orchestra breaking up, making its way backstage. He finally asked the exact question you just asked: *What happened to you?* I could tell he was at a loss for how to handle me. His usual method of insults and browbeating didn't seem quite appropriate here because perhaps he wasn't sure whether I was entirely sane. Had I had some kind of episode? A mental break? He just sort of stood there—I don't know if he was really expecting me to answer but seemed braced for me to do some other savage and unfathomable thing. I said, 'I wasn't thinking. I was doing.' Which really must have meant something to me then because saying it felt so true, a paired act to what I had just done onstage. I would recall my saying those words to him afterward and feel, yes—I had just explained something essential about an essential and courageous act. And then, after a while, I would recall the words, recall that I had once felt a certain way, recall that they were meant to explain something, but could no longer remember what. It's like what I was saying just now about the book. Time sets you apart from your work, your utterance, separates you from it. Some metaphor about birth would be appropriate here. Umbilical cords, et cetera."

"But what did you do then? After that night you disappeared. What happened to you?"

Arthur tugged at his tie to loosen it and unbuttoned the top two buttons of his shirt. He sat down on a stack of boxes that sagged under his weight. "I lost my scholarship. My violin teacher dropped me from his studio. I wasn't officially expelled but might as well have been. There was no way I could have paid the full tuition, and even if I could have, after that who'd have taken me?"

I shook my head. "Why did you do it? Arthur, you lost everything. And for what?"

"I could say I did it because I wanted to do something that would be unforgettable to an audience. But then you would point out that any number of acts perpetrated on a stage might be unforgettable, though they—like the one I did perform—would none of them be music, and we'd have circled back to where we began, lo those many years ago: what is music, what is its purpose."

A nonanswer. Intellectualizing away an act that was so self-destructive, so against our basic nature as social beings. If my cousin's kids were any indication, pooping becomes a private activity fairly early on, its smells and noises associated with shame—by five or six the very muscles and nerve impulses required will refuse to cooperate if others are watching. So why could Arthur? Why *did* Arthur? These questions were not answered by his ontological ruminations.

I was going to press further, but Arthur's attention became diverted—I followed his line of sight back into the apartment. His wife had suddenly appeared and was setting a heavy bag of groceries down on the dining room table as his son, toting a bright orange gun, stalked the room shouting silently. From out here there were only the sounds of air conditioners and traffic. Arthur said, "Shall we continue this inside?"

He opened the sliding door in time for us to hear his son shout, "You'll be lying in a pool of your own guts!"

"Not if I blow your brains out first," Arthur's wife said in a cutesy voice, sorting through the mail. She looked up and smiled at us. "Who's ready for a drink?"

On my way to the diner the following week, I marshaled an argument against firing our editor, but Sri Lanka wasn't in the mood. "This shoestring budget needs all the lacing it can get," he said. "Is it my fault? Hell, yes, it's my fault! But what am I going to do? I'll tell you what I'm not going to do. I'm not going to keep this guy around because you don't want to hurt his feelings."

Our eggs arrived, and we ate in silence. When the check came, he told me he'd forgotten his wallet. I paid with a twenty I'd swept up from one of the theater's dark aisles the night before, which left it up to our editor to pay the delivery guy for the sushi we ordered for lunch.

We elected to shelve the Winnebago stunt in lieu of something simpler. It was a two-shot in a pickup truck between the young reform-school Hamlet and his yokel best friend Horatio, who is telling a story about some roadkill venison his father had once brought home to feed the family, to hilariously disastrous results. Punch line: *Projectile vomiting!* The scene had been done in one long shot with a car mount, the budget only allowing us a few hours with the thing—we had originally conceived and shot it in Horatio's living room but decided when screening the dailies that it would be more dynamic if it were told while some action was taking place (the speech was long). It was squeezed into the reshoot schedule as an afterthought—a few hours, a predetermined side road, followed by cutaway footage of telephone poles and passing farmhouses. These shots would be used to cobble together the best moments from each of the half-dozen takes.

But even this fairly straightforward cutting-room task became, in the atmosphere of this place, an occasion for conflict. The editor wanted to do away with the cutaway footage, which he said was overexposed and blended poorly with the much-darker footage in the cab of the pickup, and instead intercut the earlier takes as shot in the living room with the later car-mounted stuff. It made for a rather edgy and stylized edit, but one that Sri Lanka argued did not fit with the aesthetic.

"I don't get it," the editor said. "You keep saying to get creative with this thing, and here I get creative and you object."

"Explain it to the man," Sri Lanka said. I echoed back what Sri Lanka had already said, that while it worked on its own, it needed to blend with the other scenes.

Though Sri Lanka hadn't given me any explicit order to fire our editor today, the subject hung heavy over me—each look he gave I took for a signal. It was clear that I had two choices here: go through with the firing or offer my resignation.

So when Sri Lanka excused himself to go to the deli for a late-afternoon soda, whether he meant it to be or not, I used the moment to do what I had to do. After I was sure we were alone, I said, "He wants me to fire you."

We were facing each other, but I was looking down, rolling one of the brushed-steel coasters along the glass coffee table like a wheel.

"Fine by me," he said. "I've been figuring on a way out here for a while."

"For what we're paying you, I'm sure it can't be worth your time."

"It'd be one thing if I really cared about this project—not that I have anything against your guy, but this thing already feels dated, and it's not even finished!" He laughed. "Besides, he's impossible to please. You see how he is. He has no idea what he wants. Is this for festivals or late-night cable? He wants the prestige of the one but the instant market of the other. I've seen it a dozen times with these first-time directors. They start out intending to make some groundbreaking piece of cinema, but now that the bills have come due, the money gone, they don't have the courage to follow it through. It's a shame—the script is good."

Why did this hurt my feelings? He was just saying what I'd been thinking—plain truths—but it offended me to hear him say it. I let the coaster roll to the edge of the table and drop to the floor. "The script is the script," I said. "The movie is the movie."

"You should just start over."

"That's a helpful suggestion." I got up. "I'll be sure to pass it along."

"Listen," he said, but didn't get to finish the thought because just then the power cut out. The blinking AV rack went dark, along with the three monitors. A new silence replaced the drone and whir of equipment-cooling fans. Suddenly traffic noise could be heard, the creaking of footsteps above us. The editor left the room and went to the front door.

I followed.

There were already several residents out, feeling their way along the walls, asking one another what was going on. It had been hot for days, unbearably so, with warnings from the city for people to ease up on their AC usage, but if my mother and this editor were any indication, the warnings had gone unheeded. The movie theater kept its cavernous spaces just a little warmer than bone chilling. Two years later, this same situation would have provoked a wild-eyed panic among the residents of this city, an assumption that we were once again under attack—but back then we made no such assumption. A citywide crisis like this was a time of fun, of mischief, and had a way of making that border we must erect for the sake of sanity in a city of nine million seem porous, somehow, allowing for a deep and satisfying sense of connectedness—an occasion to feel grateful for the human beings around you.

So in spite of our conversation just moments earlier, we were suddenly giddy. A crowd gathered by the red emergency light of the open stairwell. A slow line shuffled past, down the steps, clinging tight to the banister. Echoes rang up from below, traveling word-of-mouth reports from street level. In the hallway, the neighborly sharing of a cell phone, good-natured lamenting about melting ice cream and raw meat. "I'm supposed to have people over," a woman said. "My husband's on his way right now with people from work." The rose glint of eye whites and teeth. Booming laughter from the stairwell, the heavy chunk of a door opening and closing and with it the arrival of more residents, Sri Lanka among them. He found us.

"I heard it's all of the city," he said.

Another new arrival said, "On the radio they say it's into Connecticut, New Jersey too, though a guy I just talked to said some blocks in Queens still have power."

"There's a grill up on the roof."

"Why are people so fixated on spoiled food? Just keep your fridge closed, and it'll be fine for at least forty-eight hours."

While we were talking, a discussion had taken place between the woman with the imminent cocktail party and those with raw meat. A coalition was formed, a larger shindig. We were invited to join, to empty our freezers and meet up on the roof. I declined.

"Oh, come on," Sri Lanka said. "Don't tell me you're going to the theater today. Projectors and popcorn machines run on electricity."

"Unless they're using alien technology." From out of the darkness, Arthur's son appeared, orange gun in hand. "Which most people think isn't real."

Sri Lanka said, "Most people are idiots and can't believe the truth that's right in front of their eyes."

The boy said, "In a book I'm reading it says that Thomas Edison was an alien, which would mean that everything is alien technology. The lightbulb, the telephone, the compact-disc player. It's not really a book-book—it's more like a comic book."

"What's your name, little man?"

"I'm Will, even though I shouldn't be telling you my name."

"Is it a secret?"

"It isn't a secret, it's just you never know. That's what Tyler's mom says. You never know. But she needs to worry less about other people's influence on Tyler and more about her own."

Adjusting to the dimness, I saw that the hostess of the imminent cocktail party was Arthur's wife, Penelope—at the moment handing Will several sloshing ziplock bags of marinated meat. She was short, not much taller than her son, with chopped black hair and a small upturned nose, through one nostril a silver loop that glinted orange. She had cherubic cheeks and full red lips. She was wearing jeans and a black tank top that exposed a sleeve of tattoos the length of her arm. "Hold them by the tops," she said, "like this. Give me the gun, thank you very much. Here's the flashlight. Go ahead. I'll meet you up there."

Sri Lanka and I helped the editor empty his fridge of its beer and frozen dinners, and we felt our way back down the hall. On our way up to the roof, Sri Lanka riffed on the submarine, red-lit stairwell—its creative possibilities as an opening location for a low-budget short. "That's what we need to shake things up," he was saying to us. "Get back to basics. Just the three of us and a camcorder. Forget all that other crap. Cut it in camera." He was squinting, framing with his fingers as we made our way upstairs.

The editor and I arched eyebrows at each other. A playful eye roll. A grin.

(How can I describe that feeling, jogging up the stairs after this wordless exchange—that welling up inside? It doesn't come too often as I am a natural wallflower, closing off the petals of myself to people instinctively, a tendency that has become more pronounced the older I get. But as a child the feeling came to me quite often: the simple desire to be someone's friend—and the simple hope that this someone felt the same way, too.)

A sign on the roof door read NO PUBLIC ACCESS!, yet the door was propped wide by a rusty beige folding chair. Gravel crunched underfoot and the tar floor beneath had a springiness that made it feel, with each step, like you were about to break through somebody's ceiling. Clouds of grill smoke and the smell of charcoal and lighter fluid. The rising swell of horns from down below, a massive island-long traffic jam. There were no railings—it was just roof and thin air. A water tower loomed in the center of the space, an everywhere city thing rarely seen this close up—a giant homage to the water towers of New York. Already plenty of people were up here, looking out over the roof, bodies tense and rooted, marveling at the sight of a city without power, eerie even in the light of day.

I considered calling my ex-girlfriend, who still worried over me. An and I met during freshman orientation and immediately settled into a domestic bliss that lasted until the day we received our diplomas. After the breakup, she insisted on our continued acquaintance, checking in weekly. Our most-sought-after bassoonist at school, An had afterward gone abroad to study Byzantine frescoes; like so many others at conservatory, myself included, she had shed the habit of music upon graduation. But she had taken the high road, gunning for a master's at the most prestigious institution that would have her. An was horrified to learn I had taken up the movies and was doing everything in her power to dissuade me. It was, she said, an aesthetic and intellectual ghetto.

"Aren't you interested in art anymore? That quintet, oh! I could see it entering the repertoire." She was referring to my senior thesis, and I knew An well enough to know her praise was meant only for rhetorical effect: she wasn't pointing out how good a student composer I'd been but rather how little potential there was for me in film. I told her that I was having fun, which was more than I could say for the time spent in the practice room, sweating over that quintet.

"Fun," she said.

"Sure," I said. "Fun."

Arthur arrived with his work colleagues, two men who looked like they might be twins. His wife greeted them, his son circling as Arthur droned on. I approached but was forced to wait alongside Arthur's wife as he wrapped up his train of thought.

She gave me a sympathetic look, as did the twins, who seemed to be looking for a way out of this conversation. "It's the fundamental mistake with the reader-oriented model," Arthur was saying. "Just because a readership wants a certain kind of literature doesn't mean it's a literature that should be written—a literature that *literature* wants, so to speak. The reader model assumes the reader knows what's best. But this just encourages fad chasing. And it reinforces existing tastes, which in turn ensures the same kinds of stories get written over and over. Readers can't be trusted with that kind of responsibility."

One of the men Arthur was with, upon closer inspection, was a woman. She had on the same outfit as her colleague—plaid short-sleeved shirt with jeans and Day-Glo sneakers. They both wore crew cuts and horn-rimmed glasses. Penelope introduced us and, having just met them herself, messed up their names.

"I'm Leslie," the man said, "and she's Lucien." It was unclear if they were related in any way other than their place of employment. Leslie toyed with the strap of his canvas tote like he was adjusting a seat belt.

Lucien said, "You can call me Lucy."

I was looking to chat some more with Arthur, but he was already being pulled away by Will ("You've got to come look at this, trust me, it's really cool"), leaving me alone with his work colleagues and his wife. I excused myself to find Sri Lanka and the editor, who were sitting in a folding-chair semicircle with a half-dozen others.

"Geography," the editor said, "Entertainment, Literature, Science, or Sports and Leisure." He was holding a deck of Trivial Pursuit cards.

"Entertainment," someone across from him said.

"Make sure you're rotating them."

Sri Lanka, when I sat down, said, "So I've been on this website lately? And it's given me some really good ideas for our next project. Why-Frame-the-Juice-Dot-Org."

The editor read from the card in his hand. "Here's your question. *What actor played immigrant Latka Gravas on the television series* Taxi?"

"There's a theory circulating that the murders of Nicole Brown and Ronald Goldman were masterminded by Andy Kaufman to help O.J.'s flagging career."

"Andy Kaufman!" someone said. "That's his name."

"That's a wild coincidence," I said.

Sri Lanka, deadpan, "There are no coincidences."

"Anyway, isn't he dead?"

"He faked his death, dude. Everybody knows that." Then hushed, "Listen. Are you ready to head out?"

"We're just settling in."

"But these are adults. If you want to have fun, I know a couple of places we can go." He took a pull on his beer and belched. "Plus I'm kind of hungry."

"Why don't you go ahead then," I said. "I'm going to stay here awhile."

Leslie and Lucy joined the circle.

"Okay, this one's up for grabs," the editor called. "Entertainment, of course: *How many* Rocky *movies were made by 1990?*"

"Who on earth would admit to knowing that," said Lucy.

"Oh, here we go," Leslie said. "Let's hear it."

"What," Lucy said.

"It's such familiar ground you're covering. Generations of old people have been there before you, kvetching about what heathens we've all become."

Sri Lanka said, "Five! That's easy."

I watched Penelope some yards away cuff a small brown paper bag and set it down on the ground. Will was helping. He held the bag steady while she filled it with dried beans from a large bin and set a small candle inside. Will lit it for her and then handed her another bag from the stack he was holding. By the time they were done, the place looked like a proper roof garden.

"I'm not going to apologize for having a problem with this, Leslie. I mean, am I really wrong?"

"Yes, you're really wrong. Besides, aren't poets of your generation supposed to have embraced pop culture?"

"Is there even such a thing anymore? Everything is pop. Fucking semiotics."

Leslie turned to me and said, "Departmental politics. Not all that different from seventh grade, actually."

"It's the very thing that bothers me. Trivia. It's what the age has reduced us to. World knowledge as nothing more than a set of browsable, meaningless facts."

"Wine," said the woman next to me, handing a bottle to Lucy. Lucy thanked her and took a Dixie cup from the stack on the ground. The woman, who had introduced herself as Marsha a few moments ago, said, "It's a good point you make. Didn't it used to be that only the people in power had knowledge? Keepers of special knowledge?"

"The Church," Leslie said. "Who had it on good authority that there was a big hole in the South Pole where a race of giants lived."

Arthur had come over and was standing just outside our semicircle. He said, "You're thinking of Poe's novel."

"Based on a going theory of the time."

"It used to be that knowledge was power," Marsha said. "But now knowledge isn't powerful. It's—"

"Trivial," Arthur said.

"Fine," the editor said, "but can you answer me this: *Do porcupines masturbate?*"

"That's not a question!"

"No?" I offered.

"Wrong. Guess again."

"What's the question?" This was the man next to Marsha.

"I'm Marsha," she said to Sri Lanka. "And this is my husband, Greg."

"Greg and Marsha?" Sri Lanka said. "Are you serious?"

"Except we're not brother and sister."

"Neither were your TV counterparts—they totally could have fucked."

Arthur stood there for a while—large hands shifting from under his armpits to his pockets to his elbows—as he looked around for a way in. After some time, he took a cross-legged seat on the gravel. I became engaged in some lighthearted repartee with Greg and Marsha, then looked over again to see Arthur staring out blankly, the way one does when caught in an awkward social situation. The people on either side of him were involved in other conversations, leaving him alone in this now-boisterous group. Eventually, he got up, brushed at the bottoms of his chinos, and wandered off. I excused myself.

I caught up with him at the base of the immense water tower. We talked for some time there, wandering the labyrinth of an idea I kept losing the thread of. In my tipsiness, I didn't really care, content enough to drink my beer and nod away as he pursued a train of thought. Then he said, "I'm not good at this."

"At—"

"Being with other people. I don't know how to relax. To chat casually about the world. I do this, what I've been doing with you, which seems to alienate most people."

"We can talk about the weather if you want."

"Penelope is different. She thrives in these situations." We regarded her as she stood by the grill some yards off with two others, gesturing wildly with a pair of barbecue tongs. The couple she was with held paper plates, onto which Penelope delivered two blackened pieces of chicken off the grill. She caught us looking and waved with the tongs.

"How did you two meet?"

"On a bus. If I think about that day, I can still smell it, the air inside that bus. That's memory! The humid earth, the coffee, the cologne. It had been raining. Sometimes I wake up next to her, amazed. A wonderful thing, marriage is—no longer having to navigate the baffling bureaucracy of life alone. To have a partner. Someone who believes in you. Her belief is so strong. Sometimes I wonder if, without her, I'd exist at all."

"How'd you manage it—if you're so bad at small talk? She turned on by long tracts about the reader-driven model of literature?"

"I got her pregnant."

"I like your technique. Effective. I'll have to remember that. And being a father? As wonderful as marriage?"

"The boy's a born artist—all children are, I suppose. But you get to see just how natural the impulse is to invent things out of thin air. His most recent project has been Tug, imaginary Rottweiler. Sublimating his desire for a dog through endless drawings of one. We are in the Tug period of Will's artistic career. Pencil sketches, clay models, glazed tile. Opening a book I'd been reading the other day, I discovered a Tug on the bottom corner of every page: a flip book of Tug running through a meadow. *Tug*, because Rottweilers are ugly yet powerful—like tugboats. You'll look through any of the sketch pads in Will's room to find page upon page of family portraits, featuring Tug front and center. Tug is being willed into this family through sheer force of imagination. Isn't that right, O Son of Mine?"

Will had been beam-balancing the waist-high railing around the water tower as we talked, giving us each a duck-duck-goose on the head every time he passed. He jumped down between us and said, "I'm over the whole dog thing. What I want now is a poltergeist forensic kit. It's for discovering unexplained phenomena."

Will brought us over to see some "suspicious evidence" he and some of the other tenants had found. As we walked off together, I thought of myself at Will's age, ten or eleven, with my own father. I have vivid memories of our time together — the day we toured the island of Manhattan on the Circle Line, just the two of us, and the hours spent constructing an elaborate scale-model space station I'd gotten for Christmas, heads bowed together at the dining room table, passing a small tube of glue back and forth. Strangely, I don't much recall playing with friends, although I must have; I spent most of my time at the local playground and at school with those my own age, but I have only the most generalized memories of these as places — sandbox, sprinklers, courtyard — not what I did there. Maybe it's for their rarity that I remember those moments with my father. He was generous with the time he had for me — but there wasn't much for him to be generous with. His professional life took so much of him — pedaling twice as hard against the lack of even a high school diploma — that I often found myself on the sidelines having just missed my chance to hold out that cup of water as he passed. At Will's age, I yearned toward my father, found myself interested in whatever interested him — his favorite television show (*Star Trek*) became my favorite television show; his favorite author (Isaac Asimov) became my favorite author. This didn't seem to be the case with Will, I noticed. He was his own man. In this rooftop investigation, Will was the lead detective — Arthur the staid partner with only two weeks left to retirement.

The problem was Arthur didn't seem to know how to play along. Will, kneeling, picked up a handful of gravel wet with an iridescent sheen—I think it was hand soap—then let the gravel slip through his fingers, back onto the ground. He rubbed his index finger and thumb together, brought them up to his nose. He squinted up at Arthur and said, "This substance has no basis in the natural world. Let's bag it, have our labs check it out." And instead of telling his son that the technicians at the labs couldn't be trusted or that he had no idea what he was getting himself into, that this conspiracy went all the way to the top, Arthur instead began a lecture about how even artificial products were technically part of the natural world because man himself was part of the natural world. And when Will countered that this particular stuff looked like it was of *alien origin*, Arthur tried arguing that aliens, though they might be from Mars, were themselves still "naturally" occurring, if one included the universe as part of nature.

As the last of the daylight faded, the votive bags shone more brightly. The gathering around the semicircle took on a campfire glow, which is to say it felt intimate—faces flickering in and out of view, everyone drawn into the radius of light—and yet at the same time it felt vast: the dark dancing shadows beyond each light's small cone a suggestion of the great void above. I found myself standing with Penelope, both of us slurry with beer. Sri Lanka had described her as a MILF, and I guess she was, though she was our own age. She was curvy, and her playful green eyes complimented a high, singsongy voice. The arm-length tattoo was sexy, I had to admit; after she caught me staring, she held it out for inspection. "It's a snake," she said. The beast's mouth was open around her wrist, its scales like chain mail. The illustration was made to look as though her limb was being devoured. "I got it so this would be less noticeable." She touched three raised patches on the snake's body each the size of an infant's palm print and made of what looked like the pebbly skin of a nipple. I hazarded a feel. "The guy who did it is an artist. His ink work costs triple what anyone else on the East Coast charges. The dishwasher where I was working at the time had his back done to look like one of those old anatomy drawings, skin peeled to show the veins and muscle and all that?"

She spoke of Arthur's mother and father, whom she described as "totally batshit." She said that Arthur wisely steered clear of them. "They're Manhattan fixtures. They live downtown in a loft and keep their front door open for anybody to walk in off the street. In fact they encourage it; they welcome everybody in. That place was a madhouse back in the day. Arthur tells me stories. Once, when he was maybe thirteen he was taken by a couple—they came in right off the street and Arthur wandered back to their Lower East Side apartment with them. And here's the kicker: his parents? Didn't even realize that he was gone—and he was gone for two days. *Two days!* Arthur laughs when he tells that particular one, so I don't think anything too bad happened to him while he was away, but there are other stories he doesn't laugh about. And a few he refuses to even talk about. I've dropped by their loft a few times but didn't mention who I was. Kind of fun being undercover!"

"They've never met you?"

"They've never met me, never met Will. They don't know he's published a book—even though the bookstore around the corner has it in the window!"

"I've been meaning to read it."

"Oh, you should. He's brilliant. You read the crap from those people he teaches with, and it's so clever you want to vomit. Art's the only serious one of the bunch, definitely the only one those students should be taking advice from."

"Said the wife about her husband."

"It's true, though! Those others?" She cocked a thumb at a clutch murmuring behind us. "They're just trying to keep up with their careers. They spend as much time sleeping with each other at MacDowell and schmoozing with known members of grant committees as they do thinking about what they write. Art's different. He could care less about career, about tenure—if he continues to teach, he'll be an adjunct for the rest of his life, and I say fine. What, you're surprised hear me say that?"

"You're living in the city and raising a child. Health insurance and a steady paycheck? That doesn't interest you?"

"You're thinking about some other man, some other marriage. I knew what I was getting into when I picked Art. He's barely employable. He thinks too much, takes too much to heart. But it's also what I love about him. I figured out long ago that if we were going to be together, I would have to do the breadwinning, so to speak—" She told me earlier that she was the head baker at Balthazar. "It's okay, though. I'd rather him be brilliant and happy than a miserable so-and-so. Better for me and better for Will."

I didn't have a bedside lamp—reading in bed was not a habit—and so I took the gooseneck from its perch on the piano's music stand and clipped it onto the radiator's knob by my bed. Pointing it at the wall gave me plenty of light to read by. I slid Arthur's book from the bookcase and sat back against the pillow.

It had been ages since I last enjoyed a book. As a child I read voraciously, above my grade level, to my mother's great pride. She was fond of repeating an anecdote my kindergarten teacher once told her, that on my first day when asked to choose a book from the bookcase—arranged in ascending difficulty from lowest shelf on up—I grabbed a chair and nearly split my lip climbing for a selection at the very top. I suppose the bookworm is a common only-child type. But in college I learned the vocabulary of arm's length. The book was a *text*. To like or dislike something was to say that it *worked* or *didn't work*, as though we were a classroom of repairmen. The profusion of pages and deadlines made enjoying any of it as likely as savoring a hot dog at a hot-dog-eating contest. And so I lost the habit.

Arthur's book is about an intense high school guidance counselor, divorced, living alone, who takes an unhealthy interest in a troubled boy he's convinced is being physically and sexually abused. He calls the boy to his small cubicle daily, trying to get him to talk, but the boy does not want to talk. The counselor tells the boy that abuse has to be dealt with, that unchecked it will

eventually eat the boy alive. The boy denies that anything has happened, but only vaguely, in a way that encourages the counselor.
His interest in the boy takes on the quality of an obsession. We
sense a train wreck on the horizon as the counselor goes through
with the purchase of a gun and begins trailing the boy to his home
and lurking behind dumpsters. There will be a confrontation
between the counselor and the boy's mean drunk of a father; we
see it coming from a mile off and read on to witness the collision.
But the head-on never happens. What we don't see coming is the
moment the boy—having been convinced by the counselor over
the course of weeks that it was imperative for abuse to be dealt
with—arrives at school with his father's shotgun and blasts a hole
in his coach, who, as it turns out, has been the one molesting him,
and makes a getaway with the counselor. It ends with the two on a
motel room bed, kissing, boy and man, the counselor unbuttoning
the boy's pants and pulling them off.

What's so shocking about this ending is that although we are
unsettled, we find ourselves somehow rooting for it. Arthur has
achieved that sleight of hand the best authors make us fall for: we
want things to work out for the narrator, whatever kind of person
he turns out to be. It's jujitsu, using the natural momentum of a
reader's desire to see his protagonist's desires fulfilled to launch
us over the line into this transgression, to want this transgression,
in a sense. What's troubling is where it departs from the stories of
other reprehensible literary characters. Raskolnikov is crushed by
his own guilt in spite of himself; Humbert, though unrepentant,
tells his story from a prison cell. But in Arthur's we have no such
assurances of the moral balance of the universe.

I wondered what would have motivated Arthur to invent these
characters, to take them—and us—on this journey. That Arthur
had written it, not only written it but also essentially performed
the role of this character himself—the counselor is the "I" of the
book—seemed bold and dangerous. Penelope was right. He was
a terrific writer. I disappeared down the hole on page one and
emerged 196 pages later, wide awake, disturbed by his vision.

# 4
# VIKTORIA

AT THE THEATER, DOOR WAS a special pleasure. You were given a microphone and a copy of the schedule. Before you, a zigzag of velvet ropes like at a bank—and the moment you flipped the switch to make your announcement, all the people chatting cross-legged in the massive carpeted window casements, leaning with a smoothie at the café's marble bar, would suddenly jump to attention and jostle their way between those ropes. It was amazing, the power you wielded with that microphone and that schedule. *Now seating, the six forty-five showing of* Buena Vista Social Club, *please have your tickets ready.* Standing at the far back corner of the lobby, you observed the effects of your booming call from a puppet master's distance. For these few hours you were the man behind the curtain, giddily yanking each hipster yuppie to attention by his string. The microphone transformed you. Through it, you became an auctioneer, an anchorman, a cabaret act bantering with his audience between sets. You began embellishing, adjusting your timing, discovering funny accents. You could be afraid of public speaking or open spaces or crowds; it didn't matter. Hearing your own voice over a loudspeaker and seeing its effects were enough to make the shrinkingest violet pick up that mic and be transformed. It was a sound that was related to you and that you were responsible for, but it was not you. It was like a rumor, or a child. You enjoyed seeing the way it could charm people or make them laugh. I made the most of my time at the door.

After I sent through the nine-fifteen showing of *The Minus Man*, pondering whether to risk stealing a ham-and-cheese wrap from the café or gorge myself on the unlimited popcorn I was allowed to have, someone tapped me on the shoulder. It was a girl, my own height, with long platinum hair and alien amber eyes. I had encountered her earlier that evening, during my stint in the ticket booth. She had ordered a ticket but was short a few dollars. As she was rummaging through her purse, embarrassed, I slid the ticket out to her. I said she could pay me later, not really thinking she would, yet here she was. She had a folded bill that she now pressed into my hand. When I unfolded it, there was a slip of paper with her name and number tucked inside — *Call me*, it read. I looked up just as she was disappearing into the crowd. She glanced back and gave me a little toodle-oo with her fingers. I was too stunned to respond.

No girl, unbidden, had ever given me her number before. *A complete stranger!*

Looking more closely on the bill itself, I could see she had written the same thing in the margin — *Call me*, with her number — but then crossed it out, presumably thinking better of it. I pictured her reasoning through this hasty gesture: What if I didn't notice and just put the bill back in the register with the rest of the fives? That endeared her to me even more. As if her shocking beauty weren't enough.

Our first date was at her apartment. She had a golden retriever puppy that she kept gated in her kitchen who barked incessantly and gave the place a peculiar smell. I brought flowers and the makings of pasta and tomato sauce. She said she didn't usually eat, that she was a picky eater, but was "superimpressed" by my cooking. It was basic stuff, but it seemed to baffle her, the food, cooking in general. She watched me sauté onions as if I were demonstrating some rare skill. It seemed I was the first person to use her new pots. The dog scrabbled at the gate and yelped the whole

time, and she would periodically scream at it. It was a disconcerting scream, a note of unrestrained hysteria in it. She was a recent
high school graduate—she had gone to UNIS. Absentee parents.
They had paid for the place, obviously.

She explained that she didn't drink or do drugs. She was a member of NA. She had to spell it out for me: Narcotics Anonymous.
That's how much I knew of the world, for all my "experience" as a
born-and-bred New Yorker. She wasn't yet eighteen, I don't think.
She had been institutionalized, she explained—not without a certain amount of pride—after attempting suicide. BPD. Again, she
spelled it out: borderline personality disorder. I got the impression
she was telling me things about herself she'd only learned weeks
before from the people in the institution.

She told me she needed to take things slowly, that she was starting over, from scratch. She described herself as a "reformed party
girl." She liked going to clubs and doing coke and drinking and
staying out until dawn. She told me all of this on our first date, sitting in her new chairs at her new table, eating spaghetti off of her
new plates, the puppy barking the entire time. There were awkward lapses in conversation. We had nothing in common. I was
more than a decade older than her. Her only CDs were dance-club
compilations. But she was by far the prettiest girl I had ever dated.
Her teeth were crooked in a way that made her seem especially
beautiful. I got the impression that she thought her diagnosis was
glamorous, or maybe she was clinging to it because it was all she
had. Her parents were in Germany. She was on her own. She was
due to enroll at NYU in the fall, but she talked about it tentatively,
and I got the impression she wouldn't go through with it or that
she would drop out midsemester.

Talk of firing our editor ended. I was still working at the theater,
still living with my mother, and spent most of my awake time day-
dreaming on the plush leather couch. Sri Lanka was still strapped
for cash; it had been weeks since I'd been paid. Our editor was having trouble financially, too. Something to do with the indie market

drying up, stiffer competition. It had been almost three months since he'd worked a paying freelance gig. His reserves were depleted. But in spite of this, and in spite of Sri Lanka's inability to afford to pay him any longer, the editor continued working on our film. He'd grown attached to it, he said, to us. When I talked to my mother about my day, I found myself calling each of them by name: Suriyaarachchi and Dave. We went to Dave's daily and stayed all day. Suriyaarachchi had his film-related correspondence forwarded to Dave's address. I was given a copy of the mailbox key; it was my job to get the stuffed wad from the box in the morning, along with crullers and coffee from the diner.

I don't want to give the impression that the two of them had stopped fighting; they hadn't. In fact, these fights became a defining characteristic of their friendship. But now they were like an old Hollywood pair, filling the air with their lively, sharp-witted banter. Occasionally, it would get heated, but just when I thought I needed to step in to break it up, one of them would say something that would cause them both to burst out laughing—and that would be that. I loved it. As an only child, I wanted a brother, someone to show me the ropes or someone to whom I might show the ropes. I yearned after the fraternal pack; and sometimes, after a meal, sitting in silence and listening to the two of them squabble, I felt like I finally got my wish.

I came to admire them. Suriyaarachchi's determination was infectious. Like Arthur's son and his imaginary dog, Suriyaarachchi was willing this movie into existence by the sheer force of his determination. It made me ashamed of my own doubts about the project. His confidence made him seem much taller than the five seven he was, and the rough cut, when we'd watch it together, seem better. Each sentence he uttered was filled with optimism. *Here's an idea.* Or: *You know what would be cool?* In Dave, too, I saw traits I wanted and was ashamed I lacked. Dave was a consummate craftsman—always turning the cut over in the back of his head. We would be at his PlayStation, deep in the bowels of a dungeon, slashing our way through a thicket of skeletal ghouls, the movie right then the furthest thing from my mind—and out of the blue Dave would say, *You know what might work?* Then go on to describe some technical issue about pacing or continuity. Whereas Suriyaarachchi and I were always striving for something more than what we had, our daily grind a means to some grander, more glamorous end, Dave was different. He was content. He wanted to continue doing exactly what he was doing right now, what he had been doing for the past ten years—his only goal in life to make enough money to keep doing it until the day he died. He had found his true calling.

And Arthur? What kept me returning to his end of the hall?

Years later, long after it was all over, people—those who remembered Arthur's brief moment of fame—would ask me that same question, how it was I could stand to be around *that guy*. What did I see in a man *who could do what he did*? In my defense, his second book had not yet come out, so all I knew of the depths of Arthur's—let's call it *creative stuntsmanship*—was still the comparatively minor stuff of that cadenza. Still, it's true I remained friends with him even after the second book and kept steadfast through it all, following him down into the abyss—so I suppose this deserves a preemptory explanation.

Back in those days, I was searching for the answer, capital *A*. I didn't have it and looked to everybody else for clues. My mother didn't seem to have the answer: as a poet, she dwelled in the humdrum; her insights were the insights of a different generation—using the shock of fresh language to wake people up to the daily beauty of a dog's bark, a sinkful of dirty dishes. This wasn't what I was after. These weren't my concerns. Almost a generation older than flower power, my mother watched that short era of hope bloom and die its cynical death from a relatively safe soul-preserving remove and was able to adopt the discoveries worth adopting—namely a sense of liberal self-expression, the only good thing to come of those times besides *Abbey Road*, she thought: a quality she hoped to instill in me, all too eager to encourage my slightest creative inclinations.

My father was an early mentor, a man who held sacred his own childhood and through me was able to recapture some of its magic. He taught me a love of collecting—stamps, baseball cards, little-known facts—and fed my interest in science fiction. At the age of nine and ten I was thrilled to spend those rare school-free weekdays at his office on Fifth Avenue, only a dozen blocks south from where I now spent my days with Suriyaarachchi and Dave. He was a draftsman by trade, my father—one of those trades that simply vanished with the advancement of computers. He toiled away at a steeply angled table, tracing intricate ductwork and wiring onto sheets of vellum with a special metal pencil whose soft graphite set down marks as dark as ink. The windows—the office was on the top floor of an eighteen-story building—looked out onto a scale model of a busy street scene: toy cars and buses inching along the replica avenue, complete with tiny streetlamps and blinking crosswalk signs. I can still feel the simple pleasure of sitting near him as he worked, taking up the adjacent table. The person who sat at this desk was invariably in a meeting in the conference room whenever I was around. It only occurs to me now that this man was probably not in a meeting but rather vacating his normal post to allow me to sit beside my father, bringing his work to the big conference table for the day as a favor to us. In my room, next to my piano, is a large cardboard tube, the kind used for architectural drawings. It is filled with poster-sized vellum plans for intergalactic cruisers, light-duty zero-gravity suits, and lethal dense-particle plasma rifles. If you look closely at my 2s, you can see how I tried to undo the loop in them so that they would be more like my father's 2s, a practical and efficient arrowhead V pointing down at the base of a curve. Next to his, mine looked dopey, the 2s of a student puzzling at the sum of a pair of them. And in the bottom right corner of each of my plans, copying his sturdy caps, I put the name of the project, the name of the drafts-man (myself), and the project's lead architect (my father).

But while I might have been entertained here of the occasional weekday afternoon, on the weekends—every weekend—I was making my pilgrimage on the Uptown local, plus the six uphill blocks farther by foot, to lock myself away in a practice room in the service of great art. By the time I was able to thunder through a Brahms rhapsody on the keyboard, I had left my father behind. Through my teens, my mentor was my piano teacher, an enormous man, six six easily, as round as he was tall. He had an enormous bald head and enormous hands. To see those fingers move across the keyboard was to understand why people use athletic terms to describe some classical musicians. His fingers were galloping horses, running wild and yet nailing every single note. Mr. Masi. His tastes became my tastes. Fred Astaire, Arthur Rubenstein. These were the greats. I diligently collected all the classic recordings and every old musical he praised with the same feverishness of my days collecting stamps and cards with my father. At the same time, Mr. Masi taught me a sensitivity to grace and beauty — and that such a sensitivity could be a masculine trait. To speak with confidence about how *gorgeous* a particular passage was and to, upon hearing it, close one's eyes in submission to it. Artur Schnabel playing *Kreisleriana*, Maurizio Pollini rolling through a Chopin étude. Some lessons would begin this way, him putting on a recording and letting it fill the room. I would watch him go limp at these climactic moments and then, snapping out of it, turn to me and shout, "See? Good God! Do you *see* what this is all about?" And I did. He taught me to seek out these moments, to feel the shiver down the spine.

But then I went off to college and left Mr. Masi behind as well.

In my twenties, I was adrift, in search of a new mentor — someone who could help me make sense of this new territory I found myself in, disillusioned with university-level music making but still desperate to do something with my life, make something of myself. But how? For a while, it seemed that Suriyaarachchi had the answer: even though he was young, younger than me, his sheer enthusiasm made him a candidate. To him, creativity was an entrepreneurial endeavor, imbued with the possibilities of great profit and renown. I was drawn to his confidence but saw also that much of that confidence was based on wishful thinking. Which is when Arthur showed up, with his *astonishing feat of language*, his *uptown* professorship, his sexy wife and precocious son, and I saw that maybe, just maybe, I had been too hasty in my dismissal of art. Here was a man who seemed to have it all: prestigious job, family—and an audience. What more could one want?

And then there was the business of that cadenza. In the middle of my formative stages as a young artist, to witness that act on that stage. It was so shocking, so out of the realm of what I knew art to be—even compared with those sixties experiments involving pianos rolled off stages. Thinking back on it, I can see that it was both the catalyst that propelled me onward, down the path toward a bachelor's degree, as well as the poison pill that had slowly, over the course of my four years at conservatory, forced me back off that path, dissatisfied with the smaller and smaller territories academic composers were mapping out for themselves. Nothing I had experienced in those four years lived up to the sheer enormity of that act. But what did it mean? The memory of that incident had troubled me—for years afterward—remaining a knotted question in my brain that I didn't even realize was there until bumping into him again after more than a decade. And here he was; it was an opportunity to work out that knot. I was happy to have been given a second chance with him.

So then: A mentor. And answers.

I arrived at Dave's exhausted. Strange dreams involving Arthur and a shotgun. The gun would go off, and I'd wake up. This happened several times. Finally, I gave up and turned on the light. It was three in the morning.

Suriyaarachchi was on the phone with his father, a one-sided conversation in which he stared down at his feet and plucked at his eyebrows, grunting occasionally. After he got off, he was in a foul temper. Dave, too, was in a mood, which had to do with losing a big contract he'd been counting on. We sat around the suite barely speaking. Interestingly, neither of them seemed upset at each other.

At this point, we had a rough cut that was too long — two hours and twenty minutes — and were looking for places to trim. Dave suggested we watch it from the beginning and, after a few clicks of the mouse, shut off the desk lamp and sat down between us.

Halfway through, Suriyaarachchi said, "What else do you have to watch around here. This movie sucks!" He leaned forward and used the remote on the coffee table to mute the sound and turn up the lights. He put his head in his hands and groaned. "God! What am I going to do?"

Dave got up. "I think I have just the thing for today. I'll be right back."

After he left I said, "So what did your father say?"

"That it would have been better if I'd spent four years in an insane asylum, rather than film school. At least, he said, they teach you practical skills like basket weaving. He'd be half a million dollars richer by now and have some place to put his dirty laundry."

Dave came back with a VHS and popped it into one of the decks. He said, "How do you feel about baseball?" As it happened, Suriyaarachchi loved baseball. "World Series, game three," Dave said. He had set it to record before going to sleep and made a concerted effort to avoid learning the outcome this morning. Suriyaarachchi had learned the final score but hadn't seen the game; he promised not to tell.

I left the two of them to their mutual interest while I went downstairs for another coffee and a copy of the *Village Voice*. When I returned, I spread the rental listings out on the kitchen counter. It was time for a change. I needed a place of my own — spending time at Dave's and Arthur's helped me realize that it was more than just a thousand-dollar-a-month hole in your pocket. It was where you could, if you so desired on a Saturday afternoon, pop the cap off a cold beer to be savored with a smoke in the wide-open comfort of your own living room. Where you could entertain a certain lovely tall girl with alien amber eyes and appealingly crooked teeth.

I made some calls with the wall-mounted phone, sipping my scalding coffee through the sharp snapped-off hole in the cup's lid. On the face of it, hundreds of landlords around the city were vying to rent their cozy studios to me; however, all calls led to the same three brokerages, none of whom would get specific until I had filled out an application. Today was one of my two days off at the theater. I had been hoping to explore a lead or two during the late afternoon, but it wasn't looking good. I popped my head into the editing suite and caught the roar of the crowd.

"You don't have a fax machine, do you?"

The editor came out in his bare feet to microwave some popcorn and revealed it hiding in plain sight under a stack of books. I sat cross-legged on the floor, using the receiver to communicate with the realtors. The application was a joke. It asked for my occupation and income but for no other information that might tie me to these answers. I could have put down anything, and did, and by three thirty I was lined up to see half-a-dozen places. The broker asked me how soon I could get downtown. I told him to give me an hour.

I pulled out my wallet and removed the slip of paper that Viktoria had given me that day, the words *call me* in her loopy school-girl hand. I dialed the number. When she answered, I said, "How would you like to go apartment hunting with me?"

"Who's this?"

"The guy who hasn't called you back in a week."

"Hey! I was wondering about you. I almost didn't pick up because I didn't recognize the number. It's been a very upside-down world I've been living in. Usually, I'm the one who doesn't call *you* back. Interesting feeling, being blown off. And by interesting, I mean it sucks. Apartment hunting, why not? Where should we meet?"

I put my head into the editing suite again to announce I would be leaving early. Suriyaarachchi, engrossed in the game—it was apparently a nineteen-inning nail-biter—said, "Why don't you just take the rest of the day off?" I was about to tell him that he was paraphrasing what I had just told him, then thought better of it.

I thanked him and left.

I met Viktoria on the corner of Third Avenue and St. Mark's Place. I was struck anew by her beauty. She was stunning. Tall and thin, with long blond hair that today she had divided into twin pigtails. She wore a skirt, high-heeled Mary Janes, and a cardigan over a button-down oxford. I felt both sheepish and overjoyed to be walking down the street with this sexy jailbait. Every man we passed without exception was dumbstruck, even the two holding hands. She was, to say the least, out of my league. She seemed at ease with the attention, absorbing it and deflecting it in equal measure, returning a smile or lowering her gaze or staring straight ahead. There was something electrifying about being the guy she was with, like riding a motorcycle for the first time—power, danger, lack of control.

We met the broker outside a tenement on Fifth Street and Avenue A. He had to correct himself when telling us his own name. "Hector, I mean. Viktor is my brother. Hector Villanova." He handed us his business card with trembling fingers.

"Villanova," Viktoria said. "That can't be your real last name?"

"What do you mean?"

"*Villanova* means 'new house.'"

"Yes, it does," Hector said, not catching her drift.

Viktoria looked at me poker faced.

Hector fumbled with the keys before letting us into the lobby. It was a five-floor walk-up, past dimly lit hallways and the smells of cat pee and frying onions. Hector described the apartment as "newly restored," but all that seemed to mean was the stove had been cleaned. A sponge and a can of Ajax stood on the counter. One of the walls had been given a recent touch-up; the smell was intense.

One couldn't really be given "the tour" because there wasn't anything, properly speaking, to tour. The place was a kitchen.

Nevertheless, Hector tried his best. "These are the original linoleum floors," he said, and tapped a buckling tile by the refrigerator with his tassled dress shoe. I went to the windows and looked down at the street corner. Hector came over to narrate the view for me, as if to revise what I was seeing. "What we have here are two exposures, unusual for the building, but this is a corner apartment. North facing and east facing. You will get very nice light here in the morning, and it should maintain an even brightness throughout the day. You can see the features of the neighborhood from here. Restaurants, nightlife, shopping. It's very safe at night. There are people around all hours. Eyes on the street, we call it in the business. Keeps the criminal elements at bay."

Viktoria said, looking out, "Oh my God, *that* place!" She pointed to the bar directly across the street. "We used to cab it down there once the clubs closed. Nice thing about it—only thing about it, really—is that there's no last call. They'd just let us hang out until we had to go to school in the morning. I don't know how many times I barfed in that garbage can on the corner." She took me by the hand. "Come look," she said, and brought me to the bathroom.

She sat down on the toilet. "Try closing the door." I tried, but her knees protruded past the threshold and the door bumped into them.

I turned to Hector. "Small bathroom."

Hector came over, and we both considered Viktoria as she sat on the toilet. "But you have very long legs," he said.

"Taking a shit in this apartment would be a public act," Viktoria said. "It's okay, I don't mind." She got up, keeping her bare knees together.

"I will ask the landlord what he can do about that," Hector said, making a note.

Apartment hunting in New York City, I came to learn after Hector had shown us the others, is a special kind of hell. Each was more depressing than the next. If Viktoria hadn't been with me, I would have quit after the first two. She was sweet and game and helped me see that, yes, I could build shelves over here or have a loft made over there and put a desk right under it. She showed me the cool thing about this place: a safe, built right into the wall! Or that one: roof access! Or: Couldn't I just picture a cross-legged, candle-lit cocktail party in here?

By the end, six turns deep into the realtor's labyrinth, I began to see these apartments not for each one's objective awfulness but for the way each stacked up against the others. It was a trick of the eye that fooled me into believing that maybe number 4 wasn't so bad after all.

Only to be told that if I was interested, I would need to act fast.

"What does 'act fast' mean, in this situation? Me saying, 'I'll take it'?"

"And filling this out completely." He handed me a form that required my divulging all of the relevant information that the initial application hadn't, including bank account numbers, landlord references, and a signatory waiver for a credit check. "Get it back to me as soon as you can," Hector said. "And confidentially," here he handed me the faxed copy of the form I had filled out earlier, "I would suggest putting something steadier sounding on your final application than 'filmmaker' and"—he pointed to the number I had listed for income ($300,000/year)—"make sure you have a figure here that can be verified."

After parting ways with Hector, we strolled back west, toward Viktoria's apartment. Now that the sun had gone down, it was much cooler, and she hugged herself against my arm as we walked. We stopped at the front window of the St. Mark's Bookshop, a storefront I'd passed dozens of times on my way to the movie theater, never once having the urge to slow down, to take in what was on display.

We went inside. I took pleasure in losing Viktoria for a short while as I wandered the store—to discover her again, at the far end of an aisle. *She's with me*, I thought, just to make myself flush. I showed her Arthur's book, which was on display. "I know him," I said. This didn't seem to impress her, though.

She said, "Is it any good?"

"Very good."

"Reading isn't really my thing. I've got nothing against people who read, there's just so much else to do in life. Do you think they have any books on BPD? I need to figure this thing out better."

She went to the counter and asked. Even the hipsters who worked here in their tight flannel shirts and horn-rimmed glasses were not immune to Viktoria. She shook them from the heights of their affected boredom to the very core of their once brace-faced, high school selves—stammering, tripping over their own feet to show her what she was looking for. It was a joy to watch.

She brought a book to the register. *Girl, Interrupted*. "I hope it doesn't suck," she said.

I offered to pay for it. In my head while she was picking something out, I practiced a line about how paying for her book would be my contribution to the fund for her enjoyment of reading, but all that came out was "No, seriously. I insist."

The clerk had already rung through her credit card. "Do you want me to void this transaction?"

"Forget it," I said.

We continued on our way, through a crowd outside a velvet-roped place on Ninth Street. Viktoria looked at her watch. "What are these losers doing out so early? It's not even eight o'clock! Remind me to tell you about that place one day. Crazy story!" As we passed the crowd, I noted the slight shift in Viktoria's gait, taking on a bitchy catwalk.

As we approached the corner where I would have to turn left and she would have to turn right—trying to work out in my head how to land the good night kiss, practicing it, visualizing it—Viktoria invited me over for dinner and a movie.

"It's my turn to cook for you. And by cook I mean order pizza. My treat. It's what normal people do, right? They order pizza. They don't snort coke off a guy's asshole on a dare. Not me, a friend of mine. Logistically, it's hard to picture. But he swears it happened, and I believe him. He's a crazy motherfucker."

She dialed ahead for the pizza. We took our time at the video store. We chose a Hollywood drama about recovering alcoholics and watched it while we waited for the food to arrive, listening to her puppy yap in the kitchen. When the delivery man appeared, I paid and brought the box into the kitchen and put two slices on a pair of new plates. She played with hers but didn't eat it. When I asked she said, "I don't really like pizza."

"But you suggested it!"

"I was thinking about what normal people eat." This would become a common refrain for her, what normal people did or did not do.

Neither of us was really paying much attention to the movie. She kept turning the volume down, inexplicably, whenever she would scream at the dog. "Shut! The! Fuck! Up!" she would scream, and then pick up the remote and turn it down a few notches.

She lit a cigarette and went over to the window. I joined her. She said, "I used to only smoke a couple cigarettes a day, but at rehab that's all everyone ever does, is smoke. So now I'm up to two packs a day. It's sick." We finished our cigarettes, stubbed them out on the sill, and tossed them out the window. She said, "I need to take things very slow. Do you think you handle that?" It was something she had said on our first date as well. I said I could take it slow. "Good," she said and squeezed my hand.

We went back to the sofa and watched as the film drew inaudibly toward its conclusion, which clearly was imminent because the main character had hit rock bottom and seemed to be in the middle of a teary reunion with an estranged son. Viktoria leaned against me, and as the credits rolled, we kissed. Her face smelled like peach candy. The television screen, once the credits ended, bathed us in blue. We went on kissing for a while like this. I reached into her shirt and unhooked her bra. I brushed my thumb against her nipple, back and forth, until it became firm. Her eyes were closed, her breath a string of sighs, one after the next. She did not stop me, and the dog, miraculously, was quiet except for some scrabbling now and then at the gate, a stray whimper. With my other hand

I felt my way along the long path of her leg, up the inside of her thigh, and into her skirt. I reached into the humid warmth of her underwear, then reached up farther, with two fingers, and held her like this, my palm against her bristly mound as she rocked herself to climax.

We lay there for some time afterward, and from the way her head was turned, away from me, I could tell I had gone too far. I got up to pee, and when I came out, she was in a pair of boy's pajamas. Without saying good night she went to her bedroom and closed the door.

I let myself out silently, so as not to disturb the dog.

It had been the summer of *The Blair Witch Project*, and after three solid months of sold-out shows and lines out the door, the moviegoing public seemed to have awoken from the hype of this little "gem" feeling swindled and took a pass on the fall season. I sat on the glass popcorn display case cross-legged, watching over the empty theaters while the other ushers engaged in closing duties ahead of schedule in anticipation of an early night. The person in the ticket booth, entirely against policy, turned off the marquee lights and lowered the gate partway so that we would appear closed to those who might be considering a late show. This rarely worked. Either a manager would catch us or someone with a Moviefone ticket purchased ahead of time would foil our plans, but tonight it worked, and I found myself back home by nine fifteen. My mother was up watching television, and I sat with her awhile. This activity had gotten to be tricky, as I had to fake a sense of continued enthusiasm for every bit of my day that I chose to relate.

My mother wasn't fooled, of course. "I spoke with Ann today."

"My ex-girlfriend?"

"Brody. Down the hall?"

"Right."

"Her daughter's looking to take up the piano. I told her that you might be interested."

"In what? Giving lessons?"

"I didn't say you would, I just said you might be interested. I thought it could be a nice opportunity for you."

I was still momentarily stuck on my mistaken impression that my mother had been talking to my ex-girlfriend about me and what that conversation might have been like. There was a lot they agreed on, namely that I couldn't be trusted to make career decisions and that I needed to shave more often.

Seeming to read my mind, my mother said with a sidelong glance, "I don't know about this in-between look you've got going. Either grow a beard or don't, but this just makes you look like you forgot to shave."

"I did forget to shave." I pointed the remote at the television and notched up the volume on an episode of *Law & Order*. I could sense her continuing to watch me as I pretended to watch the screen.

During the commercial she said, "Give it some thought. It would be some steady pocket money for you and a way for you to reconnect a little with your music, which might not be the worst thing in the world."

"Mother dearest," I said, turning to her and taking her hand. "I love you and have nothing but gratitude for the twenty-odd years you've sheltered me—"

"Uh-oh."

"—but I think the time has finally come for me to move out."

"Again."

"For good this time."

"Any place you find, you know, is going to want first and last. Even a sublet."

"I'll figure it out."

I stood, gathered my mother's dirty plates from the coffee table, and went into the kitchen. I rinsed the dishes and set each on the rubberized-wire drying rack. "Bring the box of cookies on your way back," my mother called. "They're on the windowsill!"

Back in my room, I got into my pajamas, a gift from An way back when. I used to sleep naked, but she claimed the oil and sweat I secreted required her to launder the sheets too often. An liked things clean. I would find my pajamas washed and folded every few days on my pillow. They were falling apart now from so many washings, the waistband losing its elastic, threadbare, the cuffs coming unhemmed. I could sleep naked nowadays if I wanted to, but I'd come to see it her way.

My mother stopped in later to return the book I'd lent her.

"What'd you think?"

She turned it over in her hands. "This was that boy you knew from Morningside Conservatory? What a terrible thing, doing that onstage. So destructive. I don't know. What did I think? It's hard, knowing nothing else about him but this book and that performance, to avoid trying to link them somehow."

"What do you mean?"

She took a seat on the piano bench, leaned her elbow on the closed lid. "It feels very personal."

"It's not a book of poems, Mom."

"Still, there's a rawness about the material. As though he were still working through it. That guidance counselor. *You've got to deal with this thing or it will eat you alive.* Dire pronouncements. It's like the author's giving himself this advice."

I adjusted the pillows on my bed, leaned back. "I liked it. It's creepy, in the way Beckett is creepy. And I think he's kind of fascinating. Totally intense."

"What do Suri and Dave make of him?"

"Oil and water."

"Ha. I'd suspect so. Art and Commerce, at opposite ends of the hall."

"They're not as crass as all that, Mom. Maybe Dave is, but Suri wants more. You read the first draft of his script."

"How about your script?"

"I gave it to him. He promised to read it. Once we're done with this project." I watched my mother run her hand along the closed lid of the piano. "It's got to seem like a terrible waste," I said, "me giving up on music after all those years. The money you spent on lessons. Not to mention the four years of college tuition."

"If this is about Mrs. Brody's daughter, forget I mentioned it. And forget money. You're looking for something. I get it, honey. I do. It's not music, and that's fine. You'll find it. Whatever it is. Whatever end of the hall it's on."

The realtors wanted nothing to do with me. My income did not meet most landlords' minimum requirements, and my credit history revealed a long and contentious battle with my college lenders to collect monthly payments.

"What am I going to do now?" I was at Viktoria's, in her kitchen preparing a dinner omelet while her dog snuffled at my crotch.

"You could stay here with me and Sammy. We'd love that, wouldn't we? Oh, wouldn't we? He could be our little slave, cooking and cleaning for us while we went about our business." It actually didn't sound bad at all.

I took the potatoes out of the oven, which I'd tossed with a little oil and rosemary and set up on a high rack to broil under some aluminum foil. I divided these on the plates with the eggs, which I set down on her rickety Ikea table. Viktoria opened the gate and let the puppy roam. "I think he can be trusted by now."

I shook some ketchup into a small dish and set it between us for dipping our potatoes. I demonstrated.

She clapped. "Yay, like normal people!" She forked a potato and blew on it. "You really should be proud of yourself," she said after a few bites. "I usually don't eat, but this smells so good. My parents would be shocked." Despite this claim, she only made it through a quarter of the omelet. Most of her potatoes remained untouched. It occurs to me now that on top of her other troubles, she might have been anorexic as well. I had no experience with this, as all the women in my life were good eaters. She was very thin, her hips narrow, her breasts the buds of a prepubescent girl. Her stunning beauty was not a voluptuous one but rather the angular, androgynous beauty of a runway model. Thin limbs that extended out to her very fingertips. Clumsy, but the clumsy of a swan on dry land, of Annie Hall. It wasn't her breasts you noticed or her rear end. It was the graceful hollows, the scoop of her clavicle, the dimpled backs of her knees.

Viktoria lit a cigarette and dropped the match onto her plate, where it sizzled. I cleared and upon returning was struck by the distinct stench of dog shit. Viktoria smelled it, too. We followed it to its source.

On the little entryway rug, Sammy had left a wet-looking pile.

"Oh you stupid fuck!" Viktoria screamed at Sammy, who sat shivering on the bed.

# 5
# N O V E L

ARTHUR AND PENELOPE HAD BEEN expecting me. "Here," Arthur said, handing me a stack of paper held together with a binder clip. "Tell me what to do with this."

"Him? You're giving it to him? What does he have to do with this?" Penelope was holding a glass of white wine. She said, "Put that down and let me get you something to drink. It's a good cheap fumé." She left the balcony and went into the kitchen.

Arthur said, "Don't put it down. Don't put it down. I'm asking him a question, Penelope. One that you don't seem to have the nerve to answer."

She returned with two glasses and took a sweating bottle from the dining room table and poured some wine into each. She handed one to me and one to Arthur. "I'm assuming you want." Her right hand was swaddled in gauze. "Work related," she said when she saw me looking. "I'll live. Let's go onto the porch."

I was wearing a turtleneck and a wool blazer — a yearning toward the professorial poise in Arthur, I suppose. It was crisp out — pure, I want to say. When you're above the exhaust pipes and manholes and dry-cleaner steam, just breathing the air, New York City can smell as clean as a lungful from a ski lift in Vale. It's a fairly short period, though, a week or two at most, after the garbagy musk of summer and before the burnt chestnut chill of winter.

Arthur brought out three dining room chairs, and we sat. I set the stack of pages on my lap. It was maybe three inches thick. The center of the top page read *The Morels: A Novel*.

"Is this your new book?"

"He wants me to read it."

"And why don't you?"

"I will. But not like this. Art thinks I won't approve and—no way. I don't want any part of that. You wrote what you wrote. I'm not going to be your conscience or your censor. Do that for yourself. And you know what? Fuck you. For trying to make me play that role. I don't want to play that role. Anyway, what am I supposed to say? I read it, I don't like it, I tell you, *Art, don't publish this. Burn it*."

"I'd burn it without a second thought."

"But what about me? I'd be nothing but second thoughts. You're saddling me with this burden? That's fair. And like I would ever say such a thing. You know this. You know I would never tell you to do that, so what are you really doing here? You're forcing my hand. It's a bluff. You don't want me to tell you what I really think. You want me to tell you to go ahead, and you know I'll tell you to go ahead because what kind of supportive wife would tell her writer husband to burn his manuscript? It's a free pass. You know how I know? Coming to me now. It's sold, your agent has seen it, he's gotten a publisher to agree to buy it—this thing is already out of your hands—why not come to me when you were still working on it? When you could have done something about it?"

I thumbed though the pages. On first glance, it appeared to be a string of emails. Three hundred and sixty-two pages of emails.

"But you don't understand. That's not it at all. I'm asking you for help. I don't know what I'm doing. You give me way too much credit. I'm not in control over what I write. This isn't some piece for a travel magazine or some restaurant review. It's not a mystery, it's not a romance, or what have you. This is—excuse the pretentiousness of saying it—literature. I'm looking for good, for true, for dangerous. This is my mandate, my only mandate. There is no formula. It's a direction, the vaguest sort of destination, a kind of compass that, if I know how to use it, will show me the way. And here is this thing I found, and I know it's all these things, but I also know it will hurt you and Will."

"Art. They're words. It's a novel, yes?"

"Technically, yes."

"There is no technically. It is or it isn't."

"I guess that will be the question, won't it?"

"Look. You can't please everybody. You can't. You make sac-rifices. You think this is any different than what a doctor goes through? A top surgeon? The procedure develops complications, and he has to miss his son's graduation. Or I don't know, at least that's the way it goes on television, but it sounds about right. These are the trade-offs. This is what happens to a family man with a career. You're not special. You just have to accept that your wife and son may never forgive you."

"I can't do that. That's unacceptable. It can't be either-or."

"You're such an only child, Arthur."

"I have half siblings!"

"You want it all, but you can't have it all."

"Okay," he said. He took the manuscript from me, got up, and went inside.

Penelope crossed her eyes at me. "Do you see what I'm dealing with? He turns into a crazy person sometimes. I want to pull my hair out."

Some people would say they avoid being around couples for precisely this kind of cross fire I was in, but I found it comforting. It made me feel closer to them, that they should have let me into their lives enough that I could see them argue. I took a mouthful of wine. "This is good," I said.

Arthur came back empty-handed and sat down.

"So," Penelope said quietly, "what are you going to do?"

"I'm going to call Doug in the morning and tell him to forget it."

"Oh, Jesus! I didn't realize I was talking to someone's Catholic mother. Poor Arthur! Going to martyr his magnum opus for the sake of the family."

"What do you want from me, Penelope?"

"I want you to be realistic. You've brought this thing into the world. You can't undo that. Destroying it—the original file, all copies, whatever—doesn't change this fact. You wrote it. Period. Deciding not to publish doesn't change this. Even if you could take it back, even if nobody had read it, it wouldn't change a thing. It exists. What's required of you now is to be a man about it. Own it. It's yours. To hell with me. To hell with Will. Is that what you want me to say?"

"You should read it. You should know what you're getting into before you say a thing like that."

"I don't care what it's about. Do you love me? Do you love Will? Does this story change that? No, so go forth and publish."

Arthur looked at his watch. "I need to go pick him up."

In the elevator I said, "So Penelope doesn't know anything about this new book."

"Not from me withholding it, believe me. She doesn't want to know. She wants to go out on the day it's released, walk into a bookstore, take the thing off the new-arrivals rack, and pay top dollar for the hardcover. Be the first in line, as it were. It was the same with the other one."

Arthur explained that the release date of a book is a rather anticlimactic affair. There are launch parties and readings and three-way conference calls about first-week numbers, but this is somehow beside the point. With a movie premiere, the auteur has the satisfaction of sitting in a back row and seeing the effect his efforts have, connecting the dots of that triumvirate uppercase $A$ — Artist, Art, Audience—the reaction is immediate, visceral. He can stand with the ushers as the moviegoers file out and hear just how enthralled or bored they were. A gallery opening, although more of a ceremony, achieves this same function, plugging together viewer and object for the benefit of its maker, so she can see her achievement realized. And likewise with the composer, the choreographer, the architect, the chef. The spaces they describe are traversable such that the artist can witness the traversing. Not so for the novelist. The book launch, though it pretends to accomplish this—invited guests, signed books stacked on a foldout table, a reading, and, at the end, applause—is a sham. Because books are different. They can't be consumed in one sitting. The narrative arc takes many hours, days if you're a slow reader, to travel, and it's a journey that happens alone. This was the other difference about literary art. Theater, music, dance, dining, are all communal arts, the experience enhanced when shared with others. Reading is an entirely solitary activity. Even a subway car full of straphangers all reading the same bestseller is a hundred separate people alone with a book. So where does that leave the writer? He can't watch over the shoulder of a stranger, gauging his reaction. And the author's wife has likely already read a draft or two, or at the very least knows too much about the endeavor and its author to enjoy any pure reading experience.

But this is exactly what Penelope wanted to do: enjoy a pure encounter with Arthur's book. To be told nothing about it, and on the day of its release buy a copy in the bookstore, spend all day reading it, and return through the apartment door so he could have the satisfaction of seeing her reaction—helping him to close that circuit. Audience. Artist. Art.

It occurs to me that Will's absence from these get-togethers may seem like a writerly convenience. The truth is, though, the only memorable conversations I had with them, as a couple and individually, were those that happened in Will's absence—indeed, were only possible *through* Will's absence. There were any number of other occasions when I might encounter Will and his mother in the hall or the three of them in the elevator, and I would hear how they were off to see *Star Wars: Episode One* for the third time or were just coming back from Leandra Williams's birthday party. Will would be the focus of these encounters—children, I've noticed, become the center of gravity in a room—talking rapidly about something *hilarious* Tyler said at the party or demonstrating the proper way to avoid the jaws of a Tyrannosaurus rex. It wasn't that Will was especially precocious or that what he was saying was especially interesting; it was just that he was the one with the most energy and with it he commanded the most attention. It was like this on the few occasions I knocked unannounced, to encounter the three of them preparing for a typical evening in: Will on the floor staring up at the television, Arthur at the table trying to concentrate on a stack of papers and Penelope picking up stray clothes and toys around the apartment and yelling at Will to *turn it down!* Even with Will occupied, it was hard to keep the thread of a conversation going, as our attention would gravitate to what he was watching. When Will wasn't at the television, he wanted to be a part of our talk, and soon enough we would find ourselves learning about something hilarious Tyler had said about Mr. Boinkman today or the absolutely true story he'd heard about the vampire living in the school basement.

And it's not that I don't like kids. It's that they make me nervous. They're unpredictable. Their problem with personal space is no different than that of a crazy homeless person's. One minute they're saying you remind them of creepy Freddy Krueger and the next they're trying to shimmy your torso for a piggyback ride. Other people don't have this problem. Dave, for instance. He had a rapport with Will, which began, I suppose, that night on the roof. Will would show up randomly, without notice, to discuss movies or video games, and Dave would let him in, offer him a soda, as though he were Seinfeld and Will were Kramer.

"The kid's got pretty sophisticated taste for an eleven-year-old. His favorite movie? *Reservoir Dogs*. He says *Pulp Fiction* is too stylized for his tastes. He used that word: 'stylized.' I asked him, 'So your parents let you watch movies like that?' I mean, this is pretty violent stuff. And he's like, 'I get to make my own decisions.' He's a funny kid."

Will would appear while the three of us were working in the

editing suite and plop right down on the couch next to us. Suriyaarachchi didn't seem to mind. He liked Will too. Will would
be in his costume, black suit and tie with a badge that read FBI.
Orange gun in one hand and a large policeman's flashlight in the
other. "Trick or treat," he said the first time I encountered him at
the door.

"Who are you supposed to be?"

"Special Agent Fox Mulder, he said, shining the flashlight in
my face.

"You look like a Jehovah's Witness."

"Jehovah? He's under federal protection because he knows too
much."

"You're lucky I'm not a truant officer. Shouldn't you be in
school?"

"Half day. I'm looking for Agent Suriyaarachchi and Agent
Dave. They around?"

Dave told me that Penelope would occasionally call on him to babysit last-minute, which entailed getting twenty bucks to have Will
come over to do what he normally did. Dave used the money for
takeout, which the two of them would eat while blasting the limbs
off of zombie hordes.

Will took after his mother, slightly plump with thick black hair
and the delicate lashes of a pretty girl. He liked to eat and often
came prepared with a knapsack of Tupperwared food Penelope
had packed for him.

Will said to me one day, quite out of the blue, "Mom and Art
are fighting a lot." I was looking through the sublet listings in the
Voice. Dave and Suriyaarachchi had gone out to the post office.
Will had come in during their absence and asked if it would be
okay if he played a video game. It had been intended as a rhetorical question—he was already kneeling in front of the console—but
I said that he would have to ask Dave's permission when he got
back from his errand.

"When will he be back?" Will was used to being adored by

adults, but I had made it clear I was immune to his charms. He would often find himself blinking at me, unsure of how to proceed. I had hoped my answer would discourage him from sticking around, but instead he took a seat next to me and picked up the entertainment circular of the paper and held it out in front of him, as if to read. Cute. I resumed my task of starring any long-term sublets within my budget — there weren't many — when Will said what he said about Penelope and Arthur fighting. I waited for him to go on, bracing myself for a discussion about how he shouldn't worry, sometimes parents fight but it doesn't mean that et cetera.

Will said, "Mostly it's Mom who does the yelling. Art listens. I think it's because she loves him more than he loves her."

"What makes you say that?"

Stray hair floated up off his head from the static of the hat he'd just removed. A crust of mucus ringed his left nostril. He set down the paper and opened his knapsack, removing a round bin that contained apple slices, a little browned. "I've always thought that. She does the hugging and the kissing. He accepts it. It's not like he doesn't like it. He's like me that way. And I don't hear them doing it anymore, which is another thing. Not since we moved here."

"You know what 'doing it' sounds like?"

He rolled his eyes and popped an apple slice into his mouth.

"What kind of son are you, who doesn't hug his mother?"

"I hug her. Of course I hug her. But sometimes I need to play it cool."

Suriyaarachchi and Dave returned. "Will, my man," Dave said. "Let me score some of that apple. I'm surprised to see you just sitting there. Thought for sure I'd find you warming up the PlayStation for me."

Will looked over at me as if to say, *See?*

After dropping Will off at school, Penelope stops in at Barnes & Noble to pick up a copy of Arthur's new book. Crinkly green bag in hand, she heads up and east along Sixty-Sixth Street, into Central Park. She'd planned to find a quiet spot under a tree, but the benches are wet from the overnight rain. Somewhat at a loss, she wanders around and ends up ordering a pretzel from a vendor cart even though it isn't yet ten in the morning. It's an autumn smell, it beckons her, but the pretzel leaves a pasty taste in her mouth with overtones of ashtray and makes her instantly sleepy. She finds a line of dry benches under an eve, above and behind the old proscenium band shell around which people Rollerblade to music on their headphones in bright colored spandex. There is the distant treble of a faraway boom box. She sits and shrugs off her coat, humming a tune that takes her a moment to realize is the song on the boom box. She slips the book from its bag and cracks it open, giving it an involuntary sniff before turning to the first page.

She is shocked anew by the power of Arthur's writing, its ability to take her in. Is this just the power all authors have? The mere mention of a *red shawl*—like a command you are powerless to resist—and there it is, the chenille soft in your hands. Even though the title prepares her somewhat, it's also a shock to be taken into the fictionalized realm of her own life—a version of déjà vu, not unlike hearing her own voice on an answering machine. She reads, and winces, reading, and reads on, and then falls asleep.

In her dream, she is twelve and in braces, self-conscious of her breath and of being naked. She is in a stable, shivering. There are horses stamping and farting around her. Something terrible has just happened, or is about to happen, but she can't figure out what. She wakes herself so that she can remember and discovers that her coat is on the ground and her shirt is hiked up and she is freezing.

She finds the book, which has fallen under the bench. She returns to the last page she remembers reading and continues, but she can't shake the feeling that something is terribly wrong. Her dream has entered the atmosphere of the book, or maybe she is picking up a subtle atmosphere from the book itself? It's hard to tell now. She puts her coat back on and zips it up and continues reading.

In the manner of other contemporary fiction, there's little story to speak of—the dilemmas of everyday life—and yet it's also compelling. It's the sentences, the train of thought—it's persuasive. So she turns the pages to see where it all might lead, because it does seem to be leading somewhere, each scene a preparation for some defining moment. How could he call this a novel? She checks the cover again. *The Morels: A Novel.*

The main character is named Arthur Morel, who is married to a character named Penelope, and their child's name is Will. The voice is conversational, less formal than the I-voice of his previous book, closer to Arthur's own. Main-character-Arthur works as an administrative head at a university library, a job real-Arthur had for a short while, before being let go. It had not been a good time for them. Arthur was miserable. This was three years ago, before his first book was published. Will was eight.

We find ourselves at the beginning of *The Morels* with Arthur struggling to make meaning from what has become a mundane domestic existence—he works; he comes home; he washes dishes and bundles garbage. The burden of fatherhood puts a strain on him, on the marriage. Manhood does not come naturally; he is not a natural father. What to say, how to behave. His father-in-law tells him not to worry, that it's eighteen years of on-the-job training, to follow his heart and he would be okay.

The only problem for Arthur is that his heart is a mystery to him. Most of the time, Arthur doesn't know what to feel and suspects that deep down he feels nothing—for anyone. In the meantime, he fakes it. He watches Penelope for clues, imitating her expressions of affection, her declarations of love—and as such, Arthur feels as though he's making up his feelings, inventing them as he goes along—careful to feel whatever is appropriate for the situation. His job brings him little satisfaction—it requires a kind of leadership he does not possess—he must motivate his staff as well as those he answers to. He dreads work, feels in over his head daily—the suits he's required to wear have been given to him by Penelope's father, his father's suits, as it were. He looks in the mirror to see that he is no longer himself, but with every passing week, living the life he is living, he is no longer sure who that is anymore.

DEVOTED HUSBAND, LOVING FATHER. It feels like an epitaph.

His thoughts turn morbid. He feels like the walking dead. A man of no consequence. He has given up the immortality of Visionary Artist for the mortal and inconsequential role of Family Man, indistinguishable from eighty-three million others just like him. It is a long slow march toward the grave, no doubt on which will be written DEVOTED HUSBAND, LOVING FATHER. Within two years, less, his family will have moved on, forgotten him. It would be as if he'd never existed. His struggles at his job and at home take on the proportions of life and death — it's a struggle he is waging — and losing — for his own survival.

In lieu of lunch, Arthur goes into the library stacks, and here he can finally breathe again, a fish returned to water. He drifts among the sea of words, stopping randomly at an unfamiliar or interesting title. Opening the book, he allows himself to dream for a while inside, and when it's time for him to make his way back to work, he feels as though he is leaving a part of himself there — that part of himself has become trapped within the covers of the book he'd been browsing — and so he must go back the next day, and the next.

He tests his limits. He skips meetings in which he is not expected to speak. He spends entire days lost in the stacks or behind his desk, holding all calls, in front of his computer. When someone enters, he does not look up.

He begins writing emails to himself.

At night, unable to sleep, he fires up his laptop to find his inbox full. The messages are addressed to himself, from one part of his brain to another. Cries for help from a man in the trenches. He details his troubles at work. His restlessness, his suffocation. He used to be able to shut the stall door in the men's room and with a visual cue of Dean Bartholomew's secretary — her parted legs under her desk, the small patch of hair — masturbate to climax in less time than it took most men to wash their hands. These days it is a different story entirely. He works at his flaccid penis there in the stall, trying to fully picture the space underneath the secretary's desk — unsuccessfully — until the bathroom door bangs open, the sound of unzipping at a urinal, and Arthur's concentration would be fully broken. What has he become, that he can't even give his secret work crushes their proper due? That this last refuge of freedom, his sexual imagination, is closed to him?

Arthur reads these emails from himself in the monitor glow of the darkened bedroom, Penelope asleep not five feet away — addressed as though he were someone else, an estranged friend. So he does what any friend would do: he writes back.

He commiserates. He relates his various miseries on the home front. His life with Penelope and Will is just a series of small lies — from the moment he walks through the door. *I missed you,* she says, and he says, *I missed you too.* But he has not in fact thought about Penelope throughout the day — should he have? He feels guilty, and so when he tells her that he has missed her too, he is lying. Or maybe willing himself to have missed her, not so much a lie as it is a kind of apology. When he says, *I missed you too,* what he really means is *I want to have missed you too.* He means *I will try my hardest tomorrow to miss you too.*

She asks him how his day has been, and when he says that it was fine, when he doesn't tell her that it was decidedly not fine, this is another lie.

These overtures about their day are no more prelude to a real discussion of their true feelings as the peck on the lips as he's taking off his coat is a prelude to sex.

This is married life.

It isn't what it used to be. Back when he was just shelving books — infant Will at the apartment with his mother-in-law — Penelope would show up in an easy-access skirt and no underwear, and they would fuck right there in the stacks. They used to get such a kick out of playing house, out of peeling the blistered skin off of a butternut squash and placing it in the new Cuisinart; add a little cream and look — soup! Now dinner is just another chore, the Cuisinart a tool like any other in the kitchen, no longer a novelty. A pot of chili on Sunday for a week of leftovers. Frozen portions of split pea in individually microwavable containers. Life at home. Asleep by nine thirty, up at six to do it all again.

Back in his office, he shuts the door and checks his emails; deleting those from his boss, he opens the one from himself. He reads it over, then spends the rest of the morning crafting a reply. *Why is it so hard, just living?* he writes. *I am married, my wife is healthy and beautiful. I have a son who is healthy and beautiful. I, too, am healthy and have a job that supports us, that allows us to live in relative ease. So why am I not living with the ease in which I live?*

His troubles at work, his miseries on the home front. With these out of the way, he moves on to other concerns, to the darker corners of his mind. He reminds himself of a passing childhood acquaintance, a boy his own age. Acts of sexual pleasure engaged in with this boy. How old had they been? Nine? Arthur used to worry over the thought of being gay. Did these acts he used to perform make him so? He would think of his time with this boy and become aroused. Even now — as a husband and a father — when he remembers these encounters, he becomes aroused. In fact, it's the only image potent enough these days, sitting there in the men's room stall, to get him off. What does this mean? How is he to reconcile this with the life he lives as an average family man?

Arthur finds that by pursuing this correspondence with himself, he feels better. The more he commiserates, the less miserable he feels. Airing dark truths help lighten his spirit; and writing obsessively to himself these long dark weeks cures him of the need to write obsessively to himself. In one long last email, he talks about his new contentment, about how at peace with himself he has become. He thanks himself for listening, for commiserating. He describes venturing out of his office now to engage with fellow staff and administrators, a new desire to tackle the overflow on his desk. He tells of a home life in which he is now fully and happily engaged with Penelope, with Will. His heart is brimming with new love for them, a love he does not have to fake anymore. He brings in pictures of them and tacks them up on the board above his desk, puts one in his wallet.

The big shock comes on the final pages, suddenly, although in some way it seems to be the culmination of all prior moments in the book, the destination that all sentences point to.

Penelope reads the final scene, then reads it again, and before she is aware of what she is doing exactly, she is on her feet, running out of the park. The people she passes stare at her. She can hear herself panting. She is jogging down Central Park West, past Lincoln Center, past the Theater District, past Port Authority, left at Madison Square Garden toward Manhattan East Middle School.

Will does not appear to be among the small clusters of children playing here. It is a brisk autumn day. The sun is overhead, warming her shoulders and gleaming off the windshields of parked cars. The air is still. There is a basketball hoop, boundary lines painted on asphalt. Older kids are yelling their way through a game, though in the long moment that she stands there, nobody seems to be able to make a basket. Those about Will's age are involved in some version of tag at the far end of the yard by a muraled wall. Two girls sitting down are tagged, then leap up and join the fray, letting out blood-chilling screams; others, who have been hopping around, dodging outstretched hands, lose focus and drift off. And then Penelope sees him, sitting against the wall with three Hispanic girls. She searches Will's face for any trace of trouble. What is she looking for? He seems to be enjoying himself, totally at ease with these girls. This always surprises her about Will, his ease with people, it didn't matter who. Was that a function of his age? He certainly didn't get it from Arthur. Even around people he knows, Arthur is shy and stern. At parties, he suffers from social exhaustion, his tolerance for small talk low; before long he grows restless and needs to be home again with her and Will. He doesn't like meeting new people. Will, on the other hand, can talk to just about anybody. He is charming, precocious in that way of only children. It breaks her heart how at ease he is with people.

A male teacher, who has been sitting on a bench, notices Penelope and saunters over. Hello, he says. You're a parent, but I can't remember whose.

Will Morel's mom, she says.

That's right, of course. Checking up on him?

Just making sure he's safe.

I was coming out of Dave's, done for the day, when I ran into Penelope ascending the subway's stairs. She took me by the arm.

"What are you doing now? Let's have coffee."

She led me across the street into the Galaxy Diner and walked us toward the back. These were the last days of smoking in New York City, and there were a few reserved booths by the restrooms that were usually empty. She took a seat and asked me for a cigarette.

"I'm not the girlfriend type," she said, lighting up. "Other women have girlfriends they complain to, go to for comfort. I have Art. And my parents. And I can't talk to either of them about this. So who do I talk to?"

The waiter came with menus and a dishrag that he heaved in two swipes across our table, leaving behind a mildew stink. His borderline hostility brought my attention to the emptiness of the place. The cooks behind the counter were watching us as they sudsed down the griddle and mopped the floors. This was a lunch place, and lunch was over. I ordered a Coke. Penelope ordered a tuna melt. The waiter stiffened at this. "I'll have to see if that's still possible."

"You do that." She pulled on her cigarette, watching him go, then said, "Have you read it? Of course you haven't, it came out this morning." She put the book on the table. "Take it, I don't want it. Shit. You need to read it, though, I've got to talk to someone."

"Talk to me, now. What's so wrong?"

She told me the story of her day—dropping Will off at school, buying the book, reading it in the park, then running back to the school to check on him—as if the solution to her dread were to be found here, in the minutiae of the day's decisions. "I mean, the thing of it? It was exactly like I said. You were there. I called it a mile off. He set me up. That motherfucker set me up." This word— *motherfucker*—it sounded in her cutesy voice as though she were invoking the name of a fairy-tale villain. "Now he can always say he gave me an out. But even if I had read it back then, I couldn't have told him to destroy it. I wouldn't have."

"What's so bad about it?" I turn the hardbound book over in my hands. The dust jacket showed a photograph of Barbie and Ken and Young Ken standing naked in a toy bathtub, genital areas blurred out.

"I don't want to say. You'll read it. You'll find out, and you'll probably like it—admire it for its unflinching whatever."

"So you're just mad that he wrote it."

"Yes! And what am I going to tell my parents? Not to read it? They've been so happy Arthur's finally made something of him-self—they'll be crushed. And furious."

"That's Arthur," I said. "It's not good unless he's pissed some-one off."

"Ugh, I sound just like them. Listen to me. Falling for the same bait. My parents like art but have weak stomachs. They're easily outraged. Mapplethorpe at the National Gallery, I tell them it's supposed to provoke, but they don't want to hear it."

Penelope stubbed out her cigarette. "Ah, Christ. Art."

"Whatever it is you don't like about it," I said, "remember, it's just a story, words on a page. You said it yourself."

"That's just it, though. So much of it's real. Our names, the loca-tions, the situations. But I know. Even as I say it, I can hear how naïve it sounds. Of course it's possible to have a book that uses the people in the author's life as characters—and the author himself— and for every word of it to be made up. Right?"

Our order came, and Penelope went at her tuna melt hungrily with her hands, pizzalike, baring her teeth at it before each bite. My soda was flat, but I drank it in small nips through the straw.

"Art can't know we've had this little chat."

"Why not?"

"He needs to know that I support what he does a hundred percent. If he doubted it, that would be the end of his writing career."

"You realize you're describing a paradox."

"I don't want things to go back to the way they used to be. Before he was writing, he was miserable. When he thought he had to be the man of the house, he was such a sad sack. And my family was relentless. Holidays were an ordeal. 'Still at the library?' my mother would ask—half question, half accusation—knowing full well he was *still at the library*. The humiliation of having my brother offering Art career advice—a man who's never worked an honest day in his life, who actually describes himself as an *entrepreneur*. My sister's husband eventually joining in, Dad, too, and by the end of the evening, they'd all be at him with their *advice*. It was cruel. Oh, but they were being *helpful*. Their comments and suggestions were *not* veiled criticisms designed to point out Art's ineptness, his lack of any practical skills. And what could Art do but thank them for their concern?

"Now he's a star in their eyes. Oh, yes, my mother says, he's a *published novelist*. She's so funny. And I can't say it wasn't nice coming across Art's writing for the first time. We'd been married some years, Will was six, maybe?"

To see all of Arthur's hallmark qualities—fixating over odd moments, taking nothing for granted, coming at everyday objects like a tourist in his own life, his capacity to deconstruct even the simplest instructions into a paralyzing metaphysical dilemma—these qualities that made him a drag at cocktail parties and all but unemployable here on the page served him well, made for exquisitely rendered scenes, well-observed prose, good writing. It pleased her to be reminded of Arthur's talents, to be surprised by him. Wasn't it refreshing, after years of seeing everything Arthur wasn't, of having pointed out to her everything Arthur could never be—and the kind of family she could never have—to be shown what her husband actually was?

"So, no. I don't want to go back to an Art who doesn't make art.

I'd rather he offend my parents, offend me." She wiped her mouth with a paper napkin and tossed it onto her empty plate. In a flash the waiter swiped it and my empty cup and everything else on the table. The check had been waiting, stuck facedown on the damp counter, since the food had arrived. Penelope put down a twenty and got up.

The staff followed us out in their street clothes, and as soon as we were over the threshold, the shutter rattled down at our backs. I lit a cigarette, and Penelope had one more. We smoked, watching the big brass revolving door across the street trade one person for another, taking them in and letting them out in equal measure.

She said, "I feel a lot calmer now, thanks."

I assured her that I'd done nothing.

"Well, you should continue to do nothing again. It will keep me sane through this. And bring your cigarettes."

# 6
# THANKSGIVING

ENELOPE AND I MET SEVERAL times over the next couple of weeks. She used the time to reminisce, determined to recover some more flattering image of herself and Arthur, of their life together. "I had a boyfriend when I met Art, but he was mostly a way of saying no to boys I wasn't interested in—long distance, rarely saw each other, got a weekly call. When I told the guy that I was seeing someone else, he said, 'What's his name?' 'Art,' I said. 'Do you love him?' 'Yes,' I said—and just admitting it felt like vertigo. Art was my secret. People thought he was an asshole, but that's just because he doesn't know what to say most of the time, especially when he gets nervous. People didn't know him like I knew him, didn't know his touch, never saw him at his tenderest or most vulnerable."

Basement auditorium of the Queens College Film Club, circa 1988. First date. Showing is an Australian release about neo-Nazis that has caused some controversy. It features the debut performance of an actor who will become Hollywood's baddest bad boy. In it, everyone's head is shaved. Not a single woman actor. Penelope notices this and holds on to the observation for something to talk about afterward. Staying focused is hard, like watching opera—the main thrust of the plot has to be gotten through body language. With those accents, it's anyone's guess what people are actually saying. This is made more difficult by the two men sitting directly in front of them, talking full volume. The small auditorium is full, and its attention, she can feel, is tangled around this disturbance. There is shifting, mumbling from all corners.

After some time, Arthur leans in between their heads. Hey, he says. Be quiet. Both men are bald; one is wearing an earring that glitters in the dark from the light of the projector.

Penelope's stomach tightens. She knows where this will go. These guys are older, not like grad students. Like people with jobs, who go to bars and beat people up.

The men pause, and Arthur leans back. Penelope tries to relax, to focus on what is happening on-screen. But after a few moments the men start up again.

Arthur leans forward again and says, Did you hear what I just asked?

The two pause again. Maybe we should go, Penelope whispers, although she doesn't want to go. She is out on a date; she is watching a movie. Why should they be the ones to leave? Who do these assholes think they are! Suddenly she is trembling with rage.

Yeah, one of the men says, maybe you should listen to your lady.

Maybe you should just shut up and let us enjoy this movie, Arthur says.

This seems to be the cue the men are looking for.

Okay, he says, now we're talking. The one who says this swivels in his seat. What do you propose, huh? Interestingly enough, the man is whispering now.

But Arthur laughs. Oh! What do I propose! You mean, "What do you propose to do about it, *punk*?" Isn't that your line? You cannot be serious.

Serious as they come, the man says, and stands. Get up, he says.

Arthur stands. Some brave soul from a far corner shouts, *Shut up already! All of you!* The images on-screen flash. There is a chase, the shuffle of feet, camera wobbly, disorienting. But Arthur seems entirely undisturbed. He is nose to nose with the man. It is like they are on the verge of kissing.

Come on, the man says. Let's go.

Arthur says, That's right, you and me. I'll meet you outside. But first I'm going to finish watching this movie.

How about I break your nose right now and get it over with?

Arthur snorts. If it will shut you up.

Two sounds follow: a snap of fabric, like someone quickly shrugging on a jacket, and a crack, like someone cracking their knuckles.

Arthur stands cupping his face.

Enjoy, the man says, and clomps with his friend out of the row — perhaps not as gracefully as they might have liked — and down the aisle. One takes a bow before banging open the double doors.

Arthur sits.

Here, Penelope says, let me help. She digs in her purse, for what she doesn't know. Her words come out hollow, like she is acting them out. She can feel everyone's attention on them. She urges him to go. Arthur is bleeding; she can see the glistening down his lip on his chin and neck. His nose is swollen; even in the dark she can see this. They need to go to a hospital.

But he refuses. He wads her scarf, which she has handed him, and puts it in front of his mouth and faces the screen with wet eyes. I just want to finish watching this movie. Okay?

That was Arthur. He wore his hair long in those days. It was wavy and hid half of his face, while the rest was tucked behind one of his large ears. He was pretty, even in his unshaved scruff, and the crush Penelope had on Arthur had about it the crush for a girlfriend, a crush of envy — what she wouldn't do to have that jawline, those eyes, those thick natural curls! His nose never healed correctly after the punch. She tried getting him to go to Health Services for it, but he refused. What's done is done, he'd said. It went from a nauseating gray that first night, to olive, to jaundice. The swelling of course receded, but it was still bent oddly, and a knot under the skin at the bridge remained. Penelope thought of it as her nose. Its new shape marked the beginnings of their lives together. She would touch it sometimes and shiver.

The way he towered over her. She was reminded of a school trip
to a farm, the way she felt putting her twelve-year-old hand on
the flank of a horse. The damp hair, the shiver and twitch of that
muscle's power beneath her hand, a synchronous twitch in her own
groin. This moment formed the basis of her early sexual fantasies.
She wasn't one of those horse girls who read *Misty of Chincoteague*
and collected Breyer models; she had girls in her grade, in art class
they drew nothing but horses, at lunch they carried their horse
lunch boxes and horse backpacks, in their rooms they papered their
walls with horse posters. Penelope made fun of those girls. Hers
wasn't an interest in horses, or even this horse per se, but rather
this particular moment in this particular stable, with the brute feel
of horseness in general. It was a small grain of shame that she worried over and returned to until her interest in boys replaced it, and
she later learned somewhere, overheard from someone once at a
party, that this was a common girlhood phenomenon, and when
she felt Arthur hovering just over her, or when being drawn into the
power of his writing, she felt that old twitch. He shared that equine
contradiction of beastly and pretty—the beautiful monster—blind
trampling power of hoof at the end of each slender, precarious leg.
She liked to think of Arthur as a green stallion, barely broken, the
one the ranchers called her crazy for even bothering with. He was
wild; he had fire and terror in his eyes.

Arthur was an infuriating kind of ecstasy. As the baby of the
family, Penelope had always been cooed at and coddled, show-
ered with encouragement. And even though in time Penelope
came to understand that much of this attention was a form of con-
descension, she nonetheless grew up with a healthy sense of self
and an expectation from a loved one of a certain amount of coo.
So Arthur was a rude awakening. His affections were sporadic,
unpredictable. He had the ability to undo her with a single word.
With Arthur, she became a wallflower and found herself craning
toward any glimmer of affection as though her survival depended
on it. Her brother, never known for pulling punches, had told her
she could have done a lot better. She had the goods. She knew this

about herself, and even without her own esteem there was proof in the stares she got, not to mention the offers. Stopped on the street or alone in a café. Even pregnant, even afterward with her post-partum paunch. They just couldn't help themselves, they would say. Then how was it Arthur could? The one person from whom it mattered. Cruel irony! And this indifference, these surprise attacks of affection and long stretches in anticipation of affection, made her hypersensitive to Arthur's needs, quick to compliment him on the simplest accomplishment, quick to come to his defense.

They honeymooned—she eight months pregnant—in her parents' timeshare in Maine, an A-frame cabin with a wood-burning stove and a steep set of steps that led from the deck to the clear blue lake the cabin overlooked. They drank water out of a well and shat in a shack without a door into a hole onto which they'd sprinkle lye from a bucket when they were done. A Boston whaler and a kayak tapped against the dock, a reassuring sound at night that lulled them to sleep.

She came home to their brand-new empty apartment in Queens fully invested in her brand-new life. She indulged her role as wife, unpacking the registry gifts that were waiting for them, setting them away in the cupboards, in the sideboard, in the closet. It was a fairy tale, and she indulged it. She was never one to play house or dream about weddings. Her childhood was spent in tom-boy competition with older boys, proclaiming her disdain for all things girlie. Girlishness, when it came in her late teens, was about dress up—black lace and black eyeliner, an ironic subscription to *Cosmo*—but now she saw what she'd been missing out on. Playing house was fun! She enlisted her mother's help, which her mother was thrilled to offer.

And in this way, maternity was a kind of surrender, too. A giving in. She relinquished her body to this being inside her and found the rest of her following suit. This was uncharted territory. She was vulnerable and in need of help. Wasn't there something thrilling in this life she suddenly found herself in? Something oddly transgressive? In the kitchen, pregnant, barefoot? So this was the thrill her mother got out of her winning jello molds and Tupperware parties. And finally her surrender to Arthur. She tried out different cocktails on him: sidecars and martinis and sours — when he came home after a full day at work — and sipped her virgin versions of them, gauging his reaction. She cooked for him and was thrilled when he asked for seconds, hurt when he didn't. She washed his socks and his boxers and his T-shirts and his sweats and folded everything neatly into the dresser drawers for him to discover and marvel at, gratefully. She was grateful for his gratitude. This was the idyll of newlyweds Arthur and Penelope.

Her brother Ryan was appalled. You're so young, what are you doing?

I'm happy, she said.

But what happened to your brain? You're a poster child for the pitfalls of marriage! In one fell swoop you've managed to get yourself pregnant and enslaved. What happened to apprenticing in Provence? What happened to owning a restaurant?

I can still do those things, she said.

How? You're grooming yourself to be somebody's maid.

What about Martha, Penelope said.

Martha's different. She has the ankles for it, the double chin. From my baby sister, I expected something different.

But Penelope was proud to be engaged in this fertile life of hers, this fertile marriage. Her brief status as biological celebrity. There were maternity clothes that attempted to deemphasize the belly — dark colors, loosely fit — she didn't understand this. Why would anybody want to hide the only clear evidence of her biological worth — her fifteen minutes of fame? She walked down the grocery store aisle grandly, like royalty. She bared herself, weather permitting, in spandex scoop-necked tops, pulled up so that the crown of her belly was showing, belly button like the tip of a thumb.

Neither, though, was she one of those hippie freaks who went on about how "beautiful" this all was, about "body wisdom," who hennaed their tummies and braided their hair and performed their deliveries in rivers while chanting in time to a drumming circle.

Nor was she like those yuppie freaks who invited their girlfriends to make papier-mâché pregnancy casts over sparkling grape juice and Manchego. She had no illusions about the ordeal of pregnancy. The morning sickness was brutal. She had to breathe delicately through her mouth because any smell, savory or otherwise, would have her groping for the bucket, and not just in the morning, it turned out—it was constant, unrelenting—it was a twenty-eight-week hangover, a boat cruise in bad weather. She lost her balance, her composure, her sense of dignity, and when it finally went away in the beginning of her third trimester, she was left with this thing inside her, floating, ravenous, feeding on her from the inside out—it had gills, apparently, and fed on her blood—it was an alien implant, sucking the life out of her, bleeding her dry, growing stranger every day, and it would eventually emerge triumphant, tearing its way through and leaving her a shell, a lifeless shell of spent meat. The sonogram reinforced this image—it looked like an ancient fossil, some extinct creature from a time when the world was more dangerous, or a satellite photograph of life on one of Jupiter's moons. The technician handed it to them and, sure, she and Arthur stammered over it, cried over it, and, yes, in part that blubbering was because they were stunned by this ancient biological miracle that had visited its everyday magic upon them, but it was also the blubbering of the sole survivors in a horror movie being chased by the monster. She tacked it on the fridge. My God, what was this thing they were about to unleash?

And then came her Will. Her reason for breathing. New parenthood was an ordeal but a different kind of ordeal. Will was on their side. They were in it together. It was them and Will against the world. They battled their health insurers for coverage for the emergency room visits they were forced to make—Will was prone to febrile seizures. She battled her family's stubborn refusal to wash their hands before touching Will. Her mother: *Do you think your grandparents washed their hands every time they handled you kids?* They battled pedestrians and restaurant-goers who'd give them dirty looks every time Will so much as gurgled from his stroller—as though he were a *boom box* they'd brought in, as though *they* were the selfish ones! Arthur battled his employers— for paternity leave, for more vacation time, for more sick days, for more compassion for the new father whose wife had all she could do to keep from going crazy in the house alone with a baby who wouldn't stop crying because he, well, who the hell knows why he won't stop crying! They called the pediatrician, whom they liked, whom they trusted, but who frankly was of no goddamned use. New parenthood was a fire alarm that wouldn't stop, that followed them around wherever they went, even into their sleep— Penelope would wake at three in the morning in a sweat and rush to Will's crib to find him fine, he was fine, happily asleep. It was one unfixable thing after the next—it was everybody wanting a piece of them, but they barely had enough for each other—and when Will was crying, when he wouldn't sleep or take the nipple or jump through the hoop in the next stage of development like the book said, it was a total nightmare they couldn't wake from, but when he smiled or the moment he finally said, "Da," when he slept through the night or finally got up onto his wobbly fat little legs and took those five, six, seven steps before toppling over, it was a dream they never wanted to end. How could this be? This miracle, how was it she could be so lucky?

And when she felt this way, she guarded the feeling; she didn't tell her family or Arthur even. It was hubris to feel this way. If anybody else knew, the word might spread, and then anybody could just come and take it away from her. So she told her mother that she was struggling, that it was hard, which was true enough, but she didn't tell her mother how her heart ached for Will when he was in another room or in another person's arms. Her mother thought she was doing Penelope a favor when she drove up from Virginia to babysit, insisting that she and Arthur go out, have fun, treat themselves to a hotel, but really all they did was sulk over their candlelit dinners, fidget through the movie distracted, until neither of them could take it anymore and canceled the room reservation and took Will back, relieved to be home, to be a family again.

It was hard, though. Arthur was right. It was life altering, mind altering, they were no longer the same people they once were, not older exactly but different. To be a mother wasn't merely to have a child; it was to have weathered a fundamental change of chemistry, of identity. She looked back on the years before their marriage, before Will, and thought, *Who was that girl?* Not meanly. Like a compassionate big sister. She finally understood that contradiction in her parents — was able to reconcile those disjointed impressions she had of them — the hip teenagers they claimed to have been with the prudish fuddy-duddies she knew them to be now. It made perfect sense. She'd read somewhere once that humans shed their old cells every seven years — or maybe it was that humans renewed their cells at a rate of every seven years — so that after seven years one was literally no longer the same person. If that was true, then why couldn't both versions of her parents coexist? And she, Penelope — why couldn't it be that she had been both of these people? That she had evolved?

This was the idyll of motherhood, of the family life of Penelope and Arthur and Will.

I'd emerge from these talks at the diner confused. My friendly crush on Arthur's wife had flared into a chest-burning ache, and with it came an equally hot jealousy of Arthur, who clearly didn't deserve this woman's love. I felt guilty. It was like we were having an affair, meeting clandestinely twice a week. We'd sit in our "reserved" smoking booth, and Penelope would go through half a pack of my cigarettes while she talked.

On Halloween, we all put on suits and homemade FBI badges and followed Will's flashlight trail down the long corridors of the building looking for *unexplained phenomenon*, which mostly took the form of Reese's Pieces. Penelope played Scully while Arthur sat by the open apartment door with a large tray of her homemade peanut brittle. There were apparently four other kids who lived in the building, somewhat younger and with whom Will had no interest in playing. These kids and their parents, all in Rite Aid costumes, tagged along with us warily, not sure what to make of our little mafia clique. We went around ringing bells to mixed success. A few on any hall were anticipating our arrival with a cobwebbed door or a red-lit foyer, generous with the treats. Others we'd catch genuinely by surprise, a look of panic on their faces—was there a fire?—until they processed who we were. But mostly, nobody was home.

By the first week in November we had a final cut of *Dead Hank's Boy*. I set Suriyaarachchi up with a fellow composition student I knew from conservatory. She was getting her DMA now in Ann Arbor and agreed to score the film for very little cash and a bullet point on a résumé. We collaborated over the course of weeks via Express Mail. With a darkly atmospheric sound track, trimmed to within an inch of its life—a lean eighty-seven minutes from title card to final fade—the movie was more than watchable: it was downright entertaining! Suriyaarachchi went out and bought a giant dry-erase calendar on which to mark the deadlines of every film festival we were eligible to enter, and two, as it turned out, we weren't—being neither Latina nor Canadian. We put together a "press packet," with synopsis, production stills, headshots, and résumés. We went at this project with painstaking care, spending hours on these ancillary materials to accompany the tape in the mail, as though these things might make up for any unexcisable failures the film still bore.

On one of my errands, juggling an armful of stuffed envelopes, I ran into Arthur. He invited me to Thanksgiving dinner. His in-laws were coming up for the long weekend. Penelope wanted me there, he said. "She thinks we can use an ally."

That afternoon Will came over. The central heat in the building hadn't kicked in yet, and we were all sitting around in our coats. Dave said, "My man Will! Is it three o'clock already?"

Will said, "Where are you guys going?"

"We're freezing."

Will noticed the hardcover on the couch. "That's my father's new book," he said.

"Have you read it?"

"Not yet," he said ponderously. "I plan to, one day, but I decided it would be better to wait awhile. And anyway, I already know what it's about."

"And what's it about?"

"Art. And Mom and me." Will sat down by my side. His puffy jacket wheezed a smell of banana and ham sandwich. He picked up the book and flipped through it.

"Your hands are filthy," I said.

"I'm eleven years old. That's what happens when you're eleven. I don't like the cover."

"I don't know," I said. "I think it's kind of clever."

"Is that supposed to be us? Art's hair isn't blond, Mom's hair isn't blond, and my hair isn't blond either. What were they thinking?"

"So you're not the least bit curious to read what your father's written about you and your mom?"

"I mean, I could. I told you, I make my own decisions. It's called *delayed gratification*."

I arrived at the Morels' empty-handed, something I noticed only as Penelope was welcoming me in. Seated on the sofa was an older woman with a square crop of coiled hair and an embroidered velvet jacket.

Penelope said, "This is my mother."

"Mrs. Wright," the woman said. She did not hold out her hand for me to shake. "Tell me, dear, is this a convertible sofa I'm sitting on?"

"Yes, Mother, it's a convertible."

"I was just wondering—it's very comfortable."

"Why don't we get you a drink," Penelope said to me, rolling her eyes with her back turned so that only I could see. I followed her into the kitchen. "'Is this a convertible'! Meaning, why couldn't she and Dad have stayed here?" She poured out some champagne into a fluted glass and told me that this was the first time her parents were visiting since the move. They didn't understand why they couldn't stay with Penelope and Arthur. Her mother was hurt; her father was angry. "It's not Queens, for crying out loud! But that means nothing to them." They were used to a certain kind of hospitality — and budget — from living below the Mason-Dixon Line and were put out to be spending so much on a hotel when they could be staying with family for free. And indeed when I sat down with Mrs. Wright, she spent a good ten minutes comparing their hotel room with her daughter's "three bedroom."

"It's a one bedroom plus den, Mother."

"It's a palace compared with where we're staying."

The patio's sliding door opened, and Arthur entered with a stocky older man. They trailed a distinct whiff of cigar smoke. Penelope's father, who introduced himself to me as Frank, crew cut and upright, looked like he had kept up a twice-daily regimen of sit-ups for the past forty years excepting no holidays. Frank regarded me with a certain amount of suspicion. His questions about who I was seemed less to do with getting to know me and more to do with getting to the bottom of what my motives were, intruding on this family gathering.

He said, "So what was this fella like back in his school days?"

"He hasn't changed much," I said.

"Once a troublemaker, always a troublemaker. Could have used you around a decade ago, warn us what we were getting ourselves into." He didn't crack a smile. If he was being humorous, the humor was of the driest sort.

"It would have been too late," Penelope said, going around the room with a platter of deviled eggs. "He already knocked me up."

"Okay, now," Mrs. Wright said. "Not in front of the boy, surely!"

Penelope gave me a wink.

It smelled good in the apartment, juices caramelizing in a roasting pan. The air was steamy, festive. Cinnamon candles flickering on the windowsills, doorways trimmed with lights and pine branches. The dining room table was set and twinkled like a department store display. Holly shaped rings coiled around each red cloth napkin.

The first part of the evening was pleasant. Penelope's mother proved easy to talk to, despite the frosty first impression. She asked me what I did, and for the first time, I was honest. "I work at a movie theater," I said.

"My friend is being modest," Arthur said. "He's also a movie producer. He and his cohorts work here in this building, down the hall from us."

I told a couple of anecdotes. Though Frank remained cool to me, Mrs. Wright warmed up some—she was an eager listener, or at least an obliging one, responsive with a gasp or a laugh, with wanting to know what happened next. I was aware of myself in her eyes as Arthur's long-lost childhood friend—it seemed Penelope had billed me as such—and right then I allowed myself to indulge the illusion.

I went out onto the patio for a smoke, and to my surprise Mrs. Wright joined me. We stood side by side, looking out. I offered her a cigarette and, with a glance over her shoulder, she nodded. She kept her back to the door and her elbows tucked in and smoked with small movements so as not to betray what she was doing to those inside. Without looking at me, she began to talk about the predicament the Wrights found themselves in with their son-in-law.

Although they both had their reservations about Arthur's left turn into fiction and worried over his ability to be a financial asset to their daughter and grandson, they were nevertheless supportive of his need to express himself creatively and of his decision to make a go of the writing life. Especially Frank. Give the boy some room to breathe, he said. After all, the family had some money, and whatever drain it might be on their daughter's finances to have a writer for a husband certainly would be made up for by the buzz it would bring.

"We are strivers, you know," Mrs. Wright said. "Our friends, too. As a group, we're a competitive bunch." And the contestants in this competition, she explained, were the children. Whenever she would get together with her friends, they traded their

children's achievements like they were playing a game of cards —
a graduation, a new job, a child on the way — keeping the failures close to the vest. Arthur's first bloom of success was a coup
for her and Frank as well. There was something giddy about it
she couldn't explain and something generous that allowed their
friends to participate without being jealous. So she perceived.
Whereas Ginny Morgan's new grandson was a success only for
the Morgans, and subject to the petty jealousies that they were all
helpless to, Arthur's minor splash as a debut novelist was something they could all share in, as a community. And it was a success
that promoted itself — neither she nor her husband ever had to
mention it — their friends would come to them with news, sight-
ings of the book in a magazine or in a bookstore. It was the prestige felt at the blackjack table during a winning streak — proud
in a shy way of the table's attention — even though you knew it
was only luck that brought this about. They admired Arthur's
success in a way they wouldn't have had it been their own child.
Of their children's success, they felt differently. They would have
counted it as their own, as owed — a success they were at least
partly responsible for. But Arthur's success was a gift, and for it
they were grateful.

  Then came the new book. That passage at the end.

  She didn't want to think what kind of recesses such writing had
come from in Arthur, or what life experience had led him to write
it. She wished she could undo having read it; she didn't want to
associate Arthur with those words on those pages.

  What are we supposed to do about this? Frank had wanted to
know. He was worried, as was she. They were together in this at
first — in their concern, in their confusion at their son-in-law, in their
attempt to reconcile this young man who married their daughter
and of whom they were so fond, with the man he revealed himself
to be in this book.

  They tried out explanations on each other: he was merely voicing a part of himself we all have, the id. Or Arthur could have been
abused as a child, and this was his way of coming to terms with

it. Frank reminded her that Arthur was an artist, and this is what artists did. They pushed buttons, pushed boundaries. And what about *Lolita*? she added. Wasn't that book banned in this country? Maybe it hadn't even been Arthur's idea. There was an agent, after all, and a publisher. Maybe somebody along the way had told him his story wasn't risky enough, "artistic" enough. They couldn't sell some boring old book about a sad sack. And so they insisted he spice it up. Maybe Arthur didn't even write the passage—it could have been added after the fact, to make it more marketable to a reading public who expected extremity in their literature. Or could it be that Arthur was referencing some other work of literature? Maybe it wasn't at all about what it seemed to be about. It was an allusion—the real subject hidden, subtextual. The way Joyce was really writing about Greek heroes when it only seemed he was writing about drunk Irishmen. She had always been too literal minded when it came to literature.

Whatever it was, and whatever the reason Arthur wrote it, it was something in their lives that they couldn't resolve, that couldn't be settled, as most unsettling things in their world were settled, with one of Frank's conversational one-liners. Global Warming: Buy property in Siberia—it'll be worth a fortune! The Massacre in Texas: Is it Waco or Wacko? Somehow, at the end of the day, having done their moral obligation of watching the news open eyed to its daily dose of horror, mulling over the tragedies of the day, to have Frank pronounce his one-liner was a real comfort. It was a way of closing the door on the world's sadness, for the time being. It meant that they were no fools; they knew how cruel and hopeless humanity could be, and by addressing each sadness they were paying tribute to it. Joking about it was a way of distinguishing their own lives from the lives of others. She would groan at Frank's bad joke, tell him to knock it off, these weren't issues to joke about, but this just part of the ritual, a way to have Frank say that if you couldn't joke about something serious, then you were really in trouble—if you couldn't laugh at the world, then you might as well put a bullet in your head. She didn't know what this meant, but Frank said it in a way that seemed powerful and true.

There was, however, no one-liner for what Arthur had done. The matter remained in the air, unsettled, floating between every pause in conversation.

Her friends grew conspicuously quiet on the subject of the book. But Frank's "buddies," the men at the veterans' lodge, were a different matter. She didn't know why he insisted on going to that hole-in-the-wall twice a week—three times a week, now that he was retired. It was the stomping grounds of the local bigmouths. She refused to learn any of their names—they were not friends of the family; they were men Frank drank with, nothing more. And unlike the people she counted as her friends, these men were not quiet on the subject of Arthur or his book.

For a while, Frank cast himself as Arthur's staunchest defender. You should hear what they're saying, he said. Bunch of ignoramuses. Ignorami? You'd think the kid was another Hitler. I said, Ever heard of Oedipus? If these guys had their way, the only books in the library would be car-repair manuals. I mean, thank God for Arthur, am I right?

But then Frank stopped relating these arguments to her; even though she was fairly certain the talk about Arthur at the lodge hadn't stopped. Three times a week now, Frank came home in a dark mood and fell asleep in front of the television. He avoided talking to Arthur on the phone. He would call Penelope's cell to speak with her and had her put his grandson on. If Mrs. Wright was talking with Arthur, Frank would wave the phone away when she tried handing it to him.

"You should talk to him, I tell him. What is he supposed to say, he wants to know. Say you're angry. You're confused. But Frank's not the type."

As we sat around the table with our empty plates waiting for Penelope, Will rallied us into a game. "We played it on our first day at school," he said. "You don't need a board or to learn any complicated rules. It's simple. We go around the room and tell three facts about ourselves. Two of the facts are facts, and one of the facts is a lie. Then everybody has to guess which one is the lie. It's fun, you'll see."

Upon hearing this, Penelope—who had just come out of the kitchen with the turkey—looked on the verge of dropping the platter. From the flurry of wordless looks—for reasons that will in a moment become clear—you would have thought we were all in a Bergman film. Had Will read the book, in spite of his claim to the contrary? Or was this just evidence of the emotional telepathy in children that allows them to ferret out the supposedly hidden affairs of grown-ups? Will said, "What's the matter?"

Arthur said, "We know too much about one another for it to work. That game's best played with strangers."

Frank said, "I'm going to say no—for the same reason I say no to poker. Can't bluff to save my life."

"And I'm no liar," Mrs. Wright said, "so I'm afraid I will have to sit this one out as well."

Despite these protests, and despite Penelope's attempt at diverting us with the front-page controversies of the day—developments in the Lewinsky scandal and a recent push by our mayor to cut funding for the arts—ten minutes later Will had us bluffing our way around the table.

I went first. I told them I had never learned to ride a bicycle, which was the truth. I told them I had once found Robert De Niro's wallet at Katz's Delicatessen—also true—and that I had been arrested twice: the lie. There was unanimous consent that nobody *didn't* know how to ride a bicycle—and so I managed to fool them. Will reminded us, looking sternly at me, that the game depended on everybody being *honest* about their lies. I assured him that my lie was the truth, and so we continued.

Will went next. He told us that his math teacher had once been a famous R & B singer, that he had lied about doing his homework yesterday, and that he had just last week seen the ghost of the dead boy who haunted the school's stairwells.

Frank said, "Only two of those facts are verifiable."

Mrs. Wright said, "Obviously it's the third one. There are no such things as ghosts."

Will protested vehemently at this and described the sighting in great detail. "I swear on my mother's grave."

"God forbid!" Mrs. Wright clutched her heart.

Penelope said, "You lied about doing your homework?"

Will hopped off his chair excitedly, padded off to his room, and a few moments later returned with a xeroxed flyer of a black man with a large afro crooning into a microphone, and a loose-leaf sheet—the homework in question.

Arthur said, "You lied about *lying* about doing your homework. So the lie's the lie. Very clever!" He smiled approvingly at his son. "Okay, who's next?"

Mrs. Wright went next, despite her earlier protests. A momentum had developed. She told everyone that she had never been to Europe, that a close childhood friend of hers had only recently learned she was adopted, and that her favorite color was blue.

After we had exhausted our guesses, Mrs. Wright revealed that all three of these things were in fact true.

"That's not the game!" Will protested.

"I told you," Mrs. Wright said, "I'm no liar."

Penelope, during her turn, lied about a latent allergy to eggplant, and Frank—who seemed to have missed the point of the game—kept trying to fool us with little-known facts about Abraham Lincoln. Then it was Arthur's turn.

He sat at the head of the table, a mischievous twist of a smile, in his element. He said, "I have thirty-four teeth. I have a vaccination scar on my left upper arm. I have a bruise on my right shin."

Penelope said she knew Arthur's vaccination scar intimately— it was on his *right* arm, not his left. Frank said that thirty-four teeth sounded like too many and checked this hunch against his own teeth, which totaled thirty-two. My money was on the bruise. When we were all done guessing, Arthur opened his mouth and confirmed a vowely thirty-two, just as Frank had said.

"But I know that scar," Penelope said. Arthur rolled up his right sleeve to confirm that Penelope too was right. "That's two lies," she said. "You're only allowed one."

"Three lies, actually," Arthur said, showing us his hairy, unbruised shins.

Will said to me, exasperated, "Didn't I explain the rules clearly enough to these people?"

Arthur said, "For the sake of symmetry—Constance's three truths to my three lies."

Dessert was served: apple cobbler and Linzer cookies that the Wrights brought with them. "In my luggage," Mrs. Wright said. "I'm amazed they survived." Penelope brought out coffee and cut fruit.

Will took some coffee, refused the fruit. "I think I'm ready for bed," he announced, and got up.

"Is it that time already?" Penelope said.

He hugged his grandparents, patted his mother and father on their heads.

Once Will had gone into his room and closed the door, Mrs. Wright said, "Is bedtime really a question, dear?"

"We've been letting him make his own decisions."

I took another cookie. The center was pure Smucker's, so sweet it made my fillings hurt. I ate around the edges and left the middle on my plate—I did this with all three of the cookies I took. Frank watched me do this.

"What sorts of things are you letting him decide about?"

"You can't let him decide everything. He's a child."

"It's an experiment. We haven't set limits on what he can and can't decide. If this is going to be a lesson about the responsibility of free will, what kind of example are we setting by telling him, essentially, there are times when you can't think for yourself? Times when, arguably, it's most important to use good judgment."

"Penny, darling," Frank said, "I love you but that's absurd. If he decides he wants to take up smoking, obviously you're not going to let him. So what's the point?"

"Hold on," Arthur said, "not so obvious. So what if he wants to try out smoking? Okay, he's a little young—but all the better, really. His lungs won't be able to handle it, and he'll find it repulsive. Lesson learned. Why would I deny him that experience?"

Something in both the Wrights' demeanors changed. Mrs. Wright frowned and looked down at her hands. Frank opened his mouth for a moment and then closed it again. Their expressions registered something, a fear confirmed.

"I wouldn't hand him one," Arthur said, "and good luck finding a smoke shop that will sell to someone Will's age."

Penelope gave Arthur a sharp look. "Anyway, it's illegal. We're mostly talking about decisions within legal boundaries."

"And your book?" Frank said, quietly.

"This hasn't changed," Penelope said. "He's agreed to wait until he's older."

"*He's* agreed," Mrs. Wright said.

"Well, we can't very well stop him, Mother. If he wants to read it, he will find a way to read it. The best we can do is help him see the wisdom in waiting." This seemed to be a subject they'd talked about at length, judging from Penelope's exasperated tone.

"Look," Frank said, "I don't want this to become a territory issue. We know our place, and we don't want to step on your toes here, and Lord knows your mother and I understand better than you would think that raising a child isn't a black-and-white issue. But the boy is eleven years old."

"And."

"And he needs—"

"Discipline?"

"He needs structure. He needs to not be the one driving the ship. He can't be his own role model."

"I refuse to brainwash my son," Arthur said. "I want him to have the courage to make hard choices, to think for himself."

"He needs limits, boundaries. You can't just do and say whatever you want!"

"Everybody has to learn to be part of society," Mrs. Wright said, "or they end up in the nuthouse or in jail."

"Or an artist," Arthur said. "Picasso spent his whole life trying to recapture the free spirit of his five-year-old self before he'd learned to paint."

"Oh, for Christ's sake! The free spirit is a myth. Even the artist has his place in society."

"The artist who works for society isn't an artist; he's a propagandist. A real artist is an outsider. If he has any hope of making real art, he needs to remain that way."

"You are a father and a husband," Mrs. Wright said. "Where does that fit into the model of the real artist? And what's so bad about being useful? The propagandist is a craftsman. He serves a valuable purpose. We need slogan makers as much as we need slogan busters."

"There will always be someone to make slogans. Everywhere we turn, we're being sold something, via slogan. And dissent is only heard when it's made palatable by actors and rock stars. Real dissent? Real dissent is marginalized."

"And what are you protesting exactly? The rights of pedophiles?"

"Lower your voice, Dad."

"I have no message."

"Arthur, you don't have to explain yourself. He doesn't have to justify what he writes to anybody."

"Oh, come off it, Arthur's employed by the university. Art is a mill, just like any other. You've got a market, a demographic. Just because it's smaller doesn't mean it's more legitimate."

"For God's sake, Arthur!" Mrs. Wright said suddenly.

Everyone was quiet for a moment.

"Why did you have to go and—? What kind of smug, self-indulgent—I'm sorry, Penny. I can't pretend anymore. It's disgusting, what he wrote. Where is the self-respect? The decency?"

More silence. My instinct, of course, always to smooth things over. A joke, a non sequitur, anything to lighten the mood, anything to right this train that had suddenly gone off the rails. I could think of nothing.

Arthur said, "What good are those traits? Will they make me a better writer?"

"You have disgraced your family. You are aware of that, aren't you? What you have done is disgraceful. Do you have any idea what Frank has to put up with when he goes to the—"

"Constance, don't."

"He should know. He should know how it affects us. We live in a small community. You have the luxury of living in an anonymous place. Nobody cares what you do here. But fine—forget about us. What about your wife? What about your son? How could you do this to them? Explain it to me so that I can understand."

It's the last scene in the book.

Arthur is taking a bath with Will. Will is eight. They sit facing sled fashion in the tub, Arthur in front, Will behind. Will plays with his Hot Wheels, using Arthur's hairy back as an island. Will asks for the shampoo, with which he sudses Arthur's back. He whips up some clouds on the bathwater. It's a recurring setting— bath time in this bathtub—which makes these final pages feel like a culminating moment.

Will announces that he is done, and they stand and shower off the suds. Shower spray at Arthur's back, the bathwater drains at their ankles, toy cars floating and sunken underfoot.

Quite out of the blue, Will reaches for Arthur's penis. He caresses it. Arthur flinches, but does not pull away.

It's soft, Will says.

Yes, Arthur says.

Mine is small.

You'll grow up and it will be just like mine, Arthur says.

It looks like a mushroom.

It does, kind of, doesn't it?

Will lets go of Arthur's penis and touches his own, a newborn gerbil of a thing.

The prose is vivid here, in stark contrast to the rest of the book. It is the only scene described in this much detail, the only full conversation that takes place between two people. The rest of the book is just thoughts, interiors. It comes on almost like awakening from a dream.

Is it *whack* that my penis grows when I touch it? Will asks. Lamar says it's whack that my penis grows. I told him that it's perfectly normal. It *is* perfectly normal, right?

It's perfectly normal.

Everybody's penis does this. That's what I said. Even yours, right?

That's right.

And when you make it grow on purpose it's called *whacking off*.

As Will is talking, he is fingering his own penis and walnut scrotum, and when he takes his hand away, his small hard-on is as stiff as a pencil shaft.

It feels good when I touch it, Will says.

Yes, Arthur says.

The air fills with Will's boy breaths and Arthur's own thumping heartbeat. The moment becomes strangely charged. In the way that an enticing smell can make someone aware suddenly that he is ravenous, this moment stirs in Arthur an appetite that has lain dormant until this very moment. Arthur becomes aware that his hand has been mirroring Will's at his own penis. He looks down at it, the speckled mushroom cap of the head poking through his fist. Arthur lets go and it stands out stiff, quivering. He is aware of himself as a father, of Will as his son, but they feel like arbitrary designations, suddenly, or as Arthur puts it in the text, he loses the *moral relevance* of their roles for a moment.

There is only arousal.

He feels the bulge of ejaculate, wanting release, and when Will reaches out and touches the underseam of Arthur's penis, a single soft stroke, it comes—an initial startling shot of sperm that hits Will in the face.

The rest pulses out into the now-empty tub.

# 7

# E N D I N G

**M**Y FACE HAD BECOME HOT and my heart hammered in my chest. I felt like I should excuse myself from this moment but feared that, if I did, Mrs. Wright would cast the spotlight of her fury on me, that I'd be called on to defend Arthur, to explain his actions. And at this moment, I couldn't. Arthur, on the other hand, seemed relatively calm. I was reminded of his easy demeanor at the Concerto Concert, just moments before he pulled down his pants.

The refrigerator shuddered, cycled off. In the new silence I sensed Will behind the closed door of his room, listening.

"I was writing out a deep-seated fear I had." Arthur looked down at his plate. His sleeve was still rolled up, hairy arm bared. "By writing about it, I was hoping to dispel it."

Frank said, "You're afraid that you might molest Will?"

"Dad," Penelope said, "it's a work of *fiction*."

"It's got his name, your son's—our *grandson's*—name. Don't tell me about fiction. Your husband's telling me he's worried about molesting *your* son. Doesn't that alarm you?"

"No," Arthur said. "What I mean to say is—okay, take this knife." He reached across the table to the platter and picked up the carving knife. Everyone flinched. At his empty plate, he began slicing imaginary vegetables. "You're going about the ordinary

business of making dinner. You're chopping and you're cutting—
and the knife slips, almost slitting open your thumb. But it doesn't
slit open your thumb. So you continue about the business of slicing
and dicing, dicing and slicing, and yet now you're thinking about
your thumb, slit open by that knife. It's an image, suddenly, that
you can't shake—it's visceral, gory—it makes your gums ache,
makes your knees weaken with its bloodred vividness. You try
thinking of something else, you turn on the radio, but that image
persists, still in your mind as you continue to chop and chop and
chop. At times like these, when your brain is stuck like this, the
only way to get that image out of your mind is to touch that knife
to your thumb"—and here Arthur touched the carving knife to
his thumb—"lightly, so that it doesn't draw blood, because after
all you *don't* want to cut yourself, but just firmly enough to satisfy
whatever compulsive itch your brain can't seem to scratch. And
once you do, once you've pantomimed that act of cutting yourself,
the image vanishes. Do you see?"

"You married a lunatic," Frank said. "You realize that, don't
you?"

"Art has nothing to apologize for. It's literature; it's not real life.
You're all confusing the two."

"Your mother's not asking for an apology, Penny. She's asking
him to help her understand. But once again he offers this psycho-
babble. It's meaningless. Arthur, don't you see? We need to hear
from you that this *did not happen*."

"Of course it didn't happen," Arthur said, almost grudgingly,
as though he were giving something away. "It's fiction."

"Then tell us why—*why* this was not just some pointless stunt."

"They're just words. Come on, Frank. I'm still me. Nothing's
changed."

"I wish that were true, son. But saying something doesn't make
it so." He stood, stared down at his plate. "I've got to get out of
here. I need to think." He grabbed his jacket off the back of the
couch and strode to the front door.

"Frank, you'll freeze," Mrs. Wright said.

As soon as Frank was gone, Will opened the door of his room. He stood there in his powder-blue pajamas and yelled, "Stop fighting about me! I didn't do anything wrong!" He was crying. He held his pillow clenched in his fists as though he might smother any one of us seated at the table.

"Honey," Mrs. Wright said, but Will had already retreated and slammed the door.

I looked at Penelope, who was looking down at her plate. Arthur was observing his mother-in-law steadily. She was shaking her head, looking back.

Arthur turned to me and said, "I think I might have a cigarette."

I patted myself down and pulled a pack from my back pocket. "Two left."

"I didn't know you smoked," I said, once we were out on the patio.

"I don't. I tried once and found it disgusting. But the moment seems to require it, don't you think?" I gave him one and lit it, watching as he sucked and coughed doggedly. He stepped out past the overhang and tilted his face to the misting rain. "Thanks for coming," he said. "Sorry to get you involved in the drama."

"Looks like Penelope was right. You really did need an ally."

"Don't get them wrong about art. They like art. They're genuinely curious people. To browse their bookcases is to know this about them. Edith Wharton, Hemingway, Michener, Mailer. Writers who tell us the story of ourselves as Americans. Who entertain and enrich our understanding of the world. They are avid readers of American literature. *House on Mango Street, Interpreter of Maladies.* Asian writers, gay writers, black writers. They allow in the great democratic bounty. They're not snobs either. Tom Wolfe and detective fiction—Hammett and Chandler." Their bookcase, Arthur said, was evidence of the usefulness of art, each book a powerful statement in support of its usefulness and, when it came down to it, damn fine reads, each and every one. If there were any evidence required to prove society's enrichment through literature, one had only to look at the books in the Wrights' bookcase.

They were living proof of the relevance and power and usefulness of literature.

"So? What's the problem?"

"What's not there," Arthur said. "The gaps in their collection speak for themselves." There was Steinbeck but no Stein. Bellow but no Burrows. No Faulkner, no Pynchon. None of the great American experimenters. Gass or Gaddis, Barth or Barthelme. And with the exception of a single hardbound volume of the complete Frost, no poetry. "What good are they? They are books that tell difficult stories — if they tell stories at all! — that are difficult to follow and that don't necessarily make you feel better for having read them. The Wrights' belief about the usefulness of literature makes no room for these books. They are not useful books. They do not confirm our understanding of ourselves and in fact often leave us more confused about ourselves than we were to begin with. They are voices from the margins that are better left to the margins. Society would not be worse off without them."

"So it's the limits of their taste that prevent them from liking your book."

Arthur smiled.

This talk pissed me off. At the time, I didn't know why, but later when replaying the conversation in my head, I imagined myself shaking Arthur, just taking him by the shoulders and shaking him. *Cut the intellectual bullshit! Your family's in real trouble here!* I said, "So what are you going to do?"

"Do?"

"They're pretty upset."

"Should I apologize?"

"What would be the harm in it? Even if you don't see eye to eye, they're important people in Will's life, in Penelope's life."

"But I'm not sorry."

"Does it matter? Convince them you are. For the sake of peace."

"I can't undo what I wrote, and apologizing won't make it disappear. An apology is an admission I've done something wrong. It would only further justify their anger."

"You don't think you've done something wrong?"

"The book is good."

"That's not what I asked."

"I don't see how anything else matters. We don't read Hemingway any differently because he was a bully and an absentee father. Do we? The author is human and has human failings and eventually dies. He is irrelevant. Mortal. In the end the book is judged on its own merits. It is judged not against the author but against other books. The author is the husk, out of which the book sprouts."

"This is an evasion, and you know it. I'm not talking about your book."

"You think this is some quarter-life crisis."

"I don't know what to think, Arthur. Why do you need to make things so complicated? All these years have passed and, as far as I can tell, you haven't changed a bit. Still squandering your good fortune. Still dumping on the people who champion you. Of all the subjects in the world available to write about, Arthur. Why would anybody choose to fictionalize the incest of his own prepubescent son? It's self-destructive and, as a statement, opaque. What's the point? I'm going to have to agree with your in-laws on this one—I get the fear part, voicing a fear in order to dispel it? Fine, so you see a therapist, or you write it down in your supersecret journal. And then *burn* that journal. You don't *publish* it! I don't understand it, Arthur. I mean, is Frank right? Are you mentally ill? Or is there something you're not saying, some key to understanding all this?"

"He's back," Arthur said. Through the window we watched him as he was greeted by Mrs. Wright at the front door. He paced the room, saying something that only came to us out here as a deep humming. Penelope appeared from Will's bedroom, and Frank stopped pacing and beckoned the two women to the dining room table. The ember of Arthur's cigarette reflected on Frank's chest.

"What's going on?" I said. We watched through the sliding glass door as Frank unsheathed a stack of papers from the copy-shop bag he'd been holding. Frank looked up, and his eyes met Arthur's.

"The other shoe," Arthur said.

I suppose another explanation is required here. Why, after reading Arthur's book, wouldn't I have just walked away? Not only *not* walk away, but accept an invitation to a holiday dinner with his in-laws? And then, after that dinner, continue to subject myself to the family strife? (For to spend time with them—to be in the same room with them—was to know just how deeply in trouble they were.)

Here, I suppose, I will have to confess: I was in love with Penelope Morel.

It started the day after, Friday. On my way home after a busy matinee shift, I found myself passing Balthazar's. I loitered by the bakery's menu out front. I was about to leave when Penelope appeared from the back and, recognizing me, waved.

She came out. "Thank God. A man with cigarettes!"

The following day, and every day after for the next seven days, I found excuses to be on Spring Street so that I could pass the bakery and catch a glimpse of her through the swinging door beyond the glass display cases. She'd flash in and out of sight in her starched chef's whites, red bandanna around her black hair. I'd stand at the front window pretending to look at the menu but really watching the swinging door. Each time it opened, I scanned for her red bandanna. I could have done this for hours. I could have done nothing but this for an entire day. Invariably, she would see me and come out wiping her hands on her apron to give me a hug. We'd sit on the bench outside and smoke and talk.

"I keep going back to that day," she said. "You were there. He *handed* me the damn thing. Said read it, tell me what to do with it. I don't know what I was thinking. I saw the look in his eyes. He really did want me to read it. He wanted me to stop him. And what did I do?"

"It's not your fault he wrote that book."

"I told him to *go forth and publish*. Those were my exact words. I should have read it! I should have thrown it across the room, thrown it at his head, told him to shred it! Shred the damn thing! I should have told him that if he published it, I would divorce him. But I let him *go forth*, even though I knew there was something wrong. I could sense it. What stopped me? And what stopped me when he did publish it, when I did read it, from immediately kicking him out of the house? I should have told him that he was crazy, that he was too toxic for Will to be around, and filed for divorce."

"Well? What's stopping you?" The air was frosty and damp — the forecast called for snow — yet under her apron Penelope had on only a T-shirt, and her clogs exposed her bare heels. She hugged herself against the cold. I unzipped my down jacket and draped it over her, feeling even as I did it the awkwardness of this chivalric gesture. I could feel Penelope's eyes looking me over, appraising me — maybe wondering what I was up to. She thanked me and pulled the jacket's flaps around her.

"Who else would have him," she said, "if not me?"

Then there was Viktoria. After our night on the couch, I was respectful of her need to take it slowly, happy to enact a chaste domestic bliss with this gorgeous and troubled girl. Lying next to her at night, I would imagine that I had found my Penelope, my other half, who would come to love me as much as Penelope loved Arthur, despite the havoc I might cause in our lives. She would see my failings as an essential, even lovable part of who I was. But in this relationship, unfortunately, she was Arthur and I was Penelope. I pictured meeting her German parents, winning them over, and perhaps even forgiving them for being so criminally neglectful of their daughter. I pictured Viktoria bearing me a child whom I would love absolutely, for whom I would give up all notions of art making without a second thought.

She talked about a man, her "best friend." He was her dealer and had once raped her, she said. But she also had sex with him willingly. The chronology of their relationship was confusing. She had broken off contact after getting out of the hospital. He would call her, but she wouldn't answer, wouldn't return his calls.

Viktoria was at her best in the presence of gawkers. When we were out, even though she was talking to me, it seemed she was playing to some other person at our periphery listening in. She didn't seem to know how to behave when it was just us, alone in the apartment. She was always telling me how *nice* I was and how she didn't deserve someone as *nice* as I was. Nice was new to her, it seemed. She wasn't used to it. I got the feeling I annoyed her with my niceness, that she was doing all she could not to bait me into an argument, to get us on footing that was more familiar to her. Our tame evenings with takeout and a movie and the barking dog must have felt, in comparison to her previous life, like just an extension of the white, antiseptic flatline of the hospital. She said that I was good for her. As though I were a kind of root vegetable.

She brought me to a certain Midtown nightclub — *her* nightclub, she called it. It was one of those places whose advertisements I would come across while browsing the housing listings in the *Voice*, ladies in fishnets, disembodied DJ turntables floating above them — I'd pass these ads and wonder who on earth actually went to places like that. Answer: Viktoria. Nightclubs are excruciating when you are sober. It seemed like she was doing it to punish herself — or maybe tempting herself back into a relapse. She told me to go ahead and have a drink — she didn't mind — but I wouldn't.

There was a friend, a girl, but I don't remember what the friend looked like. Who could tell what any other girl looked like in the presence of Viktoria? She eclipsed all other girls. These two would dance for hours, and Viktoria would shout to me places in the club that were meaningful to her — the bathroom stall where she used to do blow, the stage where she would be invited to dance, and the time she was dared to take off her top in front of the orgiastic crowd, the bar where they'd sometimes hand out glow-in-the-dark necklaces. It was hard to understand what she liked about these places — they were so loud — big empty black-painted rooms that stank of stale beer and cigarettes. It was all noise, a noise that tried to fill the void. Or maybe it was meant for something else entirely; maybe I fundamentally didn't get clubs; maybe it was a space for people to be their sexiest, to show off their ideal selves.

We met up with Rich, the best-friend-drug-dealer-ex-boyfriend-rapist. Rich. He was, somewhat unexpectedly, old. Old and fat and poorly dressed. He kept calling her *darling*. He spoke with an affected lisp. He had red hair and a beard. He looked me up and down like he wasn't sure whether he wanted to stab me or fuck me. Rich took her aside and talked to her while I waited, watching them.

After that encounter with Rich, Viktoria changed.

We would go to a club and now Viktoria would have a drink. Or two. I wouldn't go home with her. She would tell me to go on ahead, she wanted to stay a while longer. I didn't know how to react to her drinking and felt parental and judgmental when I said anything about it.

She started classes at NYU and would bring home her course books and line them up neatly in her empty bookcase. She bought enough stationery supplies to turn over a new leaf and color-coded her schedule with highlighters. She talked about the new people she was meeting — teachers and fellow students — and this gave us something to talk about when I came over and ate takeout with her.

I should have broken things off. I don't know why I persisted. Domestic routine comes so naturally to me. I have always had a nesting instinct. I fantasize future life histories with girls I barely know. I love homemaking, burrowing in. An and I, when we both were freshman and living in the same dorm, would sign out the party room — we both had roommates — and lock the door and build a fort out of the couches and cushions and chairs.

One evening I came over and Viktoria was dressed to go out, a short skirt with sparkling earrings. She had a nose ring — a single tiny diamond sparkling on her nostril — and a belly ring. Her stomach was firm and flat. Her top exposed this part of her. We were supposed to eat at home and watch a movie. I had rented a couple of new releases and brought them in my laptop case. She suggested we go out, meet a few of her friends instead.

We went to a lounge in the East Village and sat on a low couch and drank cranberry vodkas with one of her new NYU friends, a girl, a total blank to me now.

Viktoria spent most of her time on her cell phone and made frequent trips to the bathroom, returning to her seat to proclaim to both of us how great this place was. "Isn't this place great? Don't you just love it?" We agreed that it was great.

Viktoria's friend smiled at me with pity.

A couple of other NYU friends arrived and drank and then left. Viktoria was agitated, restlessly tapping her foot and chain-smoking. I had never seen someone under the influence of cocaine before, but it was clear to me that this was the source of her restlessness. She made a phone call and said that she wanted to go to a club. Did I want to come?

I told her to go ahead.

"Are you sure? Okay."

I told her that I would call her tomorrow. To have fun but not too much fun. I kissed her. I felt like her father. Then I left, walked home.

In my room, sitting on my bed and taking off my shoes, it suddenly hit me that I'd left my laptop (and my rented videos) at Viktoria's apartment.

I called her cell, and a man answered. It was Rich. It was quiet, no thumping club music. I asked to speak with Viktoria.

She came on the line. She asked if I couldn't just wait until the next time I was at the apartment to pick up the laptop.

I told her that I needed it now. For work. I sounded petulant.

She said that she was at Rich's apartment and wasn't planning to return to her apartment tonight, but she agreed to meet me at her place the next morning.

I couldn't sleep. I was livid. By the time I arrived in her lobby the next morning, I had a speech mapped out. I was trying hard to remember to say everything that I had fantasized about saying while lying awake in bed. I may have even written something down so that I wouldn't forget. I was trying to remember my anger. I have trouble with this. My anger goes underground fairly quickly, and I wanted to keep it on the surface, to use it to say what I felt I needed to say.

I arrived before her and had to endure the humiliation of waiting for a long time in her lobby, an hour, maybe more. This helped with the anger.

She arrived with her sunglasses on. She seemed tired, or bored — and sober. We took the elevator up to her apartment. She told me how tired she was. She said it several times. I had to fight my impulse to be sympathetic and kept my mouth shut. The dog yelped and yelped. She must really have been tired because she didn't scream at it.

She sat on her bed and suggested we talk later about this. So far she hadn't admitted any wrongdoing. Her apology was limited to keeping me waiting.

(Writing this now, years later, clearheaded, I realize that there really was no wrongdoing — we were not married, had made no vows to each other. But what did this mean to me, who had spent hours in her kitchen, fantasizing a distant future in which she would be telling our grandkids that I had rescued her, that she used to be a bad girl until I had come along?)

She collapsed on the bed and said again how tired she was. Her sunglasses were still on.

Again, I felt like a parent here, dealing with an unruly teen who'd stayed out past her curfew. I picked up my laptop bag and checked its contents and then delivered my speech. It was fairly short and ended with the line *And I don't like being made to feel like a fool!* In my head the line sounded powerful, a perfect expression of my pain, but when I said it out loud, I just sounded sad.

And I didn't get the feeling that she was listening too closely. She told me that she didn't think I was foolish and that we should definitely talk later, after she'd had a chance to catch up on some sleep.

I told her that I had nothing else to say, that there was nothing left to talk about, that I didn't want to talk later.

I left. Walking down the street, I felt good. I felt the righteous anger of the wronged. I felt a certain power in rejecting Viktoria. I savored it on my way to work.

Suriyaarachchi was there, browsing the Web. Dave was making a pot of coffee. I could have hugged them both but instead handed them the egg sandwiches I bought and spent the morning in the editing suite, watching the rented videos on the one-hundred-thousand-dollar editing machine.

They took me out to lunch and let me mope. They told me that I deserved better, that we would go out tonight and get drunk, the three of us. Suriyaarachchi said he would help me pick up any girl I chose, whichever one my heart desired, that he had a way with women, and he could see to my wishes. Dave joked that the only women Suriyaarachchi had a "way" with were the ones who advertised in the back of the *Voice*. Forget girls, Dave said. Tonight was just for us guys: scotch and cigars. A round of steak dinners on the house!

Whatever I wanted, Suriyaarachchi said. Today, I was the boss.

That night Viktoria came to see me at the movie theater and insisted on us talking. We sat in the carpeted window casement, and she took my hand and told me how she'd never wanted to hurt me and that she had things she needed to work out in her life, and she was working on them. She said she would understand if I didn't want to see her anymore.

I told her I didn't want to see her anymore.

She seemed surprised at this. I got the sense that there was a way this was supposed to play out for her—that she was supposed to be contrite and that I was supposed to forgive her and that I would come back to her apartment and pick up where we left off. But I wasn't saying the right lines in her drama. Or at least that was what I hoped she was feeling. I was stone, Teflon. I told her good luck with her recovery, with her life—I hoped things would work out for her.

She thanked me and got up. She hugged me, and then she left, somewhat dazed, saying that she would call me.

I told her not to bother, that we didn't have anything to say to each other.

A few days later she called and left a message on my mother's answering machine.

The humiliation of this experience would come back in waves. I spent weeks coming over, cooking for her, cleaning the dishes, listening to her stories of her attempted suicide and her recovery, encouraging her against relapse. I was like her puppy, eager for her affection, frustrated at not getting it, caged off from her bedroom, from the rest of her life. Meanwhile, she was out having sex with her ex, while I was waiting at home. I was convinced of my worth as a boyfriend, baffled that any girl who had experienced the full warmth of my goodwill would want to squander it. Why would she want to squander it? I was such a good listener! She said she thought my pasta was delicious! She said I was the sweetest person she'd ever met! So what was any of that worth, in the end?

I erased her message, hoping my mother hadn't yet heard it. But she called again the following day, and again the day after that. She didn't sound bored anymore, or tired. She was wide awake. She said that she was sorry, that she needed me, could I come over. She sounded desperate, each message more urgent than the last. She called a dozen times over the following week. By the end she was weeping into the phone, begging me to return her call.

After the first couple of messages, I felt good, satisfied. It was a balm to my humiliation. But each successive message made me feel worse. I became alarmed. She had talked so abstractly about her condition — its symptoms and causes — and it seemed so hypothetical, like it no longer applied to her specifically, as though she were talking about someone else. But here it was, revealed in these messages. They were frightening. I felt guilty, like I had caused this, and fought an urge to call her back, to go back to her and try to make it all better. I erased each message as it came.

And then the messages stopped. I thought she might have done something drastic. But, I also reasoned, it was just as possible that she'd found someone else, another me. And then I stopped thinking about her at all.

After breaking up with Viktoria, I felt a loneliness deep in my bones. At first it seemed the result of losing her, but as the days passed, I saw that, in fact, it was the other way around. In the way of certain drugs, whose side effects may include the irritation of just those symptoms one is trying to relieve—an anti-inflammatory, say, that in fluke cases causes one's swelling to worsen—so dating Viktoria had made my existing loneliness more profound. My only relief came now from the time I spent with Penelope and Arthur. They welcomed me. They wanted me between them. With Penelope I had an audience for my misadventures in love and with Arthur—suddenly interested—my misadventures in film. I think they needed me there. I kept their focus off each other, off their problems; hearing about mine was a way for them to forget their own, and in that sense I became the ballast holding them together.

As an only child of divorced parents, I was adept at the art of diversion, an art I noticed Will was good at, too. We worked as a team. Will's strength was games—board games, tile games, card games, puzzles and all manner of brain teasers—and mine was anecdotes. Between us we were able to keep Arthur and Penelope distracted through most of an evening. Then Will would go to bed, and I'd have to work twice as hard to keep the subject trained safely on me. I told them about the hair and makeup artist I fooled around with on the set of *Dead Hank's Boy*, the one with the insanely jealous boyfriend rumored to own a hunting rifle—and how, when the jealous boyfriend got wind of me, I had to hide under a desk in our production office to avoid his wrath. I told them how ushers amused themselves on any given night at the theater: by lip-synching as lewdly as possible the closing ten minutes of *Good Will Hunting* and *Shakespeare in Love*. Or by performing cross talk at the rear doors as the audience filed out, loud enough to draw attention: *Did you hear, Emma Thompson is upstairs!* Another usher: *That crazy bitch? Last time she was here, I was an hour in the ladies' room cleaning up her meth-induced rampage!* The trick, I told them, was in making the actor and the outrageous act as unlikely a pair as possible: Steve Martin fistfighting a man for trying to cut him in line, Dame Judy Dench thrown out for spontaneously barking during a show. Paul Newman's petty theft, Angela Lansbury evading arrest.

But then I would run out of stories, and things would go south. "Tell me again," Penelope would begin. At this point into her third or fourth glass of wine.

And Arthur would say, "We've been over this a hundred times."

"Is it like you said in your book? Because you were dissatisfied with me? With us?"

"That had nothing to do with it."

"Then what?"

"I told you, I was speaking out a fear—"

"Don't give me that fear bullshit! Answer me. Do you want to do—*that*—to him?"

"Of course not!"

"Well, I don't understand. Am I phrasing the question correctly? Asking the right question? How can you be afraid that you'll do *that* if you don't want to *do* it? It doesn't make any sense."

"I wanted to write a book that would take great courage to write—that no other writer would write. Think of Henry Miller. De Sade. Burroughs. I wanted to be unafraid. These writers looked into the abyss and wrote what they saw."

"Were any of those writers married? Were any of them the primary caregiver of an eleven-year-old child?"

"I wanted to do something bigger. To sacrifice something."

"Yourself, that's who you've sacrificed. And your family along with you. You're telling me you're a terrorist, is what you're saying. The kind that blows himself up on a plane."

"We live an age where you can write almost anything. The only way forward is to utter what can't be said. That which carries personal cost. If I were just risking my professional reputation—who would care? Who outside of my professional circle would take notice?"

Other times, Arthur would be the one on the offensive. In fact, Penelope's relentless questioning seemed to help him find his voice. "The death of transgression is the death of art—don't you understand? That an individual artist might do enough damage to be dangerous. This is hopeful, this means that art can still have an impact. If an artist is permitted to do or say anything, it's proof that art no longer matters enough to care about. An artist becomes the cursing lunatic on the street whom people just shake their heads at. *I want to wake people up!* You've said it yourself, Penelope. The writers around me are writing such little books." He looked at me. "I warned you about music; it was dying its last breath while we were still in school—and despite all attempts to rouse it, it's dead. Irretrievably dead. Look at it now—you've been there, you've had four years of it—an academically sealed mausoleum, written and picked over by graduate students. The same is happening now with literature. Dying its slow death in academia. Its life drained away by writers describing smaller pieces of the world. Dying the death of clever, of marketable. *Literature* is no longer a word we use anymore. *Literary* is the current term. '*Literary* fiction,' quote-unquote. Demoted to an adjective. And rightly so. Little of what's being published these days deserves the noun. If the endeavor is to survive at all, it needs a shock to the system."

"And you're that shock," I said. "You haven't lost your flair for hyperbole, I see. Or self-aggrandizement."

"We worry about the rainforest when we should be worried about the extinctions closer to home. We are fast approaching a culture without art."

"Arthur. You can't seriously believe all this. The Pulitzer Prize committee. The acquisitions department at the Whitney. They have no trouble finding great art to celebrate."

"Do you think I care about what the institution's patent office and zookeepers think of the crisis we're in? Don't you get it? A culture without art is a culture without a soul, nothing but a lifeless machine. To answer your implied question, yes, I do believe it, and I will take your feigned nonchalance as a sign I'm getting through to you. Do you have any idea how hard it is to get a fictional account of incest published—if you're writing from the point of view of the perpetrator? Have you ever heard of Varmes City Press? Neither had I, until they emerged, the sole fringe press that would agree to print my book." He said this with a kind of incredulity, as though he himself could scarcely believe what he had done. That it hadn't escaped his notice that perhaps this entire thing had been a colossal miscalculation. The shock of it was in his eyes. But then he went on. "My agent begged me to remove that last section. He said he himself had done this and shown it to Random House, to my previous editor, who said she'd buy it on the spot. But that would have been a little book, a small book. Which would have just contributed to the problem."

Penelope stared—no, watched—she watched him. As though he were a stranger. "So," she said, clearing her throat. "You wrote the book to save literature."

"Yes."

"Can't you just say you're sorry?"

"Sorry?"

"Do you see what you've done? You've killed us, Art. You've destroyed this family. Nothing will ever be the same."

I should have left them alone to their arguing, but, as I said, I am a child of divorced parents, and old habits die hard. I wanted to get between them, to referee. But all I could do was watch. I could see how much pain they were in, both of them. Arthur could not explain away what he had done. And Penelope couldn't accept the explanations Arthur gave. Just like Penelope, I, too, returned to that day. Arthur had put the manuscript into my hands as well. *Tell me what to do with this.* I'd sat out on the balcony holding it as they talked away about its fate. I now imagined chucking the stack over the railing, the pages scattering and flapping out before me like a flock of pigeons. But I didn't do that. Instead, I came over to watch Penelope burn with the rage of a Homeric war widow. And Arthur, again and again, fail to offer any kind of solace. He would blink at her, big hands dangling stupidly at his sides, baffled to be having this same conversation yet again. *Didn't we resolve this one already?* Because, just as abruptly as things would go south at the beginning of an evening, they would, despite Penelope's dire pronouncements moments earlier, return to normal. Taking Arthur by one of his big dangling hands, she'd say, "Let's go to bed, hon. I can't think about this anymore."

# 8

# PENELOPE

**W**ERE IT NOT FOR THE twin poles of Thanksgiving and Christmas to guide me, I'd remember all this as having happened over several seasons. But it was days, not months, from the holiday blowout around the Morels' dining room table to my time with Penelope on Balthazar's outdoor bench—from Viktoria's first relapse to her haunting messages on my answering machine. The weather was no help; wild swings had gusts of sleet blowing through in the morning and snowmelt streaming in the gutters, baking hot by the afternoon—a time-lapse development to match the overclocked developments in my own life.

It was the first week of December.

Here was another thing: Will no longer made me nervous. His maturity amazed me. Were all eleven-year-olds like this—like little men? He seemed fully formed, with thoughts and feelings very much his own. The way he furrowed his brows when worrying over his parents. The way he sighed and rolled his eyes when I failed to understand a point he was making. The way he said *actually,* the way he said *by the way* and *maybe so* and *just between you and me.* And yet he still had all the features of a little boy; he could fit his fist easily inside my hand. Still thrill at the rifle crack of an empty heel-stomped juice box and make kazoo sounds with his empty lunch-sized carton of raisins. He would say, "Do you think they'll get a divorce?" With eyes that said, *Say no.*

I told him that everything would be okay.

"It's no big deal if they do. Twenty-one out of the thirty-three kids in my class have divorced parents. I asked them. That's more than half. Statistically, it makes sense."

"Both of your parents love you very much."

"It would work out better for them if they did. They wouldn't have to fight anymore. And they could marry other people. Most of the divorced kids in my class have four parents. I figure that's twice the number of presents at Christmas." I remember giving my uncle the same spiel when he tried having a heart-to-heart about my own parents' divorce. He told me that it was okay to be angry, to be sad—but I gave away nothing. I told him that it was for the best, that they'd be happier, and that I was better off if they were happier. Two homes were better than one, I said, using the same equation Will used to solve this terrible unsolvable mess.

But divorce was not our usual topic. Mostly we tackled the more complicated problem of the Smoking Man and the Syndicate— the great mysteries Mulder and Scully struggled every week to unravel. Will orchestrated his life around that hour of television— abandoning all else at exactly nine every Friday evening for a front-and-center position on the couch, remote in hand. It was a needed retreat from the hardships and humiliations of being eleven. I'd forgotten how hard, how humiliating, until spending time around the boy. You could see it on his face after a full day at school. The puffiness around the eyes, the sweat-dried hair that clung to the sides of his face. They spoke of the punch to the stomach for no reason whatsoever. They spoke of the dark-eyed Maria Gutierrez who didn't (not once!) look at him yesterday. They spoke of the stack of comics that disappeared from his backpack between lunch and recess, and the unsuccessful attempt—after a soccerball to the face—of not crying in front of his entire class. Despite the saying to the contrary, time resolves none of our wounds; it only occludes with more recent ones, one on top of the next, burying what was once so painful until at last we forget. And his parents weren't helping any with their living room storms. Although I couldn't see him behind his closed door, I had no doubt he was sitting on his bed, comic book in his lap, trying to shut his ears to what he was hearing — yet craning to catch every word. On the occasions when he needed a partner in make-believe, I found myself caught up in action-figure dramas about young heroes rescuing women from mad-scientist husbands.

Penelope said that Arthur had planned a date night. "Any chance you're free?" It took me a moment to realize that she wasn't asking me along but rather if I'd take care of Will. "A sinking ship still needs its water bailed. That's something my father likes to say. I'm not sure he'd agree in this particular case, though. Art got us tickets to something at the Circle Rep. Dinner beforehand, maybe drinks afterward." She rolled her eyes. "We'll see how it goes."

We started out at Dave's, navigating big-breasted, narrow-waisted Lara Croft across a mossy precipice toward the promise of ancient Mayan treasure, but Will bored of this activity soon enough. Dave offered to show him our festival-ready cut of *Dead Hank's Boy*, but Will declined. He suggested instead that we follow him back to his room so he might show us something *totally hilarious*.

We sat down on his bed while he rifled through his backpack and pulled out his Discman. He popped the lid and fumbled the CD into the boom box on the shelf above his desk. He hit PLAY and the room filled with the caricature voices of Johnny Brennan and Kamal, better known as the Jerky Boys. As we listened, we laughed along with Will. But it was because of Will we laughed. He was the main attraction here: trying desperately and unsuccessfully to control his giggling fits as Big Ole Badass Bob the Cattle Rustler berated a lawn-mower salesman or Nikos, the Greek-immigrant delicatessen owner, mumbled incoherently to a bewildered telephone operator or the nebbish Sol Rosenberg complained to a nurse about his acute case of genital warts.

"Isn't it the funniest thing *ever*?"

We told him that it was indeed the funniest thing ever, which seemed to please Will and extend him the permission he needed to really abandon himself to his laughter, great weeping hysterics of it.

"Okay," he said after it was over, taking a shuddering breath to calm himself—followed by a giggle—then by another breath, "let's do one ourselves." He left the room, giggling as he went, and returned with a cordless phone.

"I don't know," I said. "Dave?" Imagining Dave would support me in putting the kibosh on this mischief.

But Dave said, "Who would you call?"

Will said, "You can call anybody you want. You tell me. Who would *you* call?"

Dave and I looked at each other—and moments later Dave was giddily dialing Suriyaarachchi's cell. Though Will made out like this was his first ever attempt at this, he took the veteran's precaution of dialing in the ID-block code before handing Dave the phone.

When Suriyaarachchi answered, Dave in a high falsetto stuttered, "Hello? Is this the famous Suri—yaar—yaaraah—" before erupting in a fit of giggles.

"Hang up!" we hissed. "Hang up! Hang up!"

Dave handed me the phone. "You try."

I called the theater and asked to speak to the general manager, discovering my throat constricting quite naturally around the froggy voice I used to use for just this sort of thing when I was Will's age. Back then, pay phones were a wonderful free source of entertainment. There was a pair just outside the playground where I spent most of my childhood and at which my friends and I would routinely harass the unlucky operators who answered our calls. After a pause, the theater's general manager was on the line. "This is Nelson, how may I help you?"

"Who the hell is this," I demanded. Will covered his face with a pillow. I went on to lodge a complaint about the Almodóvar film currently showing there. "That movie's nothing but titties titties titties, as far as the eye can see! And let me tell you something else—they're not speaking any language I ever heard. What is that, *Chinese* or something?"

"It's Spanish," Nelson explained.

"Well, it's not English, that's for damn sure!"

Not my best work, I'll admit, but we were just getting warmed up. Will got a phone book. Dave got a notepad and jotted down a list of colorful names for us to audition. We came down off the dizzy high of our first two calls and began anew, approaching the task before us with discipled professionalism. We made stern faces at the one who was calling, to keep them from laughing, and cued them with hastily scrawled notes. We put the calls on speakerphone so that all three of us could enjoy them. Will did a wonderful doddering grandmother—his goal with this character was to frustrate the person on the other end into swearing so that the grandmother could shout, *Language!* which, for some reason, Will thought was the funniest thing. Dave developed a hapless Ukrainian cabdriver named Wassily who insisted to his poor victim that she had left her *vibrating penile toy* in his taxi. Another favorite was an exceedingly polite British salesman calling to offer a fabulous deal on a magazine subscription. Then, following the inevitable rejection, an ear-splitting primal scream. We all enjoyed doing this one—there was something tremendously satisfying about it. But mostly I stuck to what I was good at—customer complaints.

When Penelope and Arthur came through the door, we emerged from our collective prank-call fugue state to discover we'd been at it for three and a half hours. I felt an adolescent's exhaustion—stomach bruised from laughing, throat sore from the contortions of caricature voices. Penelope tried paying Dave, but Dave scruffed Will's head and said, "Lady, friendship can't be bought. It's got to be earned." Will asked if we could have a sleepover, but Penelope diplomatically declined on our behalf. At which point Will stormed off to his room without saying good-bye. At the door, Arthur greeted me with red-rimmed eyes and boozy breath. He shook my hand and clutched my shoulder. "Thank you," he said. "This was—this was good. You're good to us."

On our way down the hall, Dave said, "What's going on with those two?"

I stopped by the bakery before work the following day. Penelope came out to sit with me on the bench. She brought a puffy orange coat, taking from its front pocket a crumpled pack of cigarettes.

"So it's official then?" I said.

She shook out one for me. "This is the least of my worries, at this point."

We smoked for a while side by side, watching customers stuff themselves into Balthazar's small bakery annex, hot air from inside fogging the windows. "How did it go last night?"

Penelope sighed through a long exhale of smoke. "He admitted that handing me his manuscript was a free turndown. Not exactly *I'm sorry*, but we're getting there. He spent the evening with his hands on me—rubbing my back, caressing my hand—like he was literally trying to smooth things over. But now when he touches me, all I can think about is the ending of that book, and my skin crawls. What's wrong with him?"

I shook my head. "Has he ever seen a therapist?"

"Are you kidding? He has a theory about them like he has a theory about everything else. I realize that I don't pay much attention when he talks anymore. I used to be so in awe of him. But these days I listen as he goes on and on and think, *Huh?* I mean, how was writing that book supposed to change anything? It's a small press, they've printed five thousand copies. Art. I used to think of him as my mad genius. So romantic—now I'm not so sure about the genius part." She was quiet for a while, and I thought she was just thinking things over, but I looked over and saw that she was crying. "What's wrong with him? God! I don't know what to do."

"I want to help," I said.

"I know you do." She took my hand, laced her fingers through mine. "You're good. Will loves you. He couldn't stop talking about how much fun he had with you two."

I wasn't good. I was feeling the damp warmth of Penelope's palm and feeling my heart race. Wondering what would happen if I kissed her. If I just turned, leaned in. To touch her smooth round cheeks, her broad freckled face, her full red lips.

Seeming to know my mind, she said, "I was very young. And stupid. I wanted to piss off my parents. You've seen my tattoo. But if I had to do it over again, I'd be smarter. I'd let myself consider all the possibilities." She bumped my shoulder with hers, then let go of my hand, patted it. "I've got to get back."

After she left, I continued to sit there, dazed. I brought my hand, the one she'd been holding, up to my face, to my nose, to my lips. I got up and walked, not really aware of my surroundings, and when I finally looked up, I was at the base of the Manhattan Bridge, twenty minutes late to work and a mile from the theater.

"I'm going to teach you how to offer a mea culpa to your lady American style," I said, leading Arthur into the tented crafts market at Union Square. "It involves the simple application of cash and a roll of wrapping paper." It was another whiplash day, weatherwise—the morning's balmy springlike breeze turning icy by noon, carrying with it a gust of silver flakes that accumulated on car hoods and awnings.

Arthur loped beside me through the densely crowded aisles. "I don't see why we couldn't just go to Macy's," he said. "It's two blocks from the apartment."

"Prepackaged isn't going to cut it, sir. What you need is something unique, something special for your special woman." Most of the stands had their lights and heat lamps going inside their enclosures, the white noise of a hundred individual generators shutting out even the sounds of traffic. We threaded our way through the stands, browsed the jewelry and handcrafted finery, and, to his credit, Arthur seemed a willing student. He'd turn over a necklace I'd chosen for Penelope, and, rather than offering a long tract on the problem with Christmas in the modern age—which is where I worried this venture would take us—he instead would inquire quite practically about its price. He'd hold it up to the light, compare it with similar necklaces in the velvet display cases, ask if perhaps I liked this one better than that one. I browsed as well, picking up any number of semiprecious objects—a bracelet, a pendant, a ring—and imagined fastening each around a corresponding part on Penelope.

Arthur was being sued. The night of the Thanksgiving blowout, Penelope's father had said he needed to *think*. What he meant was *decide*—because he had already done enough thinking. He had spent the weeks following the publication of *The Morels* thinking—about what his son-in-law was up to, what it was all about—and at the end of this period of thinking concluded that it was not about art. It had nothing to do with art. It was about shock. Arthur making a name for himself. He was no better than those loudmouthed radio jocks who said anything about their mothers for a bump in the ratings. Making a name for himself, yes, on the backs of the good names of his daughter and his grandson. And Frank was damned if he would sit by and do nothing about it. A longtime friend, an attorney, was more than happy to draw up the papers. The friend said that it really was his daughter's case to make, that likely nothing would come of the suit were he to file it himself. But this wasn't important. He had to do something. He came to New York undecided about what to do, willing to give his son-in-law a chance to explain himself, but instead his worst fears had been confirmed. He stepped out into the chill November evening and walked and walked until he found an all-night copy shop and printed out the email attachment his attorney friend had sent and returned to his daughter's apartment to serve the papers on his son-in-law himself.

"My publisher is thrilled. The publicity! He's contacted every paper in the country, praying it gains traction." Arthur shook his head. "Poor Frank. Certainly not what he had in mind. If he persists, he'll invoke a self-fulfilling prophecy."

We emerged from the market laden with bags. In addition to the necklace, Arthur had picked out a silk scarf, a pair of cashmere gloves with a matching hat, and an immense framed poster of a license-plate collage, each license from a different state, spelling out in shorthand alphanumeric chunks the opening of the Declaration of Independence. He also found several shadowboxed pressed flower arrangements, a set of table linens, and an exorbitantly expensive cuckoo clock. I imagined him presenting each one to his wife, hoping to give his life a makeover after the mess he'd made of it. Arthur admitted to me that two nights ago, lying awake in bed, he'd actually contemplated redacting the book.

"It would be feasible, I thought. After all, there have been so few copies printed. And sold? Probably a fairly short list." He could contact each customer, one by one, and undo what had been done—what *he* had done—to buy back this mistake, and with it a stake in his marriage, the stake he'd so recklessly gambled away. The following morning he called his publisher, but the man claimed it couldn't be done. Impossible, he said. Arthur started naming sums: he'd pay back his advance, twice that amount— three times, even four. How much would it cost? But it wasn't about the money. Didn't he understand? The book existed, like it or not—already cataloged in the Library of Congress database, reviewed in more than a dozen newspapers, named in a pending lawsuit against him, and situated permanently on the household bookshelves of customers who paid cash and whom Arthur would never be able to reach. This was friendly advice—the publisher said he would be happy to help Arthur attempt this Sisyphean task, more than happy to, but he was giving him fair warning. Such an unprecedented act, recalling a work of fiction, would have the opposite intended effect. It would cause more of a stir than his father-in-law's suit.

Arthur saw this was so, even as he was asking the question, even before, as he was dialing the number, clutching the receiver to his ear, breakfast curdling in his stomach. What he was really feeling was regret, and this was just a bout of wishful thinking.

There was no buying back what he'd done. Though he could feel regret for it, he could not undo it. He had caused an explosion. Penelope was right. He was a terrorist. He had detonated something by publishing *The Morels*. Each copy out there a hot piece of shrapnel. And like it or not, there was no way to make a thing unexplode. The damage had been done. The only thing he could do now was make it up to her — to Will. "American style, as you so aptly put it."

Arthur directed us with our market's armload through the small triangle of park, into the chain toy store across the street. We traveled the slow escalators with the rest of the shoppers, stopping on each floor to audition games for Will. How lost Arthur seemed under the harsh fluorescents, gripping our shopping cart for dear life. He was truly a man from a different age. There had been a spate of movies around this time with a similar premise — one involving a man from Victorian England transported to contemporary Manhattan, another about a Neanderthal teenager thawed and released into the wilds of modern Los Angeles — and watching Arthur aisle after aisle puzzle through the bewildering maze of blinking beeping gadgets, I thought he seemed just as out of place. Although this has got to be something of an exaggeration, doesn't it? He was, after all, the father of an eleven-year-old. This certainly wasn't Arthur's first time in a toy store. And yet, how was it possible for him to seem so unskilled still, after eleven years of practice?

The stuffed bags Arthur emerged with barely fit through the exit. We hailed a taxi and headed back to the apartment. For the first few stoplights on our way uptown, it hadn't occurred to me that I lived elsewhere — and Arthur seemed too preoccupied to notice. When we came through the front door, Penelope was at the answering machine, playing a message that bore a distinctive grandmotherly voice I'd become well acquainted with two evenings before. This "grandmother" wanted to speak to the famous Mr. Morel — she had a *bone to pick* with him. Was he responsible for this *smut* she'd been hearing so much about? Well, it just made her want to reach into her purse and play with her *vibrating penile toy*!

"Three messages like this since you left," she said to Arthur, who was stuffing the gifts up on a high shelf in the hall closet. "The third message is just screaming. It's frightening. Who the hell is it?"

I asked where Will was.

"Spending the day with a friend," she said.

I had gotten my mother a jade pendant necklace from the crafts market while shopping with Arthur, but when I got home and turned the thing over in my hands, it seemed all wrong — too intimate, the kind of jewelry one got for a lover, not a mother — so I put the necklace back in its box and wrapped it up, presenting it to whom it was really intended the next time I saw her, bench-side.

Penelope looked down at the little box I had just put in her hands and said, "Uh-oh. What's this?"

"Just open it."

She tore the ribbon off and lifted the lid to reveal the pendant sitting on a tuft of cotton. "It's beautiful," she said. "And who am I supposed to say gave this to me, when Art asks?"

"You can say I gave it to you."

Penelope chuckled. "Okay, good idea." She closed the box and handed it back to me. "Look, I'm flattered. Seriously, you have no idea. But I can't."

"It's just a necklace," I said. I put it back in my pocket.

She looked at me for a while, letting her gaze travel my face, and then took a deep drag of her cigarette and shook her head. "You're sweet. But my life is very complicated."

We sat for the rest of the time in silence, almost touching And when I got up to leave, she surprised me — herself as well, perhaps — by giving me a peck on the lips. "Now get out of here," she said grinning, and slapped me on the butt.

I visited her every day for the next five days. We spoke less and less. I sat there and she sat beside me, both of us smoking, both of us seeming to feel through whatever this was between us. We sat with our elbows touching, our knees touching, our shoes touching. On the fifth day, Penelope gave me a tour of the bakery, which shared its kitchen with its parent restaurant next door—a war zone of shouts and clangs, the flare-ups of small grease fires lighting the corners of my vision. Everybody knew her, but as she talked into my ear about the role each of these people played in the greater chain of command, she did not introduce me. I thought I might have detected a knowing glance pass between herself and a few of these people. About what? I wondered. About me? The thought set my body into a faint tremor that lasted the duration of the tour. It ended out the back door, in an alley by several enormous metal dumpsters. She had a seat on a milk crate and lit a cigarette. She stared at me frankly without talking for some time. I went for my pack, to give my nervous hands something to do, but my pockets came up empty.

Keeping her eyes on me, she took the cigarette out of her mouth and held it out. I put it to my lips, my every fiber aware of the dampness around the filter's tip. She said that she wished she could stay out here all day but had to get back to work—afterward, I realized it was meant to be a joke, taken in the context of the trash bins and the gaseous stink around us, but at the time I said quite earnestly that I wished the same. She walked me down the narrow alley and gave me a hug. She pressed her ear against my chest, and I let my lips rest on the top of her head, breathing in the intimate smell of her hair. When I spoke, my whispered words tripped over hers, so that together we sounded something like *I wish we can't I know me too.*

(Writing this now, years later, I think about Penelope—how young she was, in her late twenties, with an eleven-year-old and married to a man like Arthur, how she must have felt, hearing day after day her coworkers' after-work exploits, their carefree couplings and uncouplings, the total ease with which they were able to live. How she must have longed to be as free—to call in sick because she felt like catching a movie or to punch out at the end of a shift and walk off into the night with everybody else to a karaoke bar, to an all-night noodlery for *yakisoba* at three in the morning. Not to worry whether Art forgot to feed himself or let Will go through a box of Frosted Flakes for dinner. Not to worry what these two boys weren't telling her, what she was so in the dark about.)

I stood out in the bright sun blinking into the mouth of the alley from which I'd emerged, disoriented. Where was I? It took a turn around the block to reconnect with the bakery's main entrance. I walked on, past it, back to work.

I was loitering in the café with my sweep set toward the end of my shift when Penelope showed up. The nine o'clock crowd had just dispersed. She greeted me with a long look and a slow hug. Her puffy orange coat squished like a stuffed animal in my arms.

I took her on a wordless tour of the theater. Where were we going? I didn't have a destination; I just let my feet take me places. Penelope followed, coat swish-swishing in my ear. I showed her through the swinging door behind the café counter to see fellow employees hurrying through their closing duties. I brought her down the escalator into the stockroom to see the hissing carbon-dioxide tanks that fed the soda machines. I brought her into the cement break pit, into the locker room, and up the narrow flight of stairs into the projection booth to see the great platters of spooled film feed each of the six flickering projectors. We held hands as we did this. Penelope's hair was damp and freshly combed, her lips glistening, face flush with a recent application of makeup — something I noticed, I think, because she didn't normally wear makeup, or this much of it. My heart leaped at the thought that she might have done this for me. We bumped into the general manager coming up the stairs, and we must have looked caught in the act of something, because he teasingly singsonged, "What are you two lovebirds doing?"

As anyone who has found themselves in a similar situation knows — or who has allowed such a situation to get as out of hand as this one had — I was not thinking about whom I might hurt. I was not thinking of Arthur sitting at the dining room table, eating the dinner Penelope had prepared for him out of its Tupperware container. I was not thinking of Will in his room with his earphones on listening to the Jerky Boys while doing his homework. I was thinking only of Penelope's hand in mine, of her arm brushing against my arm, hip brushing hip.

We took a seat in the back row of Theater 6, showing a new adaptation of a Thomas Hardy novel. It seemed, despite the period costumes and candlelit interiors, that those on-screen were enacting our story: unhappily married woman carrying on with another man. Knowing glances, long knowing silences, long lingering walks alone. Moments before the two on-screen gave in to their desires, our lips were feeling out for each other in the flickering darkness. I kissed the contours of her face, her eyelids, her ears, her nose with its tiny cold stud—and her mouth. Our teeth clicked, our tongues met, the musk of our shared saliva inhabited the air between each kiss. Her puffy coat was a hindrance, rustling loudly in the dark. I tried pulling it off.

*Where can we go,* she breathed into my ear.

There was a place the ushers used for napping, one of those secret spots that nobody discussed but about which everyone knew, a folding canvas cot set up in the bowels of the stockroom behind a blind of stacked boxes. The spot was ideal, as the only access to it was down a long corridor, which gave you ample time to straighten your clothes, wipe the sleep from your eyes, and grab a sleeve of cups out of one of the boxes, the feigned object of your excursion to this out-of-the-way place. I led Penelope by the hand through the darkened theater, down the center aisle to the front row and out through the emergency side exit behind the screen. My teeth were chattering. We stumbled down two interconnecting passageways, through a back door into the stockroom, then farther, down the long corridor and around the corner wall of boxes.

I took off Penelope's coat and spread it out on the cot. I unzipped her fleece and peeled it off, pulled her T-shirt up over her head. I unhooked her bra and held the miracle of her bare breasts in my hands. She kicked off her clogs. I unbuckled her belt and stripped off her pants. "My turn," she murmured. I watched her tattooed arm, that chain mail of snake scales, pull off my bow tie and work its way down the buttons of my white work shirt. Her fingers trembled through this, her arm a stucco of dark blue goose bumps. Her normally green eyes were dilated black. Her cheeks burned, bringing to the surface the tiny all-over scarring of teenage acne. Through our fucking—the warm damp press of naked bodies, the penetration, the rocking and rocking and rocking to climax—she breathed hard into my ear but didn't say a word.

In the drowsy afterward, she lay curled against my chest. Pulling back, I saw that she was crying.

Writers have the luxury of elision. They can excise what causes too much discomfort to relate. And were I to take such luxury here, I would skip over the moments that followed, pick up the next morning with Suriyaarachchi and Dave and a fresh cup of coffee. Cut away, avoid the pain of waking from our lust. Because, as we sorted through the aftermath of shed clothing, with each article redonned, it was as though we were clothing ourselves in the terrible wrongness of what we had done. We walked a long slow march back down the corridor, not holding hands and not speaking, avoiding a brush against the shoulder or a hip as though a force field had come down between us. We emerged from the stockroom into the salty popcorn air of the empty lobby. I walked her over to the exit doors. She stepped out into the cold and before walking away looked back at me briefly, bleary eyed, and shook her head.

In my dream, Arthur held a shotgun. He pointed it at me and told me that he knew what I had done. I apologized, I broke down weeping, and woke with the sound of the blast ringing in my ears, the cry still stuck in my throat.

Leaving for lunch, I heard Arthur in the hallway with Will and ducked into the stairwell to travel the fourteen flights on foot rather than stand with him and his son in the elevator. A part of me wanted to come clean, to get it off my chest. Another part of me reasoned that it wasn't my decision alone to make. I needed to speak with Penelope. But Penelope remained unreachable through the swinging door behind the bakery's counter. I waited on the bench outside for an hour. I went through most of a pack of cigarettes. I pretended to look at the menu and watched for her red bandanna. I went inside and asked to speak with her. The cashier disappeared for a few moments and returned to tell me that she was busy.

Penelope showed up later at the theater. I invited her to sit at one of the café tables, but she didn't want to sit. She said it would be best if I stopped coming by the bakery. And, while I was at it, the apartment. Just avoid that end of the hall altogether. It was best. I suggested we tell Arthur. Absolutely not, she said. This was not something to hash out. It was something to box up, to toss out as though it never happened.

But I felt terrible, I said.

"Well," Penelope said, "keep it to yourself." And then she did sit down. And put her face in her hands and wept. "What have I done? I am so fucking stupid!"

I sat down and put my hand on her knee, but she jerked it away. "No, don't touch me." She dug in her pocket for a tissue and blew her nose. "I thought I could get back at him—balance things between us. But all I did was make it worse."

I respected Penelope's wishes. In the days that followed, I avoided the Morels' end of the hallway. A part of me was relieved. How could I face Will? He would take one look at me and know. I used the same stairwell, across from the garbage chute just past Dave's apartment, that I'd ducked into earlier to avoid Arthur and Will. The long jog down led me to the side exit by the loading dock, which allowed me to steer clear of the revolving door.

Suriyaarachchi had begun sleeping at Dave's, I noticed. I would come in to find him on the editing-room couch covered in a blanket or exiting the bathroom with a toothbrush in his mouth. At first

I thought it had something to do with the long nights of drinking they were always inviting me to participate in and I was always sheepishly though firmly declining. To be their *wingman* — or I think it was used as an enticement, that they would be my wing-*men*. The bars they liked were all of a piece: the former beauty salon, the former pharmacy, the former grocery store. Rather than gut these places, the proprietors thought it better to polish the fixtures, dust off the wares, and restore the signage to simulate a heyday, circa 1957. The ladies who got drunk here were pierced and tattooed and wore dresses carefully curated off the racks of Goodwill. Like Penelope. They did their hair up in the styles of an era to match the décor.

"Don't you have an apartment?" I asked.

"Can't afford it anymore. Found a guy to sublet it for plenty, though. I pay half of Dave's rent now and with enough left over to see this movie into the hands of a distributor. Crawling to the finish line, just barely."

The twin betrayals in this statement left me winded. I want to say that my face went "dark." You read writers using this word to describe a character's expression, but I couldn't see myself so I can only say it felt this way. The usual tension in my facial muscles that holds my social exterior together, that tries to project a certain friendliness to make me appear, as people have said about me, eager to please — these muscles went slack.

Suriyaarachchi must have sensed this change, too, because he was already backpedaling defensively. "There's no way you could afford what I was asking for my place. It's a prewar one bedroom on Park Avenue, dude. I have a doorman! Anyway, aren't you shacking up with your boyfriend and his wife, down the hall?"

I glared at Dave, who was standing in the kitchen with a bowl of cereal. "You knew I was looking for a place," I said. "Haven't you noticed the desperation with which I've been using your fax machine?"

Through a crunching mouthful, Dave said, "I don't know why

you hang around that creep Arthur. Did you read what he wrote about his kid? What's up with that?"

"It's not what you think," I said. "He's trying to save literature."

I gave my mother the pendant.

"She didn't want it then?"

"She was married," I said.

"Her loss, my gain, I suppose."

I helped her with the clasp at the nape of her neck.

"I don't know what I'm doing, Mom."

"It's okay," she said. "Nobody does. The ones that say they do are just fooling themselves."

"I meant about this clasp."

"No, you didn't."

We were standing in the kitchen. My mother was tall, with a dancer's graceful posture, though she had never been a dancer. She liked to boast of the casting directors who used to mistake her for one. I have a framed studio headshot of my mother in my room—a teenager from the fifties harboring dreams of becoming a starlet. She dismisses these childish ambitions when she talks about her past, of that time before she *knew who she was*, as though poetry were the inheritance to a kingdom and she were its heiress.

Mom checked herself out in the reflection of the toaster, letting her fingers play over the small jade teardrop against her chest. "It's lovely, honey. Even if it is a hand-me-down." She turned and kissed me on the forehead, patted my cheek. "I won't tell you that it gets easier, because it doesn't. It just seems to matter less, the older you get. It's an improvisation. Think of it that way. And there are no wrong notes, because it's your tune. You make it up. It's not ideal, but what other choice do you have?"

In my room, sitting at the piano bench, silently sounding off notes on the keyboard, I thought of my An of the Byzantine frescoes and wondered how she was faring. The days when we were together seemed so far away now. Senior year we rented the parlor floor of an old Victorian town house not far from campus. It was rundown, the landlord a reclusive man who lived on the garden level among a maze of bound magazines and stacked newspapers. The rent was cheap. His only stipulation was that we leave our shoes at the door, something I was already used to, as An had this stipulation, too, when I would spend time in her dorm room. I turned that place into a home. An argued against it, as we were only renting — the supplies cost a great deal, more than we could afford — but I couldn't help myself; as I said, the nesting instinct is strong in me. I ripped up the old threadbare wall-to-wall and waxed and buffed the hardwood planks beneath to a golden luster. There was a set of French pocket doors dividing the living room from the kitchen that were permanently stuck partway open and in total disrepair. I spent weeks restoring those doors, getting each to run properly along the track, stripping the paint and replacing the plywood squares with matching panes of frosted glass from a local glazier. I installed custom shelves in the kitchen, hung a thrift-store chandelier in the bedroom, and planted a garden in the dead patch of dirt out back. I loved my life then, coming home to An, stretched out and reading on the couch, or waking up next to her on a Saturday morning, the weekend wide open before us. It was a much simpler time, compared with the thorny brush I was hacking through now.

I went into the living room for the old rotary and brought it on its long extension back into my room and closed the door. After three foreign sounding rings, An picked up — much to my surprise. And, much to my surprise, within moments I was blubbering about how much I missed her, how terribly I missed our life together. I confessed everything. I told her about Arthur and his book, about what I had done with his wife.

"Get out," she said. "Get out while you still can. This situation you're in now is destructive. You can see that. Why don't you move out of the city? Start over somewhere else. Baby, listen to me. Just get on a bus and go!"

She was kind. She let me reminisce, participated in the reminiscing herself. She did not tell me about the boyfriend she no doubt had. Or how wonderful the alpine air in Baden-Württemberg was this time of year.

Lying in bed, awake, I resolved to quit. An was right. The movie was done. There was no reason I should be spending my days there anymore. The time had come to move on. But what would I do? I had no marketable skills, other than those I had picked up as an usher—sweeping, counting change, making announcements over a loudspeaker. Skills that might have served me well in Communist Poland but that made me at the age of thirty in the entrepreneurial capital of the world an increasingly pathetic figure. My only option at this point was grad school. A doctorate in music composition. I could teach, get the occasional local symphony commission. It seemed almost glamorous now, after being confronted with the realities of moviemaking and the realities of being an iconoclastic novelist with a wife and a child.

# 9

# RUSHDIE

THE FOLLOWING MORNING, AFTER I offered my resignation, Suriyaarachchi said, "But you'd be turning down a full-fledged
producer credit, which would be a real shame."

"On *Dead Hank's Boy*?"

"That ship has sailed, my friend, no. I'm talking about our new
project."

"A documentary," Dave said.

"About?"

"Your boyfriend down the hall. Dave, show the man."

Dave held out a copy of yesterday's *New York Post*. "Page nine."

I looked from Dave to Suriyaarachchi to the *Post* in my hands.
The headline: "Brick Suspect Rips Rudy's Homeless Policy." I
thumbed past the movie listings. Page 9. There were three stories
here. One involved a retired television weatherman convinced
that a coming storm would wash away the sins of the city and was
building an ark on the roof of his Cobble Hill brownstone. The
neighbors had filed a court injunction against it. The man's name
was, improbably, Fludd. Another was an update on the kidnap-
ping of a Queens woman's two-year-old — it turned out the whole
thing was a hoax. To what end was not made clear.

The third story was about Arthur: "Local Writer Sued — by His
Own Family." The article began, "Herald Square resident Arthur

Morel, who has made waves in literary circles, now finds himself in deep water with his family upon the release of his latest effort, *The Morels*. Franklyn Wright, Mr. Morel's father-in-law, has filed a defamation suit on behalf of his daughter and grandson. Mr. Morel's openly autobiographical book makes explicit mention of an act of incest between himself and his then-eight-year-old son. Mr. Wright claims the portrayal of his daughter and grandson in such a manner constitutes unfair and damaging use of their names for the express purpose of furthering Mr. Morel's own career. Mr. Morel could not be reached for comment."

"And?" I said, handing the paper back to Dave.

"And!" Suriyaarachchi spread out his hands and jumped. *Ta-da!* "There is no *and*. This is it, baby! This is the movie that's going to make us famous."

"But we're out of money. You said it yourself."

"Let me worry about that. Tell me you're not itching to get out there and shoot again. Look at me and tell me honestly."

"But a documentary? They lack something. Michael Moore on the red carpet looks like a boom operator who wandered in by mistake. And you're forgetting what production was like. We're not equipped."

"But we are equipped. A camera, a subject, a place to edit. That's the beauty."

"What about my script?" I said.

Suriyaarachchi gave me a look: *What script?*

"The one I've given you three times already but you keep losing!"

"That one. I don't know. Dave, what did you think?"

"It was a little derivative."

"Too many long speeches. And Mexican standoffs. Leave that stuff to Tarantino and John Woo. I keep telling you, you want to make your mark, you've got to do something different."

"Anyway," Dave said, "that's a narrative feature. It would be months before we could begin shooting. Even if we did it on the cheap."

"With this documentary we could be shooting tomorrow. Tomorrow! And be wrapped with a final edit in time for next year's festivals. We wouldn't have to reenter a movie that's already been rejected"—the envelopes were already coming back to us—"we would have this new effort, a film that would be even stronger for us having been through *Dead Hank's Boy*. And if we got the attention of a distributor? It could only be good news. It's leverage."

"A two-picture deal."

"I was up all night thinking about it."

"The only problem is your subject," I said.

"Arthur?"

"He's awkward."

"He is awkward," Dave said.

"And," I said, "he's a writer. This lawsuit aside, I don't think you're going to find he's much of a subject. It's not like he's Salman Rushdie or anything."

"Rushdie would be a subject," Dave said.

"I think he's still in hiding."

"He came out for a cameo on *Seinfeld*."

"That wasn't Rushdie. I saw that episode. That was someone who Kramer *thought* was Rushdie."

"It wasn't Rushdie? Are you sure?"

"Look," Suriyaarachchi said, "you don't have to have a price on your head to be interesting."

"It doesn't hurt," Dave said.

"What about the crazy weatherman," I said. "I think he'd make a great subject."

I was dissembling, of course. From the moment Dave handed me the paper, I knew where this was headed, and I didn't want any part. Despite Suriyaarachchi's claim, we couldn't start shooting tomorrow because, for one, we didn't have Arthur. And this was where I came in: the one who could bring him around. Luckily, I was still feeling hurt and angry at the both of them from the day before, or I wouldn't have had the presence of mind to refuse. It struck me as unseemly, trying to capitalize on the very real turmoil the Morels were going through. And then there was the mess with Penelope; just thinking about it tightened a knot in my chest. But Suriyaarachchi worked on me all day long. He bought me lunch, kept calling me "the man," laughing hysterically at any little thing I said.

"Just think," he said, "this would be your project. No more running errands, no more 'associate' producer. You'd be a full partner in this. An equal voice in all creative decisions. And I'm planning on funding it without my parents' help, which would make your license in these decisions that much more free."

A few days later, against my better judgment, I went to knock on the Morels' door. To say that I had *refused* Suriyaarachchi may be an overstatement. In fact, I told him that I would have to *think about it* and, having thought about it some, came around to the idea of a documentary about Arthur. Although they lacked the glamour of narrative features, there was something pure about documentaries; they were more serious, higher-brow. And despite what I had said to Suriyaarachchi, Arthur did seem to be a good subject—the perfect subject, in fact. He said and did things that got him into trouble. What could be more entertaining than that? And to the question of using the misfortunes in his life for our gain, I thought: this is what artists do. No need to make it sound so sinister. It offered a way for me to face Arthur again, a way for me to make it up to him. In my fantasy—a fantasy that Suriyaarachchi encouraged—this movie would make Arthur famous. I would be doing him a service, I reasoned, while atoning for my sins.

The door was open. A red suitcase blocked my way in. I stepped over it and called out, "Hello?" There was someone here. I could hear sounds coming from elsewhere in the apartment. I called out again and walked down the short corridor toward the bedroom. The light was on in the bathroom, door partway open, and when I peeked in I saw Penelope crouched at the cabinet under the sink. Stuffing things at random, it seemed, into her purse. I tapped my knuckle on the door.

She screamed, wheeled around. "What are you doing?" She stood up, then elbowed past me out of the bathroom.

I followed.

She said, "I thought I told you to stay away."

I told her I had been, but something had come up, an opportunity—she could be a part of it. That I'd like to make her a part of it, if she was willing.

She didn't appear to be listening. "Look," she said. "Something's happened, and I'm just, I'm on my own. I have to deal with it on my own." She was in the bedroom now, pulling open dresser drawers and tossing clothes by the handful into an open suitcase on the bed. I want to say she had been crying, but her eyes weren't red or puffy. I might say they were a little shiny, and in her high sweet voice there was a new throatiness, a new depth.

I said, "I read about the lawsuit in the paper. How are you holding up?"

"The lawsuit," she repeated. "Oh, the lawsuit. That's just my father being crazy." She zipped the suitcase and jerked it up off the bed onto the floor. "Will!" The place was ransacked. The dresser's drawers remained yanked open, a pair of stockings spilling out. The closet was empty but for a few full-length dresses.

"I hope this isn't because of us," I said. "Please don't leave because of us. You two can still work it out."

Penelope glanced past me to make sure nobody was there and then narrowed her eyes at me. "I told you never to mention that," she hissed. "There is no us. I told you that, too."

"Then where are you going?"

"I tried," she said. "I tried with him, but there's only so much I can do. At a certain point, I've got to start being a mother. God, why did it take me so long to figure that out?" She clicked the suitcase handle into place and rolled it out of the room. "Will," she shouted down the hall, "are you ready?"

*I tried with him.* Was she talking about Will or Arthur? I followed after her into the living room.

Will was kneeling at the television. "Hey," he said to me.

Penelope said, "Where is your sleepover stuff?"

"I want to make sure it tapes. It's the second episode in a two-part—"

"I told you, Will. We're not coming back for a while."

"But when we do come back—"

"Your sleepover stuff. Now." Will got up and marched into his room.

"I know you have your hands full here," I said, "and I don't want to make things more complicated for you right now. But I have a thought—not a thought, more of a proposal—for you to think about on your way to wherever you're going. Where are you going, by the way?"

"Jesus, just ask what you're going to ask already."

"I want an interview with you."

"An interview."

"We're going to make a film. About Arthur, about your lives. You can be famous."

"What is this? You want to film me? What for?"

"And Arthur. It would be a documentary."

"Fucking unbelievable. You people are fucking unbelievable. It's like a steamroller, a runaway steamroller. Will!"

Will stomped out of his room. "I'm packing," he yelled. His voice was angry, but his eyes were afraid.

"Forget it. We're leaving. Now. Out the door." She ushered Will into the hallway. "Hit the button," she called, following him, leaving me standing in the center of the room. She didn't bother to close the door on her way out.

I related this run-in to Suriyaarachchi, who said, "Don't worry about her, she'll come around." He rubbed his hands together. "So the plot thickens!"

The next day, I tried knocking on their door again, half expecting it to be open, but it wasn't, and nobody answered. I had Arthur's cell number and tried that a few times, but it was going straight to voice mail. The campus directory at Columbia put me in touch with the Writing Division, and the woman who answered the phone said he had office hours on Thursdays. It was Friday.

"Isn't he around any other day?"

"He's here now, but I couldn't say how much longer he'll stay. Most people leave early on Fridays." I thanked her and told Suriyaarachchi that I would be back later.

I arrived at the doorway to Arthur's office, flushed and out of breath. "I've been looking for you."

He was seated at his desk, stack of papers in front of him. He looked up. "What do you want?"

Despite Penelope's claim, it seemed clear to me that the frantic business of her packing was the direct result of our affair. I was certain it had caused this final tumult in their lives—a shouting match that ended with her throwing the fact of her infidelity in his face. Arthur's abruptness appeared to confirm it.

"Nothing urgent," I said. "Mostly just concerned."

He gave me a frown. The office was dim and windowless, barely big enough for one of the two enormous desks here. Whoever occupied the one opposite Arthur was not here now, though there were signs of a recent vacancy: unfinished email on the monitor, a plastic takeout container open next to the keyboard: pasta, fork with a bite twirled neatly around resting on the lid.

"That's Don," Arthur said, seeing where I was looking.

"I tried calling. And knocking and ringing your doorbell. Where have you been?"

He was unshaved, hair uncombed, shirt untucked. He watched me for a moment and then, as if to wish me gone, returned his attention to his papers. I sat down at the unoccupied desk, waiting for him to tell me what he knew, readying my apology.

"Don's coming back," he said without looking up. And then, putting down his pen, "Penelope left me. She took Will."

"Oh no," I said. Then, testing the waters, "What happened?"

"I came home last night," Arthur said. "There was a reading up here, over at eight. I thought she might be picking Will up from the neighbors'. Then I saw the bedroom."

Closet empty. Dresser empty.

He called her cell—straight to voice mail. He sat down on the bed, pulled a coat hanger out from under his seat. He tossed it on the floor with the others. He had always thought that he would one day end up alone—that his luck would one day run out. So in this way, the discovery was not an unexpected one. After all, who could love someone like him? What was there to love? He was too literal, too humorless and detached, with a self-destructive streak a mile long. Arthur would say to Penelope during their first year of marriage, *You're going to leave me.* At first she would protest, reassure him that she wouldn't, then later it would provoke an argument. *Do you want me to leave? Is that it? You can't handle being married? Is it too hard for you?* Somewhere along the way he'd stopped saying it, though he hadn't stopped thinking it, which was maybe why this scene he'd walked in on was not shocking, why it felt like some piece of bad news he'd known for some time though hadn't been officially told to him.

What did surprise him was the panic. He'd recently gone after a student for describing a character as being *in the grip* of panic. Why does panic always have to *grip*? Can't panic do other things? Can't it *flog* or *pinch* or *startle* or *finger*? Why always *grip*? But sitting there on the bed, he felt very much in its grip. His ribs pressed in on him, he had trouble catching his breath, he felt squeezed, felt his pulse ticking loudly in his head, his thoughts trapped in his skull. He got up, paced the apartment.

Will's room was similarly ransacked of things.

He called Penelope again, and again got her voice mail, again stopped short of leaving a message.

Where had she gone? Where had she taken Will?

He dialed the Wrights. Constance answered. She doesn't want to speak with you, she said. That was it. She hung up. Arthur called back, but this time got the recorded voice of Frank declaring that nobody was home.

Arthur was not a man of action and would not have imagined he'd be one to hail a taxi to the airport, no plan other than to see his wife and son, to wait standby for a flight to Dulles, yet there he was, no overcoat, no change of clothes, still gripped—yes, gripped—by a feeling that some terrible change was taking place, had already taken place, while he wasn't paying attention, and that he was entirely at fault. It was up to him to make it right. But what could he do, what could he say to make things right? He had tried. For the past two weeks, he had tried—but had obviously failed miserably.

"Why didn't you just take the train," I asked.

"Haven't you been listening? I was in a panic. And we usually fly when we see Penelope's parents—Will's not good with sitting for long periods."

His name was the last to be called, his seat between a pair of squabbling young boys. Their mother came over to apologize several times and to scold each into sitting quietly in his seat, but Arthur couldn't help noticing that she didn't offer to switch places with him. He felt a sudden pang of sadness for Penelope, who didn't have the luxury of this mother—her ignorance of him or her freedom from him. Penelope was stuck, forced to carry with her the burden of knowing him and sharing a child. She wanted out—her parents had finally convinced her—and here he was, following her. She wanted to be left alone. To be free of him. Why couldn't he leave her be?

But this empathy for his wife passed, and in its place came a wave of self-pity. His students loved him; he was their hero. He stood cornered after the reading the night before by a gaggle of them, eager for his esteem, eager to prove that they too understood literature's power and importance. The fluorescent overheads were too bright for a cocktail party, but under their glare he had a cup of white wine, and then another. He enjoyed their belief in him, in what he'd written; it must be how a revolutionary feels after leaving home—family furious at being abandoned and put at risk—to arrive in the basement of his comrades, welcomed warmly as a fellow soldier, admired for the sacrifice he's made of his family for the greater good of the cause. These were his true believers, fellow revolutionaries. They regarded him with awe, with respect. He stayed as long as he dared in that corner with a second, then a third, cup of wine, just to hear them talk, to have them ask him questions.

Overheard at the start of the semester, while passing a fellow faculty member's office: *One book does not a writer make.* Had they been talking about him? Probably. He had not made friends among his cohorts. It was more important to have the alliance of faculty than his students. Full-time positions were not determined by student evaluations. Penelope urged him to invite his colleagues to dinner, to get to know the dean. Penelope was smart in these matters. It was all Penelope's dream — the novelist husband, the distinguished professor — not his. *One book.* Whoever said it was right. He should have quit while he was ahead.

But he didn't quit. Something compelled him to keep going, to seek publication. What was it he was doing? What was he trying to say? It was something Penelope had asked relentlessly, day after day, these two long weeks, and when he answered her, she assumed he was hiding his true intentions. But he wasn't. If there were other motives, motives behind the reasons he gave her, then these motives were hidden, even from himself. Yet he could say this for certain: whatever he was trying for in that book, whatever possessed him to write what he wrote, these ambitions were not the same as, or even related to, the ambitions Penelope wanted for him — the academic ladder, lucrative book contracts — they were not the ambitions of even his most idealistic students either: he wasn't aiming for great literature, to add to or dismantle the canon or reveal some hidden aspect of human nature or prove some political or philosophical point or make innovative use of language or form or style. They weren't necessarily the ambitions of a writer at all. They were, if anything, related to his notions of art from many years ago, when he was studying music.

His old composition teacher worshipped at the feet of the

"great" composers. He played Arthur recordings of the estab-
lished living masters, "bearers of the torch," he used to say, as
though each of these men from different parts of the world, from
different generations, shared the same aim, an aim that his teacher
could never articulate clearly to Arthur. As if Bartók's curatorial
notions of his countrymen's folk music were in any way related to
the playful, kaleidoscopic symmetries that flowed from Mozart's
brain. For a while, Arthur would allow himself to become enam-
ored of a composer or a certain contemporary school of thought—
new serialism, indeterminacy, minimalism—feeling each time that
yes, this was the answer. But then he would decide that the theory
fell short in some way, didn't account for some music, unwritten,
that was inside of him, needing only to be unlocked.

However these composers and schools of thought failed individually, they failed collectively in the same way: the music was all
dead on arrival. For every piece of music, once written down, was
merely a description of itself, its true purpose a set of instructions.
And to perform that set of instructions was merely to describe the
description. It was to confuse the act of cooking with the act of
reading a recipe out loud. True music was not created by instruments squawking out noises specified on a page. It was not to be
written down. It was not to be thought about, codified into some
school of thought—somewhere along the line, music found itself
divorced from one of its more powerful, primal purposes.

Catharsis.

"It's an antiquated notion," Arthur said. "The lost art of ancient
bards with their lyres. It's been replaced by a more general suggestion that music should quote-unquote 'move people,' that it should
activate the emotions in some way, but on the whole, people who
make music—composers, performers—disown themselves from
this responsibility: it's up to the audience to feel what it will and is
generally out of the hands of the person onstage. And many contemporary composers have taken it a step further—they reject the
notion that music should do anything at all, that, in fact, to actively
try to provoke a feeling in a listener is a futile effort at best and, at

worst, a manipulative act better left to the hacks who score movies and, as such, something any serious-minded composer ought to avoid. So freed from any and all obligations to a listener, the contemporary composer is free to annoy—or more likely bore—that listener to death."

Catharsis: to cleanse, to purge. According to my dogeared college dictionary, "an emotional purification through art, intended to renew the spirit." Or "to rid oneself of a fixation by allowing it direct expression." An appealing idea for Arthur, one that came to him not through his time at music school but at home, in the process of teaching himself French.

His parents' bookcase at home was a special kind of library. Guests were free to take any book they wanted as long as, in its place, they donated one of their own. It was a tradition his parents began before he was born and continued to this day. It was better than any public library, they claimed, bringing them into contact with titles they would never have chosen on their own. (The spring of 1976 saw the sole, important amendment to the rules: the book donated must not already exist in the bookcase—after they noticed their shelves overrun by dozens of copies of *Zen and the Art of Motorcycle Maintenance*, threatening to overtake their entire library like a virus.) They received books of all kinds, many in languages other than English, and during Arthur's foray into the French language, he scoured the bookshelves for titles a little more challenging than *Le Petit Prince*. Arthur found a book by one Louis Moulinier entitled *Le Pur et l'Impur dans la Pensée des Grecs*, which seemed to describe, if he was reading correctly, cathartic traditions and rituals in ancient Greece.

In it, he learned that Greeks practiced music as a kind of medicine, as a way of keeping the "humors" in balance. In order to purge evil humors, the musicians would invoke them through their music—similia similibus curantur, "like curing like"—in the way that Achilles cleansed himself of the murder of Thersites by washing his hands in the ritual blood of a sacrificed piglet: blood purified through blood. In this way, Arthur learned, the Greek purged himself, through music, of all sorts of bad stuff. And it wasn't only the audience that was the beneficiary of this treatment: the musicians themselves and the composers were cleansed as well.

As Arthur read this (as it happened, at the same time struggling with a cadenza for the concerto he was to perform), it seemed he had unearthed an essential truth about art, long forgotten — a truth he himself knew but had never been able to articulate before.

It was a notion that came to inform his writing once he found himself engaged in the activity. When he'd finally gotten around to Aristotle's *Poetics*, he was struck by this sentence: "Tragedy is an imitation of an event that is serious, complete, and of a certain magnitude, being found in action, not of narrative."

So, then. The main thing was *action*, not narrative.

Then what was one to do with a novel, which was narrative in nature? Even scenes that "showed" rather than "told" in a novel were, at core, narrated. How could you overcome what was in essence, your very definition? Was there such a book that could achieve this ideal and still be a book? Actions, however well described are still descriptions of actions — narratives — and not the same as the actions that unfold on a stage, witnessed by a live audience. Books amounted to nothing but fancy stage directions, all potential, no action.

If a book were to overcome such a shortcoming, it would have to be less about what it contained — its story — and more to do with the action on the part of its author — what the author himself was doing or appeared to be doing.

"Like Hemingway," I suggested. "The hunter who writes about hunting."

"No," Arthur says. "Not like Hemingway." He makes a face. I can see I've gotten it totally wrong. He's disappointed.

Arthur had written several shorter pieces of fiction and with each one felt his craft improving, and although he enjoyed a certain satisfaction in writing them, he was unable to get any closer to this notion of what he felt literary art should be. It was only after he had completed his first novel — in the doldrums between books, ready to give up—that it came to him. In fact, it had been there all along, on his bookshelf—seen so often that it had become invisible.

He had discovered it as a college student, shelving books at the Queens College Library, a job he was terrible at. He'd wheel a full cart into the small rickety service elevator with every intention of doing his job, and yet there he'd be, three hours later, kneeling in the PQs, paging through the unexpurgated *120 Days of Sodom*, shelving cart parked in a corner, still full. Yet when, at the end of a shift, he slipped out having only put away half-a-dozen books, nobody seemed to notice. It was a place to daydream literature. It was during one of these daydreams that Arthur discovered PR6068.U757 S27. He was about to shelve it when he noticed the title: *The Satanic Verses*. Rushdie back then was a prominent news story—the ayatollah only a year prior had levied the holy bounty on the author's head. Arthur imagined the book—from the furor it had caused and his misunderstanding of the facts—to be some slim document written in Arabic, an unrelenting tirade against Iranians and all that they stood for, whatever that was. His half-brother Benji, whom he was living with at the time and who was outspoken about all matters of cultural debate, declared it only fitting that the book should have sent him into hiding, for it was so poorly written—and when the issue came up in a class Arthur had been auditing the semester prior, he parroted Benji's condemnation of the book. Yet to Arthur's surprise there in the library, the book was nothing like what he had expected. First of all, it was in English. The "About the Author" on the last page revealed that Rushdie wasn't even Iranian—he was from India. The book was big, bursting at the seams. It was at turns lyrical and funny and crass and intellectually challenging.

The burgundy clothbound tome, its library call letters on a strip of white adhesive at the bottom of its spine. Arthur was still on record for owing the eighty-dollar replacement fee. He had kept renewing it, intending on finishing it, but never did. In fact, he hadn't gotten any farther than he had in that initial enthusiastic burst at the library so many years ago.

He took it off the shelf and reread the opening passage. It begins with a startling image—two men falling out of the sky—suicide bombers who have leaped from a rigged jetliner just before an explosion. Do they get their wish? He couldn't recall and did not read on to find out now, for it wasn't the words or their meaning that interested Arthur—it was the action behind them. Here was a book that managed to achieve a certain cathartic ideal. It wasn't the plot that was the power of this book. Or rather the plot managed to generate the actions that made this book into a powerful creative act. It had caused a series of events that flowed reflexively back to the author. The book, in a sense, was generating story. This he liked; this was interesting literary art.

"So write a book that will get banned. Is that the idea?"

"Not exactly." Arthur described a man in Florida, a serial murderer, who wrote "stories" in which the protagonist rapes and strangles his victims, the protagonist matching an idealized version of the author and murders tactically similar to the murders he himself would commit, the victims of a similar type he himself might choose. When he was eventually caught, these stories, found on a shelf in his closet, were used as evidence against him in the trial. This, too, Arthur thought, was ideal fiction, powerful fiction, authentic documents of authorial action. It didn't matter if these stories were poorly crafted—Arthur managed to obtain a copy of them, published by a fringe press under the title *Killer Fiction*—odd point-of-view shifts, basic grammar and style errors. The craft didn't matter—the abrupt nonendings, the woodenness of dialogue, the flatness of character. They were essentially snuff fantasies, a kind of morbid pornography. Yet there was an Aristotelian perfection about them. It was an example of narrative catharsis—*similia similibus curantur*. Blood washing blood. It was why de Sade remained such a potent figure: it wasn't the writing—for, really, the work, shocking though it is, in the end is just downright tedious—but rather the image of the author imprisoned for engaging in such acts, dreaming up these pages on his only available writing implements: toilet paper and his own blood. The writing becomes synonymous with the author. It's not what's written that matters; it's *that* the author has written such a thing—the writing of the book as a performative act, a purgative, purifying act. Catharsis.

If Arthur had to define his modus operandi, it would be this: *writing as performance.*

Arthur disembarked from the plane at Dulles and found the rental counter. His only option that evening was a bright yellow Camaro, a stick shift. He'd never driven a stick before. The attendant made Arthur sign some kind of waiver before giving him a lesson around the parking lot.

Arthur lurched out. The seats were very low. It felt like he was driving lying down. Several cars on the highway honked and flashed their lights at him. He waved tentatively as they passed, thinking that perhaps he looked as ridiculous as he felt and these people were laughing at him, but after a while he realized he hadn't turned on his headlights. He groped around the dashboard, swerving, until he located them and flipped them on. When he arrived at the Wrights', the window lights—dark upon his approach—went on one by one as he idled, trying to remember how to turn the headlights off.

He had brought the gifts for Will—on his way out the door he pulled them down from the closet shelf before putting on his coat. As he hoisted himself out of the car, he dragged the enormous bag from the backseat, loaded down with two video-game consoles, three board games, and a poltergeist forensic kit. He limped with it up the front walk.

What had changed? Why had Penelope chosen this day to leave him? He could only think that her father was at the bottom of all this. His lawsuit, his corrosive anger. Since he'd filed the suit, he called the house daily. If Arthur answered, Frank would hang up. When Penelope answered, she would take the cordless into the bathroom and have long conversations from which she would emerge cantankerous, spoiling for a fight. Had her father finally gotten to her? But why wouldn't she speak to him about it? It was unlike her. She was usually so vocal about things.

Arthur swayed there for a moment after pressing the bell. He pressed it again. He hadn't imagined this scenario. Somehow, he thought that Constance would open the door to let him in, that he would be able to ascend the stairs to Penelope, to Will. He didn't know what he would do when he saw them—his imagination didn't go that far—but the important bit would be to have them there in front of him. Something would come. Their very presence would see to that. She would say something, and then Will would say something, and then Arthur would say something—at which point they would be talking and, from there, all roads led home. He would do whatever he had to, say whatever he had to, to have them back. But none of this could happen out here.

He stabbed at the doorbell, banged at the door with his fist. He yelled, Penelope! Will! He paced, banged some more. It was no good, no good! Even if Penelope did come to the door, it would be no good. To speak to her out here would be to lose them both. All roads, from out here, led to rift, to divorce. She would say something, he would say something, it didn't matter, it would end, whatever was said, with her walking back inside and closing the door on him. These were the essential truths of body and action: to cross the threshold, to breach her father's castle, was to win; to stand out here in the cold was to lose. He had to get in.

The lights came on downstairs by the entrance, but he remained staring at the closed door. He pressed the bell again, followed by a few raps with the door's knocker. This produced some whispering on the other side of the door. Arthur tried peering through the lace gauze in the narrow side window. Constance, he said. It's Art. Please. Let me in.

The curtain was yanked back by a hand, and Frank's face appeared suddenly, sternly, nose to nose with Arthur. He shook his head slowly—so that it could have stood both for refusal as well as disappointment—and then disappeared again.

Arthur banged on the door, so hard it rattled the frame, rattled his teeth. He bellowed, Penelope! Will! Let me in!

He marched around to the rear, trudging the gift bag at his

side, to the enclosed porch. The screen door was locked, but the door was outfitted at its base with a swinging panel for Curtis the Cat.

Arthur crawled down and managed, by turning himself sideways, to wedge himself in. Strands of spiderweb tickled his lips and clung to his face.

Hands planted, legs still outside, he heard the swoosh of the sliding back door and a sound that, never having heard it before in person nor ever having felt the cold steel of it on the back of his head, he knew nevertheless to be the cocking of a shotgun.

Back, Frank said.

Arthur moved to stand up.

No. The way you came. He nudged Arthur back with the tip of the gun.

Come on, Frank! I need to see my wife.

Not tonight, you don't. Now go.

Arthur was forced to shimmy back out through the unyielding pressure of the gun barrel on his head. He stood up, facing his father-in-law through the screen door. He said, I can't leave until I see them.

They don't want to see you.

Why?

If you have to ask, then I don't know what to tell you.

Just open the door, Frank. They stood staring at each other. It was clear Frank had no intention of letting Arthur pass. Arthur grabbed the handle of the screen door and rattled it.

Frank shouldered the shotgun and firmed his stance. I will blow your head off.

Arthur was suddenly furious. Do it! Do it! Shoot me, Frank. Go ahead — Penelope!

The whoosh of the sliding door again, and Constance, in pajamas, came out. Okay, okay, she said, her voice low, calm. Frank's not going to shoot you. Frank, put down that thing. But you can't come in, Arthur.

Constance, Arthur said.

The police are on their way, she said. A cordless phone was in her hand — she held it out, as if this were proof of what she said, and then brought it to her chest. Now go, she said. Penelope will talk to you when she's ready.

I need to see her. I need to see my son.

Will, Constance said, her voice suddenly different — still calm but no longer soft. As long as I can help it, you will never lay another hand on that boy.

Up until this point, Arthur had been in the dark about Penelope's sudden retreat with Will, her refusal to see him. He had been raging out here under the impression that he was raging at — raging against — his in-laws, that he had come out here to win her, and Will, back from them. But this wasn't it — he was still in the dark, but he saw now that he was not in the position he thought he was in — they were not barring his entry as much as they were protecting their daughter and grandchild. Penelope had not been lured to this place — she had fled here for protection. From him.

He was not the hero; he was the intruder.

Tears pricked his eyes. What is this? he said. He looked at the old couple before him as if for the first time — frail, frightened of the man standing before them.

Arthur walked back around to the front just as the flashing squad car pulled into the driveway. An officer who could have been one of Arthur's students took down his name on a pad and asked him some questions, each one a spoonful of grief: what was his relationship to the Wrights, what had transpired between them, what was he doing out here. The questions framed this situation as a domestic dispute. They treated Arthur generously, compassionately, even — though he was made to stand by his Camaro with one of the officers while the other was admitted into the house by Constance.

Neighbors emerged from their houses and stood on their lawns. Ones who were too far away came up the road and stood watching with their arms folded.

A man approached the officer by Arthur and said, Everything okay here? He gave Arthur a penetrating glare.

Thanks for your concern, sir. Everything is under control — just go back inside. The man walked back, keeping his eye on Arthur, to his position on his lawn, arms folded. The officer rolled his eyes. Everybody wants to do something when there's nothing to be done. Makes me laugh. Same guy passes a dark alley during a mugging, and he just keeps walking.

I just want to talk to my wife, Arthur said.

I understand, man. I really do. Believe me, I've been there. But if she don't want to come out of there and talk? There's nothing you can do. The officer had seemed merely a kid at first, but getting a longer look, he estimated that the man was older than he was by several years.

He pulled a gun on me, Arthur said. And threatened to blow my brains out! Isn't that against the law? He didn't like how he sounded — he was tattling on the old man. His body had begun to tremble, and a twitch in his stomach was threatening to force up the egg salad he'd had on the plane.

The officer pulled out his pad and made a note. Depends on the circumstances, he said. He who? The owner of the property? Mr. Wright. Your father-in-law, correct? And what were you doing at the time?

Never mind, Arthur said.

The officer cleared his throat and repeated his question, more forcefully this time, and Arthur reluctantly described the scene at the back porch. I don't want to press charges, if that's an option even.

These sorts of things rarely come to that, the officer said, returning his notepad to his pocket.

They were silent for a while. Nice ride, the officer said.

It's a rental.

That's the way to do it. In style. The officer stirred up some small talk to pass the time. He spoke enthusiastically of the car: his uncle had an earlier model, same color; how the man had been bequeathed the car by a dead relative and spent his spare time modifying it. He'd gotten to comparing his uncle's earlier model with this current one when the other officer emerged from the house.

He approached them, nodded to his partner, was abrupt with Arthur. No question which one was the bad cop here. He wondered what the Wrights had told him. Bad cop didn't let on. He told Arthur that he'd have to move along, that loitering here was forbidden, anticipating an argument, but Arthur didn't argue. He bid the officers a good night, opened the driver's side door, and stuffed the gifts in back. He stalled twice on his way out of the subdivision. He watched the police cruiser in his rearview, colored lights flashing silently, all the way to the highway.

He got himself most of the way back to the airport before turning off 267 and into a motel. He sat on the bed and called his wife. This time, she answered.

Arthur, she said.

Penelope, thank God!

It's over, she said. She told him to stop calling her parents, that they were all tired and needed to get some sleep. He begged her to stay on the line, to listen to what he had to say but was relieved, in spite of himself, when she said she couldn't and hung up. Because, the truth was, he didn't know what to say. He would apologize, he would say whatever she wanted him to say, but after his encounter with the police and the barrel of her father's shotgun, he was feeling defensive.

To apologize for what he had written was tantamount to apologizing for what he was thinking, and could he, in all honesty, do that? He could be sorry for allowing it to be published, but Penelope admitted that she had encouraged him. He could be sorry for allowing himself to be encouraged, but that was just a passive-aggressive apology: *Sorry you feel that way, sorry you're displeased.* These were no longer apologies.

If he couldn't be sorry, what could he do? He couldn't recall the book as though it were a faulty laptop battery; the publisher had made this clear. He couldn't unwrite it. Penelope would have to set the terms of the amends, but she was refusing to speak to him.

Arthur called the airline and booked the first flight out the next morning. Afterward, he opened the door to his room and stood out on the balcony that overlooked the parking lot. Three shadows by a red pickup truck—two men and a woman—smoking cigarettes and drinking from a shared bottle. He watched them for a while—the woman sat cross-legged on the hood, the men leaning deeply onto the passenger side door, discussing something serious. Arthur watched them long enough to decide that getting drunk looked like a good idea.

He found his keys and got on his jacket and, asking directions from the trio by the pickup, drove to a nearby liquor store where he purchased a bottle of something called Duff Gordon, which turned out to be cooking sherry.

By the time he returned to the motel parking lot, the red pickup was gone. He uncapped the bottle and had a swig. This was what you were supposed to do when your wife and child left you; you got drunk in a motel parking lot. The circumstances required it. He adjusted his seat, turned off the engine, but kept the key in so that he could listen to the radio. He found a station playing "Waiting for the Man," by the Velvet Underground. He thought of his mother.

He was woken by the sound of an electronic bleating that turned out to be his cell phone. It was his agent. He flipped open the phone. Hello? The morning's glare from the windshield aggravated the cracked plates of a headache.

Arthur, it's Doug. Are you sitting down? I hope you are, friend, because I have some news that's going to knock you off your feet.

# 10

# M E M O R Y

"HOLY SHIT," I SAID. "CONGRATULATIONS!"

"You sound like my agent. Lord. I haven't won any-thing. I've been short-listed. Besides, it's not a real prize. It's a vanity award, the kind they give out to small-press books in order to make us feel better for our dismal sales numbers."

"Still, it sounds very prestigious."

Arthur said, "I got off the phone. As I said, blinding headache. I turn the key, and *chug-chug-chug*, goes the engine. It won't turn over. I'm late for my flight, my wife has left me, taken my son. I have a hangover, and I miss my plane waiting for a tow truck to jump-start my car."

"Well," I said, "that's the bad news. The good new is your career's taken off!" I meant it as a joke but felt genuinely jealous as I said it. "I'd trade places with you."

"You would because you're used to hangovers and because you have neither a wife nor a child, so you have no idea what it means to lose them."

"Right, and I have no career to speak of. Thanks a lot. I feel much better now."

"What I mean is be happy with what you haven't got to lose. And I don't have the career you think I do. Fiction writing is not a career. Adjuncting at a university, I don't care what its pedigree, isn't a career either, despite what my wife thinks. This isn't my office. We adjuncts get to share the space left unoccupied by the full-timers on sabbatical." He looked at the takeout container by my elbow. "And I'm not liked. I haven't made the effort. I'd be surprised if I were teaching here in the fall."

Arthur walked me out, and I don't know whether it was Arthur's suggestion or if it really was in the air, but I felt us being stared at by those we passed, a curiosity that bordered on malice. Arthur stopped at his cubby and looked through the various notices and flyers. The woman at the reception desk offered a tight smile. She didn't say hello to Arthur, and Arthur didn't introduce me. At the door, we shook hands.

I said, "Have you explained to Penelope this notion of art you have?"

"An explanation won't do what she wants it to. To give her comfort. No explanation will do that."

"Maybe I don't envy your misery," I said. "But I do envy your spine. The way you follow through with your idea about art—strange though it is—is impressive."

"Okay," he said, "out with it. You didn't come here to listen to me talk, and you didn't come here because you were worried. You came to ask me something. So ask."

"Fine. Here it goes—how would you like to be in a movie?"

Arthur snorted. Then he said, "You're serious."

"You could be yourself because it would be a documentary."

"About?"

"About you."

Arthur seemed ready to refuse—he tipped his head back and made a sour face—but he didn't refuse. "Documentary," he said, measuring the word. He said it a few times, sounding out its syllables. "Come back to the office for a minute," he said.

We retraced our way upstairs, and I stood outside the door while he rummaged around the top of the desk. "She's always sending me these things here at the school, but now for the life of me I can't—aha!"

He held aloft a postcard, brought it over to me. On it was a photograph of a necklace made from what looked like human molars. On the other side: *Cynthia Bonjorni, Artist @ Carriage House Crafts, Greene & Grand*. Cutout letters, mixed fonts like the liner notes of a Sex Pistols album.

"Cynthia Bonjorni?"

"My mother. If you want to make a movie about me, she would be the best place to start."

On the subway ride downtown, turning over Cynthia Bonjorni's card in my hand, I puzzled over Arthur's explanation—his modus operandi—pieces of ancient art theory I didn't fully grasp. It all seemed so arbitrary. That quote of Aristotle's, for instance, that Arthur should put the emphasis on the word *action*. He wrote it down for me when I asked him to repeat it. I looked at it now. First of all, wasn't the real key word here *tragedy*? Aristotle was describing an ancient form of dramatic art, not literary art. And in emphasizing action, he seemed to be overlooking the more important word: *imitation*. Surely Aristotle wasn't advocating that novelists write novels that brought about their ruin. And anyway, what was he was trying to purge?

The day she left, Penelope had received a call from Will's fourth-grade teacher. She got the call while she was brushing her teeth. It would be years before the act of toothbrushing—mint lather, bristles on gums—would decouple itself from the ugliness this phone call would bring.

She was escorted to Will's classroom by a tall black girl in a full-leg cast, swinging ahead of Penelope on her crutches. Through the small square window in the door, she could see the class in session. The teacher, a wiry woman with cornrow braids, was enthusiastically telling them something while the students at their desks—popping up and down, bursting with energy—passed around a pail into which they dropped slips of paper. Will was in a seat toward the front. Penelope's heart leaped. When the teacher

saw Penelope, she instructed one of the students to stand up front
while she opened the door and stepped out.

Mrs. Santiago, Penelope said.

Angie, please. She looked at her watch. Five minutes to lunch.
She directed Penelope to wait for her in her "office," which was
a cubicle, one of a dozen created from low carpeted partitions set
up in in a repurposed classroom. Penelope took a seat at one of
two chairs next to a small desk. As predicted, the period bell went
off, an earsplitting electronic buzz, and a few moments later Angie
returned with Will.

I'm not in trouble, he said to Penelope, though from the look on
his face she could see he wasn't so sure. He sat down in the empty
seat next to her.

Angie took the desk chair, setting down the book she was holding. She said, We had speaking skills today and Will here gave us
a report on Dad's book.

Will picked up a block puzzle from the desk and began fiddling
with it. Penelope put her hand on his knee, the little knob.

During one of the many conferences Arthur and Penelope
had attended this fall, they brought up the topic of Arthur's
new book. Angie explained back then the futility of trying to
control the flow of information around the school. They could
lock down their Internet portals as well as hard sources that
might come through the doors, but they had no control over
what students told one another. The spirit of keeping Will from
the book wasn't about the words in the book but rather the
scene that the words evoked, and this couldn't be kept from
Will. Ideas and images were airborne things, carried and spread
by his classmates or anyone else with whom Will might come
into contact. A mere Google search of *Arthur Morel* pointed to
online reviews that paraphrased the scene in all its disturbing
detail. What sort of inoculation could they provide against it?
They considered telling Will about the scene but couldn't think
of a way of describing it — or why his father would have written
it — that would make any sense to him. They decided instead to

do nothing but be prepared for the moment, whenever it came. Which appeared to be today.

Why don't you tell your mom what you told the class about the sex part, Will.

I was joking, Will said. I was just messing with everybody.

Angie said, It didn't sound like you were joking.

Will's knee jittered under Penelope's palm. She squeezed it to reassure him, but Will tugged his leg away. He looked down at his puzzle—for some moments it appeared as though he'd shut them out, this whole situation, and devoted himself entirely to solving it. It looked simple—there were only four pieces, discrete shapes that would, when fit together correctly, form a neat cube.

Penelope and Angie looked at each other. Angie's shimmery green eye shadow matched exactly her green running shoes, which in turn matched her green nails. Though Angie seemed buoyant and easygoing, there was something else about her—a fastidiousness that suggested she was barely keeping it all together. Or maybe Penelope was thinking of herself. Angie nodded at Penelope, indicating some kind of cue, but Penelope wasn't sure what she was being asked to do.

She cleared her throat and turned to Will. Honey, she began. What were you *only joking* about?

Will said, not looking up, I read it.

This she was prepared for. This she had an answer for. What she wasn't prepared for, what she had no answer for, was when Will told her what he had told the class before Penelope had arrived, what prompted Angie to call Penelope in, and what prompted Penelope to say to Will, You what?

Remember. It's okay, right, Angie? You said I wasn't in trouble.

You're not in trouble, Will.

What exactly do you remember, honey?

I was just showing him how. I asked him to.

Him who?

Art.

Art. You were showing Art how to what?

To you know.

I don't know, Will honey. You have to tell me.

Penelope. I think it might be best if —

Are you *joking*? Are you *messing* with me?

I guess not. You're mad, though.

Will, I'm not mad, but I need you to tell me — exactly — what you mean when you say that you *remember*.

Will, your mother and I will be back in a moment — you work on that puzzle.

Angie took Penelope out into the corridor and said, We have to be very careful here. If I can make a suggestion? I think before we jump to conclusions, Will should speak with someone about this.

Someone? Penelope couldn't think; she was aware that her mouth was open, aware of the thought, *Close your mouth*. She closed her mouth. She thought, *This is it*, though she wasn't sure what *it* was just yet. She needed to call Arthur, yet she was afraid to. She was, in fact, trembling, though her forehead was perspiring. Her mouth had gone dry, she could barely swallow, she could still taste the toothpaste, its grit coating the roof of her mouth. This woman, the teacher, was still talking. She was handing Penelope a card. She wanted Will to talk to this person, a child psychologist. She was waiting for Penelope to respond, but Penelope couldn't respond. She was done talking; she needed to go now. She needed to get her son and go.

They left out the side exit into an alley off York Avenue. She hustled Will along (Where are we going, Mom?), pulling him by the hand, Will's backpack jiggling on his back like an excited monkey. (I'm in trouble, aren't I? You're not in trouble, honey.) She had the urge to pick him up and carry him in her arms.

Where were they headed? What was she supposed to do?

Arthur was teaching. He turned off his cell phone when he was in class. She could call the office, and the work-study girl who answered the phones could go to Arthur's classroom, get him to come speak with her. Or. She could go up there with Will now, in person, pull him out of class. But what would she say?

Not with Will. She should have let Will finish the day, as Angie had suggested. Anyway, what was there to say to Arthur? Plenty, although she couldn't think, she couldn't think — she needed to think! (Mom, the light's green!)

No. She couldn't talk to Arthur now.

Besides, there was nothing Arthur could say that would make this better. The psychologist. Maybe the psychologist could help.

Joyce Mandelbaum, Ph.D. Did Dr. Joyce take walk-ins? It was worth a shot.

Dr. Mandelbaum explained over the phone that her next free appointment for new clients wasn't until the end of February, but when Penelope explained why she was calling, she found herself an hour later sitting in a waiting room, arranging a wicker nest of *Condé Nast Travelers* at her side by country. Italy was overrepresented. There were several closed doors and a small dim window across from her that let in the cooing of pigeons and the occasional groaning of a passing truck. A side table by the entrance held a dried-flower arrangement that gave the place a mentholated smell.

When Dr. Mandelbaum emerged, she did so without Will, ushering Penelope through one of the closed doors and into an empty office. Dr. Mandelbaum told her to sit.

Will is angry, she said, taking a seat herself, that much is clear. Most of which seems directed toward his father.

What did he say?

It's not so much what he said as what he did. You see, in my practice, unstructured play speaks louder than words. Dr. Mandelbaum was holding a stack of Polaroids that she now handed to Penelope. Working with children is different than working with adults, she said. The tools one uses are different. With adults you have a couch and a box of tissues. With children, tissues won't cut it. You need things, a closetful of things. Dolls and toy trucks and water pistols. You need clothing for dress-up, hats and scarves, pocket mirrors and long cigarette holders. You need kitchen utensils and buckets and mops and a full porcelain tea service for eight. I often say very little. I'll just open the closet and watch them play. Today, a stuffed dummy, a plastic knife, and a Polaroid camera. As you see, this can be very revealing.

What Penelope was holding were "crime scene" photos. Will had set up the scene, Dr. Mandelbaum said, and then took the pictures as if he were an investigator. Various angles on a stuffed human-sized dummy sitting in an armchair. The dummy is wearing a dinner jacket, gloves, no pants. His head lolls back, and out of his lower abdomen protrudes a plastic knife, the dummy's mitt of a hand touching the hilt. Several closeups of the wound. I asked who did this to the man, Dr. Mandelbaum said, and Will told me the man did it to himself.

Penelope must have looked alarmed because Dr. Mandelbaum said, Don't worry. This kind of play is perfectly normal. Healthy, well-adjusted kids at one time or another will fantasize about off-ing their parents.

Do you think Will is telling the truth?

I put the question to him directly, and he answered quite straightforwardly. Yes, he insists. It's true. And while he showed no obvious signs that he was trying to deceive me, neither did he exhibit the sorts of signals I'm used to seeing that help to confirm such abuse.

What kind of signals?

Oh, embarrassment, for one. Usually, a child will not readily admit to something like this, and if they do, it is a deeply cathartic experience, bringing about great shame. But Will seems—nonplussed by it. A little nervous maybe. This doesn't mean he's lying, however. It's a tricky business. I would be very wary of contacting the police at this point—before I've spent more time with him. Their default position I'm afraid is to take the testimony of the child at face value—admirable, I'm sure, but one which unfortunately leads to a miscarriage of justice in too many cases. Not denigrating the important work they do. They're heroes, many of them. I happen to be married to one, and he has put away some very bad people and saved countless children from some pretty awful situations. It's just that the bureaucracy of the Justice Department has no use for the subtleties of the adolescent heart. It takes time to get to the bottom of these things, to piece together what's really going on. The memory plays tricks. And there are any number of reasons for Will to make something like this up.

Because he's angry.

Perhaps. 'I hate Daddy, he makes Mommy cry all the time, he's the reason they're getting the divorce.' And so forth. If you can think of a reason, there it is. The mind is a very complicated place. I have to say, however, as concerning as this is, I'm just as concerned about your husband. So he's written about this in a book?

It's a work of fiction, he says.

Still—it's quite disturbing. Quite disturbing. Well, maybe Will's getting back at your husband for writing lies—in a book that pretends to be the truth. But it's not the truth. So he decides to tell the lie right back at him. To get even.

After struggling unsuccessfully with a broken seat belt (This is totally illegal, you know!), Penelope ordered the driver to take them across town.

Will was concerned. When they arrived at the apartment, he followed her around asking what he could do to help. God, he was so much like Arthur! When Penelope was angry or upset, Arthur would always ask, What can I do to help? Even though usually it was something Arthur had done to piss her off in the first place. What can I do? What can I do to help?

She said to Will, You know what would help tremendously? If you'd empty the dishwasher and load up what's in the sink.

Will needed a specific task; his eyes, wide and wet and overblinking, were asking her for help. Will seemed relieved. He went through the swinging door of the kitchen and, soon after, the clatter of plates, the rushing of the sink, the knocking of cabinet doors.

Penelope paced. She sat down. Will's colored pencils were strewn on the dining room table, sheets of paper with half-finished drawings inspired by the book he was reading in school, an abridged version of *The Odyssey*: Telemachus with a machine gun, Zeus in a helicopter—the world of ancient Greece processed through the mind of a twentieth-century child. She was reminded of the craft works she'd seen recently from a street vendor near work: traditional baskets and jewelry done by women in tribal Africa—using electrical cord and Coke cans.

Penelope took a pencil and on the blank sheet of drawing paper in front of her drew a question mark, filled it out, gave it shape, until it became a long curved road, the point at the bottom the final destination.

She had to talk to Arthur. She needed—she hated herself for having this thought—she needed him to tell her what to do. If this were television, she would be disgusted with her character's weakness. *Grow some balls!* she might yell at the screen.

She took her cell phone from her purse and speed-dialed Arthur. He would be out of class now—he might have turned his phone back on. She got halfway through the automated instructions before she realized she wasn't listening to Arthur's voice mail but rather customer service for Avis rental car.

She looked at her phone's faceplate. Strange wrong number to have gotten—then saw that it was an adjacent entry in her contact list.

She was about to hang up when an operator came on to ask how she could help. This was a sign. This was what to do.

I'd like to reserve a car, she said.

For which dates?

For right now.

She went into the bedroom and pulled open dresser drawers at random. She counted out one, two, three balled sock pairs—a fistful of underwear, stockings. She upended the drawers onto the bed. She added to it an entire hugged armful of clothes on hangers from her closet. This activity developed a momentum, the physical act of doing it brought on a kind of desperation. She lugged a suitcase from under the bed.

Will was standing in the doorway.

Penelope said, We're taking a little trip.

Mom?

I need you to do me another favor, honey.

Mom?

Get down your suitcase for me and pack like you were going to Magic Mountain.

We're going to Magic Mountain?

We're not going to Magic Mountain.

Will said, I take it back.

Honey, it's going to be okay. Listen to me. Hey. You didn't do anything wrong. We're just going on a little trip.

But I take it back! I take it back, I said.

It's not something you can take back, Will.

But I don't remember anymore. I forgot, okay?

That's not the same as it not happening.

Why not? Before I remembered, it hadn't happened. So I'll just forget. We can go to a doctor, and he can hypnotize me. I don't want to go on a trip.

Penelope walked over to Will and gathered him into her, pressed his head to her chest. It's just a little vacation, a little break. You like it when we stay at Grandma's and Grandpa's. We'll talk about what you do or don't remember later.

Will relented, packed a bag, but they became mired in the practical problems with leaving: What about piano—he had a lesson tomorrow afternoon—and the Harry Potter party Azucena was throwing—Will had campaigned for weeks to be invited to it—he was the only one in his grade who was going—and he was supposed to dog sit for a neighbor over the weekend—what about that? Penelope made the calls while Will gathered his books, his handheld video game. What about—and what about—and what about?

That was when I arrived, an encounter she was in no mood for.

Eventually, Penelope just ushered him out the door. He insisted on "helping" her with one of the suitcases, the results of which on any other day would have been endearing to watch: each crack in the sidewalk caused the thing to tip sideways and take Will with it. He tried pushing it in front of him like a wheelbarrow, tried facing forward and pulling it behind him like a rickshaw. It was crowded on the subway. Penelope lost sight of him for a moment and screamed his name, and the subway car went still. People looked up from their papers. But Will was standing right behind her.

She grabbed his wrist.

Ow!

Don't do that again! she cried.

They walked to the rental-car lot in silence. It was bitter cold, and the wind out here in this neighborhood of low industrial buildings and parking lots and wide unprotected avenues was fierce. Though it was only three avenue blocks from the subway station to the rental lot, it took half an hour. Will stumbling over the suitcase on the cracked slabs of sidewalk, Penelope refusing to let go of his wrist.

It was dark when they arrived. The sign was a beacon of safety.

The woman behind the counter reported, without looking up from her screen, that there was no record of the reservation. But now there was no choice. She had to go, get out of town. You don't understand, Penelope said, this is an emergency!

The clerk was unmoved.

What was she supposed to do? She couldn't go back to the apartment, not now. She had to get out of this place, to get away. From Arthur. What am I supposed to do now, she said, to nobody in particular.

A man with a southern accent asked her where she was headed.

Thanks, Penelope said, but I'll figure it out.

The man had a sunburn and no chin. He was wearing a yellow windbreaker. I'm headed to Atlantic City, so if you're headed to points south along the Garden State Parkway, I can get you partway there at least.

Penelope stared at him for a moment before saying, You've got to be kidding me—I'm not getting into a fucking car with you. What do you think this is, the sixties? Come on, Will. Let's go.

—⁓—

Penelope looked for a cab but couldn't find one. A green Dodge Neon passed them, in the driver's seat the man with the sunburn and yellow windbreaker—he looked at her and shook his head.

They walked the dozen blocks to Port Authority, and she bought them two tickets to DC. By this time, Will had stopped overtly fretting and seemed to be enjoying himself.

They ate at the Au Bon Pain in the terminal. Will wanted a chocolate croissant and a chocolate milk. Penelope didn't fight it.

They sat in silence. Will used a plastic knife to cut his croissant in half and gave one of the halves to Penelope. This, more than anything else today, made Penelope want to weep.

That's okay, honey, you save it for later, when you get hungry on the bus.

They went to a newsstand. Will chose *Mad* magazine. She paid for this and a copy of *Us Weekly* and they traveled the escalators down to their gate.

It was 5:45 by the time they shuffled through the line and took their seats. It was 11:05 by the time they arrived in DC. Her father met them at Union Station and drove them out to Annandale, to her childhood home.

Arthur's postcard led us down into the cobblestone heart of Soho, to an unassuming carriage house that stood between two new clothing boutiques.

Arthur's mother, Cynthia, greeted us from its open archway, ushering us inside. "Friends of Artie! I knew those postcards would hit their mark one day. Next time you can bring him, too. Doc! Where are you?"

Cynthia had an enormous amount of hair, a weeping willow of hair, and spoke expansively with her whole mouth, each word enunciated so that it might be unmistakable to people seated in a theater balcony. She was dressed in a flamboyant purple scarf, and her bony arms jangled and clacked with bracelets running up and down, arms that flailed as she spoke. Her teeth were large and perfectly white—perfectly fake, I could only assume.

Doc—Arthur's father—was lean, pockmarked, and bald. He wore a Hawaiian shirt and a backward Kangol hat. They were both old, but he was much older. If she was fifty, he was seventy, at least. But there was something about his eyes; he had the eyes of a teenager—mischievous, attuned to our smallest gestures. It was Cynthia who did most of the talking that first day. Doc was restless; he got up and disappeared for stretches of time before coming back, settling in, and listening to Cynthia—nodding, grunting assent, or frowning when something she said took a turn he didn't like. It wasn't clear that he knew—or cared—why we were here or what our relationship might be to his son.

They lived in squalor. Though their address carried with it New York prestige—neighbors with Robert De Niro and David Bowie—they embodied an older kind of city shabbiness, from a time when you could be a poor artist in New York. They used to have the whole building to themselves, Doc explained, but when property values exploded in the eighties, they were forced to rent out the upper floors to a graphic designer. They lived on the first floor, which opened via a garage door onto the street. At nine every morning, the door came up, and the elder Morels played host to all of downtown Manhattan, as they had done since moving in more than thirty years earlier. This open space was part living room, part artist's studio; there was a broken-down couch, a lounge chair draped with a dingy sheet, a coffee table, as well as easels, a painter's taboret, a wood block midsculpt in the corner. The floor was built up with overlapping threadbare rugs, irrevocably paint stained. On the wall hung paintings that varied wildly in style. Seeing me scan the walls, Cynthia said, "This is my trading post. Keith stayed with us for a while after his boyfriend kicked him out—paid for his stay by painting me that." She pointed to a toilet seat hanging on the far wall that bore the unmistakable jigsaw graffiti of Keith Haring. "And that one?" She pointed to a blurry color photograph of a drag queen pursing her lips. "Let's just say that one didn't nearly cover the damage caused by those assholes Nan brought in with her."

As we talked, we were interrupted constantly by people walking in off the street. Doc insisted on getting up and greeting each as a potential customer, yet it didn't appear as though anything was for sale. "Come on in," he said, "look around!" And we'd resume our conversation with these strangers loitering silently behind us. "Mostly what we get these days is tourists—they come, snap a few pictures. It's okay. The Japs especially—we've been told we're in a guidebook: 'hidden gems' or something like that. The old days was different. We had real guests, all kinds. Neighbors, drifters, politicians, artists. Come to stay an afternoon or a week. Real orgies."

Orgies? Dave and Suriyaarachchi gave each other wide eyes.

Though they'd been here for years, and its furnishings seemed a part of the place for as long as they'd lived here, the arrangement felt temporary, ramshackle: there was a hot plate in the corner on which sat a charred espresso pot. Doc, always moving, unscrewed the pot and filled it with water and a few spoons from a coffee can nearby. A floral bedsheet separated this public living room from the rest of the apartment, which consisted of a kitchen and a sleeping loft perched over a desk space cramped with books and antiquated office equipment, including an old mimeograph, a typewriter, and a spiral-bookbinding machine. Dave helped himself to a peek into the sleeping loft—a rickety construction of unpainted two-by-fours. I think Dave must have realized a step or so too late up the ladder that he was intruding into a stranger's "bedroom" and came quickly back down. He gave a shake to one of the ladder rungs. "Sturdy," he said.

"Sturdy enough." Cynthia gave him a sly smile. I noticed in the course of our conversation that she had a tendency to hold eye contact a few beats more than was comfortable, something I only later connected with Arthur, who had a similar tendency. With Arthur the effect was one of frankness, that he was seeing into you, past what you were saying with your words and into what you meant in your heart; whereas Cynthia's lingering eye contact suggested something sexual and gave the words she was saying the quality of innuendo. Disconcerting, being hit on by Arthur's mother.

Doc, after opening the fridge and walking away, said, "Help yourself to whatever you find that's edible." Not much was, as the fridge wasn't on. It was being used as a pantry. Room-temperature cans of root beer, a net bag of clementines, rolls of toilet paper. The freezer — also warm — stocked batteries of all shapes and sizes.

"Doc worked it out," Cynthia explained, "that it was cheaper to just let Con Ed go and live on portable power."

"You know how much those cocksuckers wanted from us? How much was it, Cyn?"

"I don't remember. Three thousand?"

"At least! Can you imagine?"

"A month?"

"A month? No, that was over how many years? Lost count."

"You haven't paid your Con Ed bill for years?"

"Years."

"And they didn't cut you off?"

"Eventually they did. Which is the situation we find ourselves in at present."

"Off the grid."

As we continued on our tour, I noted just how much of their lives ran on batteries: TVs, fans, radios, clocks, lights — heavy-duty flashlights fitted with shades. The hot plate and the makeshift hot-water heater, which Doc showed me with great pride, ran on butane. Once we got out of the chill of the open-air living room, my senses thawed. It smelled like dirty socks in here and something I couldn't identify until I saw one: cat. Cynthia claimed there were six, though I saw only one during our time here. She picked it up on our way down to the basement, an explosion of gray fur. "And this is my pussy-pussy!" She brought it to her breast and buried her face in it. The cat indulged this sleepily, limbs drooping down as though it were a stole.

We descended a narrow wooden staircase and found ourselves in an open concrete space that felt like a parking lot. "This is what we refer to as the Permission Room. Down here you have permission to do anything you want."

"It was Artie's idea."

"What do you want to do?"

As my eyes adjusted to the dark, I could make out a solid mass of things, all hugging the wall—broken furniture, tangled clothing, musical instruments, boxes collapsing under their own weight. An accretion of years of neglect.

"You can scream to your heart's content," Cynthia said and let out a piercing shriek. The cat who had been in her arms bolted. "Nobody can hear."

"Or," Doc said, and lit a flat ceramic pipe that he'd been holding in his hand. We all waited as he held his inhale, eyes squinched, holding our own breath until finally he exhaled a cloud of pot smoke. He held out the pipe. Suriyaarachchi shook his head, but Dave took it with a shrug before having a hit.

Though the suggestion was that this place was for sex and drugs, the Permission Room gave me the serious creeps. There was something of the serial killer's lair about it, and I was relieved to be escorted back upstairs.

When we finally got around to explaining who we were and what we wanted from them, Cynthia said, "That's great, look at that. Artie's got people who want to do a movie of him."

Doc said hoarsely, "As long as it's making him happy."

"That's the important thing, it's true," she said. "Doing what makes you happy. How is Artie? Is he happy?"

I said, "When was the last time you saw him?"

"Oh, Doc, how long's it been?"

"What is it now, thirteen years?"

"At least."

After we had done a full circuit of the house, we stood outside the open garage door's threshold on the sidewalk. It was cold, and I wondered how these two survived the winter on battery power, one of their four living room walls essentially flung open to the wind and rain. Neither wore outerwear. Cynthia was in sandals,

Doc in socks. Neither did they seem fazed by the wind that had me digging my hands in my coat pockets. Doc was pointing to the windows on the second floor. Suriyaarachchi and Dave looked up, making visors of their hands. "It was nice having the whole place to ourselves, but the taxes? Forget it! With Con Ed, the worst thing they'll do is leave you in the dark. The tax man will put you in jail. This guy's done wonders up there, all glass and bare hardwood. Brand-new computers, top of the line. Nice guy. I check in on him most days, we chat. One of the new breed. Been here several years now, but still I don't think he's figured out what to make of me."

They happily agreed to be filmed and seemed eager for us to return with our equipment. The idea of being in the spotlight activated something in Cynthia. She became fluttery in the eyelids, hands going up to her hair and down to her clothes, adjusting the fit here and there. "I don't know what I'll wear," she said.

"Something that shows off your rack. She's got quite a pair, even at her age."

We rented production-quality gear on Dave's credit card — the not-so-secret industry secret was to rent for two days beginning Friday; as the rental houses were closed on Sunday, you got the third day for free.

When we returned the following Friday, Cynthia was outside at a folding table with her jewelry. Similar to the piece on the postcard, the earrings and bracelets and necklaces and pendants were all made from teeth strung through bent paper clips. Creepy, but also kind of beautiful.

"I found a box of Doc's old stuff and just went from there," she said.

The four of us chatted while she fiddled with the arrangements. People stopped and looked, but Cynthia ignored them.

"Let's go inside," she said.

"Don't you need somebody to mind this stuff?"

"It's fine. People like looking at it, but no one actually wants it."

It seemed they'd straightened up for the occasion, which for some reason I found touching, and set two armchairs next to each other facing the sidewalk, so that after we unpacked our equipment and the Morels took their seats, it appeared that, in answering our questions, they were addressing not only us and the camera but all of New York City's passersby.

It was agreed that Dave would handle the sound, Suriyaarach-chi would handle the camera, and I would conduct the interview. As this was our first real break in the project and the first footage we would get, we spent a great deal of time planning in the days leading up to it. We watched *Grey Gardens* several times and all of Errol Morris's films. We brainstormed a list of questions that we hoped would bring out their craziness. We wanted to hear about the wild seventies, their theory of parenting, the Permission Room, and what Cynthia fed her six cats.

But, in the end, they insisted on answering their own questions and, in so doing, related to me, to us, to the city at large, the peculiar story of their lives.

# 11

# W A R H O L

I T BEGINS IN NEW JERSEY, early fifties. Doc is a husband. The wife is not Cynthia but rather someone named Dolores. They have married young, Doc and Dolores, when he is just out of dental school. Happy years, these first living in Trenton, an apartment near Cadwalader Park. Dolores bears him a daughter. The birth of their second coincides with a move out to the new suburbs of Plainfield. This occasion also marks for Doc an end to that happy period in their lives. This second child, a boy, brings with him a deep and lasting depression for Dolores. Doc comes home to find four-year-old Sarah racing around the house naked, infant Benji in his crib, screaming. His wife can be found in bed with a pillow over her head, weeping. When they leave the children with her parents for the evening and go out to a nice restaurant, she ends up staring mutely into her salad, weeping. When they invite their friends over for drinks, Dolores ends up locked in the bathroom, weeping. When they drive to her parents' for the holidays, Dolores won't get out of the car because she doesn't want her parents to see her weeping. Benji is weeping; little Sarah is weeping; the whole goddamned car is weeping! Dolores is not unhappy with Doc; in fact, as she tells him again and again, he is the only thing keeping her sane. If she didn't have him, she just didn't know what she might do.

Dolores had always been needy; it was what drew him to her in the first place—that and her enormous breasts. In college, her neediness was romantic. He'd sneak her into his dorm room, and she would refuse to leave. He humored this, enjoyed it even. It appealed to an essential quality in his maleness to be relied on like this, to be needed—that her need bordered on dangerous? All the better, all the more exciting. Before the kids, before the suburbs, when they were free—they'd indulge in weeklong "vacations" in which they wouldn't leave their Trenton apartment. Out, he would forage the grocery for ice-cream sandwiches—fifteen minutes, ten if he hurried—and when he returned Dolores would pounce on him, and they'd have sex; she would tell him that these minutes he'd been gone had been too long away from her. After sex, they would pick up the book they'd been reading aloud to each other—Dickens or Brontë—an ecstatic mixture of gloom and comfort that, in those first years, felt so much like the love they read to each other about. After a men's night out, having stayed overnight on a buddy's couch, he came back to the apartment to find Dolores had downed a bottle of aspirin with an entire bottle of cough syrup. The cough syrup in those days had codeine. She was in a near coma, facedown in a pool of vomit. This incident should have sobered him, should have warned him against kids. But he was in love.

Over the years, through the birth of their two children, the move to the house, the start-up of his practice, there were moments of peace, of happiness. But the neediness, the dependency, out here in the suburbs, calcified into a jealousy of all people with whom he came into contact—men and women—but women especially: women patients, other mothers, her own women friends. His receptionist becomes a particular point of contention, and after firing three, he decides to live without. Where he worked, back then it was difficult to find a man with that particular skill set who would work for what he could afford to pay.

His home becomes a prison, his wife the warden. They are alienated from their friends. The children spend increasing amounts of time at their classmates' houses. Home life is reduced to minor repairs and fighting with Dolores. His one solace is his practice, and he spends as much time there as he can, booking appointments as early as six forty-five in the morning and as late as seven forty-five in the evening. She is jealous of his patients, too, the time he spends with them, in intimate contact with their open mouths, their tongues, their pain. What do you want from me! he exclaims. Are you married to me or your patients, she asks. He points up, which has become in this recurring argument shorthand for the mortgage, the maintenance, the food and clothing and general well-being his salary can afford; and in response she gives her shorthand, a different finger.

"It wasn't even like she wanted to spend time with me anymore," Doc said.

This need for him to account for his whereabouts replaced her need for his actual presence. Jealousy replaced desire.

"And these were arguments I couldn't win, of course. The conversations were rigged. They were torture. Really, they were a form of psychological torture. There's a woman in the supermarket parking lot. Drop-dead gorgeous, dressed to kill. 'You think she's pretty,' she says. First off, it's not a question. It's a statement, so already I'm trapped. To deny it is to disagree with her. But to agree with her is to admit feelings for another woman. Second, it's a fact; she is pretty. To deny this is to deny your senses. Like if it was raining and Dolores had said, 'It's raining.' Of course it's raining! You bet your ass it's raining! So I offer a noncommittal, 'She's okay.' Not good enough. She wants a real opinion, a firm opinion. Then it's on to 'Would you have sex with her?'"

It's no use. Whether or not he engages her in the discussions, the outing would be ruined, and depending on his performance, later there'd be broken dishes or appliances. A best-case scenario is a black hole of days without speaking to each other.

Inevitably, this suspicion becomes a self-fulfilling prophecy. Her statements—*you don't love me anymore; I repulse you; you want to have sex with her*—become facts.

"You know, Doc," Cynthia interjected, "it's entirely possible that she was just ferreting out something you were already feeling. Maybe the way you looked at women was dangerous in some way. Some men look—and that's it, nothing threatening about it. Other men look, and it's predatory, a prelude to something else. You don't think it's possible that she was attuned to things about yourself and your marriage that you weren't ready to admit—she wasn't just helping you along?"

Doc shrugged. "Whatever the case, I found that sex—and I was never an especially horny guy before this—was suddenly all I could think about. Every girl on the street or who'd pass through my office, every magazine ad—it was as though her jealousy had unleashed this in me, had woken up something in me that had lain still for a long time. I was all of a sudden masturbating three or four times a day. It used to be a couple times a week, most, but no more. And before I was okay with having sex with my wife—our sex was fine, in spite of everything. Not fantastic, but fine, perfectly fine. Well, no more. 'I repulse you,' she said. Well, yeah, now she repulsed me. 'You don't love me anymore.' It was true. I wanted to leave, but I was afraid of what she might do. At this point Sarah was fifteen, Benji was eleven. Mama's boy and Daddy's little girl. This was where the lines were drawn."

That year, Sarah and Dolores were having a particularly difficult time, and perhaps as a way of hurting her mother, or maybe just out of loyalty to Doc, she began to take particular interest in what she saw as her father's plight and would relate daily updates to her best friend, Cynthia.

Cynthia said, "Sarah and I lived across the street from each other. She spent many nights at my house—and I spent many afternoons at hers, listening to Sarah tell the saga of her poor daddy and her evil mother. To tell you the truth, I tuned it out. They were grown-ups: What did I care? I had bigger things on my mind. It was 1967. I wanted out, I was going to the city. I was going to be an Andy Warhol Superstar! There had been a screening of *Chelsea Girls* at the old Criterion. Do you remember the Criterion?"

"Sure. Beautiful Greek columns outside."

"It was a big event, this screening. Rated X. The manager was young—he'd been a star of our drama club. God, what was his name? Rudy Jackalone. Jackalane? And he had notions of making our theater into a kind of art house. Ha! They got halfway through the film that first night before the cops raided the place, confiscated the film, arrested half-a-dozen people. On obscenity charges. It made quite an impression on me, and I thought if this is what art can do, cause a stir like this — everyone was talking about it, months after — then count me in! I learned all I could about him, about the Factory. Earlier that year, or the year before, he had staged a happening. He called it the *Exploding Plastic Inevitable*. I read about it in the library — they had bound back issues of the major newspapers. There in one volume, six months' worth of news, and I could see it just reverberate out, in stop motion, column after column. Like what happened in our town, but on a much-larger scale, from the announcement the day before to the review of it in the arts section, to the op-ed pieces that appeared weeks later, how mention of it showed up on the fashion page, a music review, a piece about local politics. It really did explode. That one event reverberated outward for six months, a year, reaching as far out as here, our small New Jersey theater, and who knows how much farther out? Well, that was it—I wanted to be at the center of the explosion. I sent away for a silver wig and patent-leather boots from a mail-order place in Van Nuys, California. Remember those?"

"You looked like a Forty-Second Street hooker."

"I don't remember you complaining back then."

"Who's complaining?"

"I had that Velvet Underground record, the one with the banana on the cover? I played that album constantly. It drove my mother nuts. She banned it, so I had to come over to Sarah's and play it. Sarah had no idea. She was innocent. She thought I had a crush on Andy Warhol. She wanted to make this some teenage heartthrob thing, which was sweet. She decided that she was in love with Lou Reed — as though these were the Beatles we were swooning over.

But it wasn't about that for me. Not at all. I mean, *Blow Job* was a movie in which Warhol films DeVeren Bookwalter getting a *blow job*. His oxidation paintings were done by putting copper paint on a canvas and then inviting underage boys drunk on wine to *piss* on them. This wasn't about love—this was about freedom! I felt so much older than Sarah, though we were the same age. I want to say she looked up to me, but that may just be fantasy. I don't know if she really knew what to make of me. We would lie there in her room—she would be on the floor on her back—and she would tell me about her poor father and her evil mother, and I would sit in front of her dressing-table mirror, puckering up, putting on makeup, getting myself ready for my fifteen minutes. When did I first notice Doc?"

(This is what she would do—what they both did—throughout the interview: ask themselves questions and then proceed to answer them.)

"I think it was when I caught him watching me undress. That time I think it made me angry. Later, I thought maybe I was angry, not because my best friend's dad was a pervert violating my privacy, but because I felt that my privacy was being violated. You see, I thought I was *enlightened*. Here I was, walking the walk in these boots and that wig and some nobody watching me undress has the power to send me scurrying into another room! How bourgeois can you get? I don't know for how long he'd been watching me—"

"A while—"

"—before I noticed. But after I noticed, I thought, Okay, let's give the old perv a show. Why not?"

"Our houses were directly across the street from each other, and all of the houses in the neighborhood were the same—"

"So from my bedroom window I could see Doc there watching me from the upstairs bathroom. I don't know what you were doing in there while you were watching me. You weren't brushing your teeth, that's for sure."

"I was masturbating."

"There. He was masturbating. I found it terribly exciting, to tell you the truth. I did it as a kind of lark, a what-the-hell sort of thing at first, but it was tremendously arousing. My whole body came awake, my skin was alive. I felt nervous and self-conscious and sick to my stomach, but, oh, terribly excited! When did we first fuck?"

"She's no romantic, this one. Don't you remember?"

"Oh, I remember. I just think you should tell it."

"She showed up—for an appointment. I saw her there in the waiting room—those boots and that hair—I mean there was no mistaking her, she was one of a kind. The kids were beginning to dress wilder by then, long hair, fatigues, and those long shape-less flower dresses—it was like your generation was trying on cos-tumes."

"We were. We were trying to figure out who we were. It's no different now."

"It is different. It all comes prepackaged."

"Okay, whatever, moving on—you don't want to get him started."

"I could barely contain myself with some of the girls that came in, girls who feared the needle, girls I knew from the age of six and seven, to them I'm the same old white coat, the same old nightmare in a face mask, but to me they're—in that chair, grown up, vulner-able, beautiful, eyes closed, mouth open, supplicating. That's what it was, almost religious, a blessed offering. They had no idea. But this one, sitting in the waiting room. She knows me. She's seen my desire, stoked it even. She puts down the magazine she's reading when she sees me, gets up. 'Right this way, Miss Bonjorni.'"

"The appointment had been made for me a ways back. My mother, she took care of those things. I was going to cancel it, but then I thought—why? Let's see what happens. I knew I was going to fuck him."

"She knew. I didn't know. I left her in the chair for—"

"An hour!"

"While I tried to pull myself together in the bathroom. I

brushed my teeth several times. I flossed. I gargled mouthwash. I was very paranoid about my breath, I remember. And my hands. I scrubbed my fingernails. I filed them down and buffed them. I don't know why — I wore gloves. I come back in. 'And how are we doing today?' All formality. 'Lean back for me, that's it. Rinse, if you please.' I had an assistant, where was she? She wasn't there that day, that's right, which must have been why I was so nervous. With my assistant around, it would have been an entirely different encounter."

"I would still have fucked you."

"How could you?"

"I would have found a way."

"She's very persistent. She *would* have found a way. So, routine examination, all tact, very gentle with the instruments. Nothing is said out loud that betrays our, um, relationship. It's all in the eyes. I say, 'That wasn't so bad,' and she says, 'It was fine,' and it's the eyes that say everything. 'You're a bit too big for a lollipop, I think,' and she says, 'I'll take one anyway, if you don't mind.' We did it right there on that chair."

"It wasn't the most comfortable place to have sex."

"It was very awkward."

"Knocked over a tray of tools, hit my funny bone on the sink. Banged my head on that articulating lamp. But it did the trick."

"For you. It was over very quickly."

"That's always been a problem for me. Imagination gets me too excited for the actual deed."

"I made a follow-up appointment, which I ended up canceling."

Back at home, Doc waits by the bathroom window, but in the days that follow the curtains in Cynthia's room remain shut. He thought that the encounter in the chair was the start of something, but for Cynthia it was the end of it.

Doc is beside himself. Cynthia still comes over to spend time with Sarah, and Doc makes sure now to keep a Wednesday or Thursday afternoon appointment-free so that he might come home early and catch glimpses of her when she and his daughter come into the kitchen for a snack or the living room to watch *American Bandstand*. Dolores has discovered therapy and is getting out more, reconnecting with old friends, making new ones.

Doc notices one day that Dolores has stopped focusing so intently on him. She tells him, I've come to realize that you're not responsible for my happiness. It was her attempt at a blanket apology, some nonsense she had learned from her therapist, but it made him want to cry.

How could he tell her that it was too late, the damage was already done?

She takes a needlepoint class and stitches a slipcover that reads HOME SWEET HOME, with a picture of a house. She goes on a diet so she can fit into *those outfits you used to love*. She takes a class in Indian cooking at the local community college so they might *introduce a little of the exotic into our lives*. She no longer grills him on his whereabouts. If she catches him staring at Sarah's best friend like the dirty dog that he is, she refrains from saying anything. She crawls on top of him in the middle of the night and rides a cock that is already stiff from dreaming about Cynthia.

"She had really turned around, the poor thing. She wanted to make things work for us so badly. I think she figured Sarah's almost out the door (that girl was college-bound from her first day of kindergarten), and Benji wouldn't be too far behind—with the kids gone, we had a second chance at happiness. She would talk about future trips we might take, romantic places, retirement bliss, growing old together hand in hand. Shit like that."

So with Dolores at one of her therapy sessions or at an afternoon class, Doc has free rein at home to watch Cynthia watch television or make a sandwich—to be in the same room with her, to have her brush past him on the stairs, or to enter a bathroom she has just left. Even the lingering waft of her shit can bring about an erection. Cynthia finds Doc's silent desperation sweet and a little sad. She turns to see him watching her and, making sure Sarah isn't looking, gives him a quick wink. Is her pity the result of Sarah's influence, tales of her poor father? In part, maybe. But she is also moved by his situation in general as a married man. It's the pity she has for the beasts at the zoo, pacing their cages. All that desire and nowhere to go—it breaks her heart. And for the same reason she wouldn't unlock a tiger's cage, she does not indulge Mr. Morel any further. She doesn't want anybody to get hurt.

"That was until you found out you were pregnant."

"God, yes. But that didn't make me want to sleep with you again. I needed to talk to you."

"How did you know it was mine?"

"How many times do I have to have that conversation with you—forget it! I was not a virgin, no. Nor was I having vaginal intercourse on a regular basis. It was you—you, baby, you!"

"She gets touchy. I like to tease her."

Doc and Cynthia declared it time for lunch. Suriyaarachchi opened his wallet and handed me three twenties. "Anything but Chinese," Cynthia said.

Doc said, "There's an Indian on Wooster that does knockout *palak paneer.*"

It seemed that even full-partner producers got the takeout around here. A motley crowd had developed outside of the entryway: tourists with cameras, construction workers with blue deli cups of coffee, locals with dry cleaning slung over their shoulders. They parted to let me through. One of the construction workers wanted to know what the deal was with these two.

"That's what we're trying to find out, I guess."

We regarded the set together for a moment, and that was what it was, with the beat-up equipment boxes stacked to one side and cables taped to the floor. Suriyaarachchi squatted facing the camera, mounted on its low turret, lens in hand, blowing out the gate with a can of compressed air. Dave was crouched with a pair of enormous headphones, staring down at the audio equipment. I breathed deep of the manhole steam that drifted past us.

One of the tourists said, "This place, Japan, very famous." He held out his guidebook, and we all crowded in for a look. Sure enough, on the open page was a small photo and above it in English *Carriage House Theater* with its address. Everything else was in Japanese.

We all nodded, impressed.

I found a place that sold soup out of an old clapboard newsstand. The line was long, but I waited, using the opportunity to pull out my list of questions and revise them. I thought of prompts that might get them talking about Arthur. I was glad to hear their story—they provided a good starting point for the puzzle of Arthur Morel, product of a teenage Warhol groupie and a philandering suburban husband—but worried about its direct connection to Arthur's present dilemma: so far, there was none. Would it continue like this, running parallel but never connecting? This was, after all, Arthur's story. I was reminded of *Grey Gardens*, the documentary about the Bouviers, the crazy mother-daughter pair that was obliquely related to Jacqueline Kennedy. The story went that the filmmakers intended to make a movie about Jackie but, quite by accident, hit on this pair in a vine-choked falling-apart mansion in East Hampton and decided to make the whole movie about them instead. Like the Bouviers, there was something monstrous and compelling about these two, hearing them relate this adulterous statutory rape like a pair of old lovebirds. But would Arthur, like Jackie, end up on the cutting-room floor?

I also had to wonder why Arthur had sent us here. I did the math and calculated that the last time he had seen them he was performing his "cadenza" onstage. In all that time—wife, child, career—with all of them living in the same city, not once had they seen one another? That took serious determination. So why now?

By the time I returned with the food, the crowd had dispersed. Doc offered us utensils. "It's okay, they're clean," he said as he chipped bits of dried food off the edge of a spoon. They sat in their armchairs, hunched over their bowls, slurping away, wordlessly passing a bag of bread back and forth. It was hard to reconcile these two with their sexed-up sixties selves. They seemed so sweet here, with their heads together, murmuring to each other. But then Cynthia would open her mouth and the connection became clear.

I gathered the empty containers, and Dave did a sound check. Suriyaarachchi examined the gate one more time, and we were rolling again.

"It was May of '68," Cynthia said. "I was getting ready to leave. I had no interest in finishing high school. What for? I didn't need a diploma to be a Superstar! I hadn't been feeling well for some days. I had been out sick. I was rifling through the medicine cabinet for I don't know what, feeling lousy — I saw the tampons and it hit me flat. What a wallop! I mean, teen pregnancy I'm sure is no picnic these days, but back then, where we lived? It was a death sentence — "

"Or a life sentence," Doc said with a chuckle.

"You could take your pick. Either way it was permanent. I mean, to be sexually liberated at the age of fifteen is one thing, to be thought of as easy, a slut? Fine — I'll wear that, and proudly even. Some girls in school, myself included — not that we were a group or anything — we weren't too bothered by what we were called behind our backs or to our faces. We got our power from it somehow. But to be pregnant? That was a whole different matter. That was *disgrace*, plain and simple. And there was no other option, no Planned Parenthood. Abortion was a horror story you heard about, somebody's uncle taking manslaughter for trying to help some poor girl in her second trimester. Or the girl in our class who survived a malpractice butcher — the look in her eyes when she told you what he did, what she went through. Legal abortions were something new, in only a couple of states. I sat there on the toilet, box of tampons in my hand, racking my head for which ones. It had been on the news, one of the C states: California? Colorado? How would I get there? How would I pay for it? How much safer would it be? And how could I keep this from my parents — though I made much noise about not caring what they thought about me, I very much did not want them to know about this. I didn't want to know about this. So I did the only thing I could think to do: I made an appointment with my dentist.

"I said it was an emergency. His receptionist put me on hold and came back on the line to tell me they could squeeze me in. Ha! I don't know what you thought you were getting."

"I thought we were going to fuck."

"Boy, were you disappointed."

"I sent my assistant out on an errand. I brushed the hell out of my teeth. Floss, rinse, repeat. Moved the tray of tools out of the way this time, and that stupid light! And then you came in." It was, to put it mildly, not welcome news to the beast in Doc's pants.

She was not wearing her wig or her boots. She was in jeans and an old Rutgers sweatshirt that smelled like men's aftershave. She walked into his examining room and punched him in the jaw, then sat down, vomited neatly into the porcelain sink attached to the chair, and wept.

If he had felt the wrongness of what he had done and what he had continued to feel, it was never more acutely felt than right there with this young girl crying in his chair, wearing her father's sweatshirt, face damp with sweat. It was his daughter, sitting there. He held her hand and smoothed her hair, her real hair, and murmured fatherly words of comfort.

"I would be lying if I said I wasn't turned on," Doc said.

"I was your daughter, and you were turned on."

"I had the hardest erection."

"Fine. You felt what you felt. Moving on."

He took a urine sample ("What are you going to do—make a painting?" "A what?" "Never mind.") and sent it off to a colleague of his. He wasn't entirely sure he could trust the man, who was more of an acquaintance, but it would be senseless to go through with all of this on a false premise. It would take a couple of days to get the results, enough time to prepare, to plan. Doc agreed that doing nothing was out of the question. He also agreed that she needed to be rid of the thing growing inside her. But how? California, Colorado, Oregon, North Carolina. These were the states they might go to for the procedure. They could make Charleston in six hours, have the procedure the same day. Post-op recovery would have to be done there, at the hospital or in a motel room nearby. There would be no hiding what she had been through for at least seventy-two hours following the surgery. It would cost thousands. It would involve elaborate lies—he would have to pose as her father. He could make up a conference to attend; she could "run away" from home, leave a note about going to the big city—only to return the following week. She would look bedraggled; her parents would be angry, worried sick, but happy to have their daughter back, lesson learned, none the wiser about her real whereabouts. She would head to the bus station on the morning he left for his "conference," and he would pick her up at the station. At the hospital, he would pay cash, in full. He would bring equipment with him to monitor her condition at the motel and if necessary drive her to a nearby emergency room.

But a hospital stay was to be avoided—for the expense and the added scrutiny they'd be under. It would be dangerous, but they just might, with a little luck, get out of this intact. He goes home to his wife and kids, dark cloud of worry following him through the front door.

Dolores has cooked a Mexican fiesta. *Happy Cinco de Mayo!* she says. She has made a pitcher of margaritas, decked out the dining room with streamers. She is wearing a sombrero. Grilled steak, tortilla shells, beans and rice, and guacamole. The table is stacked with platters. They sit down to it as a family, the first time in a while they've eaten together. Dolores is beaming and a little tipsy.

Dinner, he is sure, is good, delicious even—it smells fine—but he has no appetite. He may as well be eating wet cardboard and library paste, for this is what the food feels like in his mouth. He leaves a large portion on his plate. Dolores asks him if he's feeling okay, and he says he just doesn't have the stomach for spicy food, which is certainly the wrong thing to say.

Benji, ever the pleaser, helps himself to what's on his father's plate and exclaims how he himself enjoys spicy food. He heaps second and third servings of refried beans and rice onto his licked-clean plate and eats as though he is having a wonderful time, pretending to be drunk on the pitcher of virgin margaritas his mother has prepared for his sister and him — performing slap-stick pratfalls off his chair. Sarah is openly helping herself to the other pitcher, which her mother is pretending not to notice. When Doc starts to say something about it, Sarah fixes her father with a withering look.

"She knew," Cynthia said.

"You didn't tell her."

"I didn't have to tell her — she knew what you were up to. She was a smart girl."

The phone rings, and Sarah storms out of her seat to get it. She comes back in and says to him, It's for you. It was Cynthia.

"She was getting cold feet."

"I did not have cold feet."

"You didn't want to go through with it."

"It wasn't like I changed my mind. I still didn't want to keep the thing; it wasn't that. It was just — there was so much lying involved. I didn't know that I wanted to be a part of it. I had been doing some reading." She tells him this on the phone. She says that it's true that in New Jersey, as in most other states, abortion is illegal. Except in cases of *rape or incest.*

There is a long pause on the line while he waits for her to go on, but that is all she says.

He says, So?

So, you turn yourself in.

For what?

For rape. You say you raped me.

But I did no such thing.

You don't have to put it that way. Put it however you want to. I seduced you, you seduced me, it was entirely consensual. In the eyes of the law, it doesn't matter — it all amounts to the same thing. You see, it'll be so much easier, and we can be honest about it — and I can have an abortion here without all that lurking around.

If Doc was lying before about why he wasn't hungry, his

stomach is now making it true—he belches and feels a sour sting in his throat, the spicy steak and beans lodged, burning, in his chest.

But your life would be over, he says. You told me that you wouldn't want people to know about this.

I'd rather live with them knowing than live with this lie buried inside me. Look, I'm on my way into the heart of total liberation, man. I don't want to meet Andy Warhol with this thing on my—

Fuck Andy Warhol! Will you get real for a minute? This is my life, okay? It would be my life you'd destroy.

There is another long pause, after which Cynthia says, You're the one who needs to be real. Call me back when you're ready to do that. She hangs up.

He sets the phone back gently in its cradle. When he returns to the dining room, everyone has gone. Dolores stands in the kitchen sudsing the pots in the sink. Benji is shuttling dirty dishes to her side from the dining room table. He looks like he is going to cry.

Dolores says, I'm trying here. You see that I'm trying, don't you?

I see that you're trying.

And I'm willing to try harder, as hard as I can to bring us back together. But I can't do this alone. You have to want this, too. Do you want it, too?

Look, he says, babe. He is about to say something, some auto-pilot reassurance to end this discussion—nonsense that he doesn't even believe—but stops himself. He looks at his wife, who has turned to face him.

They have known each other for so long—since they were kids, almost Sarah's age now. They are kids no longer. She looks so old, so tired and sad. Maybe it's the booze—her eyes are droopy, her hair matted to her forehead—she has taken off the sombrero, but it's left a thin red line across her forehead. Her face has become so wrinkled—under her eyes, around the corners of her mouth. When had that happened? She isn't old, yet she has the face already of the old woman she will become before long. She has always insisted on a full face of makeup—it's something his mother has been warning her about for years, whenever she visited. *All that*

*makeup, dear. It'll make you old before your time. You're young. A little
love is all you need to make those cheeks rosy. A kiss from that fine man –
that's all you need to get color in those lips.* It seems his mother was
right—the products are taking their toll on her. Her hands hang at
her sides, dripping suds.

A year ago—a month ago!—he would have welcomed this
moment, would have rejoiced in it, would have gladly taken his
wife into his arms, kissed her, and said whatever he had to say.

She says, I'm not stupid. And I'm not deaf. I don't want any
admissions, any explanations either. Not interested. Keep it
between yourself and whoever. I'm only interested in hearing if
this is something you want, something you want to work.

It is, he says. I do want this to work. Which is true enough. But
it won't, which he knows, too.

Dolores looks so relieved at hearing him say it, and so on the
verge of collapse, that he has no choice but to take her into his
arms.

He lies awake the entire night. He watches day brighten the
window, hears the birds begin their morning noises. He had his
opening. He could have said, *No – it's over.* He could have told her
the truth. But to do so would have been to end the marriage, end
their lives—the lives of the four of them—as they all know them.
Harder than it seems, to utter the word *no.* To tell the truth.

And what is he to do about Cynthia? She is threatening to end
his marriage, this life as he knows it, even if he can't do it himself. He finds himself plotting her murder, something that, when
he thinks about it, is actually easier than getting rid of the fetus.
He would have to convince her to let him perform the procedure.
Have her sneak out in the middle of the night to his office. He
would put her under a general anesthetic and then give her a second, lethal, injection. He wouldn't have to go as far as North Carolina for all this either. Drive out to Newark Bay to dispose of the
body. But where would that get him? He'd be without Cynthia. So
instead he plots his wife's murder, which then brings him around
to the easiest solution of all: suicide.

"All of which he tells me about the next time we're alone! The man was not well. It was clear he hadn't slept in days. He hadn't called me back. The thing about him turning himself in, I don't know that I was totally serious about it. I mean, what did I want? I didn't know that either. Lying, sneaking. That was all I was opposed to. I hate secrets. They make me ill. I was sure he'd call me back later that night, try to convince me of some plan or other. But he didn't call. A week I didn't hear from him. I was getting concerned. I thought maybe he'd actually done it, gone to the police, because I didn't see him around. Then I thought maybe the lab results came back, and the mouse was still alive! Maybe I wasn't pregnant after all.

"Sarah had been keeping her distance, but I still spent time at the house, out of habit, I suppose. I should have had it out with her. Well, we would have it out soon enough. Instead, we said awful things about other people who thought they were our friends. I think it made Sarah feel better about hating me, and it made me feel better about not opening up about this whole affair with her father.

"We heard the car in the driveway, and then he was in the room with us. 'Out,' he said to Sarah, and she obeyed. He closed the door. He told me he'd been contemplating murder, he'd been contemplating suicide."

He tells her these are not good options. But neither is going to the police. Has she really thought this through? (She hasn't.) Has she considered that it will involve a trial, in which she will have to testify? (She hasn't, no.) That it could drag on for months? Longer, with appeals? That she won't be free to go to New York to become a Superstar until this is all over? He won't give in, he tells her. It'll be his word against hers. What evidence does she have, besides her word? He will fight it every step of the way. And whom will people believe? He is a respected member of the community, the friendly neighborhood dentist—and what is she? A promiscuous young girl who dresses like a hooker. It will be months before she can get the abortion—if she somehow manages to win, and by then it will be too late. The rape clause pertains only to first-trimester abortions. She will be forced to keep the baby and now be center stage in a messy trial. She will be famous — people will talk — but is this how she wants to spend her fifteen minutes?

No, she says meekly.

He feels sick. This is not how he meant for this to go. He botched a routine filling that morning, badly, and, after canceling the rest of his appointments for the day, had been driving around aimlessly. He pulled into the driveway expecting to throw himself on her mercy, to beg her not to make him turn himself in. He was on the verge of tears when he burst into Sarah's room. He watches himself talk. He hardly knows the man who is saying these words, the man who is standing over this poor girl and browbeating her half to death.

So what do we do, she says.

He doesn't know. He has to think. He will call her later.

When he leaves, Sarah returns, "And we finally had the fight that had been brewing for weeks. By the end of it, we were no longer friends, at least as far as Sarah was concerned. She called Lou Reed a fag and snapped my Velvet Underground album in half. She kicked me out of her house before I had developed a full-enough head of steam to storm out on my own. I went across the street, back home, slammed the door, stomped upstairs, and proceeded to trash my room.

"If I wasn't quite ready to call this town quits, after that afternoon I certainly was. There was nothing left for me here."

"What about your parents?"

"You mean my mother and her string of boyfriends? I would have moved out of her house at the age of twelve if I had the means — or knew where my father had run off to.

"I packed a duffel. If I hadn't gotten the call from Doc that night, I would have left on my own. He asked me how long it might take me to be ready to leave and not come back. I said, 'I'm already packed.' He said to meet him out front at midnight.

"I left out the front door. I got into Doc's car, which was idling in his driveway with the lights off. Anybody could have seen us leave, but I didn't see any lights come on—in either of our houses—as he pulled away, and I watched out the back window. Where were we going?"

Delaware, he says.

What's in Delaware, I ask.

A bus to New York.

"Like James Bond, this guy! His plan was to ditch the car outside of Wilmington. And once at the bus station, pay some wino to buy us two tickets to the city. Why all the secrecy?"

"People didn't need to know our whereabouts."

"I said, 'I can't get an abortion in New York,' and he said, 'You're not getting an abortion. You're keeping this baby.'"

It's the first time he has referred to the thing growing inside of Cynthia as a "baby." And doing so is like casting a spell. They both can feel it. After he utters the word, it's no longer something to be gotten rid of, to be dealt with. It's a life—to make room for, to figure out.

Okay, Cynthia says. But you're not leaving your wife for me. That's not what this is—you're not ending one family just to start another. I'm not going to be your wife. And this is not going to be your son.

Fine, he says. But I'm coming with you, wherever you go.

Fine, she says. You can be a Superstar, too.

# 12

# COLLECTIVE

THEY ARRIVE AT PORT AUTHORITY a little after six in the morning on Tuesday, May 31. They find a motel room on Forty-Ninth Street and Tenth Avenue. The rates are designed for use by the hour, more time than most customers seem to require, from all the coming and going. They sleep in a windowless room that smells like a urinal and bad breath. The bed is narrow and surprisingly clean for what this place is—the sheets bleach white and fresh. They sleep next to each other but do not touch.

When they wake, it's night. The place has suddenly become very active.

They go out to a nearby diner. We need a plan, he says, and outlines his idea for how to proceed. The day before they left, he withdrew half the family savings—he slides the cashier's check across the counter to her now. And I have enough cash in my wallet for us to get by for a couple of weeks without making use of this, he says.

Will he start up a practice here in the city?

No, he is through with that life. It's time for something new. He wants to make something, to use his hands, tools on a large scale—picks and drills that aren't all designed to fit in a person's mouth. He has heard of a man who went into business for himself restoring rundown properties and then reselling them at enormous profit. He can buy a place with the money, and they can live in it while he fixes it up — then they could sell it, which would net them enough for another place and enough left over to live on while they fix the new one up. And so on. It would be a self-sustaining way of life. There is something graceful about its logic — from the micro to the macro — restoring cavities in the face of a block. He'll learn as he goes. He already knows quite a bit from being a homeowner — it's surprising what you pick up intuitively about structural engineering from managing your own home repairs. And when the baby is born, he — or she — will have a roof over his head. Cynthia meanwhile can do whatever she wants — sing, dance, act — anything her little heart desires.

See, she says, I knew this is what you would do.

Do what?

You're making a family. You are not my husband. And you are not going to be a father.

Honey, in seven months I am, like it or not. Fine. So let's hear your plan.

You do what you want. My plan is simple and hasn't changed since tenth grade.

Do you even know where this place is? (She doesn't.)

And what do you imagine will happen once you get there? He waves his fairy magic wand — presto, you're a Superstar! You still don't have a place to live. (She'll figure something out.)

You're still going to need to eat. (She'll manage.)

They walk along Forty-Second Street, among a rough crowd of transients and prostitutes. They lug their belongings with them because they don't trust them in the motel. Cynthia insists on stopping every vagrant with a cup of change to ask where she can find Andy Warhol's factory. She has heard somewhere that Ultra Violet and Candy Darling — and most of the other Superstars — were, at the time of their discovery, bohemian eccentrics with *no fixed address*.

Why don't you just look it up in a phone book?

Don't be stupid — he's not going to put his phone number and address out there for just any person to see. The place is *under-ground*, man! (In fact, she has no idea whether or not it would be listed in the phone book. Thinking about it now, she imagines that it probably was.)

One man Cynthia asks leads them to a place several blocks away. The Factory? Sure, I know it, he says. But it turns out to be a jazz club called the Factory. Inside, it reeks of sweat and furniture polish. The three of them slide into a booth and listen — Cynthia enthralled, Doc skeptical — to the man's life story over the cacophonous quintet of musicians onstage.

When the man gets up to go to the bathroom, Doc says, He's just milking us for free whiskey.

Cynthia looks at him blankly. So? He's broke. What else is he going to do?

They stay until the place closes at two and then wander, drunk, back to their motel, which, when they arrive, is being raided by the police. An officer at the entry tells them to move along, and they happily comply.

They book a room at the motel next door, which isn't being raided. ("A stupid, stupid thing to do," Doc said. "It was just dumb luck the cops didn't — when they were done with the one place — move on and raid this place, too. I would have been toast. Cynthia would have gotten what she asked for — cops find a forty-year-old man and a fifteen-year-old girl in a motel room? They would have driven Cynthia back and locked me up and thrown away the key.")

This place isn't as well maintained. The carpet is stained; the sheets are not clean; a haze of cigarette smoke hangs in the air from the previous occupant, who seems to have vacated only minutes before their arrival — the cigarette butt stubbed out on the windowsill is still damp with saliva.

They sleep in their clothes, on top of the covers.

The sounds of a violent argument shake the walls. Stomping, screaming (a woman), bellowing (a man), splintering furniture (a bed?), glass shattering (a mirror? an ashtray?), outside the wail of sirens. When he wakes that morning, Cynthia—as well as all the cash in his wallet—is gone.

He waits in the hotel for three whole days, not daring to leave lest she return and not find him there. But she does not return.

He walks the Forty-Second Street corridor, from river to river, but she does not turn up. He begins to recognize the faces of the permanent vagrants, to learn names. Popcorn Jack. The Cardboard Preacher. Josephina Billingham III. Haunted faces, faces worn hard by vices, by insanity. Scars, open sores, hard callous feet.

When he reads a couple of days later that Andy Warhol has been shot by a woman, he thinks, My God, Cynthia—what have you done? He starts at every police siren, sure they are looking for him, sure he will be arrested as her unwitting accomplice. It turns out, though, not to have been Cynthia but rather a radical feminist by the name of Valerie Solanas, who had been in one of his movies. According to the papers, there had been some dispute about a screenplay.

He goes to the Factory, which turns out to be in a building down in Union Square, but he is stopped by a drag queen on his way off the elevator.

Your business?

I'm looking for a girl. He describes Cynthia, but it's clear she isn't here—clear, too, that this place it not what she had supposed. There are no vagrants here, no Cynthias. Everyone here is, in spite of some costumes, normal, adult. It is a place of commerce—a messenger handing over a package, someone signing for it, a man in a suit and bow tie sorting through artwork on a large table. Business as usual, even though their fearless leader lies recuperating in a hospital from a bullet in the ass.

What's so special about this place? Nothing, as far as he can tell. Cynthia will be disappointed when she finds it—if she hasn't found it already—just to be turned away by a man in a pink beehive wig.

He leaves and spends the rest of the day searching the meadows of the city. This seems to be where all the young people congregate when the weather is nice. In Union Square Park, Madison Square Park, Tompkins Square Park. He spends an entire day getting lost along the cloistered footpaths of Central Park. He buys a hot dog from a vending cart, and then another, then an ice-cream sandwich. He sits down in an enormous grassy field, among a ring of young people. Several have musical instruments. He is welcomed in warmly and — after being encouraged several times — joins in the singing, even though he doesn't know the words or the tune, and eventually finds himself beckoning with the others for passing strangers to join them, making room, expanding the circle.

This was the day Robert Kennedy was killed.

It grew dark, and the circle broke up. He left the park and found his way back to the room he was renting. It was time to move on. Cynthia was gone, subsumed into the great anonymous swirl.

He would occasionally wake, panic-stricken that Dolores had killed herself and still, half dreaming, imagine that Benji was calling to give him the news. He would grope for the phone in the dark and be woken by the sound of the dial tone droning in his ear. He'd hang up and go back to sleep, and by morning the dread would have passed. No news was good news, he figured. They were all getting along fine without him, he was sure. He had certainly left them all enough money to, anyway.

So however impossible it might have been to utter the word *no* and dissolve his family, it was remarkable just how easy it had been for him to forget about them entirely. That he had left them forever never to see them again was already, in his mind, a fact. In these first weeks of his arrival in the city he thought about one or another of them only in the context of how distant, how unreal, they seemed to be. He could conjure his wife's face only vaguely and Benji's not at all. The most vivid was Sarah's, but sometimes he caught himself confusing her face with Cynthia's.

He himself hardly remembered who he was anymore. Who had he been all these years? And who was he now?

It was too soon to know.

The death of Robert Kennedy turns out to be an occasion of national teeth gnashing and breast-beating; it's an event for which he himself has no particular feeling. The only politician he ever liked was Barry Goldwater, but this was only because Goldwater talked sensibly about taxes and government spending. The Kennedys are a phenomenon he doesn't get. What that family of New England socialites had to do with poor black people in the south he just could not figure out.

He is alone in this, he can see. Everywhere he goes the conversation is about the assassination—how nothing will ever be the same, how they are living in dangerous times now, how this will define the era. And coinciding as it does with an occasion of personal upheaval, Doc begins to hear the disembodied phrases of national mourning uttered by people—at a newsstand, in an elevator, on a bus—as advice. Start from scratch. Do what needs to be done. Move on.

He starts seeing a sculptor who rents an old carriage house on Grand Street. The neighborhood—if it can really be called that—south of Houston Street, had been a major base for manufacturing at the end of the last century and the beginning of this one, but most of the businesses moved away, the rest forced out through the threat of eminent domain. Early in the sixties, many of the buildings had been slated for demolition to clear the way for an eight-lane expressway that would connect the Manhattan and Williamsburg Bridges with the Holland Tunnel. Apartments could be gotten cheaply, and artists took advantage of these raw spaces—some former printing houses, others former textile factories, grand old buildings with cast-iron façades, expansive views, and enormous windows—expecting that when the city got its act together, they'd all be kicked out.

In fact, this never happened. The expressway plan fell apart due to a change in political winds, and by the time Doc arrives, it has become a thriving creative hub. It's not zoned to be lived in, but most landlords look the other way. Neither is it a neighborhood convenient for its residents. There are no groceries, few restaurants — the delis keep bankers' hours. The nearest Laundromat is on Sullivan Street, many blocks away. The buildings are not equipped for tenants — bathrooms are multistall affairs in the hallway, without showers, no kitchens, no bedrooms or closets or proper ventilation. When he stays over — which is most nights — he is reduced to sponge bathing in the large slop sink in her studio.

The woman claims to be a lesbian, but this does not stop them from sleeping together. So far as he can tell, *lesbian* just means that she enjoys being pleasured orally — fine by him — and occasionally catcalls women on the street. She also claims to be an anarchist. They initially bonded over their mutual indifference to Robert Kennedy's death. She likes to host parties, which he pays for. The parties last all night and into the next morning, and if one falls on a Friday, it lasts the entire weekend. He is free to sleep with whoever is willing, though he is often at odds with his desire to follow through with this invitation and his desire to get high, which precludes his doing anything sexually productive.

It's at one of these parties that Doc meets the lesbian's landlord, a tall man in his fifties who she says used to be an actor. Doc doesn't recognize him, but the man does use old-fashioned turns of phrase, words enunciated to the verge of British. Doc tells the man that he's interested in buying the carriage house. A month later, Doc finds himself in possession of the deed to the property and shockingly less money in his new bank account. He buys a sledgehammer and begins knocking down walls.

Don't I get a say, his lesbian asks.

If you don't like it, talk to your landlord!

He tries hiring an architect to build a kitchen and proper bathrooms, but he is told it's against zoning law — so he goes out on his own. He finds a plumber and a general contractor. He pays them in cash.

The lesbian says he's crazy. Who's going to buy a luxury condo in this neighborhood?

The contractors are young toughs from Brooklyn who spend as much time working as they do trying to catch a glimpse of the lesbian, who tantalizes them all by walking around topless. They take long lunch breaks, openly indulging in marijuana and beer. Sometimes Doc joins them. Other times he finds this irritating and yells at them to get out. *I'm not paying you to sit around and get high!*

The place, raw enough before, takes on a bombed-out look now. The lesbian remains very tolerant of the state of affairs—the haze of plaster dust and the perpetual whine of the circular saw biting into a two-by-four—in part because she is no longer paying rent. Also, perhaps, she is beginning to allow herself to be taken in by Doc's vision of what the place can become.

They had gone to a party at Vic Tedesco's place a couple of weeks prior—Vic was a self-proclaimed real estate baron and patron of the arts. He converted a warehouse on Mercer Street and West Broadway. It was immense—restored brickwork and wrought iron. He had built a solarium on the roof—accessed via a sweeping spiral staircase—which enclosed a pool. Vistas of the Midtown skyline, clear up to the Empire State and Chrysler Buildings.

She stops teasing Doc after that night and in fact encourages him—for the most part staying out of everyone's way. She even takes to wearing a shirt around the house.

Occasionally now as Doc works, in that pure, blank mind state that hard work produces, he finds himself thinking about Dolores. He can hear her saying, *I am willing to work as hard as I can.* And then he can picture her perfectly, standing before him in their kitchen, hands sudsy, hair plastered to her forehead, waiting for him to respond. He has the strongest urge during these daydreams to pick up the phone, just to hear her voice. He hates himself for the urge, for whatever forces in him bring this memory to the surface, but finds himself unable to refrain every once in a while, after he's had a few drinks, from picking up the phone and dialing his home in Plainfield, a number that he still remembers easily. On all but one occasion, he hangs up before anyone answers.

On the occasion he doesn't, it's a man who picks up.

Is Dolores there?

Who is this?

It's been only five months since he's left, less than a year. Is it possible she remarried? Maybe she moved.

And then, into the pause: Dad?

Benji?

Oh, my God, Dad, where are you?

Doc hangs up, heart thudding, his whole body gone into high alarm.

This is a mistake he does not repeat. Now, when the image of his wife comes to him, he locks himself in the newly constructed bathroom and lies in the smooth cool dry tub until the wave passes.

November brings with it another reason that the buildings in this neighborhood are ill suited for residential use: the cold. They are drafty and impossible to heat properly. A modern boiler system needs to be installed, but in the meantime they are making do with space heaters.

He is on his way out to buy two more to replace the ones that have overheated and died the night before. It's brisk, but he sees—passing through Washington Square Park on his way to the Woolworth's on Sixth Avenue—a throng gathered around a dry fountain basin.

A man in a leotard and bow tie is performing magic tricks. His assistant is a young woman in a peasant dress. It's clear that she's very pregnant. It's also clear, as he comes closer, that it's Cynthia.

When the show is over, she goes around with the maestro's top hat. She passes Doc without noticing him.

He reaches out and puts a twenty-dollar bill in the hat. When she recognizes him, sees that the bill is his, she becomes angry. She fishes it out and gives it back.

Not so fast, the man in the leotard says.

He shakes Doc's hand and offers him a business card. On it is a graphic of a unicycle and the words *The Meticulous Ticulous*. No address or phone number.

Ticulous?

At your service, Ticulous says, and bows deeply.

Where are you staying, Doc, asks Cynthia.

Around.

The Meticulous Ticulous says, Are you her father?

Cynthia snorts. Hardly.

Have you been to see a doctor?

She gives him a confused look, and he points at her belly.

My friend, Ticulous says, childbirth is not a medical procedure — it's the most natural thing in the world!

So's a postpartum hemorrhage, Doc says. Cynthia, it's freezing out. Your legs are bare. And you're wearing beach sandals.

Doc takes out a pen and crosses out what's printed on the business card Ticuolous has given him and on the other side neatly writes the address and phone number of the carriage house.

Cynthia refuses to take it, so he drops it in the top hat and walks away.

Ticulous hollers out, Farewell!

Doc, in spite of himself, waves.


When Cynthia met Ticulous, she had been trying, unsuccessfully, for an audience with Andy Warhol.

After the shooting, the Factory effectively closed its doors to the public. Warhol became much more private — and wary of strangers. She was met by a voice over an intercom and told to leave her contact information and that somebody would get back to her. She gave the number of a public pay phone nearby and had been guarding it ferociously for days.

There was a mime working the passersby of the block. He was engaged in a routine wherein he would pretend to be hurrying along wearing an invisible hat, carrying an invisible briefcase. He would stumble, and the briefcase would fall open, and invisible papers would fly out that he would scramble through the crowd trying fruitlessly to recover. Then he discovered Cynthia, stubbornly pretending to be on the phone, waiting out a growing line of impatient people.

I'm on hold, she snarled, reaching into her pocket for a nickel, pretending to insert it in the slot.

The mime liked this. He got on line and acted out extreme impatience, tapping his foot, looking at his invisible watch—and then, discovering an invisible phone booth next to the one Cynthia was on, he would step into it and make a call and, mirroring exactly Cynthia's body language, stave off a growing line of invisible people, claiming with a shrug, an eye roll, a pointed finger, that he, too, was on hold.

During a lull in foot traffic, he asked her, with hand gestures, whom she was waiting for.

I'm waiting for a call from Andy Warhol, she said.

That asshole?

Hey! You're not allowed to talk.

Pop is the death of art, the mime said, and that man is the grim reaper.

He introduced himself, handed her a business card. He explained that he was just one of several street performers in a troupe. This loose collection included former students of half-a-dozen illustrious institutions: Julliard, Oxford, Yale. We are an impressive band of dropouts, he said. Ticulous had been to Lecoq. Their shared ethos was the *renunciation of artistic professionalism*. Appalled by what they saw as a rise in the commercialization of their chosen callings, and the willing participation of their colleagues and mentors in *the greed machine*, they opted out and somehow found one another, taking a monastic vow of poverty; the only means of protest available to them in a capitalistic state was with a dollar—or its refusal. They gave the gift of their art freely, accepting donations given only in a similarly free spirit—food, clothing, shelter, or, if it was all you had, money. They prostrated themselves like monks to the generosity and goodwill of the people of New York City. Koko, who had spent three years at Academy of Art in Bonn before coming to New York, drew elaborate and lavish oil-pencil murals on the pavement. Winston, who had been dancing from the age of five and endured two years at Birmingham Royal before calling it quits, made the various platforms of the subway system his stage. They were, all of them, hounded by police. They had all been arrested repeatedly, spent time in jail. Most had been mugged; a couple had been beaten. Many nights were spent freezing—or wet and freezing—on park benches. They were not above fishing through trash for food. The fervor with which he talked drew Cynthia to him—and away from the phone booth. By the end of their conversation, he had made her vow never to return. It's not like he was ever going to call anyway, she said, so he didn't think she was too easily persuaded.

For the rest of the day, she followed Ticulous around as he performed his routines, taking an increasing delight in being his straight man. If they were able to draw a crowd, Cynthia took the bowler from his head and circled for tips. She invited him up to her room—she was renting a sublet on Thompson Street—and they talked until morning. He convinced her that art was not a commodity to be bought or sold but rather like love to be received and given freely. He demonstrated with a kiss.

I'm pregnant, she said.

Congratulations, he said, and kissed her again.

I'm a little sensitive to smell right now, she said, so if you keep kissing me I may vomit in your mouth. You're kind of ripe, if you don't mind my saying.

He convinced her to be his assistant. He had been teaching himself magic and could use one, and her belly was sure to help loosen people's grip on their wallets. In exchange, she could share in the profits.

He introduced her to the collective: Koko, Andrew, Winston, Margarita, Annan, and Brigit. They pooled their resources and—she came to find out after getting to know them and inviting them to stay—their affections.

Cynthia had somehow, by being spurned from what she thought she was looking for, ended up stumbling into precisely what she'd been looking for all along.

—

When Doc happened by, the term on her sublet was expiring. She was forced to spend the better part of a week in a makeshift lean-to over a subway grate. She disliked Doc—he gave her the creeps. He made her feel dirty about her body and her desires. And he was responsible for this beast growing inside her, which was devouring her from the inside out, making her hungry all the time, sleepy all the time, having to pee all the time. She hated him for it and wanted nothing more to do with him. But the cash she had taken from his wallet—which she considered money owed and earned—was gone. She is living on nothing, scraps, reduced to outright panhandling, but people's hearts have gotten colder with the weather. No bills. The slush of coins at the end of the day is mostly small change. Enough for a meal, not nearly enough for a room.

She doesn't bother calling, and when she arrives at the carriage house, the main door is open.

She says, If you invite me, you're inviting them as well. Ticulous has come in with her, but the other six are waiting outside.

Doc welcomes them in. There's plenty of room, he says.

He calls the lesbian sculptress out of her studio as Cynthia calls in the rest of the troupe, and they go through a round of introductions. The construction workers come out—Mario has been staying here on a more or less permanent basis since his father kicked him out of the house, and his cousins Michaelo and Cheech often spend weekends here so they won't have to take the subway back to Bay Ridge after catching a show at the Garden—and introduce themselves.

Doc makes their stay contingent upon Cynthia seeing a physician about the baby and agreeing to have it delivered in a hospital and not, as she has been threatening, in the pure waters of the Central Park Boat Basin.

He hands Ticulous and the three other men sledgehammers and crowbars and tells them they are now to answer to his construction crew.

Their first order of business: knock down the one remaining

partition in the house—the sculptress's studio wall. This is now a house without borders between public and private, between art and life. It's an experiment, one in which more or less all thirteen members of this motley crew are willing if not enthusiastic participants. They are all, in one way or another—and each for his or her own reasons—hedonists. Each enjoys the roam they've be allowed in this arrangement, each happy enough to give up privacy for the sake of the general pleasure to be had, happy to surrender daily life to art. That is the idea, anyway, without anyone having to say it. Pleasure and art. Revelry. Even the bathrooms are communal, a set of doorless stalls, one per floor.

The Brooklyn Trio, as they come to be called, is able, with the help of the eight others, to outfit the house with modern fiberglass insulation and a proper hot-water heater just on the heels of the first real cold weather of the season. They freely spend all the cash that they've been given, and by the time Doc leads a shaky Cynthia back through the front door with her infant son in her arms and a swirl of snow behind her, they are all officially broke.

They subsist through the winter on communal pots of something called frankfurter stew, a Depression-era recipe handed down from Brigit's grandmother who, with the pittance given her by her alcoholic gambler of a husband, had to feed an entire brood of siblings and cousins. Ticulous has a connection with a grocer, an admirer of the collective, who sells them dented cans and frozen goods past their expiration date. Often he throws in stuff for free. The loaves they make with the flour occasionally have mealworms, and the canned vegetables need to be cooked extra long in case of botulism, but for the steep discount it is worth it; they eat well.

Meanwhile, Doc retains a proxy to go back to New Jersey and find a buyer for his practice. The man returns some weeks later with a check along with divorce papers from Dolores. He signs them and gives over half of the money from the sale of his practice. The remaining half will go toward the renovation and living expenses, which, with a baby and a house full of freeloaders, require more money than he has.

Cynthia dislikes Doc as much as ever, but Ticulous seems to admire the man. He thinks of him as their patron and leader. When Cynthia bestows on Ticulous the honor of naming her child, he chooses the name Arthur, much to her dismay, in honor of Doc. Doc, however, still thinks Ticulous is a buffoon and takes every opportunity to rile him, which Ticulous, for his part, takes in stride. On any matter on which they disagree, Doc would say, Did they teach you that in clown school?

To which Ticulous would insist, Lecoq! Lecoq! The man is the greatest living performer in the world, and L'École—

Tell it to your pal Bozo. I'm not interested.

And Ticulous would laugh. He thought Doc was kidding and that he enjoyed Ticulous's company more than he let on.

Baby Arthur is doted on by two-dozen hands. Never was an infant more handled than Baby Arthur. There is no crib, nor is there a need for one: he is never put down; he is always in somebody's arms. Cynthia breastfeeding him, Doc burping him, Ticulous sweeping him around the room, Koko cradling him while he naps, or any of the others caressing or changing or cooing or cuddling.

He sleeps on the top floor, with Cynthia, Ticulous, and Winston. It is the warmest place in the house. On the rare occasions he is left undisturbed to sleep, it is in an old typesetter's bath, padded down with blankets. When, after months, he outgrows the makeshift manger in the corner, he begins sleeping in his mother's bed. One day Annan comes in with a crib he's found on the street and lugged all the way from Midtown, pleased with his contribution to Baby Arthur's care and well-being, but Cynthia refuses to even consider it. I'm not putting my son behind bars!

It is, most of the time, unbearably hot on the top floor where they sleep, Arthur curled against his mother's belly as though he were remembering how he used to sleep. Even in the winter they sleep with the portable fans going—the windows on the top level do not open, and so the fans merely produce a swirl of hot air. They sleep naked, mother and son, under a thin sheet, as do Winston and Ticulous, who have taken up together on a separate mattress.

The coupling and decoupling in ever-rotating pairs was a fact of life in those first years at the carriage house. And however free most felt to share and share alike, there remained something quaint about these fleeting unions, for they were always pairs that were formed — the groups came later — always discreetly consummated, on a mattress at night. There was a time to be a couple, a time for sex, and that time was night. These boundaries were understood. There were the usual jealousies and hurt feelings that came with arrangements like this — but they were feelings quickly healed through new pairings. Those that did not heal left, to be replaced by a new face, a new possible permutation in this evolving community. When a couple was engaged in sex, they were given the benefit of privacy, however illusory. For the fact remained, there were no walls. Most had gotten used to life without them. The lesbian, who came to be known as Emily (though this was not her name), insisted on keeping her area private with a series of sheets draped over clotheslines and took to the toilet and shower in the early morning while her floor mates slept, but by that point she was already halfway out the door.

And however tactful, however much people in the house deferred to a couple's privacy, sex must have been some of Baby Arthur's first, vivid facts of consciousness, lying curled against his mother's breasts to the sounds of two people grunting through their shared pleasures. And as Baby Arthur began to wobble and race, something he did at all hours, as Cynthia shunned the notion of a "schedule" for her son, guided by his own internal clock when to sleep and when to wake up, he would often happen upon two members of the house having sex, for Baby Arthur gave no such deference to his housemates' privacy. He would be greeted happily by the out-of-breath couple and then free to watch as they continued with their business or to bobble off to some other corner of the house.

With the convenience of a fixed location, the performers begin using the carriage house as a creative venue. Ticulous throws open the great arched doorway through which horse-drawn carriages many years ago used to enter and leave and, setting up a cluster of chairs along the sidewalk and acting the part of an old-fashioned barker, calls out to passersby to stop, take a load off, and behold: Brigit on point or Koko painting herself gold and wrapping herself in white bed linen or Ticulous himself hopping down off his barker stool and tumbling into a handstand.

The street-side theater, as it were, evolves. Those main doors frame a natural proscenium arch. It is perfect. Day by day, with each performance, they develop a repertoire, invite local performers to use the space, to collaborate. Ticulous directs a series of movement pieces: mime productions of *The Canterbury Tales*. Annan conducts a series of chamber ballets set to his own music. The Brooklyn Trio builds a stand of bleachers, which the police eventually make them move inside, to be set up permanently against the three walls on the ground floor. For a while, it is the Carriage House Theater, doors kept open so people can walk in off the street and take a seat and watch the show, already in progress.

This is young Arthur's living room. He eats his meals in the stands, watching his aunts and uncles rehearse. Most objects he touches in the house are used onstage as props; even the plates and utensils he eats with while watching a play might be taken from him and washed and used in the next scene. When a child is required, he is offered up—dressed and set before an audience with a few words to deliver on cue.

He is tested out, like a new instrument, by each member of the Carriage House Theater, for quality, for truing—to see where his talents and inclinations might lie. Koko thinks he has a certain raw potential with the plastic arts; Brigit declares that he will never be a dancer. Just look at his feet, they will always be in his way. Ticulous agrees but thinks his rhythm is quite good. Annan pronounces his natural aptitude in music to be extraordinary. A quarter-sized violin, among a crate of props, is strung and tuned and given to the boy. He is taught to read music, and Annan comes up with a series of fingering exercises for the boy to practice.

You're not going to force my son to learn a bunch of pointless lessons, Cynthia says, but Annan pushes back.

Come off it, Cynthia. This isn't about freedom. Arthur is happy to spend the entire day sawing away on that violin, and you know it. You just can't stand the noise.

It's true that Arthur isn't very good yet; the particular high-pitched squeaking sets Cynthia's teeth on edge and carries through the house, following her wherever she goes.

He's not to spend a minute on that thing he doesn't want to, she says.

Annan devises more difficult exercises and starts training the boy's ear. They work together at the old saloon upright under the bleachers. Cynthia asks the boy if he is enjoying these lessons, and Arthur says, Sure.

Doc jokes that his son skipped the age of two. "He never learned to say no. It was always 'sure' or 'okay,' whatever it was. He'd eat anything you put in front of him. Benji and Sarah, when they were little? If it wasn't spaghetti, they weren't interested. But Arthur, you could put anything in front of him—steamed broccoli, raw tofu, pickled beef tongue—and you ask him if he wanted to try it he'd say, 'Sure.' If he didn't like it, he wouldn't have seconds. Benji, he didn't like something, it was the biggest production, the faces he'd make, the yelling, the fits. You'd think we were trying to poison him. But with Arthur it was always 'sure.'"

Arthur becomes a regular attraction at the Carriage House Theater. Annan composes pieces for Arthur to perform as incidental music between set changes. By the time he is eight, Arthur has been playing for three years, and Cynthia no longer complains about her son being enslaved by pointless rote memorization. She is enjoying, along with the rest of the audience, the weekly recital programs he comes to perform. Arthur's virtuosic feats are paired with Ticulous's magic; these, Ticulous feels, are acts well suited for each other, as the child prodigy is a kind of magic, not unlike the talking horse or the dancing bear. One is moved to a similar awe and pity for the creature.

Ticulous in tails and top hat, Arthur in a black suit and clip-on bow tie, they are a nested set. Ticulous would creak around on the black-painted boards of the stage, barefoot, pulling live pigeons out of his hat, making various audience-supplied items disappear and levitate while Arthur, walking the perimeter would play glissandi and arpeggios — an incidental sound track meant to mirror the illusions. During longer setups, Arthur would give the cue to Annan at the upright offstage, and they'd strike up a duet, Arthur up front now, bow hopping lightly to a Mozart sonatina.

These concerts are held on Sundays for neighborhood parents and children who in the late seventies are few and far between — and as such that much more enthusiastic to find an oasis of free child-friendly entertainment within walking distance.

Annan invites his mentor, Cornelius Diamond, to hear Arthur play. Diamond brokered Annan's journey to this country from his native Afghanistan ten years earlier — arranged for schooling, scholarships, visa — and Arthur is a kind of offering, a willing and capable apprentice, new blood for the old man.

Diamond usually handles older students, but for Arthur he makes an exception. Annan's assessment of the boy is confirmed: Arthur is good. They start small, lessons once a week — a list of pieces to learn.

Doc is shocked at the cost. I don't care how great this guy is, there's just no way. But Annan pitches it as an investment in their son's future. Doc won't budge, but Cynthia is swayed by the idea.

I thought you were against this whole thing, Doc says to her.

This is my Artie. I don't ever want him to say we held him back from doing anything he wanted or becoming anything he needed to become.

For such a free-spirited household, Arthur leads a very sheltered life. Although Cynthia consents to the lessons, she won't hear of Arthur having lessons at "some old perv's apartment." So for the first year of his apprenticeship, Diamond comes to Arthur. Diamond is temperamental and explosive. When he hears something he doesn't like, he claps his hands, a sound like a gunshot in that big open space, and shouts. *For God's sake, stop! Stop!* He storms over to Arthur and grabs the little violin and bow out of the boy's hand and, hip checking him out of the way of the music stand, says, softly, Just listen. And then Diamond plays the passage, his large hands seeming all the more enormous on Arthur's half-sized violin. Arthur is good, but when Diamond plays, it's music. No question who is the student, who the master. Arthur stands at attention, waiting for Diamond to hand back his instrument.

Money was an ongoing problem. The theater, in line with the monastic ethos of its members, accepted as a fee only what its goers were willing to part with, which was—judging from the jumbo mayonnaise jar at the entrance—very little. By 1978 Doc had run out of money, which would have spelled an end to the Carriage House Theater, to young Arthur's education, and the collective in general had not his insolvency coincided with the acquisition and restoration of an offset printing press.

One was liable in those days to come across pretty much anything on the sidewalk. The printing press was just one of the many objects hauled in off the street. It would have lain dormant under the bleachers to this day had Mario not been taking a correspondence course in the maintenance and repair of industrial office machines. He fixed the thing just to practice his skills.

Doc took to using his old prescription pad for the occasional antibiotic or painkiller. But after a while he began to see its usefulness as a recreational tool as well—codeine for a mellow party, say, or Benzedrine for a more lively one. Word got around about his access to drugs and, lo and behold, there was a market waiting for him. The profits he could pull in through the sale of pills divvied out five or six at a time was well worth the outlay for a generic refill and whatever risk was involved in attempting to fly a bogus prescription. And so he began selling to make ends meet, which developed, like most activities Doc engaged in, slowly, with no particular plan beyond the necessity of the moment.

Soon enough, however, his one and only prescription pad was depleted. He kept the last page around and tried copying it—but his options were limited in those days. He sought all the readily available technologies, but photostats felt fake and mimeographs smelled fake. Which was where the offset press was of use. Not only could he make a perfect replica, he could also change his name, as well as his degree—there was only so much as a dentist he could get away with prescribing. With a minor alteration of title letters, he could have at his disposal the entire range of opioids, of amphetamines and barbiturates and benzodiazepines. The sky was the limit.

"Nowadays," Doc said, "you have tamper-resistant pads, watermarks, nationwide electronic databases—pharmacies proceed from a starting point of skepticism. You've got to be pretty ambitious to practice that kind of fraud. In those days, though, it was different. Because there was no such thing as a copy shop, to forge a thing like a prescription was more difficult, which in turn meant people weren't on the lookout for fakes—or signs of the genuine. Pharmacists were, by comparison, rather guileless; they didn't question what you handed them—or rather they questioned different things. They would call the number on the prescription, which was the only tricky bit. We had a second phone line put in. 'Hello, doctor's office.' It was written in big marker letters across the phone's handset. Anyone who answered that phone had to say it. It's amazing we got away with it as long as we did."

I said, "But those first prescriptions would have had your New Jersey office number, right?"

Amazingly, Doc explained, the dentist who took over the practice kept the number. "I guess he figured he'd save his patients the headache of learning a new one—most of them he poached from me. So when the pharmacy called, they got him. I don't know how or why he okayed those prescriptions. He could have gotten into serious trouble for that. He was young, and I guess I was able to strong-arm him a bit."

It had been mutually agreed upon that Arthur's brain would

not be poisoned by the institutions of knowledge and that each member of the collective would share in the responsibilities of schooling him in whatever he wanted to learn. Doc taught him science; Koko taught him history; Brigit taught him math. Books were procured from the public library on Canal Street, and Arthur spent weekdays, when he should have been in school, at his studies. Here, too, Arthur proved himself to be serious and determined. Cynthia was amazed.

"If it weren't for the eighteen hours of labor," she said, "I wouldn't have believed that was my kid at those books. He was a gift. I don't know what I would have done had he been a bad seed. He could have easily brought down this place of ours. So easily. I think back and can't believe our good luck."

Diamond told Cynthia that Arthur wasn't getting as rounded a musical education as he should be at this stage in his development. Arthur had long outgrown the basic theory and ear-training primers they worked out of. At the conservatory where he taught there was a weekend session for the younger students. A scholarship might be available, depending on how his audition went.

Cynthia objected. School? Out of the question.

But Arthur, who thus far had rarely expressed his wants, was very clear about wanting this, and so, from the age of nine, he began his weekly Saturday excursions to Morningside Heights. For those first few years, Annan would escort him. Arthur would return from these adventures flushed and full of stories.

Doc saw this and began expressing reservations about the boy's weekday "schooling." He should be with kids his own age, he said. Keeping him cooped up like this couldn't be good for the boy.

It's too late, Cynthia said. There was no telling what might happen if they walked him into a real school at this stage. Aren't there laws about keeping kids out of school? It's been four years. They'll end up taking him away from us for neglect.

Although it was meant to preserve and sustain it, the pill business brings the excess and decline of the theater and the collective as a whole. Brigit leaves, Koko leaves, Winston leaves — and several characters with little connection to art take their place. The only original members left now are Annan and Ticulous, and they are only here out of concern for Arthur.

On his last day, Ticulous tells Arthur, *Follow your art. It will always lead you in the right direction.* He is standing at the main archway with Annan and Cynthia. He buttons his peacoat, picks up his army duffel. He pulls Annan into an embrace with his free arm and tries kissing Cynthia, but she turns away.

You don't get to leave here on friendly terms, she says. This is desertion, plain and simple.

After Ticulous leaves, Arthur weeps and storms up to his room. The atmosphere of the place changes. One could feel it come off its axis. With Annan and Arthur upstairs — the piano had been installed on the top floor so that Arthur could work undisturbed for longer stretches of time — what else was there to do? There had been order, rhythm; rehearsals, a chore board. Without a chore board, there were no more chores. Without rehearsals, there were no more shows. And without Ticulous's magic, Arthur's Sunday performances failed to draw more than a few passersby — and so these, too, were abandoned.

The new members of the collective brought "instruments" — congas and bongos, harmonicas and ukuleles — so that when they were high they could "jam." Doc and Cynthia — the only two members of the household not trained in the arts, who until now had always abstained from art making, preferring their role as patrons — became active and enthusiastic participants in these jam circles. There was singing and dancing, which oftentimes devolved into stripteases, which devolved further into free-form group sex.

Annan is the sole holdout and protests this artless noisemaking. It's disgusting, he says, and besides, Arthur is trying to study! How is he supposed to learn with all these distractions?

Arthur suggests a compromise: Why don't they use the basement? Down there could be a free zone, to do whatever people wanted.

Doc and Cynthia like the compromise, and so the Permission Room is born.

One day — or evening, it becomes hard to tell after a while — Doc comes up from the basement to discover the bleachers gone.

Cynthia says, It's time for some real change around here. Out with the old-fashioned, in with the fun! She is naked, the main door wide open.

What combination is she on, Doc wonders, and would she give him the recipe?

If those first years at the house were a celebration directed outward, out into the street, a giving away, now is a time to turn inward again, for each to seek out his or her own pleasure — the time has come to take back. And whereas the ethos of life had been toward excellence and beauty, now it's the opposite. It's all revel, without the art, without the life. The drugs do away with any inhibitions, as well as the notion of coupling. It is every man for himself now. There are no more experts. It's an unwinding of sorts. The only thing to do is fuck.

"That was a crazy time," Cynthia said wistfully. "Crazy."

I asked, "What about Arthur?"

Doc said, "What about him? He was a big boy by then. If he lived in India, he would have been married off. If he were a Jew, he would have already been a man. Thirteen, fourteen. Almost the same age as Cyn when I first banged her."

Cynthia said, "Anyway, he kept to himself mostly. He was in his room practicing or out at the library or at a lesson or up at that music school."

I tried pressing here; what activities had Arthur seen, exactly? What might he have participated in, in the Permission Room, and with whom? At what age? But their answers were elusive. Later, I could see that this was a mistake, pressing the issue. It pretty much put an end to the interview. Cynthia excused herself to "piddle," and Doc, taking out the flat marble pipe from his pants pocket along with a Bic lighter, sparked up a waft of pot smoke that he kept in his chest along with anything else he might have been willing to say that day.

The Morels talked for six straight hours. Dave had to make a run up to Tower Records to pick up more DV cassettes after a frantic bit of whispering with Suriyaarachchi; we hadn't planned for this kind of outpouring. And, despite my failure at the end, Cynthia had come back into the main room as we were packing up and invited us to stay and continue filming—she was planning to design some more jewelry and thought we might be interested in filming her make it. Maybe stay for dinner.

We departed the carriage house after promising to return on Sunday, and, when safely around the corner, we were free to hug one another, to giggle at our good fortune. The Morels had proved to be a gold mine. Suriyaarachchi carried the cassettes in a special bag that he clutched now with both hands to his chest.

"So they're not married," Suriyaarachchi said.

"They don't sleep together. Did you see the other bed?"

"I thought that was for guests."

"It's where he sleeps. She's up in the bunk."

"Your man Arthur," Dave said, "had one strange kind of childhood."

We passed an Indian restaurant on Broome Street that met the description of the one that Doc had recommended earlier. The place was empty. Several waiters were gathered around a table in the back, wiping down menus. We sat down by the window and ordered samosas and three servings of *palak paneer*.

After hearing about the last days of the carriage house, I had to wonder at Arthur's sexual inexperience. From what he'd shared with me, and what I gleaned from his book, there had only been that one early encounter with another boy his own age. How was that possible? From the way Cynthia told it, he would have been tripping over writhing orgies on his way to the bathroom every morning. I pictured myself at the age of fifteen, with a perpetual erection, living in that household, with my pick of willing participants and no prohibition whatsoever from my parents. It would have been nonstop fucking, I would have gone insane from fucking. And, I would have thought, growing up in a household like that, Arthur would have been less shy, more at ease with himself in social settings. Another thing that didn't add up.

"Sunday will be about pickup shots," Suriyaarachchi said. "And cutaways. We need lots of cutaways. See if we can't get our hands on old photos or artwork. Signs, anything we can do that Ken Burns slow pan-zoom with. And we'll need all sorts of footage of that basement."

"We're going to need light. The gain in the shadows will be bad."

"If you bring light down there, it's not going to look like a creepy basement anymore."

"As long as we get the ratio right, we can do what we want."

The two of them argued for a while about this until our food came, and then we lost ourselves to our appetites, piling our plates high with pea-studded steaming rice and torn flaps of naan, ladling the stew from the round copper bowls. There was plenty to go around, and by the end I felt stuffed and a little guilty at my indulgence.

# 13

# S U S P E C T

EVENTS DEVELOPED FAIRLY QUICKLY AFTER this. I was present for very little of it and only put the pieces together through interviews, generously granted to us by Penelope, the Wrights, and law enforcement many months later, after it was all over.

Two officers from Fairfax County responded to the call from the Wrights' residence in Annandale. Report of an unauthorized person trying to gain entry. The unauthorized person was the Wrights' son-in-law. Officer Colonna waited outside with the suspect while Officer Fields spoke with the owners of the house.

There had been a domestic dispute between their daughter and her husband, the suspect. All parties were vague as to what had transpired.

Violence? No.

The father and property's deed holder, Frank Wright, had a pending civil suit against his son-in-law. Defamation. That man out there is a monster. He molested my grandson and wrote about it, just to smear our noses in his awful deed. He's lucky I'm a Christian and obey my Commandments or I would have blown his head off! Mrs. Wright sat by her husband's side and stroked his hand.

The officer asked to see the permit for the weapon and the weapon itself—he did this less out of protocol and more as a way of keeping them focused, of calming them all down. Officer Fields asked to speak with their daughter and her boy, who seemed to corroborate Mr. Wright's claim. The events that the boy described had taken place when the boy was eight, in their place of residence at the time, in Queens, New York. The boy was now eleven.

Officer Fields finished taking statements, checked the permit against the serial number on the firearm. Mr. Wright wanted to file a restraining order against his son-in-law. He has no right to be on our property!

There was a hush in the house. A television in the living room played out an episode of *Law & Order* quietly. Mr. Wright's statements sounded like outbursts in the relative calm. Everyone else spoke quietly, mirroring Officer Fields, who recently attended a seminar in which he learned to project the emotional calm he was looking to instill in the people he was sworn to serve and protect, something he revealed to Mrs. Wright when she noted his calm demeanor.

Officer Fields told Mr. Wright how to go about filing for a restraining order. Mr. Wright looked for a pen and paper frantically, which Mrs. Wright calmly found and set before Mr. Wright. He began dutifully copying out Officer Fields's instructions but stopped after a while. It was too complicated. Obtaining documents from this office, filing it with that office, going to court. The shotgun would do for the purposes of restraint.

As Officer Fields was leaving, he told the daughter and her parents that an investigator would be in touch. The three seemed at odds about this: Mr. Wright eager to get the ball rolling, Mrs. Wright and her daughter not so sure.

Are you going to arrest my husband?

At this point, no. We will make sure he leaves you all in peace tonight—but as to the other matter. That's serious business. We will share what information you've provided with PD in your neck of the woods back in New York. They have special investigators to handle cases like yours.

Officer Fields bid them good night and rejoined his partner, who was chumming with the suspect. Officer Fields put on his best intimidating face and told the suspect to vacate the premises.

The suspect started in about his rights to see his son, and Officer Fields told him that he did not own that house and had no right to enter it without the owner's permission, and if his wife and son didn't wish to see him right now, it was their right to stay in a house in which he was not welcome — and if he persisted in loitering, they would issue him a desk-appearance ticket, and he'd have to spend the rest of the week going between the police station and courthouse to deal with it.

Penelope is contacted some days later by phone. *Detective Ramirez,* she writes down on the back of an envelope. He would like to speak with Penelope and Will, to determine whether or not there is merit in pursuing a criminal complaint against her husband.

A week has passed. Penelope has been getting a seven-day earful from her father. It's having an effect; his rants are beginning to sound like sense. She's angry now. Furious. At Arthur and at herself. How could she have let this happen? She should fight for the apartment, insist Arthur find a place to stay, but she doesn't want to negotiate with him. She doesn't have the strength at the moment, and the truth is she's not sure she wants to bring her son back there. She calls Rachel, an old high school friend who lives in Brooklyn Heights. Senior year they'd smoke joints on the gym's roof and gossip about pregnant classmates. As adults, they got together over coffee occasionally to discuss their ailing marriages. Penelope had helped shepherd Rachel through her divorce some months earlier, and Rachel is thrilled now to return the favor — and insists Penelope and Will come stay with her.

Penelope goes to the precinct with Will. The investigators question her about her statement to Officer Fields in Virginia. They want Will to speak with one of their psychologists. Penelope's not so sure. What if it's all a mistake? She's already spoken with a psychologist, and Will has gone back and forth about it.

Has he been known to lie?

No, she says.

Would he have any reason she could think of for making this up?

Because he's mad at his father.

Detective Ramirez laughs. I can remember being all sorts of mad at my father. Kids fantasize about doing terrible things to their parents. But they don't actually do them.

Or for the same reason my husband would have for making it up, she says. I don't know. Statements, psychologists. I just don't know if this is a good idea. And a trial? I don't know if I want to put my son through all that. The family through it.

Are you afraid?

Of what?

That if it's true you'll be held responsible for letting it happen, presiding over it.

But I'm not responsible.

You're not? When your husband published his confession, you did nothing.

He said it was a fiction.

And you believed him? You just—took his word for it without asking your own son if it was true?

I didn't want to confuse him, didn't want to hurt him!

Who—your son or your husband? Who were you trying to protect? If this goes to trial and your husband's convicted, you can be tried afterward for negligence—and, if you refuse to cooperate here, obstruction as well.

Is that a threat? Are you threatening me?

I'm laying out your options here.

Do I need a lawyer?

You're not a suspect, relax. If you cooperate, let us do our jobs, we could make certain guarantees down the line, what avenues we do or don't pursue if this goes to trial, if your husband is found guilty.

She goes with Will to a room and is joined by a young man— how old is this kid? He asks Will questions. Will answers. There are toys. They have him sitting at a low table. Paper, Crayola pens. Will tries to use several of the pens, but they're dry.

You need new pens, Will says.

The psychologist hands Will the pen in his pocket. It's a fountain pen. Have you ever used one of these before?

It's heavy, Will says. He hefts it in the tips of his fingers. Can I have it?

It was given to me as a gift, the psychologist says. He explains how a fountain pen works—the inkwell, the split nib. He encourages Will to try it out, to write something. Was this a ploy? Was Will given dry markers on purpose? Penelope has to wonder.

Will writes the words: *copy, cat, tail,* and *tattle.*

Are you worried about tattling, the psychologist asks. Being a tattletale? Will is reluctant to speak. Tattling on your dad?

His name is Art, Will says.

Is that what you call your father: Art?

That's his name, isn't it?

Why don't you tell me a little about him, the psychologist suggests. What is he like? What do you two enjoy doing together?

I'm not going to say *masturbate,* Will says. I know that's what you're really asking. Do we like to masturbate together, but I'm not going to say that.

Nobody's asking you to say anything but what you know to be the truth. The psychologist asks Will if he feels embarrassed, if he might be worried about saying the wrong things in front of his mother.

Will says maybe.

The psychologist takes Penelope aside and urges her to let them speak alone for a few minutes, that her presence might be a stressor keeping Will from speaking more freely.

Is there a way I can watch?

Watch?

Through like a two-way mirror or something?

This isn't an interrogation room.

Penelope agrees. When she is gone, Will says he likes to play the Game Boy with his father, but that his father is not very good. He likes to help his father make pasta and peas, though neither of them is very good at this either. Will doesn't look at the psychologist; he doodles with the fountain pen. In our apartment we have a roof we can go up on. I have a radio-controlled UFO, which is an unidentified flying object. People believe they're real, but the government says it's weather balloons. That's what I read anyway, and I have to agree. Isn't that easier to believe? The other option is an entire race of beings from another galaxy, which scientists say is impossible, coming light-years — that's miles that are so big they measure it in time not space — to get here and do what? Crash-land in a cornfield? You would think if they had the technology to fly all that way they'd be smart enough to know how to land safely. But I guess what if the government shot them down? I'd still say it's weather balloons. Anyway, we went up on the roof sometimes and flew it out over the edge, which you weren't supposed to do, but Art said if I wouldn't tell, he wouldn't tell.

The drawing that Will has just finished looks unmistakably like a penis, though when the psychologist asks, Will writes the words WEATHER BALLOON with an arrow pointing at its shaft. People think they're round like a balloon, which in reality they aren't. They look like enormous penises. Floating in the sky.

Tell me about your father's book.

It's supposed to be fiction, but it has a lot of true-life details in it.

Like?

Like our names. And our address. I'm not sure about what people say in it because I can't remember word for word. Like now, I probably couldn't tell you what I just said. *I can't remember word for word like now I probably couldn't tell you what I just said.* But I couldn't tell you that ten minutes from now.

Will begins writing down, verbatim, everything he is saying. His speech slows as he attempts this feat, and he loses track of what he's saying and has to be reminded. There are things — in the book — that — are not true, like — I had a tantrum when

I—couldn't, *n*-apostrophe-*t*—stay up to watch *ER*. It wasn't *ER*—and it wasn't a tantrum. For instance. And there are things—that happened—that did not happen in the book. Like the UFO—on the roof.

What about those things that happened in the book and also happened in real life?

Will writes the words: *master, bait.*

I know how to spell it, he says. It's with a *u* even though it sounds like *master.* You want to know . . . did we . . . take baths.

What does the book say?

It says we did.

And did you?

He has just written his previous line of dialogue, *It says we did,* and now underlines the two words *we did.*

Each of the psychologist's follow-up questions becomes more pointed, more explicit, requiring explicit and pointed responses about what exactly Will and his father did together in the bath. Will stops speaking, stops looking up at his interrogator; instead he keeps his eyes on the page in front of him, letting the pen trace out those words he cannot utter.

The psychologist excuses himself and joins Detective Ramirez, who is sitting with Penelope on a bench outside the room.

I think we have a case here.

Detective Ramirez says, I need your son to come back and speak with one of the child psychologists.

Aren't you a psychologist?

No, ma'am. This is Detective Carvo. Detective Carvo extends his hand.

You tricked me.

No, ma'am.

But you did. You tricked me and my son into talking to you. You coerced a confession out of him.

Ma'am, we're not out to get your husband or you or your son or anyone else in your family. We're just looking for the truth here. This is a preliminary interview, information gathering, nothing

more. We don't want to falsely accuse anyone here. Which is why
we need an expert to speak with your son. Do you have an objec-
tion to that?

No.

Good.


Detectives Ramirez and Carvo visit Arthur at his place of employment. They would have preferred to speak with him at home. Talking with him here will put him on the defensive, and at this point
it would be better to have him comfortable. The tells are easier to
spot when they have a baseline of ease. But they must work with
what they have. Another case has them elsewhere in the mornings
and evenings, and they don't have time to guess at when he might
be home.

A young woman shows them to Arthur's office. She seems
thrilled that Arthur might be in some trouble. There is another
man in Arthur's office, speaking with Arthur.

The detectives ask the man if he wouldn't mind leaving while
they spoke with Arthur privately. They don't announce themselves as officers of the law. In places like this, they rarely have
to. Who else would they be? It's understood. People make a wide
berth, whisper to one another.

When they close the door, they show him their badges. Arthur
sits down. Detective Carvo stands; Ramirez sits on the edge of the
desk. They take an aggressive tack. They box him in, fold their
arms over their chests. It is Arthur who determines this, though
he doesn't realize it. Were Arthur to have remained standing, the
officers would have sat, folded their legs wide, presented him with
smiles and open palms. But Arthur is telling them, by sitting with
his back against the wall, to press down on him.

It's a tag team of questions. Arthur can't keep up with the
answers. The detectives are civil, polite even, but Arthur can feel
an icy burn expanding throughout his body. He's drowning in a
quicksand of questions, he can't catch his breath. He wants to give
them what they want, but what they want doesn't seem to have to

do with answers and questions. He stands, he moves toward the door, but can't bring himself to ask them to leave, so he leans, arms folded, in the corner by the door.

Arthur is right. The answers don't matter; whereas Arthur may determine the means, he has no control of the end. It has already been decided, at least as far as Detective Carvo is concerned. The man is guilty. But Detective Carvo is young. Hard work and intuition have gotten him this far. He is still high on his own intuition. Detective Ramirez, on the other hand, has had enough years on the job to have been proved dead wrong enough times to know that they're not all guilty, that some of them like this character Morel very well may have broken no laws, may in fact be just a run-of-the-mill pervert. Ramirez will reserve judgment because the truth is you never know. People lie, and for all sorts of reasons. It's not just the perverts, but the victims, too.

Anyway, they're not looking for concrete answers from this guy. They're after reactions. Is he outraged? Disgusted? Squeamish? Guilty? Afraid? It's how he reacts to key words, key phrases, not the answers themselves. They're looking for him to say something to complicate the story or change it in some way: maybe the boy has a history of lying, or the wife's father is a repeat sex offender. But the interview doesn't yield much.

At the same time, though, Arthur's reactions do not do him any favors or rule him out as their man. He goes from blank-eyed terror to sneering in the space of twenty minutes. He offers no damning tells, nor does he offer any complicating factors that might take the heat off him. Anyway, this case will come down to the boy's testimony. Until they have that, short of Arthur's full confession, it doesn't matter what he says.

Arthur had questions of his own, raised through these detectives' troubling line of questioning. Why were they hounding him about the "events" of a work of fiction? Where had they gotten the idea that his novel was true? Who had they been talking to? What had they been told? When had all this happened?

Penelope and Will return to the precinct for an interview with the child psychologist.

The place, in its bustle, seems less threatening this time around. She breathes a little more freely while she waits outside in the hall for her son. She feels safer, as though this place—in that impersonal yet reassuring way of hospitals—has her best interests in mind. That the people here only want to do right by her.

Detective Ramirez is a particularly comforting presence. He brings her coffee, bagels—when they go out for lunch he brings her back a sandwich. He sits down with her while she waits and explains gently, slowly, how everything will unfold. Much the way a surgeon would before a complicated procedure, with the same kindness and gravity. Unless the psychologist comes out and says something unexpected, they will ask Will to make a statement, record it on tape.

Will he also be asked to testify in court, Penelope asks.

It may come to that, yes, but there's plenty of time before we cross that bridge. First we will talk to, hopefully, Joanna. She is very nice, you'll like her. She works with the district attorney's office, and she will help us decide if and how we should move forward.

And if we do?

We will need to have a serious talk with Arthur. We will bring him in here. And at that point, it's really up to him. (Back to that idea again—Arthur in control of his own destiny or, if not his destiny, than at least the route he prefers to take to hell.) A confession may buy him some jail time. If he's not willing to confess, then we will have to make our felony complaint without it. We'll obtain a warrant for his arrest. We'll need you to be available for the whole gamut of court dates. For the next six months you'll learn how to make yourself comfortable on these benches, the art of waiting for your name to be called. I don't want to candy coat things for you, Penelope. It will be a full-time job for you, managing all of this. The court appearances will be stressful, but you have family, I hear, yes?

They're in Virginia.

If you could get them to come up, support you here, you should consider it. Mostly though, it will be crossword puzzles and hand-held video games, if that's what Will's into. My son's crazy for his Nintendo.

Reassuring the mother, this is important. She is the most dangerous person here. She can help things go smoothly or make things impossible. Best to get her on board early.

When the psychologist emerges, he says that he believes the sort of abuse described in the book, the abuse Will recalls, may very well have taken place. Penelope sobs. It comes out involuntarily, like a sneeze. She allows herself to cry, to dissolve on this bench, in front of these men who do nothing to comfort her.

Some days later, she receives a visit from Joanna Brady, the attorney who will be handling the case. She is a towering redhead with hands that could palm a basketball. She meets Penelope and Will as equals, friendly with Will without being solicitous. Will takes an instant liking.

He follows her around the apartment. Try holding this in one hand without letting it drop. He hands her a large honeydew melon. If you knew the technique of Shaolin finger strength you could crush a man's head with your bare hands, which is a lost art, apparently. Kendrick is always threatening me in the lunchroom, but I looked it up. Plus his father is a real pussy, which is a word I'm not allowed to say, so forget I said it.

Joanna is distressed to hear that Arthur is the one living in their apartment.

There's no reason for you to be hiding out here. Will should be in touch with things familiar to him. This is going to be hard enough on him as it is. She urges Penelope to take the opportunity, once Arthur is processed, to move back in, to claim the space. We'll try to have a judge issue an order of protection—he'll just have to find some other place to go.

It's hard to have a focused conversation with Joanna; Will is all over the place. He's in and out of the bathroom. It's not hard to imagine what he's up to in there. Rachel has barged in on Will twice standing in front of the mirror with his pants at his ankles, playing with himself. *Test-driving*, she'd joked. This chronic masturbating was new.

The night before, Penelope was tucking him in and could swear he was touching himself under the covers. She made him hold out his hands to her, and she took them and kissed them and told Will that none of this was his fault. That it was okay to be nervous, to be upset by all this, but to know the trouble his father was in—it was trouble of his own making. Will argued with her, using logic to condemn himself for this awful turn their lives had taken: it wasn't true that he, Will, had nothing to do with it; he was there and, by virtue of being there, wasn't it true that he was a participant and, literally, a part of it? Had he not been there—had he, for instance, not been born—

Your father is not well, Penelope said, cutting him off. And this is not your fault, but then Will wanted to explore the definition of *well/unwell*, and Penelope was forced to turn off the light and leave him to his guilt, which, God help her for thinking it, she found annoying.

His guilt, his distress, comes out in myriad unpleasant ways. Like now, for instance, while Penelope sits with Joanna on the living room sofa, Will is ripping out pages from the *Gourmet* magazines that had been fanned out nicely on the table. When Penelope tells him to stop, he argues that he is just pulling out the ads and making the magazine easier to read. It doesn't escape Penelope's notice, nor, she is sure, Joanna's, that the ads Will is pulling feature almost exclusively women in bikinis.

It's been two weeks since Will has spoken with Arthur, Penelope says when Will goes into the bathroom again—the fourth time since Joanna's arrival. Will must miss him terribly, although he hasn't said anything directly to me about it. He hasn't even requested to speak with him.

I wouldn't encourage it, Joanna says.

This advice is in line with advice she's been given by the police and by her parents. People who have vested interests in avoiding family harmony.

Joanna talks arraignment, plea-bargaining, grand jury, pretrial motions. These are television words, the vocabulary of cop dramas, and as such seem, as all of this does, unreal. Penelope can't see how these words apply to her or Will. I like to prepare for the long haul, but we'll hope for an abrupt conclusion. It's in nobody's best interest here to drag this out, especially not Will's. If Arthur is smart, he'll want to end this quickly and quietly.

Will comes out of the bathroom and picks up a remote from the couch. The television blares to life. Will, Penelope shouts, turn that thing off and come here and sit still! Ugh! She rolls her eyes at Joanna, but Joanna gives her back a blank stare.

Can I look in your briefcase, Will says, or is it attaché? Valise?

Will, Penelope says, zip your fly please.

After that visit from the detectives, Arthur redoubles his effort to contact Penelope. He goes to the bakery, only to be told that she has taken an emergency family leave. From the neutral expressions he gets, Arthur is fairly certain they have no idea where she is. At Will's school, he's told Will, too, is on an approved extended absence. These people do seem to know what's going on. They are wary of him, hostile even. But pressing gets him nowhere. Penelope's cell goes straight to voice mail, no matter how many times he calls or how many messages he leaves. The Wrights have blocked his numbers, and when he calls from a pay phone, Constance immediately hangs up when she hears it's him. He travels back down to Annandale and is told by Frank at the front door that Penelope and Will are not there.

I need to see them, Arthur says, no anger anymore, only bewildered desperation. This has all been a mistake.

You don't have to take my word for it, Frank says, but you'll want to clear out before the cops arrive. This time they're apt not to be so nice.

Arthur is at a loss for what to do, so he tries waiting. Eventually she'll contact him. He goes about his professorial duties, marking up papers, meeting individually with students, but he has trouble understanding what people are saying to him.

They come for him at work, the same detectives. He recognizes them approaching as his seminar is breaking up. He is in the hall, surrounded by several students—a confluence of those in his class and those waiting to get into the room they're vacating. The detectives click down the hall and take him by the elbow. Come with us, the younger one says. The students watch, paralyzed. The cops play at discreet, but if real discretion was what they wanted, they would have waited until he was on the street, away from students and colleagues. Or come to his apartment. They are civil but not particularly kind, the minimum courtesy they are compelled to show by law. Who can blame them?

In the car, they show no interest in challenging Arthur's right to silence. He sits with his arms cuffed behind him, trying to find a more comfortable position, but it's no use. Why have they cuffed him? He is obviously no threat. It's an act of cruelty. He talks to the officers, tries reasoning with them, but they don't answer. He threatens a lawsuit. This is abuse, he yells. One of them turns, talks to him about procedure, tells him he will be out of the handcuffs soon enough. His arms go prickly, then numb. He finds himself excited to arrive at the precinct, just to have the use of his hands again. Is he under arrest? It's hard to tell. They did not announce that he was "under arrest," but perhaps they used different words.

The room he is taken to has a mirror. He looks at himself seated at the table and knows that beyond his reflection there are people watching. Is Penelope there? Will? He imagines an audience seated, people fanning themselves with programs, waiting for him to speak. His hands tremble. He notices this from a distance. His heart is knocking at his chest. He waits here like this, alone— watching himself, feeling himself being watched—for a very long time. At first, he assumes it's a ploy, keep him waiting, throw him off balance so he will be more susceptible to saying whatever it is they want him to say. But after some time passes, he's not so sure.

Perhaps the detectives have been called away on other business, forgotten that he's in here. Eventually, Detective Ramirez arrives, accompanied by a man Arthur hasn't seen before. It's this man who does the talking.

He sits across from Arthur and tells him that Arthur is repulsive, that he shudders at having to share the same oxygen in this room with a creature like him. Et cetera. Bad cop, no question.

Arthur says that this is all a mistake, that he just needs to speak to his son.

Detective Ramirez says, If it's a mistake, straighten it out for us. You were momentarily confused, turned on. It happens. Your cock doesn't have a brain. It doesn't know wrong from right.

No, no, no! Arthur says. Didn't I tell you this already, when we first talked? It's a fiction, I made that up. The character is me, but not me — can't you understand that?

So what were you thinking there, Bad Cop says, with your cock stiff, watching your son masturbate?

You're not listening! That never happened.

Ramirez says, According to your son —

You've spoken to him?

He's under a very different impression. He says that every word of it's true.

I need to see him, I need to speak with my son.

The big cop sitting across from Arthur slams the table with his fist and says into the shocked silence, If there is any justice in this world, you will never see that boy again. To do what you did, then write about it and then walk around expecting — et cetera.

Bad Cop scrapes back his chair and comes around the table to stand over Arthur. He puts one hand on the back of the chair and the other on the table next to Arthur and leans down, a bare inch from Arthur's ear. The one thing, he breathes, that keeps your face from my elbow, my knee, my heel, is this badge. But it's okay, because where you're headed there are no badges.

Arthur does himself no favors here. He grimaces and titters. The pinched expression he wears through most of the interview comes from the immense effort of pulling on the various reins of self-control to keep from vomiting or crying or urinating, but it looks to the two detectives, as well as those present behind the mirror, like a sneer. When Detective Cliché breathes his line about badges, Arthur thinks, *Badges? We don't need no stinkin' badges!* He giggles, apologizes. The man smells like a salami sandwich.

Look, Detective Ramirez says after his partner-in-interrogation backs away and sets about pacing the perimeter of the room. Ramirez takes the seat across from Arthur. This is an opportunity for you here. The prosecutor staring at you right now, listening to us in here, once we turn you over to her, she's not going to give a shit what you have to say, why you did what you did, and what you thought while you were doing it. She's a ballbreaker. She's going to take your son and put him up on the stand and make him tell a roomful of strange adults what you made him do. You see, she doesn't care about the best interests of your child or your family. She cares about one thing: a conviction. Rack up enough, and they might give her higher-profile cases, maybe make a jump in pay grade, pay off those student loans before she retires. These are her concerns. If you're not paying attention, I mean really paying attention, to your family's best interests, and instead you're worrying about your own, thinking, What the fuck: let's go to trial, let's make a big deal about this, make it about my book, about some highfalutin point about truth in fiction or fictional truth or whateverthefuck, be a martyr, it can only help my career, right? What's a few years behind bars for the sake of notoriety? You can't buy that kind of publicity—you might even be inclined to think this is your big break. You've suddenly got a platform on which to say all sorts of things—much better than that part-time teaching gig you've got uptown there, wedged into that cramped office. Here you stand out, put yourself on the witness stand, in front of reporters, say whatever crazy shit you want to about art, about writing. People will have to listen, take you seriously. You'll be heard, loud, clear. People will be talking about you for years to come. Until yesterday, you were a nobody, really. Today? It's a whole different story. Critics will take a second look at your second-rate book and say, Wow, we've totally underestimated this guy! Let's do a profile in next month's *New York Times Book Review*. And maybe, if you can walk through the fire of a federal penitentiary, you might just come out the other end some kind of literary hero. The next book will be an instant classic! Right? Do I have the fantasy laid out there fairly accurately?

But you should really be thinking instead of your son on the witness stand. What's that going to be like for him, do you imagine? What kind of lasting effect is that going to have, reliving that incident in public like that, having not only shame to contend with but the guilt of betraying his own father, of doing him in. I don't care what kind of relationship you two have, he calls you by your first name, you call him by his last name, whatever, it's going to be, at best, rough on him. The boy's eleven. Twelve. He's hitting puberty, which is, under ideal circumstances, one of the most trying times in a person's life—and add to that a drawn-out trial of the sort you're fantasizing about. This will be your boy's living nightmare. For years. You've got court, then jail time, appeals, not to mention the civil suit from your in-laws. And you may be pleased that your book's been given a second life—publishers will be happy—everybody's suddenly reading it. Great for you. Great for your publisher. Hell for Will. He still has to walk the halls, sit with, talk with, generally be with, others of his species—and while you're wallowing around in your own filth, this boy is trying to survive his childhood! The daily skirmishes, the treacherous waters, the everyday horrors that all boys face at that age. Your fantasy trial would make that impossible. The boy will find ways to cope, few of them legal, none of them healthy or pointed toward a college degree. The friends he makes will send him in my direction, and before long he'll be sitting right where you are, talking to me about some violence- or substance-abuse-related matter. This is where your fantasy leads.

But your plea just now, to speak to your boy? To straighten this out? That sounded genuine, I can relate to a father in pain, and I know that part of you doesn't want your child to suffer or come to harm. You want your son to be safe and well. That must be true. Detective Angry over here might disagree with me, but you're no monster. Misguided, maybe. But not a monster.

What do you want? Arthur says.

What do I want? This isn't about me, Mr. Morel. It's what do you want? Do you want your son to end up in prison, or do you want him to have a fighting chance? It's up to you.

A confession is what you're saying.

It might help you, too, in the long run. I mean, I'm about as far from a shrink as you can get, but it couldn't hurt for you to get it all out, here, now, rather than having it eating away at you while you continue to keep that mask on, the veil of fiction. Give yourself some relief here, too. Who knows what that kind of peace of mind might do for you. It might free you to become a better writer! I'll give you a pen. Here. And you have a pad right there. My colleague and I are going to give you some time to consider it, to try out the pen, take it for a test-drive there, see how it feels. You might surprise yourself—inspiration strikes in all sorts of unlikely ways.

The officers shut the door quietly behind themselves. Arthur clicks the ballpoint a few times. He looks at the blank yellow legal pad in front of him.

It is ironic, what they are asking of him. Fabricate a confession that his published fabrication is actually a confession. Something like that. These people don't care if what he writes on this pad is true. Corroborate the boy's claim, that's all they want out of him. Then everybody can go home. Except for Arthur.

For the past week, since learning of his son's claim, Arthur has been trying to wrap his head around it. It's clear the boy is angry, that this "memory" is an attempt to punish Arthur for what he wrote. He knows his son to be spiteful, unafraid of putting himself in harm's way in order to harm another or gain something for himself.

There was an incident a few years ago. They were still living at the apartment in Queens. Penelope was out; Arthur was watching Will entertain a friend from school. At some point that morning the two approached Arthur — two privates at attention, reporting for duty — to solicit Arthur's permission to attend the schoolmate's family camping trip the following weekend. Arthur reminded Will of his obligation to his next-door neighbor's poodle — left for two weeks in Will's care. It was an easy refusal for Arthur, himself blameless. Will, he could see, was furious about it. There was no arguing to get his way here. Will was, at the age of nine, a master litigator, adept at winning his way by the sheer relentlessness of his logic. Will wondered if he might hire a friend to take over the responsibility, but Arthur refused. The neighbors had entrusted Will and Will alone with the responsibility. Will and his friend left, but Arthur knew this would not be the end of the issue.

Sure enough, a little while later Arthur entered the living room to see Will and his friend with the neighbor's dog — it appeared that Will's friend was trying to goad the dog into biting Will. The dog was growling, snapping at Will's ankle. Arthur demanded to know what was going on. Will said that if a dog bites a person, it has to go to the pound. It would free him of his obligation and enable him to go on the camping trip. When Arthur told the boy that sending a dog to the pound would be sending it to its death, Will burst into tears. Arthur was both appalled and impressed by the scene. The extreme he was willing to go to get what he wanted, to punish his father for not giving it to him. Was it possible that this "remembering" business was Will's way of making a point? What other explanation could there be — for it could not simultaneously be true that Arthur had made this all up and that Will actually remembered it.

Unless.

What if Will weren't lying? What if he believed he was telling the truth? Was it possible that Arthur's writing was so effective — so authentic, so vivid, so lifelike — it had actually convinced the boy he had lived it? Wasn't this, after all, the aim of a certain kind of fiction? Realism, the hypnotic spell, the continuous dream. A couple of his colleagues at the college took it for granted that the writer's work was that of the hypnotist, the spell caster—exhorting their students toward ever-more-vivid words, ever more "authentic" renderings of a place, an object, a person—Geppetto trying to turn a block of wood into a real-live boy. What if Arthur's spell had worked? His block of sentences had somehow transformed into the memories of a real-live boy?

Or here was a thought: What if what Will said was true? What if it was he, Arthur, who had forgotten? What if this had all happened, but both had repressed the memory because it was too awful? And when Arthur was spinning this fiction out of what he imagined to be thin air, he was merely recalling it? Reading the passage had jogged Will's memory. And now, the boy's claim to its veracity was doing the same for Arthur; in a sense, they were reminding each other about something they'd both tried to forget.

But how was Arthur to know? The scene in the bathtub now existed in his mind vividly, for he had dreamed it up. How was he to distinguish this from factual pieces of the past? What were "real" memories but fragments of remembered sense impressions glued together with, made coherent by, imaginative invention. And what was fiction but the inverse of this? Imaginative invention made plausible by fragments of remembered sense impressions. On one extreme there was fiction, and on the other a memory. And in the middle? For this reason, perhaps, memory was so unreliable. It was suggestible, colored by emotion, infinitely mutable.

One of Arthur's most vivid childhood recollections was of a summer afternoon in a playground in the city—he first figured the event to be memorable because of its rarity. His parents seldom took him places as a child. For some reason, he placed the playground in Washington Square Park, though it could have been anywhere. He was holding an ice-cream cone his mother had just purchased for him from a truck nearby. It was a hot day, and the ice cream, soft to begin with, had immediately begun to melt.

He was perhaps four or five at the time, and in a rage he cried out to his mother, full of blame, Make it stop! The sun is melting my ice cream! His mother laughed and handed him some napkins as it continued to melt down around his hand, and Arthur cried and cried, bitterly, blaming his mother for this misfortune. It was a favorite story of his mother's. As he got older, whenever he complained about something beyond his or his mother's control, she would cry out, Oh! The sun is melting my ice cream! Arthur learned much later from Doc that this event had not happened, or at least had not happened to him. This was an anecdote about Doc's son Benji, years before Arthur was born, in New Jersey. Cynthia had so liked the story, with its neat lesson about surrendering to things beyond one's control, that she co-opted it. It wasn't even clear that she had done this on purpose. It could have been that, in the jumble of stories she would tell about herself and those she told about other people, she had simply gotten mixed up about this one. And yet the memory remained — the hot sun, the vanilla ice cream dripping across his dirt-caked little knuckles, the hot honeysuckle air of the playground trees, the despair, the rage and blame — this memory was undiminished by the discovery that it was a fake.

But what were these sense impressions? Were they bits of other childhood occasions brought together by the suggestion of this anecdote? Perhaps. So it would follow that, if Arthur had made up the scene in the bathtub with Will, Will's "memory" would have to have some basis of truth, wouldn't it? If Arthur had never in his life visited a playground or eaten an ice-cream cone, would he have been as susceptible to his mother's suggestion? Which left him with a troubling thought: Where in Will's young life had he seen what Arthur had described in his book in such vivid detail?

Was it possible that Will had been abused, just not by Arthur? But surely this wouldn't exist as a detached fragment in Will's mind. It would be an indivisible part of that singular event. Well, Arthur certainly hadn't exposed Will to those things he claimed to have seen, on purpose at least, but what if it was something Will

had glimpsed on his own, blocked out because it was too disturbing, and then somehow unconsciously paired the image with the
one Arthur suggested in his book?

But of course all this speculation about memory is founded on
nothing but notions picked up from Hollywood thrillers and television soap operas. And in any case is irrelevant. Arthur can learn
nothing without talking to Will, and it seems Penelope is determined not to let that happen.

He can't blame her, really. What choice has he given her?

He clicks open the pen and writes:

*Once upon a time there was a man who sought peace and happiness.*

*He sat under a banyan tree because this was where wise men told him
that they had come to attain the lasting peace and happiness they themselves enjoyed — where, in fact, the original Enlightened One had come
many generations ago. So the man sat up against the tree's base and crossed
his legs and placed his hands upon his knees. He closed his eyes and tried to
empty his mind of all thought. These were the instructions of the wise men,
who had received their wisdom from other, wiser men who had received
their wisdom from the original Wise One many generations ago.*

*Once the man's mind was empty of all thought, he was free to feel the
warm afternoon breeze with its scent of earth and lilac bloom; he was free
to feel the rough bark of the tree through his robes, the tickle of branches
on his arm, the leaves whispering at his ear; he was free to see the dance of
shadows that the sunlight made as it shone through the trees, the shapes
that played across his eyelids so like a living thing.*

*The shadows were so like a living thing that the man was tempted to
open his eyes, if just to convince himself that it was indeed only the play
of sunlight on the leaves.*

*But he was just being foolish, he thought — for what else could it be?
What living thing could cast such a shadow? Such a large shadow, too.
He had traversed these woods by foot — the tree stood alone in a wide
clearing and, as of moments ago, there wasn't a soul around.*

*He tried to clear his mind once more, to feel the warm afternoon breeze
with its scent of earth and lilac bloom, the rough bark of the tree at his
back, the tickle of branches on his arm, the whisper of leaves at his ear.*

*What could it be, he wondered.*

*What could appear out of the sky from nowhere and cast such a large shadow as was playing on his eyelids?*

*A dragon?*

*He laughed off the notion — tried to, at least — as childish, as pure fantasy, and returned to the breeze, the bark, the branches, the leaves. But once conjured, the image of the dragon was difficult to dismiss. In fact, the more he thought about it, the more the breeze felt on his face like the creature's hot breath, the bark like its scales, the branches claws, the leaves its terrible voice whispering its beastly, ancient language in his ear. The man was gripped with fear. He opened his eyes.*

*And was promptly devoured.*

Arthur puts down the pen. Soon after, Ramirez returns, this time without the other detective. How did it go? He asks, picking up the pad. He reads it, then tosses it back on the table, looking disappointed. You're not doing yourself any favors, he says.

So am I done here?

What you are, Ramirez says, is under arrest.

# 14

# R E U N I O N

ARTHUR IS LED OUT OF the room and down a hall, then handed off to a uniformed officer who cites the Miranda warning to him.

I already signed a waiver when I came in, Arthur says.

Better safe than sorry.

At a bench, Arthur works on catching his breath. Next to him is a handcuffed man with his eyes closed, fingers laced over his belly. This is a main thoroughfare. Uniformed officers escorting handcuffed men and women in suits speaking in a code of cop jargon. Someone in an orange jumpsuit swabbing down the floor with a mop at the far end of a hall. This, he learns later, is what the police call processing. He is being processed. It's a peculiar combination of terror and boredom. The dangerous beyond that waits for him makes it hard to walk, hard to understand the most basic phrases people say to him.

Your name.

My name, Arthur repeats dumbly.

State *your name!*

Yet the bureaucratic formality through which he is guided has all the familiarity of a trip to the DMV and makes him, instinctively, impatient. Impatient for what? To sit in a jail cell for the next forty-eight hours?

After fingerprinting, he is invited to clean his hands with a hand-pump sanitizer that smells like Will's favorite orange soda. He is handed a white board with his name and some numbers on it and made to stand against a wall. A woman snaps a picture, asks him to turn, snaps another.

An officer hustles Arthur down a flight of steps to another room to wait at the end of a short line. Before long, he is in front of a booth where he is made to hand over his briefcase and empty the contents of his pockets, to take off his watch and his wedding ring. He is given, of all things, a receipt, presumably for all that he has surrendered, though the handwriting on it is illegible. When he is given an opportunity to use the pay phone, he dials Penelope's cell. To his surprise, she answers.

I'm in jail, he says.

I know, she says. I've spoken with the woman who is going to prosecute you.

Arthur's face grows suddenly hot, his throat closes, and he cannot speak.

Penelope says, When they release you, if they release you—the prosecutor said that depending on who the judge turns out to be they might or might not—you can't see me. Or Will. We're moving back into the apartment. You'll need to find another place to stay. They're going to petition for an order of protection.

Arthur says, I don't know what to do. I need help. I don't know what's happening, how to fix it.

You do need help, Penelope says evenly but not meanly, only I'm not the one to help you. Good-bye, Arthur. We won't be— and here her voice broke—we won't be speaking again. Oh God, Arthur! Okay? We can't speak anymore.

No, Arthur weeps. It's not okay. Please! But she has already hung up.

His jail cell, when he is finally escorted to it, is already occupied by two other men, both Hispanic. They do not speak to him, nor to each other, which comes as a small relief to Arthur. They seem as ashamed to be here as he is.

The cell is quite large and flooded with even fluorescent light. Two long white plastic benches attached to opposite walls serve for seating and sleeping. There is a stainless-steel contraption in the corner that appears to be one part water fountain, one part toilet. The men each have a bench.

Arthur sits on the floor.

There are no clocks. Terror and boredom. He waits for something to happen, anything to happen. He grows attuned to the noises. People in other cells, one man in particular, talking, it seems, to himself, a monologue of menace and threats. Drainpipes whoosh overhead, and every few minutes far in the distance the solid *clink-clunk* of a heavy door opening and closing. Time grows wildly out of control—hours and minutes exchange places. A moment is an eternity—and then the lights dim. Night, apparently.

But he does not sleep. There is shouting nearby—a scuffle, the nauseating wet slap of a body hitting concrete. Arthur's heartbeat goes wild. One of his cell mates gets up to use the toilet, and the space fills with an eggy garlic stink. He drifts, dreams that the lights have come back on and an officer has come to release him.

Then he wakes—the lights have come back on, and an officer has come to their cell, but instead of releasing him, he hands them sandwiches through a slot in the bars with a latex-gloved hand. Arthur finds he is starving and devours his in a few bites. Tuna or perhaps chicken salad. It doesn't matter, nor does it do much for his hunger. He looks on gloomily while his two cell mates savor each bite.

He goes to the fountain toilet for a drink, but pressing the button merely brings about a weak drool from the spigot.

Returning to his spot on the floor—both his cell mates are up and about, pacing the perimeter, but it's understood that the bench beds still belong to them—he draws his knees up and rests his head on the shelf they form and in this position drifts off into a deep sleep.

When he opens his eyes, an officer is nudging him awake with his boot.

There is a kind of exit interview. It is here that he learns what charges he is being held on: sexual abuse in the first, second, and third degrees, as well as course of sexual conduct against a child in the first and second degrees. The man is from the Criminal Justice Agency. He says he is here to help the judge decide whether to set bail, to release him on his own recognizance, or to remand him. He asks Arthur how he intends to plead to these charges and Arthur says, Not guilty, although it felt, just hearing the charges read to him here, as though a sentence has already been declared. He encourages Arthur to obtain a lawyer as soon as possible. He asks questions about his employment, about his living situation. The man is in a hurry. Though, like all those Arthur has so far encountered in this long nightmare, polite, professionally poised. The questions seem designed to get at whether he is going to—if released on bail—kill his wife, his kid, himself, or flee the country.

Afterward, he is escorted back to his cell. One of the Hispanic men is gone. He nods at the remaining man, but the man does not nod back. More waiting. New people arrive over the course of hours, half a dozen. Arthur finds himself longing for the good old days, when it was just the two silent Hispanics. One of the new arrivals, a bald kid with an angry clotted cut across the bridge of his nose and many earrings up the spine of his left ear, stares nonstop at Arthur, and whenever Arthur looks back, the kid asks Arthur what the fuck he's looking at.

Some hours later, he is released. No explanation, at least not to him. The uniformed officers say to one another in his presence something that sounds like *arrow hard*. He learns later this is an acronym. He has been ROR'd: released on his own recognizance.

He is given papers to sign and keep track of, information about his arraignment. He learns later that a technical hitch is preventing the prosecution from moving forward with the case until late the following week and habeas corpus grants him the courtesy of his freedom in the meantime. He is given back his clothes, his backpack, the contents of his pockets, his watch, and his wedding ring in a ziplock bag. He receives these items like the artifacts of a former life—curious, once filled with meaning, now obsolete. His clothes feel heavy on him now, ill fitting.

He walks out into the afternoon half expecting to see Penelope and Will, despite everything, and finds himself devastated that nobody's there to meet him. He puts the ziplock along with the paperwork he's accumulated into his briefcase, in with the class handouts and marked-up drafts of student work.

His classes!

What day is it? He hurries against the anonymous Midtown crush until he finds a newspaper stand. Thursday. It's two in the afternoon, already a half hour into his three-hour workshop!

He fumbles for his cell phone, but the battery is dead. He hails a cab, a mistake on two fronts: with the traffic, it takes nearly an hour to get uptown—and, two, he has no cash. The driver stops in front of a deli on 114th street with a neon-red ATM sign in the window. By the time Arthur walks through the doors of the Writing Division, out of breath, it is nearly three thirty.

Here, too, he is expecting to be met—by students, colleagues— with some sort of fanfare. After all, it isn't every day a professor gets arrested! But there is no one here to greet him. The work-study receptionist today is a young man he has never seen before, and from the blank look on his face, it seems he doesn't know Arthur either.

I didn't bother checking in on my class, Arthur says. I'm an hour and half late and assume it has been dismissed.

You're a teacher? I'm sorry—I'm usually at the undergrad office. I'm Arthur Morel.

The young man's face registers this. Oh, yes. I mean, they're expecting you. Let me—here he picks up the phone and unsticks several pink sticky notes on the desk to examine them. Here it is— just a minute.

Arthur doesn't bother waiting.

He walks into the chairman's office. He is with a student. They both look terrified to see Arthur, on their faces the same confused sick look the young man gave him when he announced himself.

The chairman, Richard is his name, dismisses the student, who seems grateful to be released.

Arthur sits in the vacated seat.

What are you doing? Richard says. Don't sit down. You can't sit down. Didn't you get the messages? I left three messages. I'm sorry, it's been a rough morning—but who am I to talk about rough, huh? Oh, boy. I'm sorry. But it's been handed down from on high. It kills me, really. I do everything I can for my fellow instructors. I do. This is a rotating chair, and you never know who will be in it next, so. But even before this latest, there'd been rumblings, up there—I've done a lot of wrangling behind the scenes for you already—which you would know if you ever came to visit! Impolitic, Arthur. But that's over with, done. It doesn't matter. We're beyond that now.

He stands, and so Arthur stands as well. Richard holds out his hand, and Arthur has little choice but to shake it. Richard seems greatly relieved to be walking Arthur to the door. He pats Arthur on the back. He shakes Arthur's hand several more times, using both hands to do it.

He says, Think of *Ulysses*. Woolf called Joyce a teenager, picking at his pimples, for writing it. Edmund Wilson thought it was an incoherent mess, as did most of the reviewers at the time. Banned in the United States for what, ten years? But who's getting the last laugh now?

The estate lawyers?

Exactly! That's exactly it. Richard laughs, clapping Arthur on the back. Oh, you crack me up. Why didn't you visit me more often? Anyway.

He sees Arthur looking at the framed photos on the wall. That's Little Freddie, he says. All pictures are of a white dog in various frozen states of romp on a field of grass. These last two are of Little Freddie III. Little Freddie Junior died in '95. The dogs are indistinguishable from one another.

You see? Everybody wants tenure—well, this is tenure. Irate deans and teachers in distress and an unhealthy attachment to

your West Highland terrier. Did you know I seriously contemplated having Freddie Senior stuffed? The day I was awarded a
full-time job here was the last day I wrote a word. Seriously. It
descended like a hex, the same one that cursed Old Man Mitchell,
poor bastard. Don't do it. I'm sure the wife is pushing you to, but
you're better off, believe me.

The word *wife* hangs in the air.

How is she, by the way? I mean, under the circumstances?

Arthur heads downtown, to the apartment. He enters through
the revolving doors. The doorman on duty doesn't stop him when
he goes for the elevator. When he gets off on his floor, there are no
police waiting outside his apartment.

He tries the lock, but his key no longer works. He knocks. He
rings the bell. Is there really nobody home? He puts his ear to the
door. Voices, indistinct, nautical. Unclear whether they are coming
from inside the apartment.

Having nowhere else to turn, Arthur turns to us, down the hall.

We let him in. We poured him a drink. Arthur was, surprisingly, a
man who could hold his liquor. While Suriyaarachchi's and Dave's
talk devolved into slurred declarations of love for Kim Basinger —
and eventually lurching trips to the bathroom — Arthur seemed
generally unaffected.

Arthur related the events of the previous two days. We were
sitting on the couch. Suriyaarachchi had returned to a movie we
had been watching in the other room while Dave sat in the lounge
chair across from us, arms folded, ostensibly listening but really
just sleeping.

"What are you going to do," I said when he had finished.

"What are my options?"

"Do you have a lawyer?"

Arthur took the mouthful of whiskey left in the coffee mug,
filling his cheeks and then gulping it down. "They don't make it
easy for you. Which I suppose makes sense. What's their incen-
tive? They're trying to put you away. One gentleman handed me

'literature.' That was the word he used. I couldn't make much sense of it, written as it is in bureaucratese. Here—"

He clicked open his briefcase and handed me a stapled packet on official New York State Division of Criminal Justice letterhead—or what had once been, several xeroxed generations prior. The state seal was an indistinct black ring, the type barely legible. It billed itself as a "handbook" of the court system meant to "demystify the due process that is every citizen's right," but managed only to, in its own labyrinthine logic, emphasize just what a maze Arthur was about to navigate. It was a kind of terrible thing, that document. It made you aware of a territory of knowledge that, unless you were law enforcement or a habitual offender, you were gladly ignorant of but that you needed to quickly become accustomed to. If you were lucky, you could forget it all as soon as the ordeal was over. It must be the same for the newly diagnosed cancer patient. I thought of Viktoria, just released from rehab with her brochures on borderline personality disorder.

"We're on your side," I said, handing the packet back to him. "Whatever happens." I reassured him that we had no doubts about his innocence and that he could count on our unwavering friendship. It might have been the liquor talking, but I also felt that welling up that I described earlier. It's gratitude, really, that feeling, a reciprocal sense of connectedness with another human being. Arthur sheepishly watched me say this, swallowing, his large Adam's apple bobbing wildly. He gripped the arm of the couch with his large hand, knuckles going white.

Then I said something insensitive, which also may have been the liquor talking. "That stuff you were talking about last week," I said, "the book doing its work, generating story and all that—isn't this exactly what you wanted to happen?"

Arthur looked at me—a long look—then, softly, so that it almost was a sigh, "God, I think so."

It was the last word he said that night. After that he just sat, staring into his empty mug. I got up to go to the bathroom, and when I came back, he was asleep.

Dave was still in the lounge chair, passed out. I checked in on Suriyaarachchi, also passed out, mouth agape, on the leather couch in the editing suite. I sat down on the opposite corner and took off my shoes.

I woke to the distant sound of knocking on a door. Suriyaarachchi was still out cold. Daylight shone through the sharp lines of the blinds' slats. I stumbled out of the editing suite, and the faint knocking revealed itself to be loud banging at the front door.

Arthur was nowhere to be seen, and Dave was racing around gathering empty beer bottles. "Quick, it's the cops!"

I stood and watched him, then went over to the front door. Through the peephole, I saw two uniformed officers, a man and a woman, one standing slightly behind the other.

"Arthur Morel," the one in front called, setting a hand on his holster.

I opened the door and told him my name, invited them in. They took off their hats, scraped their feet on the hallway carpeting before stepping over the threshold. Were they trained to do that? Dave, smiling sheepishly with his armload of empties, offered them a beer, which they humorlessly declined. They asked several questions designed to get to the bottom of who we were and what our relationship with Arthur was. Suriyaarachchi emerged from the editing suite, yawning, hand in pants, and froze. The woman officer asked his name and jotted his answer in her notepad.

"Look," the male officer said once the preliminaries were out of the way, "Mr. Morel can't be here. He can't be within three hundred yards of here. We got a call about a disturbance this morning, a male trying to gain entry to that apartment, banging on the door, carrying on."

"But I have a right to enter my own apartment." Arthur was standing in the corridor that led to the bathroom, sounds of a recently flushed toilet hissing behind him. "My name is on the lease."

"I don't care whose name is on the lease, sir. You settle things in court, once that order of protection is lifted, you can go wherever you want so far as I'm concerned. Until that time, you are not to step foot on these premises."

"Where am I supposed to go?"

"Hotels, shelters if you can't afford a hotel. What about family?" Arthur made a face.

The officers insisted on escorting Arthur out of the building. The elevators and lobby were mercifully empty. Dave, Suriyaarachchi, and I huddled quickly as the officers were parting ways with Arthur. It was decided that we could no longer afford to be without a camera rolling at all times. Suriyaarachchi would rent one while Dave, out of necessity, would cannibalize his editing suite to pay for it and the media costs long term, at least a month, through a trial if it came down to that, keeping enough of the suite intact to edit what we came up with. It was also decided that we couldn't afford to lose sight of our subject. Once Arthur disappeared into the crowd there was no telling where he might go. I would stick with him, keeping Suriyaarachchi informed of our whereabouts.

I went with Arthur to an Internet café, where he checked the prices of the city's seediest fleatraps. The Elk. The Sunshine. Each seemed reasonable—under twenty dollars—until we discovered that the rates were hourly. "We could lend you enough for a week at one of these places, maybe, but what are you going to do after that?" We had discovered that Arthur could no longer access his bank funds. It was a scene that involved our being removed from the premises by bank security. I imagined Suriyaarachchi kicking himself at not being able to get this on tape.

Arthur was reluctant to call Benji. Arthur had blown off his wedding, for which he had not been forgiven. "We haven't spoken in almost three years. It was a legitimate excuse!" He received a Christmas card the year before that showed Benji and his wife, her horsey gap-toothed smile reflected in a young child between them. They were living in Hoboken now. The card had been an olive branch that Arthur let slip from his grasp. However, with my encouragement, he made the call. It was the wife who answered. She was cordial with Arthur, just barely. She gave him Benji's number at work.

*Bastard!* came Benji's voice loud and clear through the earpiece. From the sound of it though, things were okay between them. They talked for nearly thirty minutes. "He liked it," Arthur said, a little dazed after the call. "He said he didn't find it repulsive and that in fact he was able to identify with my character. Which is so unlike him. But he said he liked it." Until now, when I have said that Arthur smiled, I suppose I really mean he smirked. It was a pinched expression, purposeful, meant to highlight an irony or to show that he disagreed with something you had just said. This smile, though, upon reporting Benji's reaction, was different. It was radiant and pure, an openmouthed, teeth-and-gums smile, an involuntary reflex that forced his eyes closed just to make room for it.

Arthur had explained his situation to Benji and asked point-blank for help. Benji seemed grateful to have been asked, to have been allowed to be the big brother, the bigger person. He had passed the New York State Bar some years back, though he was not a practicing attorney. He worked as a legal consultant to a computer software start-up that had managed—with Benji's help, he wasn't shy in admitting—to stay aloft in the turbulent aftermath of the tech bubble's explosion. He would meet with Arthur to talk about his legal options, dismayed that he didn't yet have an attorney, outraged that Penelope—was it Penelope?—had locked him out of his account. The only thing he could not offer was a place to stay. Although Benji was not put off by Arthur's book, his wife had her concerns, and with their son in the house—

"What does she think I'm going to do," he said. "But it's okay, it doesn't matter, it doesn't matter."

While Arthur had been on the phone, I asked Jeeves at the computer in my cubicle why the carriage house was of any interest to the people of Japan and discovered that in Tokyo there was a rather famous sex club modeled after it. The walls of this club were plastered with snapshots of Japanese faces between Doc and Cynthia.

"I know where you can stay," I said.

Arthur looked at my browser window. "Absolutely not."

"Why?"

"We have nothing to say to one another."

"I find that hard to believe. It's been more than a decade."

"You met them. Why would you want to send me back into that?"

"You brokered the deal. You wouldn't have introduced us if you didn't intend on using that introduction later on."

"It was a gift. I knew they'd prove willing subjects for your movie."

"I think you were building a bridge you knew you needed to cross. You see, you want to see them again but don't know how to get over the gap of those fourteen years."

"Are you sure you visited the right house? Didn't they tell you about how I was forced to fend for myself while they had orgies in the basement? It can't be those people you think I'm anxious to reunite with, can it?"

"I'm sorry, Arthur, but you have to. The narrative requires it."

"The narrative."

"Things must be seen to have traveled full circle. Your return to where you were born. Reconciliation with your parents. You'd agree that it makes sense."

"It has a certain Aristotelian logic to it, yes."

"I don't know why you're arguing. It's an inevitability."

"Fine."

"But we have to wait for Suriyaarachchi. He's got the equipment."

The footage of the reunion is wonderful. Suriyaarachchi sets up across the street so that the entire archway is visible in the frame, a blue postbox off on the left. Arthur walks into the shot from camera right, crosses the street, and stops dead center, looking around from the edge of the doorway. It's Cynthia who sees him first. She bounds out from inside and embraces him. Then Doc emerges, tentatively, smiling a kind of nervous smile, leans in — Cynthia still embracing her son, rubbing his back — and shakes Arthur's hand. Dave is out of frame with a directional mic pointed at them and catches Doc saying, "The prodigy returns, the prodigy returns!" Arthur towers over them. They welcome him in with all the ordinary, unmitigated gratitude of a pair of suburban parents. The light is diffuse, the last light in an overcast day, and covers everything in rich blues and violets. The light falloff from the open threshold is steep, so when they usher Arthur inside, the effect is stark — the three of them disappearing into the gloom. We linger here for a while. A woman enters from camera right with a stack of letters in her hand. She slows at the carriage house's threshold to see what's inside, then crosses past it to the postbox to drop off her letters. She double-checks to see that the letters haven't gotten stuck, and it's a kind of echo of her gaze into the carriage house's darkness, which itself echoes Arthur's peering moments earlier, and suddenly this gesture, flowering into a symbol, reveals itself to us: peering into the darkness.

Unforeseen cost, for which Dave must sell both his high-end Beta decks: settling the carriage house's Con Ed bill. In order to shoot, one needed light, and not just household light, but industrial-grade light. We replaced all the bulbs in the apartment with high-lumen daylight-balanced compact fluorescents, the highest wattage we dared, filling in the shadows by affixing several fluorescent strips on the ceilings. It took some getting used to. Much of the initial interior footage shows Arthur and his parents blinking glassy eyed at the glare.

Suriyaarachchi was smart. He sat the three of them down and talked frankly about what it meant to be in a documentary, that the camera would always be on, that there would be no privacy. This wasn't for Doc and Cynthia so much. Total exposure had been their ethos for the past thirty years. This was for Arthur. Suriyaarachchi waited until he had seen some footage before sitting down like this, so that Arthur could get a sense of the project's worth, aesthetically. For all of his failings, Suriyaarachchi had a great eye. The little footage we'd collected was beautiful. His was an instinctive feel for the limits of the digital medium, its tendency to blow highlights, its need for a narrower spectrum of lights to darks; he insisted on spending extra for a video camera that could shoot cinema-standard twenty-four frames a second and a zoom that allowed a wider aperture so he could get that filmlike look of sharp foreground against a lush background blur. Even on the camcorder's tiny screen, the playback was gorgeous. With this seed planted, Suriyaarachchi offered the ultimatum: all or nothing, in or out. He would have enough on his plate without having to worry about Arthur's hand going up whenever he was feeling shy or annoyed. This was the buy-in. Total access. Savvy, having Doc and Cynthia there, too. They acted like plants in a grift, leading the momentum of assent. "Absolutely," they said. "Understood. Total access." And so, Arthur agreed. Suriyaarachchi then had them sign exclusivity agreements. At the time, I thought this part was overkill, but a month from now at the height of it, I would look back at this moment and think he had been prophetic. They were not to talk to any other media outlets. This required a sales pitch. Here he talked numbers: dollars and points and box-office profits. "This film will be huge," he said. "People will be lining up to hear what you three have to say. Guaranteed. But only if they haven't already heard you say it. You start taking interviews with morning talk shows, syndicated media, you will be depleting the demand for this movie and hence any profits you might see from it. It's in your hands. You can do what you want, play your chips however you like. You won't be surprised to hear that I think you should let me hold on to them, that I will play them wisely. But it's up to you. Just remember, your silence is a very valuable thing. Don't give it up too easily."

I was sold. We all signed the papers and shook hands, and then Doc passed around the pipe, and we got high. Even Arthur. We sank into our seats and listened to Doc go on about how great Arthur's book was.

"You sound like the dust jacket," Arthur said. "I hate those raves they put all over it, like subliminal messaging. *This book is* fantastic. *You will* love *this book. The writer is a* genius. You know? It's like they don't trust readers to come to their own conclusions or the book's ability to sell you on its own merits." But Arthur seemed pleased. We ordered takeout from the Indian place up the street, and Cynthia brought us down to the basement to drum up bedding and a spare mattress or two.

It's interesting to watch Arthur and Cynthia interact in this footage. She's watching him almost continuously, touching him, caressing his face, even as she is directing us in the search. Arthur stands somewhat stiffly, not rejecting the affection, weathering it, accepting perhaps that this is how it must be, eyes down, gauging for a moment when she is not watching and only then a quick glance up, eyes bleary with pot and exhaustion, and then back to his shoes.

With the lights on, the basement seemed less like a serial killer's lair and more like a basement. Cynthia looked through the junk. "This mattress"—she patted it, leaning against the wall, went in for a sniff—"with clean sheets shouldn't be too bad. Artie, look." She tapped three large boxes, stacked precariously. "Your old stuff. We had to put it down here when we let go of the upper floor." Looking for bedding, which she swore was down here, we negotiated past percussion instruments of all types, stacked paintings, half-finished sculptures, office chairs, printing supplies, and dusty darkroom equipment, eventually locating some blue sheets inside a large Styrofoam cooler.

Although we hadn't planned or discussed the matter, the Morels assumed we would all be staying with them. We took a wordless poll, a shrug and an eyebrow wag, and agreed. The best place to make our beds, we decided, was down here, out of the way. We would keep our equipment boxes here as well, neatening and personalizing a strip of wall directly under two dim basement windows.

After the others headed back upstairs, Arthur said, "I'm glad you came. I wouldn't want to be here alone."

When we emerged from the basement, Doc was unboxing our Indian food. He seemed overjoyed at the occasion. "It's like old times, Cyn. It's like we've got our collective back."

Cynthia said, "A carriage house reunion!"

We knew there was a chance that Arthur might not return from the arraignment if the judge decided against posting bail, so we took the opportunity to get as much footage of this reunion as we could. We followed them around for the next few days, asking questions, getting them to interact. We set up the camera as we had last time, at the doorway facing in, and set up three chairs. Dave had the idea to bring up Arthur's boxed things as a tool to get him talking. Doc had found a thick snarl of Christmas tree lights in the basement that he spent an entire morning untangling — checking and replacing bulbs until the whole string was lit — and put it up around the archway. It was a pretty sight, especially when it began to snow.

They sat side by side, coats on, appreciating the general holiday swirl. To a passerby, they would have appeared to be like any ordinary nuclear family: son, shoulders hunched, between two proud parents. It was an illusion I myself indulged as I listened to them tell the rest of their story.

The afternoon following the Spring Concert, a Sunday, Cynthia and Doc receive a visitor at the carriage house, a fellow mother who had been in the audience to witness Arthur's performance. She is concerned. For many years, she explains, she was employed by the New York City Division of Child Protection as a caseworker, and although she is now in private practice and no longer working for the city, she still feels it her moral obligation to investigate and, if necessary, report her findings.

It is not a good time for a visit. The plumbing in the century-old house is in perpetual disrepair and finally, two weeks prior to the woman's visit, reached a critical state of failure. A pipe on the second floor has sprung a leak and flooded the floor below. Nothing has been done to address the problem, save cutting off the water supply. After two weeks, the smell of mildew has become unbearable, as has the smell of human waste because, though the toilets no longer flush, visitors to the house continue to use them.

But even were it not a bad time to visit, it wouldn't have been a good time to visit either. As the concerned former caseworker sits on a couch on the ground floor, two wooden milk crates end to end at her shins forming a makeshift coffee table, she counts fifteen small prescription bottles and a confetti of pills, all in plain view. Men and women stark naked saunter up from the basement and disappear into other parts of the house. From above, a sound presiding over all, the thin strains of a Bach solo partita.

Cynthia is perplexed by the stony manner in which the woman relates what Arthur has done onstage. It was a prank, she says. How brilliant! My son's like a young Duchamp, painting mustaches on the *Mona Lisa*, or that other one of his, the urinal, rubbing elbows with the *Venus de Milo*. Don't you see? Why are you looking at me like that? Oh this — Cynthia is in a robe that, despite her efforts, keeps falling open to expose her bare breasts. Should have worn a bra. Cynthia laughs.

When Doc had invited her in, the woman asked for a glass of water, and Doc is in the kitchen now, straining cloudy, particle-rich rainwater from a jug through a coffee filter, to little effect. He returns with the glass just as the woman is attempting to rise from the couch. It's on our list to have fixed, Cynthia says. There's a lot that needs fixing around here as you can see.

Doc holds out the water, which the woman takes. The three of them watch the delicate swirl of silt settle in the glass. The woman hands back the glass and tells them that she has seen plenty, too much to ignore, and that the next visit they should expect will be from Child Protective Services.

Doc would occasionally receive calls from Benji, who was all grown up and living in Queens. During that first one, he told Doc he was tired of being angry and wanted to have a relationship with his father, despite his father's unrepentant wretchedness. Doc had been overjoyed to hear from his son and asked after Sarah and Dolores. Sarah was teaching at Rutgers, and Dolores was happily remarried to a man Benji described as "well meaning." They spent almost two hours during that first phone call reminiscing about happy times, Benji filling him in on what kind of life he had lived without his father around. Benji gave Doc his number, said to ring whenever the urge struck. Doc had been moved and grateful for the call, and yet he never reciprocated. The months would go by, and eventually he would receive another call from Benji. Doc would explain that their phone service was limited to incoming numbers, which was true enough. The phone bill was among the utilities on which they were perpetually delinquent. A flimsy excuse, but Benji accepted it, not seeming to mind the one-sidedness of things.

And so Benji is surprised to receive Doc's call that Sunday and listens with dismay at their predicament. What can I do, Benji asks. I'm not a lawyer yet, and I'm not in any position, financial or otherwise, to help you fix up your house.

There's no time for that, Doc says. They could be banging on our doors tomorrow!

Arthur packs a bag, several changes of clothes, and a few books from the carriage house library. The rest he leaves in his "room," the back half of the top floor, curtained off with a sheet. The ceilings are low, and if he stands on his toes he can press the crown of his head hard against it. The windows are made of a pebbly opaque glass reinforced with wire that forms a diagonal diamond pattern on the panes. They do not open but glow most mornings with a warm light that fills the room. A music stand is planted in the center like a street sign. Mattress in a corner against the wall, above it poster reproductions of Picasso's Stravinsky and Delacroix's Paganini. Against the other wall, the old saloon upright. His violin in its case on top of it, along with a clutter of personal effects. He offers a last look but takes nothing with him.

Benji has a room ready, as well as ground rules and a plan of action. You have to go to school, he tells Arthur. That's rule one. As long as you're staying with me, you will be a full-time student.

Now, where you go is up to you. Joel Braverman High is one option. It's a short walk, and from the way my father talks, you won't have to do much to distinguish yourself as a top student. But there are obvious drawbacks, namely getting the shit beat out of you on a daily basis. The other option—he's been holding two textbook-shaped tomes and now he hands them to Arthur. Prepare for a GED and the SAT and send you to college. From the way my father talks, you wouldn't have to work too hard to make this happen either. Advantages, obvious: you don't get the shit beat out of you. Drawbacks, I'm not sure what kind of paperwork maneuvers we'll have to do to make this happen.

As it turns out, however, option 2 is unmaneuverable, which leaves option 1 as his only choice. And despite the certainty with which Benji described his fate, Arthur manages in his year at the school to avoid coming to any violence whatsoever. He has two things going for him: entering as a senior offers him some status. Also, he is tall, towering over most students and many of the teachers. He attends every one of his classes with relish. He is perplexed by those who would choose to stay in the stairwells and bathrooms instead. Why would anyone want to miss out on this? It's all so fascinating! He keeps to himself and comes home a roundabout way to avoid running into the few people who might want to do him violence, spending the waning afternoon in his room reading, typing out his assignments on Benji's IBM Selectric.

In September of 1986, he enrolls in Queens College, and two and a half years later, as the fall semester comes to a close, he has earned enough credits to graduate with a bachelor's degree in humanities. It was here, in his final semester, commuting from class one rainy morning, that he met a lovely young woman with a snake tattoo down the left side of her arm.

"Even now," Arthur said, "after everything, I'd still board that bus. Take that seat, introduce myself."

In writing *The Morels*, Arthur set out to research the mysteries of his own heart. Its central question: Did he truly love his wife and son? His conclusion, which he was only able to draw once the book had done its work in the world, was yes! He did love Penelope and Will, more than he could ever have imagined.

"You're just saying that because they're lost to you," I said.

"Does that invalidate my conclusion? Isn't this sometimes how we learn what we feel about things? From the day I left this place, I have never once missed it or anyone in it. I feel no connection with my mother or her common-law husband."

"Your father," I said.

"If you wish. He has never been that to me."

Cynthia and Doc stare straight ahead into the camera as Arthur speaks. Their faces register no particular reaction to what seem to me to be deeply cutting words.

"What about Annan," I said. "The one from Afghanistan. The violinist."

"Annan was different. I kept in touch with him after he left, after I left."

"So he was more like a father to you."

"He was a mentor."

"And when did he leave?"

Arthur thought about it for a moment and then, sensing where I was headed with my questions, said, "You're oversimplifying."

"It was spring of '85. Let me guess, a week before the concert? Two weeks?"

"About that, yes."

"And you were angry."

"Hell, yes I was angry! These two had driven everything that was good from my life. They didn't know what they had there in that house, even when they lost it. Nothing had changed as far as they could tell. They were perfectly happy to be pounding away in those idiotic drum circles. Of course, they were high all the time, so what did they care?"

"And so you thought you'd, what—teach them a lesson? Get them in trouble? What were you trying to purge?"

"I thought you were smarter than that."

"I'm looking for the truth."
"The truth is more complicated."
"Well, then explain it to me."
But that was all he would say.

# 15

# B E N J I

LAST FOOTAGE OF THE NIGHT. I wasn't aware Suriyaarachchi had been filming until he played it back the next day. We are squatting in the basement, charging batteries, labeling cassettes. Dave says, "Aren't you a little creeped out by all this? Basically, we're palling around with a child molester."

I say, "You think he's guilty?"

Dave says, "His son claims he's guilty. His wife thinks he's guilty. The New York Department of Justice is betting that twelve jurors will think he's guilty. Who am I to disagree? What do you think?"

I say, "He's innocent." Then, voicing a fear that has been brewing, one that Dave has just encouraged, I say, "Well, he's convinced he's innocent."

Dave says, "He's also a little nuts, isn't he?"

We asked Cynthia the next day. "Do you think he's guilty?"

She said, "I know men. I can look into a man's eyes and see what he wants, what he desires. And what he doesn't desire. Men are transparent that way. I look into Arthur's eyes and see he just doesn't have it in him."

We asked Doc and he said, "What if he did? I don't see the big deal here. Fathers jack off. Sons jack off. They jack off together, and everybody wants to make a federal case about it. And to the follow-up question that I know is coming—no. I never did, with Arthur. We took baths together occasionally. Did I ever get a hard-on? I mean, little boys aren't my thing, but if you're asking if I ever had a hard-on in this situation, my answer would have to be, I always had a hard-on, so maybe. But not for Artie. I mean, come on!"

When Benji came over, we asked him. Brushing off his jacket and stamping the snow off the bottoms of his shoes, he said, "It's the most natural fear in the world, when your wife's pregnant, when you hear you're going to be a father, when your mind gets down into the deep dark thousands of ways there are to fuck—to mess—things up. That was certainly the way with me. I'm not an obstetrician, I'm not a nanny. I'm not used to being around naked children. What will it be like spending part of your day touching, washing, powdering a little vagina, a little penis? There are people who are turned on by such things. Could I be one? Or okay, you're fairly sure you're not in that rarefied category of weirdo, but what about when your child gets older? At what age will that natural attraction, that natural appetite for youth, at what age will I begin to feel that kind of desire for my child? But then of course your child is born, and then you're a father, and it's the farthest thing from your mind! You can't believe you even thought such a thing."

I said, "But Arthur didn't write this book before Will was born. He wrote it when Will was what, nine? Ten? So what's the book about? Is it a what-if scenario? What if that natural fear you describe never left? What if that fear came to pass? Or did he really feel these things?"

Benji said, "I thought you were on my brother's side."

"I'm just trying to understand."

"Understanding isn't going to keep him out of prison. Now get that thing out of my face."

"Benji!" Cynthia cried. "Here to save the day!"

He offered her a disdainful squint.

Doc took Benji's hand. "Good boy," he said. "How's your mother?"

Benji was burly, fat even, the same height as Arthur. All the Morel men shared a similar hairiness. Although Benji was clean shaved, his cheeks were dark with bristles just below the surface. He was balding and kept his hair shorn in a crew-cut ring around his head. He wore a solid blue tie with a matching blue shirt. When he sat down and shed his jacket, he rolled his sleeves up to reveal his furry arms.

The news he brought was not good. A grand jury had chosen to indict. He had to represent himself as Arthur's attorney to dig up what was he able to find.

"But you are my attorney," Arthur said.

"I'm not a trial lawyer, Arthur. I can help you, but I can't try this case for you. You would be in better hands with a public defender."

"I'll represent myself then."

"That's ludicrous. You're not representing yourself. Do you want to go to prison?"

"A public defender's going to want me to compromise, to plead to a lesser charge."

"Says who? Have you spoken to one?"

"I've spent the past ten years of my life watching *Law & Order* twice a week. I know how these things go."

"From what I've heard they have a pretty good case. Will's statement to the investigating officers. A psychologist if they need one. I'll file a motion to see the rest. They haven't decided if they'll put Will on the stand yet. The guy I talked to said they were considering his welfare, but my guess is that if they're saying that, he's not as solid as they'd like him to be. In which case they may enter your book into evidence and spin it as an indirect confession. Their expert will be able to make that sound plausible."

"What about our expert?"

"You mean like a literary critic?"

"A what? No! How about someone who can prove that Will can't possibly remember something that didn't happen!"

"Oh." Benji thought about this. "There's that lady in England. She's kind of a crusader. She's helped overturn a number of these cases where twenty-five years after the fact the victim will suddenly remember an abuse from childhood? She gets all kinds of death threats and hate mail. But her thing is mostly about debunking hypnosis, that the way the therapists ask questions ends up suggesting false memories in these quote 'victims.' It's worth a phone call, but I'm not sure it can really help us here."

Doc had put together a pot of frankfurter stew so that we could get him on tape making it. Benji accepted a teacup of the stuff and slurped and chewed it while he talked to Arthur. Doc said, "Packet of franks, can of sauerkraut, can of tomato paste, potatoes, and water. That's it. A couple of bucks and you've got dinner for eight."

"It's very good actually," Benji said, "thanks."

Benji's connection with the city administration ("law school buddy") told him that Arthur's case would be prioritized on the docket. Giuliani had taken a special interest in it, rumor went. That fall there had been a group show at the Brooklyn Museum with controversial pieces apparently funded by the NEA, photographs of a crucifix in a glass of urine, a collage of the Madonna constructed with bits of dried elephant dung. The mayor was further galled to learn that these reprehensible nobodies' new notoriety, thanks to him, had caused their artwork to skyrocket in value. He was in no mood to hand out any other such gifts during his tenure. He was looking to take care of this quickly and quietly, before the city tabloids got wind of it.

"If this is true, you're actually in a good position to plead," Benji said. "But you don't want to do that. Right."

They parted ways at the open arch, agreeing to meet at the arraignment in two days. In the meantime, Benji would figure out what was involved in filing pretrial motions and file everything he could get away with.

They hugged.

For the rest of the afternoon I went around with Benji's brusque admonishment in my head. *I thought you were on my brother's side!* While Suriyaarachchi and Dave were helping Cynthia prepare dinner, I tiptoed down to the basement with the camera. Rewinding to the spot from last night, I watched myself sneer, *Well, at least he thinks he's innocent* — playing the moment over several times. What *did* I believe? Arthur had never struck me as a particularly sexual person — what mystified me as much as anything else was that he would be moved to any procreative urges at all. The idea he had gotten a woman pregnant took me by surprise at first, and some time to wrap my head around. Penelope's talk of their young lives together — the abandon with which they would give themselves over in the bedroom — was like being told of a grandparent's youthful exploits. Something that existed in an altogether different plane of reality — the distant past, another age. I had no trouble believing that passage was fiction. But then, I was just as mystified by why he would write it. There seemed no good explanation — the death of literature, *The Satanic Verses*, the French book on catharsis — all the intellectualizing in the world couldn't get at the specificity of that hallucinatory scene. There were any number of taboo topics equally as shocking. So why this? Because, Will claimed, it was true. It seemed to offer the missing piece that made everything fit. But *fit* in this case meant *child molester*. And to see Arthur talk was to know he believed firmly in his innocence. *Well, at least he thinks he's innocent.* I didn't know what to believe. I let my finger linger for a while over the RECORD button before finally erasing all outward evidence of my doubts.

After Doc and Cynthia had gone to bed, we spent some time with Arthur's old things. He knelt on the floor, sorting through a large cardboard box, arm in up to his elbow. "Something must have spilled on these," he said, pulling out a stack of old photos. "They're stuck together." He gingerly peeled the top one off and set it on the ground in front of him. He did this with the next one, and the next, as though he were dealing out a game of solitaire. "It's hard to know where to begin. They make this place sound like some kinky commune paradise out of a John Irving novel. But it wasn't, certainly not for me, and I wish I could somehow dispel that myth. Okay, now here's one." He held it out to me. It was a photograph of a young Cynthia passed out in a chair, the whites of her eyes showing, skirt hiked up to her lap to expose a thatch of pubic hair. It was forensic, the image of a cadaver. "My mother, ladies and gentlemen. Or here." He handed me a blurry snapshot of a younger Doc holding a boy of about seven. Doc is laughing; the boy is wailing. "There was a thug that lived with us who for some reason disliked me tremendously. He would mete out all sorts of unkindnesses. He would claim the others in the house were jealous of my talent or would whisper in the ear of someone he was talking to and stare at me while he did it. He would tell me of something wonderful I just had to see; excited, I peered into the corner to discover a rat, disemboweled in the teeth of a trap, its body still moving. I suppose he wasn't that different than a mean older brother. But one who had just returned from Vietnam, a little unstable, whose parents were never around to keep him in check. My father, if you want to call him that, tried to get me to laugh off his pranks, thought they would toughen me up. Here, I believe — you can just make it out in the background, that footlocker? I have just emerged from it after nine hours locked inside."

"This guy stuffed you inside?"

"Oh, no. He told me something about the cops being after me and that I should hide. And then he clicked the padlock on the lid and walked away."

"And your mother?"

"I believe she'd been trying to *get in his pants* at the time. Her words. And the threat of cops was not far-fetched. There was some tension there." He handed over a series of lurid close-ups of busted lips and ugly inflamed bruises. "A raid like that. The bellowing, my mother screaming, the sounds of splintering furniture, shattering glass. Truly frightening. There'd be outraged talk afterward about police brutality, and someone would take pictures — evidence — and threaten to sue, but it would quickly peter out."

"What were they after?"

"The cops? Who knows. Money? Some other thing? I tried to shut it out. Here." A photograph of a mutt. "That was Handsome.

I loved Handsome. One day he trotted out through the front gate into the street and was hit by a car."

"You were there?"

"I held his limp body in my arms. And this was Candy." Another photo, a cat. "I was less partial to her than I was to the dog, but not so much that I'd have wished on Candy the horror that befell her: found in the back of a closet on the second floor, dead of starvation. Her and her litter of nine newborn kittens. But hold on, you say. How could this happen in a house *overrun with people*? Wouldn't somebody have heard the cries? Heard the scratching at the door? Smelled the accumulation of urine and feces—or at the very least the ten rotting corpses? These are good questions, ones you ought to keep in mind as you consider the paradise those two describe."

As he sat there picking through his things, silhouetted against the lamplight that pooled around the strewn contents of several boxes, the image of the teenage Arthur reemerged before me—the gangly kid, unwieldy with his limbs, Adam's apple bobbling as he searched for a word or phrase. Lost, tormented, in his own home. He went on to describe other everyday horrors at the carriage house, the homeless junkies wandering in off the street, the state of perpetual, almost violent neglect—the kitchen counters crawling with mold and maggots, the bathrooms in a continual state of overflow, swarming with blowflies, the stench of rot and raw sewage in every corner of the house, inescapable—aware of it but unable to control it. The stark difference between his life and the lives of others became especially clear once he began his Saturday visits to the conservatory.

"It was a home without walls," he said. "There was little separation, little privacy. At that age when I began to develop a sense of modesty—seven or eight—I did what I could. I put up a curtain, changed my clothes when I was sure I was alone. I don't think my mother knew what to make of me. She thought of this bacchanalia of hers as a gift. She wanted to treat me to a childhood of limitless pleasures, but the more I saw of it, the less I liked. The only pleasures I truly enjoyed were those that I had to earn. This is what my own experience taught me. The fruits of a piece well learned, the pleasure in the muscles of each finger, the piece itself and its ability to bring about the stern approval of a jury committee. Even the pleasures of an unrequited crush were sweet. The borders made it pleasurable, what I couldn't have, so that pining in a sense was an earned pleasure. I wanted to remain a virgin, to remain *virginal*, and earn the fruition of that pleasure. But how could I, in this place? Hairy bodies everywhere, the stink of sex in the air along with the rot. For all their talk of pleasure, these people engaged in theirs with the enthusiasm of a nap. The moaning sounded like snoring to me; it was perfunctory, robbed by its daily indulgence of any appeal. The infantile revelry that my mother and my namesake engaged in, this was cheap and ugly, even at the age of twelve I could see it. I wanted out. To purge myself of it."

He picked up a score from a stack on the floor, a bright yellow Schirmer edition, dog-eared, its cover torn along the spine. Penciled fingerings and one-word invectives, likely scrawled in haste by his teacher: *Lightly! Fingerboard! Throat!* A foldout sheet of linen paper taped to the last page on which was typed:

CADENZA
Accept all offerings of food [24 hours prior];
Refrain from defecation [24 hours prior];
Ingest one dose laxative [39 minutes prior];
Remove pants and squat;
Think impurest thought imaginable;
Empty bowels completely.

"Lest you think it was merely an improvisatory whim up there on that stage. As you can see, it took planning. I practiced for days, so that I could better know my digestive tract and how those laxatives worked. You see? On that stage, it wasn't anger. I wasn't trying to get anybody in trouble. It was transformation I was after. *Le Pur.* Blood washing blood. And you know what? It worked. Less than a week later, I found myself living with Benji, in a normal, quasi-suburban house, enrolled in a normal, quasi-suburban school, pining after normal quasi-suburban girls. Alchemy, I tell you! Those Greeks were really onto something."

"But when I hear *purge*," I said, "I think vomit. Wouldn't it have been easier to just stick your finger down your throat? Wouldn't vomiting have been more like what you were after?" God help me, I was beginning to think like Arthur!

"Absolutely," he said. "And yet as much as I would have liked to rid myself completely of that place, I wasn't so naïve to think that I might purge it as though it were a poison. I knew it was already in me, partially digested, a piece of bad meat lodged in a fold of my intestine. And my only chance would be in showing it the other door, hoping that whatever I had already absorbed wasn't fatal."

I spent much of the night tossing and turning, thinking about that casually tossed-off litany of terrors Arthur had endured here and his unique—and uniquely disturbing—trapdoor exit from the place, yearning for what must have been to him a holy grail—a normal life with a wife and child. But by the time he found it, he was just too irrevocably broken to hold on to it.

Despite our talk about the possibility of Arthur not returning after the arraignment, we all assumed that he would not be remanded without bail. Benji suggested to the judge, quite reasonably, that as a respected educator at one of the city's top schools and born-and-bred New Yorker with parents who owned property in Manhattan, Arthur posed no flight risk. He had every intention of sticking around for the trial; there was no reason to burden taxpayers with his room and board. The ADA presenting the case, Joanna Brady, was as tall as Arthur, with sharp features and eyes whose natural wideness left her looking perpetually surprised. She conceded Arthur's status as a New Yorker but none of these other things. He had been fired from his position at the university, was estranged from his parents, estranged from his wife and son. He had threatened his in-laws and broken an order of protection. There was no telling what the man was capable of. We had been prepared for a high bail. Doc and Cynthia had calculated using the carriage house as collateral. But the figure uttered by the judge dwarfed this offering, an absurd sum that meant to keep Arthur behind bars for the duration of the trial.

We also assumed that after obtaining a press pass at the Mayor's Office we would be able to join the section set aside in the courtroom for those with such passes and be allowed to film the trial. Our worst-case scenario had only one official "pool" camera, and we would have to get permission afterward to use the footage. Trials were being videotaped in every courtroom in the country and aired around the clock on cable; it was the age of Court TV. But it was also the age of O.J. Simpson, and in the aftermath of that case judges were becoming shy of cameras, afraid of having to play ringleader in a high-profile circus. And if Benji's source was to be believed, perhaps the judge was feeling pressure to keep proceedings as low-key as possible. We considered sneaking in a hidden camera, but Benji assured us that we could be in a lot of trouble if the footage was ever made public. So, no cameras.

The last footage we have of Arthur—ever, as it turned out—shows him dressing for court in the bathroom at the carriage house: shaving, washing his face, combing his hair, tying his tie. But it's clear from the nervousness that leaves several nicks he has to stem with tiny bits of toilet paper, that has his fingers trembling as he struggles with the silk loops around his neck, that there is more to this than appearing clean-cut before a judge. He is dressing for Penelope and Will.

We have a shot of the three Morels as they exit, a kind of reversal of the exterior from a few nights before. We are inside, looking out. We don't have the whole archway in the frame—the lens doesn't go wide enough to capture it all—but along the bottom of the frame we have the rugs, a milk crate, the corner of a chair. The Morels are centered, exposed correctly, their backs to the camera, facing the street. Outside is bleached white, a bright glare made brighter by the snow. And as they walk out, the effect is one of disappearing into a brilliant field of white.

At the arraignment, Arthur stood with Benji while the charges were read. They seemed to go on forever. Arthur and Benji said in unison, "Not guilty." Arthur kept turning back to scan the room, but Penelope and Will were not here. With the exception of his petition for discovery, all other requests that Benji had filed were denied. The judge was a jowly codger who didn't seem to have full physical control of his head. It would jerk back and forth, side to side, and he would move his body around in an effort to catch up with it. He lectured from his high perch in a nasal sneer.

His lecture that day went, "The case before us has high potential for antics, to become a grad seminar in ethics and the elusive and ultimately unknowable line between truth and fiction.

"Bah! This court will not tolerate irrelevance. The truth is plain, earthbound, knowable. The line is clear. This accused is either innocent of the charges or he is guilty of them. We are talking about a man's freedom and professional reputation. We are talking about the violation of a young boy's innocence. The stakes are high, too high for such antics. So to minimize the chance, and out of respect for the stakes involved, this court will proceed carefully but expeditiously. It is Monday, December thirteenth. I will hear opening arguments the twenty-seventh, two weeks from today. Two weeks for voir dire and discovery and all matters of preparation. Happy holidays indeed."

Benji protested, said that more time was needed.

The judge said, "What's the problem? This week you line up your ducks, next week you pick a jury, and then we begin. As far as I understand it, there will be no forensic rigmarole and the prosecution will supply you whatever you require toot sweet, yes? We can continue this discussion in chambers, but you'll see I'm quite stubborn in these matters."

Arthur was remanded until he could post bail. The bailiff cuffed his hands in front of him and led him out a side door, Benji following on his heels, talking in his ear until the bailiff warned him off.

Benji came by some hours later filled with theories and rage. "Two weeks? It's absurd! Judges allow more time to traffic cases. This is a man's life! I'll tell you what I think. I think they're in cahoots, judge and prosecution. Why didn't she object? Because she doesn't want more time. She's ready to roll. She tries several of these kinds of cases a week. She's a specialist. The judge knows I'm not a trial lawyer, knows I'm out of my depth. He's trying to force my hand, get us to plead. Make this thing go quickly into that good night, it's exactly like Tomlinson said. Two weeks! But Arthur doesn't want to plead — what am I supposed to do? Fucking Giuliani. You know that prick used to be the New York DA, right? He was notorious for all sorts of underhanded shit. During those junk-bond cases back in the eighties, he didn't have enough to prosecute these guys, but he would have the police come down to where they worked and drag them out in handcuffs, out through the front door, and put them in a squad car. Just for the show of it, just to humiliate them. That's who we're dealing with here. And it's not only about the time; it's about the timing, too. Trying to squeeze us in before the end of the year. What's coming? The millennium. Oooh! This thing is generating so much noise now, with all the stockpiling and the Walmart rednecks crapping their pants over it, that's all you're going to be hearing about for the next month. By then, this case will be over and done with. But what would happen if he set the trial after the New Year? Millennium bullshit blows over, now the media's looking for something to fill the vacuum, and there it is, 'Art on Trial,' front-page news. That's why he set the bail so high. Keep Arthur away from the press, away from book signings. High potential for *antics*. Or maybe this old fucker is actually scared about the coming millennium. Maybe he wants to put away one more pervert before the lights go out. All I know for sure is timingwise, this thing stinks. How am I supposed to prepare for this? Christmas is coming, my wife's on me about gifts and cocktail parties, my son wants me to take him to

Santa this weekend. I'm a legal counsel for a software company, for Christ's sake! I need more time!"

We returned to Dave's. The editing suite looked like a crime scene, the command center dismantled, rack of blinking equipment an empty shell, leather sofa gone, brushed-steel coffee table and matching coasters gone, cockpit chair gone. All that remained was a computer, a monitor, a few stray cables, and neat divots in the carpeting where the rest had been. I was sent down the hall to see if Penelope was in the mood to talk or, at the very least, to not call the police. They wanted an interview. I told them that she wouldn't be interested, but they kept after me until I relented.

She answered the door as though she had been expecting me and, as it turned out, she had. The prosecutor's office had instructed her to make available to the defense Arthur's effects. She let me in.

"I went ahead and packed up his desk drawers. There were also a few shoe boxes on the top shelf of the closet, a plastic bin under the bed." It was all stacked neatly against the wall by the door.

We both considered the boxes for a moment, then she said, "You're not here for Arthur's things."

"I've missed you."

"Really, don't." She opened the front door. "I'm in the middle of—and I have food on the stove."

"Tell me what I can do to get you to look at me, Penelope. Just look at me."

She looked at me.

"Okay, now kiss me." I puckered up. At this, a slight smile. "Just kidding," I said.

"You weren't."

"I wasn't. It was worth a shot."

"I'm not mad at you. I know it seems like I am, but I'm just trying to survive this. I figure if I can just get through the next six months with my head down—I'll look up, and things will be saner. They'd have to be. It can't get any more insane than it is right now."

"Where's Will?"

"With my parents. They've taken him to a show. And don't think I haven't noticed that Trojan horse you're holding very non-chalantly at your side. There's no way you're coming any farther into my house with that thing."

I held out the video camera. "I thought you might want to see what's on it."

"Arthur?"

"Over the past week or so."

She sighed and let the door go. The whistling of a teakettle had been sounding, which she now went into the kitchen to deal with. She emerged with a steaming mug, set it down on the kitchen table.

While I cued the tape for playback, Penelope cracked a window and lit a cigarette. I handed her the camera. She sat down cross-legged on the couch and watched, making a visor of her hands over the small flip-out screen. I plugged in a set of earbuds for her, and she put them on. To give her some privacy I stepped out onto the patio. It was frigid. Their view faced west and allowed an unobstructed patchwork quilt of tar-black and silver-painted roof-tops, not high enough to see the Hudson River but high enough to catch a glimpse of just how broad this tiny island was. The days were getting shorter. It was not yet four thirty, and the sun was already setting directly ahead. A little more than a dozen of these and it would be setting in another millennium. Until now, if you wanted to indicate a time far in the future, you placed it here, on this horizon—or just beyond it. I was still too caught up in the sci-fi novelty to think what this new dawn might really look like. And yet here we were, on the threshold, the merger of present and future, fact and fantasy. I looked south toward the carriage house and wondered what Doc and Cynthia were planning for dinner.

I went back inside. "Poor Arthur," Penelope said. She had taken the headphones off. "How could it be that for eleven years I never saw it?" She wiped her eyes and nose with a corner of her sleeve. "He really is crazy."

"I think the stress has gotten to him," I said.

"No, he's still Art. That's my Art. I just never put it together. But how could I not have seen? Between his mom and dad he looks like a big, goofy disabled kid."

"Do you think he's guilty?"

"I don't have a choice but to believe it. My obligation is to Will. If he says this happened, then it happened. To keep second-guessing him like I have been—I can't second-guess him anymore. I'll go nuts. And I can't afford to, as I said. My obligation is to my son."

"So you hope he's convicted?"

"I'm not like my parents. The things my father says, what he hopes will happen to Art in prison, are just awful. I don't want these things to happen. And my mother is unforgiving. Art's dead to her. She says it doesn't matter whether he's guilty or innocent. The damage is done."

"Could you ever forgive him?"

"If he's found guilty?"

"Either way."

"I feel this thing has gotten out of hand. I'm not in control of it, Art's not in control of it. Neither is Art's brother or the prosecution. It's taken on a life of its own. But once it's over, we'll be in control again, and once that happens, who knows how I'll feel, what I'll do."

Our return to the carriage house coincided with a visit from Benji, bursting with good news. We had been granted more time. The first day of trial had been pushed back three weeks, to the middle of January. "We have over a month now, which still isn't enough time, but it's more than we had."

This wasn't all. He'd also been contacted by one of Arthur's former students. A groundswell of support was growing at the university for Arthur's "plight," for what some saw as yet another vicious attack in Mayor Giuliani's war against the arts. There were flyers everywhere around campus, a burgeoning Myspace page with thousands of fans. They wanted to help in any way they could. A legal defense fund was being created, and Benji had at his disposal a small army of smart young volunteers. Were these two bits of news related? Benji had to wonder. Did the judge (and the administration) see the futility in trying to keep a lid on this case and the danger of giving Arthur legitimate grounds for a mistrial or at the very least a guaranteed overturn on appeal? "Or maybe it was a schedule conflict. Who knows, who cares. I've got more than a month now and some extra hands. I'm happy."

Benji wasn't the only one. Doc and Cynthia had news as well. They'd been contacted by a few former members of the Carriage House Players. Koko, Winston, and one of the Brooklyn Trio. "They're coming out of the woodwork now that they know there's a documentary about this place," Doc said. "They're an incorrigible bunch of hams." How had these people learned we were making a documentary? This was really our first inkling, along with the student who'd contacted Benji out of the blue, that this thing, as Penelope put it, was taking on a life of its own.

Ticulous was Samuel Weintraub, currently of New Haven, Connecticut. He had heard about Arthur's arrest and sought out Benji to see how Arthur was holding up. It was interesting that he was not one of the "incorrigible bunch of hams" to call the carriage house. Several of the others, after getting in touch with Doc and Cynthia, contacted us directly to demand a part in our movie. Not Samuel "Ticulous" Weintraub. Samuel was reluctant to speak with us, and only after a hard sell would he agree to an interview. We took Metro North and were met at the station by his gunmetal-gray Camry.

"You gentlemen may find you've wasted your time," he said while we set our equipment in his trunk. "As I told you on the phone, I have no interest in reminiscing fondly about my youth or trashing those with whom I spent it. The past is the past." We assured him that we were only interested in hearing him speak about whatever, and whomever, he wanted. If he was willing, we would also be interested in getting his thoughts on Arthur's current situation.

Samuel's bald head was like shiny plastic; he had a bushy gray mustache. Under his down jacket he was wearing a suit and a tie. He was the director of Freshman Composition at the University of New Haven, which he described as a "glorified commuter school." Area students attended to take degrees in forensic medicine and fire science. His wife was a Yale professor. They lived on a lovely tree-lined street off Whitney Avenue. We set up in the bay-windowed breakfast nook by the foyer, trying not to trip over a friendly calico cat who kept rubbing against our shins. Samuel was concerned about us filming his "good" side. He wanted to see how he looked in the monitor and shifted his seat several times on the padded banquet, trying different positions with his hands on the small antique table before he was satisfied.

As promised, we refrained from asking questions, which worked out fine because he was a nervous talker, and this situation for some reason made him very nervous. He went on about a great many things having absolutely nothing to do with Arthur or the carriage house. He devoted a lot of time to the topic of national politics — Clinton's impeachment, the upcoming election. He talked about the departmental politics his wife was forced to endure at the School of Management, as well as the politics of his own department.

Eventually he did come around to the subject of the old days. "It's a shame what became of them. What became of us, really. But that's the problem of art in a country like ours. On the one hand you are stuck in a box. The only way to survive as an artist is to follow the market, no matter whether you're a television scriptwriter or an MFA grad in plastic arts. And yet, on the other hand, you are free to do what you like. Free to do anything. Anything. And this makes some people crazy, this much freedom. In a sea of freedom, it's easy to drown. Sometimes, when I was still a practicing artist, I found myself wishing that I was living in an oppressive totalitarian regime. It would be easy to create daring art under those circumstances. I would be a hero for saying anything that strayed from the party line. I could martyr myself. Such opportunities don't exist in a free society. Here, it's much more difficult to be a hero. Some think they can do it by becoming the *iconoclast*, that by declaring themselves an iconoclast, they are taking a stand, but here's the irony. Isn't it the single most quintessentially American gesture, this declaration of independence? To say you are different from other Americans is to say what every other American says about himself. Snowflakes. All unique, all identical. The American who declares himself an iconoclast ends up anything but—he's a stereotype and, therefore, an oxymoron.

"But who am I kidding? If I had been making art in an oppressive totalitarian country, I wouldn't be the dissident. I don't have the energy, the staying power. No, I would be one of those state-endorsed propagandists, extolling the patriotic virtues of the regime."

"You use the word *hero*. Do you think Arthur is a hero for writing that book?"

"It was inevitable that he would write that book. His poor wife and son. They never had a chance. When I was in school, I was always skeptical of literary time—the way in those nineteenth-century British novels a character could be so single-minded, pining after some woman for an entire lifetime, or a single childhood experience determining the course of an entire career. This just doesn't happen in real life. In real life we are not so singularly defined, so easily plotted. We pine, and then we forget; we fall in love with someone else. As children we want to be all sorts of things. I wanted to be at one time or another a fireman, a mailman, a pilot, a tennis pro, a clown, an oil baron, and a veterinarian. For some reason I'm thinking of *Great Expectations*. The character Estella, orphaned as an infant and brought under the care of bitter Miss Havisham, jilted at the altar so many years prior, never to recover. She teaches Estella to hate men, to be as cruel and unfeeling as Miss Havisham is, so that she will never have to have her heart broken on her wedding day. Too neat. In real life, Miss Havisham would have gotten over her disappointment, and Estella wouldn't have proved to be so entirely malleable to become the cruel mistress Miss Havisham had in mind. Estella would have rebelled or run away.

"But I have to marvel at just how direct a trajectory those two have sent Arthur on. That boy was wound up from conception, destined wherever he went, whatever he did in the world, to go off in somebody's face—in this case quite literally. He was Cynthia's own Exploding Inevitable, wreaking havoc wherever he went. Destined to destroy his own family."

Benji—too busy now with preparations and the particulars of his own life to visit us at the carriage house—offered his updates by phone. He had been forced to subcontract his work at the software company so that he could work full-time on the case, a cost defrayed somewhat by the legal fund. He was in to see Arthur at the detention center at Rikers every other day and was becoming concerned about his brother's well-being.

"He said a few things today that brought me over to the in-house psychologist to see about some kind of suicide watch for him. He says things that I don't understand. There needs to be a 'final confrontation,' that the only way to resolve this was by 'the son slaying the father.' I tell him nobody's killing anybody, that we've got a good case and soon enough he'll be a free man again, that he just has to hang on and trust me. Then I try to get tough and say, 'Listen, if you don't want to fight this thing, then just make a deal with the prosecution and be done with it. Stop wasting my time.' He's not shaving. The circles under his eyes lead me to believe he's not sleeping, and his cheeks are sunken, which leads me to believe he's not eating either. I thought he'd be happy about these breaks we've been given—the time, the support—but each new bit of good news hits him like a blow. The only strategy he wants to talk about is taking the stand. We've got a team of Columbia Law students who think Arthur would be his own worst enemy, but he's adamant."

Taking the stand? This was troubling news, when one considered what sorts of things Arthur had done in the past with a platform and an audience.

# 16

# C A D E N Z A

CHRISTMAS EVE, NEW YEAR'S EVE, voir dire.

Soon enough, the first day of trial was upon us.

Each day leading up to this day, it seemed inevitable that we would be saved from having to climb these stairs, if by nothing else the apocalypse, but January 1 came and went without incident. It was surreal. The broad flight before us, the massively looming courthouse blotting out the sun. There were newsvans out, telescoping satellite poles fully extended; they didn't appear to be here for us, though. Dave remained outside with the video camera, and the rest of us took up the back of the line. Doc panicked when he saw the metal detector, but Suriyaarachchi and I talked him down enough to see him safely through it. Cynthia did a little dance as the guard wanded her down. We traveled several echoey loops of marble hallway to the room Benji had given us.

The place had none of the grandeur of a *Law & Order* set. No varnished oak banisters, no ceiling-high windows blazing great shafts of dusty light. This place was small, windowless; the acoustic-tile drop ceiling deadened sound, and the fluorescent banks did the same to people's faces, making this place look more like a hospital waiting room. It was packed, which isn't really saying much, as there weren't many seats. We thought we'd arrived with time to spare, but the line at the metal detectors must have eaten through it; the bailiff had just finished his spiel, and the judge was gaveling for people to be seated. We slipped into the back row by the door.

Who were all these people who had come to watch the trial? I looked for familiar backs of heads. Penelope was up front in an aisle seat; I recognized her wild black hair. Her father sat next to her. Will was not in evidence. The familial math suggested that he was spending the day with his grandmother.

The ADA stood and pointed at Arthur, presumably — I couldn't see him over other people's heads — and said, "Some would say that this man is a monster. How else can one explain what would move a person to commit an act of incest with his nine-year-old son? To then write a book which recounts this act in all of its lurid detail, publishing it under the guise of fiction. Some might guess that this was a sadistic act meant to torment his family, to rub their noses in what he had done. But the evidence will show us that he is not a monster. Arthur Morel is a man. A very troubled man, who did something awful in a moment of confusion three years ago. The evidence will show that he wrestled with himself about this act for three long years and finally, in a way, using the publication of his book, decided to turn himself in." Penelope's mother was right. The damage had already been done. Even if Arthur was found innocent on all charges, even if Will recanted everything he had said, there was no going back from this.

After the ADA had concluded her opening statement, the judge granted a short recess so that Benji could adjust his remarks. We moved up a few rows for a better view of Arthur's orange-jump-suited back. For a week and a half now there had been enough money in the legal defense fund for Arthur to post bail, but Arthur had argued, quite reasonably, that it would be better to have the city hosting him with room and board; every dollar spent should be going toward securing Arthur with the best defense he could afford. While they were on the subject, Benji brought up the possibility of replacing himself with any of the half-dozen private defense firms who offered to try this case pro bono, but Arthur wouldn't hear of this either.

Benji stood. Even from where we were sitting, it was clear he was terribly nervous. His eyes were glassy, and the notepad he held highlighted the trembling of his hands. He approached the jury box. "The prosecutor is right about one thing. Arthur Morel is not a monster. But not because she *says* he isn't, but because Arthur Morel is *innocent*. I don't know what would possess a man to write such a strange story, whether it was a self-destructive streak in him or a touch of the crazies, and I'll leave it to the critics to explain what kind of merit there is in such a book, but I do know this. The man before you, my brother, is no child molester, and I intend to show you how and why beyond all reasonable doubt." By the end of his remarks, Benji's face was pouring sweat.

True to his word, the judge sped the proceedings along, and after a break for lunch, the prosecution began laying out its case. There wasn't much to it: Will's testimony, Arthur's book, an expert witness. The court clerk played Will's recorded statement and read the relevant passage from the novel into evidence. It seemed that Will hadn't been subpoenaed to testify, which Benji's experts interpreted as good news. It meant that Will had become shaky as a witness for some reason. Either his story had changed since he'd talked to the police, or there was something wrong with his manner—that he seemed to be lying or was unsympathetic in some way. Benji considered calling him to the stand for the defense, against the prosecution, but Arthur stood in the way of this, too. "Is he trying to get himself convicted? Is that what this is? Somebody please tell me!" The fact of Will's absence was more good news. Just sitting there, Will was a persuasive tool in the courtroom. His presence would have meant the mother was of the same mind as the prosecution or that the prosecution had enough pull with the mother to make her do it. His absence suggested the opposite. It meant Penelope had become uncooperative.

Day 2 opened with the prosecution's psychologist, who had spoken to Will, testifying to the cues Will gave that indicated his story was not a fabrication. He also gave his opinion of Arthur's book, which he saw as enough like Will's version of events to be mutually corroborative. He had also spent time with Arthur at the detention center; in his deteriorated state, Arthur seemed to him very much a man wracked by self-loathing and guilt. The psychologist admitted that, on first reading, the book was perplexing, and he hadn't known what to make of it, but after interviewing Arthur it became clear to him that it was a cry for help. Arthur couldn't turn himself in, for whatever reason, so his unconscious had done the job for him.

On cross, Benji said, "Is it possible, in your educated opinion, that William Morel is somehow confused? That he is mixing up what he's read with a memory?"

"No. That's just not feasible."

"Yet in the most recent issue of the *American Journal of Psychiatry* you write about a man who became convinced that Garrison Keillor was bugging his phone. Can you tell us how the man came to this conclusion?"

"He was an avid listener of *A Prairie Home Companion* and grew suspicious that the skits he heard resembled the contours of events in his own life. Eventually, the man came firmly to believe that the shows were direct transcriptions of conversations that he'd had throughout his day. The only explanation for this, he reasoned, was that Garrison Keillor was somehow recording his life."

"So in a sense, this man mistook fiction for real life."

"This man was in a florid state of paranoid schizophrenia."

"And how did you conclude that?" A few chuckles at this, even from the witness.

"Well—" He composed himself and began down a jargon-studded road.

Benji stopped him. "What I mean is, did you check for bugs? In the patient's apartment? Did you question Garrison Keillor?" At this point, an eruption of laughter in the gallery of the courtroom.

"No."

"And why is that?"

"I can only conclude these leading questions are designed to get me to tell you that *A Prairie Home Companion* is a scripted, fictional radio show."

"Right. And wouldn't you say that knowing this helps in your diagnosis of the man as a paranoid schizophrenic?"

"There are other ways to reach that—"

"But in this case, would you say it helped?"

"I couldn't say."

"If, for instance, Garrison Keillor were this man's father, and Mr. Keillor made skits about their life together—"

Objections from the prosecution, sustained by the judge.

The witness said, "William Morel, in my opinion, is not schizophrenic."

Benji pressed, but the man would not budge. It didn't matter. He had accomplished what he'd set out to do, planted the seed.

With the exception of rare moments like this, from the standpoint of pure entertainment, the trial was a disappointment. The ADA seemed aware of her counterpart on television and was attempting somehow to play herself in that role or remind us of it. But it came off like the stiff acting in a high school drama production. Benji, too, nervous though he was, tried to play it up in a way that missed the mark and left people groaning in pity. He bugged his eyes or furrowed his brows and scratched his chin. These were his two best moves. It was clear he'd been coached and that he was not a particularly adept student. Presiding over them, the wobbly, bobble-headed judge sustained and overruled objections in equal measure, offering the droll one-liner when the occasion called for it or a sharp rebuke, stopping one or the other of the attorneys in their tracks. Unlike the attorneys, the judge wasn't playing a role—if he was, it was a role that he had played for so long that he had inhabited it completely. Who was it who said that eventually our face takes on the contours of the mask we wear? Something I read in college, probably. I thought of it while watching these three performances. And wondered again about Arthur, his role in all of this. When the time came for him to mount the stand, what sort of performance would be required?

Mostly, the court proceedings were of exactly the sort you might expect out of a place with laminate faux-wood paneling and no apparent ventilation: interminable, bureaucratic, the narrative thread lost in the picky back-and-forth about wording and what could and couldn't be said or what this one meant, exactly, when he used that phrase. Two pigeons fighting over a piece of pretzel. I found myself glad to have been banned from filming it, as no doubt the footage, when we came to edit it, would have sat cold and inert, and the three of us would become gridlocked about what to do. It would have been the Winnebago crash all over again—a moment that seemed, when we planned it, a centerpiece, a riveting climax, but instead proved to be embarrassing and unwatchable.

By the closing gavel of day 3, the prosecution had rested its case. Benji argued for a reprieve but was denied one, and so the following morning began the defense's long parade. We came early to secure a seat up front behind the defense table.

When they brought Arthur in, Cynthia burst into tears. It was the first good look she had gotten since the arraignment. No doubt the new beard and the outsize jumpsuit had something to do with it, not to mention the sallow greenish light of those fluorescents, but there was no denying that he was a man transformed. He looked caged, some aboriginal man abducted and brought back to the civilized world to be marveled at. There were scrapes and bruises on his wrists and ankles, and his body trembled. He turned, and it seemed to take him some time to process us.

Cynthia said, "Oh, what have they done to you?"

Arthur smiled. He mouthed, *I'm fine.*

Suriyaarachchi nudged me with a folded *New Yorker*, gesturing for me to take it. He pointed at an article I was meant to read. It was an essay about the tradition of autobiographical fiction. It mentioned Arthur's book several times, praising it and its author.

From the second paragraph: "*The Morels* is one of those books that is memorable not for the story it tells or for its characters or for the quality of its prose, but for an episode within it—Don Quixote tilting at windmills, young Proust dunking a madeleine in a cup of tea—we don't remember who or what or why, but we remember this [. . .] and these actions come to stand for the book itself, synecdochically, becoming a visual thesis upon which all the rest hinges."

I handed it back to him, and he gave me a look—tugged mouth and wide eyes—that said, *Pretty good*. Meaning, for the movie. Suriyaarachchi didn't care much about Arthur's fate apart from how it might affect the fortunes of the movie. Or, rather, he did care but only in the way an art collector, heavily invested in a certain artist's work, might care about that artist's declining health. I hated him for this, in no small part because it highlighted these same feelings in me. I was not immune to the excitement of filmmaking, nor did I fail to see that Arthur's plight might be seen in a certain light as good entertainment, something ultimately that would sell.

Benji called his first witness, another psychologist. He had spoken with Arthur a few times at the prison. The man had a different opinion of Arthur and his book than the prosecution's witness, and so, in effect, these experts canceled each other out.

I looked at the roster of names on the witness list, mine among them. It would take days to get through. It seemed Benji was looking to win through attrition, and I wondered if this was what the judge had meant by "antics." If Benji had gotten the continuance he'd asked for—three months—how long would that list have grown? And the judge, despite Benji's rantings, was quite fair, to the point of permissiveness. Even I could see that Arthur's professionalism, his soundness of mind, his kindness and loyalty as a friend, had little bearing on whether or not Will was lying. Amid the unceasing calls to relevance from the prosecution, Benji persisted, and the judge allowed his witnesses to have their say. I suppose Benji had to work overtime to counteract the effect of

Arthur's very presence there before the jury—a wild creature, capable of anything.

The psychologist on the stand had also spoken with Will, but his evaluation revealed nothing that could be used to our advantage, so during questioning, Benji left it alone. The ADA, however, was very curious. She had him read several passages from his report, which revealed Will to be a somewhat distressed but otherwise normative eleven-year-old.

"What observations led you to conclude that William Morel was stressed?"

"His body language, mostly."

"What can you tell us about his body language?"

"Deep breaths, fidgeting. And he spent much of our session rubbing his genitals."

"Rubbing, how?"

"He was sitting in a large upholstered chair opposite me and held his hands clasped together, fingers threaded like this—down at his crotch. He would press them up and down against his groin when he talked. Quite unconsciously, I thought. In this context it appeared to be a response from stress. This is not unusual. He seemed reluctant to be there, speaking with me. I got the feeling that it made him nervous. He spoke of not wanting to get his father in trouble. The rubbing seemed to be a strategy for comforting himself, calming himself down."

"Did William Morel ever exhibit symptoms of a dissociative nature?"

"What sort of symptoms do you mean?"

"Trouble distinguishing fantasy from reality?"

"Not in our time together, no."

On redirect, Benji managed to bring things back in balance by getting the psychologist to admit the possibility that the diagnosis of a dissociative disorder involved more than a single one-hour consultation, that were Will to have one, he could present quite normally for days—even weeks—at a time.

It was five days of this, at the end of which came me. And Arthur.

—⌣—

If the courtroom was a bore, the same could not be said of the goings-on outside. The first day I had seen a few people with small flip pads taking notes and wondered if they might be reporters. That evening, eating dinner at the carriage house, Doc pointed at the television with a speared floret of curried broccoli. It was the final segment of the local news, usually reserved for items that would be introduced with a phrase like *Now* here's *an interesting one*. It showed a small insert of Arthur's dust-jacket photo. Doc stumbled to his feet to turn the volume dial on the small portable television just in time to catch the anchor say, ". . . but the author claims he made the whole thing up. Wonder what the *next* book will be about!" The following day, a CBS-affiliate anchor and her cameraman approached Benji and his assistants on their way up the courthouse steps, and that night we all waited impatiently through the day's leading stories for the footage, which appeared along with a court sketch of grizzle-bearded Arthur. We cheered, and Cynthia declared, "Our fifteen minutes have begun!" The day after that, it was all three of the major networks following Benji up the stairs, along with half-a-dozen photographers clicking and flashing in their faces. It became the evening's top story. The day after that it was the front page of the *Post* and the *Daily News*.

Benji had been right. In the vacuum of the millennium story, this one entered to fill the void. There were other "bigger" stories going on inside the halls of 100 Center Street that week—a grisly murder, a mafioso on trial—but this was the one that caught the public eye. The Brooklyn Museum exhibit was still fresh in people's minds. It was also a time of brazen sexual transgressions, from our president's to nannies caught on video to the several high-profile cases of teachers tried for statutory rape—both male and female—and the trial of Arthur Morel found itself as somehow the quintessence of all this, the last straw perhaps. So in spite of what the judge had said about what this trial was and wasn't, to those following its progress outside the walls of the courtroom, it became a referendum on the limits of artistic freedom. The papers took pleasure in the possibilities of his name, which—if you substituted *e* with *a*—seemed designed to comment ironically on his situation.

The announcement, in the middle of all this, that *The Morels* had been nominated for the Faulkner Award was rocket fuel that set the debate aroar and helped launch it past the local news and into the seven o'clock national slot. Two *New York Times* op-ed columnists took up the debate over several days, one arguing for literature's return to its historical imperative of extolling our better angels and the other arguing for the prerogative of literature to be whatever it needed to be.

And as unreal as this short account of Arthur's ascent may seem to read, this was exactly how it felt to live through: unreal. Dreamlike. It happened so quickly. We sat watching the news at the carriage house, the five of us, the day's papers scattered around us, scarcely believing what we were reading, what we were seeing.

Suriyaarachchi clapped Doc on the back. "What did I tell you? Okay? This movie is going to be enormous. Your two sons will see this thing through, and Arthur will come home safe—and be able to share in all of this. Just trust, just trust. And I know the phone is tempting you right now"—ringing off the hook with offers, *Hard Copy, Jerry Springer, Larry King*—"but your silence is worth more down the line. How does it feel to be the father of a rock star?"

But I think Suriyaarachchi misinterpreted Doc and Cynthia's disbelief at all of this. Because what Arthur had achieved here wasn't fame; it was infamy. He was tarred by the tabloids, already tried and found guilty by New Yorkers at large. And who could blame them? His own book seemed to convict him of this crime, and even assuming his innocence, the act of publishing it alone was thought by most who were talking about it to be a kind of abuse. It was, at best, a perverse and downright mean thing to do.

But Doc and Cynthia didn't understand the hostility. "Even if he did do it," Cynthia said. "Is it really something to get this worked up over?" They had thought themselves one with the city.

Their open door to the sidewalk had been a thirty-year testament to this. Neither of them had ever considered there were people who thought differently than they. To find out, finally, that most of the city thought they—and their son—were repulsive freaks must have been a crushing blow.

From a moving car raw eggs were pelted at the carriage house, whipping through the open doorway. One connected with Doc's shoulder. He lifted his shirt to reveal a palm-sized welt. After this the doors remained permanently closed. All through the night intermittent hollering from outside reached us down in the basement, a ghostly noise, the pounding of fists on the metal garage door echoing somberly, an uneven drumbeat. In the morning, we found scrawled on it MONSTERS in dripping purple spray-paint.

On the morning I was to testify, we pressed through a throng of jeering pedestrians before making our way up the courthouse steps. Suriyaarachchi following with the camera merged with a dozen others taping our ascent.

We were made to wait. Benji and the ADA were conferring with the judge in the emptied courtroom. A guard stood at the doors, which barred any substantive eavesdropping, but I could see the jury was in attendance as well.

I took a seat on a bench, across the narrow hallway from Mrs. Wright and Will. They were sorting foil-wrapped items out of a plastic bag. While Mrs. Wright kept a wary eye on me, Will was pretending not to notice. It was the first time since the trial began I'd gotten more than a passing glimpse. He kept a blinkered focus on his sandwich, which sat on its foil wrapper in his lap. He carefully removed the top and peeled off two soggy lettuce leaves. In his hunkered-down posture—his twitchy fingers, the dark hollows under his eyes—I saw someone utterly besieged. As though he were ducking not only me but everyone else in the world. I detected something else as well. Guilt. Not the guilt of a betrayer. The guilt of a liar.

Will and I needed to talk.

The opportunity presented itself a few moments later when, speaking to Mrs. Wright, his lips formed the word *bathroom*. Penelope and Frank were not far off, standing against a wall. Frank had been keeping his eye on me. I got up, casually, ahead of Will, and rounded the corner, making my way to the water fountain just outside the men's room door. I leaned in for a warm coppery draft, lingering until I saw Will's sneakers pass my line of sight.

I rose, wiped my mouth, and ducked in after him.

A line of enormous urinals like marble bathtubs. Will was at the one in the far corner; I took the one next to his. "You're lying," I hissed into his ear. "Aren't you?"

Will blanched, stepped back a few paces, fumbling with his zipper.

A tall gentleman emerged from a stall and walked over to the line of sinks. Will and I watched as he rolled up his sleeves, pumped out some soap from the dispenser, and washed his hands. The man became aware of us watching. He stared back through the mirror.

After he left, I crossed over to the door and kicked the rubber doorjamb into place.

Will ducked into a stall and latched it shut.

I stood for a while staring at the stall door, long enough to consider the implications of being caught in here, intimidating the lead witness.

Then, very softly, came Will's voice. "I don't care what happens to him. I hate him." His voice sounded different in here—thin, crystalline—cupped by the dozen marble basins, as though it were being transmitted from somewhere else.

"How can you say that? If you knew what you were saying, how jail would be for a man like your father—you wouldn't say such a thing."

"I wish he were dead. We'd all be better off. Mom's so sad, and it's because of his lies. Why shouldn't I lie, too? Then he'll be put away, and it'll be over, and we'll all be happy. It's what he deserves for writing what he wrote about me. Grandma says it. Grandpa says it. Joanna Brady says it. Even Mom says it."

"Will," I said. "I'm not defending what your father wrote. It's a terrible thing. But what you are doing here is wrong. Evil, in fact. You know that, don't you? Are you evil? Do you want people to think of you this way?"

"I'm not evil," he said. The stall door rattled. "I'm not evil!"

"Then you've got to make this right, Will. You've got to tell people the truth."

Someone was knocking outside. Voices.

"I tried," Will said.

"What have you told them?"

He opened the stall door, peered up at me. "I said I was confused. That I'm not remembering right."

"That's not the same as telling them you lied."

"But I can't! I'll get into trouble. Serious trouble—you don't understand. Please." Tears wobbled in his eyes. "Please don't tell Mom."

"Will, this is bigger than you getting into trouble. I have to tell her—don't you see, I have no choice."

"Please don't. I'm begging you. Listen, okay? I'll tell her myself. Let me do it. Please."

More banging. Frank's voice: *My grandson, that's who!*

"Okay," I said. "Fine. Now switch places." I pushed past him into the stall and hopped up onto the toilet, pulling the door shut. "I'm not here," I whispered, crouching.

Benji was able to get me five minutes alone with Arthur. I waited for him in a closet-sized space down from the courtroom. A glass door looked out onto the busy corridor.

Arthur was led in by a guard. The guard removed the shackles, then let himself out; he stood watch on the other side of the door. Arthur sat. He really was unrecognizable in his orange jumpsuit, with his hair so shaggy, his beard so thick.

I relayed the details of my recent conversation with Will, and Arthur nodded, frowning slightly. Then, still nodding, said, "That's not going to work."

"What's not going to work?"

"If Will confesses he was lying, then the prosecution will have nothing."

"Exactly!"

"There won't be a trial. But there needs to be a trial, for this to work there needs to be . . . you see, Will has to accuse me, to put me away for—"

"Arthur. This isn't a novel. This is your life."

He licked at the corners of his mustache. "You need to stop him," he said. He was agitated. He ran his fingers through his hair. "You need to talk to Will."

"I've already talked to Will."

"Before he confesses to Penelope! Don't you see? Once he tells Penelope, this will all be over."

"Come on. There has got to be a better way to atone for things, Arthur. Stop being so grandiose. You've hurt your wife and son, yes. And you will one day find a way to get them to see how very sorry you are for what you've put them through. But this is not it. This is suicide."

"It has to happen this way."

"You know what? I've tried. Fuck you, Arthur. If you want to stop Will, ask him yourself."

"I can't! Nobody will let me talk to him!"

"Well, figure it out. I'm done. I refuse to be a part of this game." I stood.

"Okay, okay," he said. "At least don't tell Benji. Do that for me. Please. Don't tell Benji."

"Too late," I said.

I had been put on the witness list ostensibly to speak to Arthur's sanity, to have me talk about *The Morels*—there had been debate among Benji's team on the merits of trying to explain to a jury Arthur's nuanced reasons for writing the book. Benji argued that it would be better to offer some explanation, however incoherent sounding, than none at all but had run into resistance, yet again, from Arthur, who wouldn't hear of testifying about it. Which was where I came in.

But when I told Benji of Will's confession, the plan changed. Benji was ecstatic. He clapped me painfully on the back. "We can put an end to this farce today," he said. "Right now!" He also asked me several times whether I wasn't making this up, that he would totally understand my motivation to do so, but this was not the way to help his brother. I could go to jail for perjury.

I assured him that I was telling the truth.

He nodded. "Okay," he said. "Okay!" He told me to be myself and reminded me again that whatever I did, seriously, not to perjure myself.

If such a thing had crossed my mind, the thought would have evaporated upon being sworn into the stand. It was a powerful ritual that humbled me before judge and jury and those hundred pairs of eyes in the gallery. It had been years since having this many eyes on me, and that sweaty-palmed dread brought me back to the Concerto Concert. The judge up there might have been Mr. Strasser at the podium if one swapped the gavel for a baton. Even the way he looked down at me—the slight nod, the smile in the eyes—reminded me of the way I had been looked at by Mr. Strasser, the warm good grace of being judged as sound, satisfactory. I felt the same sense of responsibility to do my best, to honor the attention I was being given.

From up here I had a clear view of every face in the room. Arthur watched his hands move in front of him on the table. Benji sat next to him, checking his notes. I looked for Penelope and found her in her usual spot up front, behind the ADA, her father next to her. I tried meeting her gaze, but she would not look at me.

Benji stood, addressed me by name. "How long have you known Will Morel?"

"Since September."

"Four months. And in that time, have you ever known the boy to lie or practice willing deceit?"

"Yes," I said.

"Would you describe these occasions for us now?"

I looked over at the jury box, a subway car of faces — black, Asian, white, Hispanic. A mute city chorus to witnesses this tragedy. At first they had been a serious-minded bunch, several of them taking their own notes, all eyes forward, ears craning to catch every word. But by day 3, several had succumbed to the boredom of the proceedings. At one time or another they would nod off, a couple openly reading newspapers. But once the story broke nationally, they seemed to snap back, to return to the solemn duty they'd sworn to uphold. At the end of the day yesterday, the judge had ordered them sequestered in a nearby hotel. This morning they sat wide awake, the full force of their attention coming at me from that side of the room like heat.

I told them about the lying game Will learned at school and had us play around the table during our Thanksgiving meal. I told them about the pranks Will boasted of once we'd gotten to know each other. The bumper prank, wherein while crouching he would slap the rear bumper of a car trying to parallel park and when the car stopped would lie prone in the street; the driver, horrified, would emerge from the car, and Will would jump up and run away. Or the overcoat prank, wherein Will would stand just beyond the edge of a restaurant's street-facing window with an old overcoat, each sleeve stuffed with a heavy sweater, and toss the coat in a high steep arc so that it would plummet right down in front of horrified diners, looking for all the world like a falling body. I told them about our marathon session of prank calls, and the prank calls I heard later on the Morels' own answering machine.

Benji wondered aloud why Will might prank call his own house but had to withdraw the question, as the prosecution objected on grounds the judged sustained. Benji asked, "Have you known Will to deceive on any other occasion?"

"Yes," I said.

"Would you mind describing that occasion for the jury now?"

I looked down at Arthur, who looked steadily back, betraying nothing. I looked up to see Penelope watching me, too. Was she trying to communicate something to me with her eyes? If so, I couldn't tell. Then I looked over at the jury box and told them what Will had confessed to me. As I was telling it, however, I sensed several members recoil. They did not want to believe me. They wanted to believe Will. They wanted to believe that Arthur was guilty. And who could blame them? If what I was saying were true, then this whole trial was, as Benji had put it, a farce. A morbid farce.

The prosecutor, when she rose to question me, helped the jurors out. She gave them every reason to suspect my testimony. I was a bully, intimidating an eleven-year-old boy. Further, I was making a documentary about the accused, which spoke of my financial interest in securing his freedom. I was currently living with the accused in his parents' house. I was a longtime friend, had known the accused for fourteen years, which spoke of my emotional interest in securing his freedom. When she was done with me, the judge thanked me, and I stepped down on rubbery legs. On my way back to the witness room, I passed Doc, who gave me a wink.

When I returned, taking my seat next to Suriyaarachchi, Benji was at the defense table, scribbling on a yellow pad and whispering in Arthur's ear. The judge called the court back to order, and the jury returned. The bailiff escorted Arthur to the witness box and closed him in. The clerk asked Arthur to raise his right hand and swear that the testimony he was about to give would be the truth, the whole truth, and nothing but the truth, and Arthur did. Benji asked the court's indulgence to allow him to establish in unequivocal terms his feelings about his son. The judge allowed it, and so Benji asked him if he loved his son. Yes, Arthur said. Benji asked if he harbored any sexual feelings for the boy, if he'd ever sexually molested him, or if the book was a confession—and Arthur answered firmly no to these questions.

"Why then," Benji asked, "would you write such a thing?"

Arthur seemed annoyed to have been asked the question. And, as he started answering, it became clear why—why Benji's legal team didn't want me explaining it and why I'd been puzzling over it this past month and a half: the answers just didn't make any sense. If Arthur was able in his living room to conjure the rhetorical flair necessary to convince me, that advantage wasn't available to him under the cold glare of the overhead fluorescents and the dozen perplexed-looking jurors in this room. Here, it sounded like the rantings of a crazy person.

When Arthur was done, Benji took a seat at the defense table and murmured that he had no further questions.

"Mr. Morel," the prosecutor began, rising, "have you yourself ever been sexually molested?"

"Yes," Arthur said. "Of course."

The words hung in the air a moment like an epiphany. *Yes, of course.* I might be projecting a little when I report this, but there seemed to follow a kind of shocked silence in the courtroom. Even the prosecutor, who'd asked the question, seemed caught off guard by the answer. How was it that I never thought to ask? In Penelope's hours of relentless interrogation, that I bore witness to, how was it that she not once had thought to ask? At Thanksgiving, why hadn't the Wrights thought to ask? Had nobody asked? How could this be? The obviousness of his answer made it seem inconceivable. I craned to see Penelope's face but couldn't from where I was sitting.

Arthur went on. "In that place, it was inevitable. Except those I lived with wouldn't have thought of it in such moralistic terms. *Early sexual experience.* What could be more natural? Man is a sexual being, after all. Children are sexual beings. Read Freud, he'll tell you all about it."

"By whom?" The prosecutor was suddenly motioning to an assistant, scrawling notes. "Who molested you?"

Arthur offered a dismissive wave. "Oh, I can't remember. I've long ago stopped trying to figure it out. That mystery is locked away inside me somewhere, inaccessible. There were any number of candidates."

"Your father?"

"No, not him. It wasn't his — thing."

"Your mother?"

"No. I told you I don't remember."

"Then who?"

Something registered in his face. He said again that he didn't remember, but this time it was less convincing.

"Have you ever performed an act of child sexual abuse?"

"Yes," Arthur said. Now it was Benji's turn to begin scribbling furious notes, motioning to his assistant.

"Would you please describe the circumstances of this incident for the court?"

"Incidents," Arthur said. "Plural." He took a deep breath. And then another. "Okay," he said. "At school. The only formal school I'd known thus far in my life. A music school, on Saturdays. In practice rooms, this was where. Sometimes bathrooms. Okay. My first was a boy my own age. Eight, maybe nine. More than touching. The use of mouths and hands and I — enjoyed — the acts, the acts I performed, we performed together. I wanted more, more touching with mouths and hands. I didn't know him, he didn't know me. This place was different from a weekday school. One didn't know one's cohort. I didn't know his name. Where to look for him again. But I wanted — more." He took another deep breath. Another. "Okay. I found another boy, same age. My same age. Another practice room. This boy, too, was — willing, a willing participant." Deep breath. "Okay. I found many willing participants. It wasn't difficult." The prosecutor pressed Arthur to clarify, and he was forced to utter the words *penis* and *anus*, the words *stimulation* and *penetration*. "It was a virus, okay? I was spreading a virus throughout school. The virus of sexual knowledge. Learned at too young an age. I was set loose on the young boys at that school. It's such a — such a shameful business. Oh, God! Eight, nine, ten. Okay? I was there eight years. Eight years, dozens and dozens of children. Boys, I should say. Only boys. Girls were not the same. It wasn't that I didn't desire them. They were just — so much more complicated. They required talking to.

A code I didn't understand. Boys were always at the ready. Curious. Willing to perform."

"When did you stop," the prosecutor asked, "molesting other children?"

"Once I began to learn the language of girls. Sixteen. High school. Once I moved in with my brother. "

"In fact, you've never stopped, have you? You have been compelled to, despite your best efforts, continue this practice into adulthood — with your own son. Isn't that true?"

"No, absolutely not. You haven't been listening." But the prosecutor was done.

On redirect, Benji said gently, "Who was it, Arthur? It wasn't Dad. It wasn't Cyn."

"I don't remember."

"You remember, Arthur. I know you do. Just say it. This is your moment."

"No."

"A teacher. You played violin. Was it your violin teacher?"

His violin teacher. I remembered suddenly. His book. His *first* book. A boy molested by his coach, who comes to school one day with a shotgun and — I almost stood up and shouted.

Arthur's shotgun. Arthur's cadenza was his shotgun.

I looked at Arthur as if for the first time. Timid, afraid. Of himself. Of his urges. The advice of the school counselor in his book came back to me now, a character of Arthur's own imagination, dredged up to give its author the advice: *Abuse has to be dealt with, or it will eat you alive.* Was this what Arthur was doing with his sea of words? Wanting to explain it all away? Hoping a manifesto about art might unravel this troubling knot inside him?

Arthur's eyes were leaking. His nose was running, and his tongue touched nervously at the glistening tip of his wet mustache. He shook his head. He shook and shook and shook his head.

"You did this for Will," Benji said, "didn't you? You worried about your own history. You wanted inoculation from this virus, as you put it. You felt your hands were unclean. You felt the need to purify them. That's what this book is about, isn't it? Purification. A purification ritual."

"I deserve to go to jail," Arthur said finally. Then would say no more.

What had Arthur planned to do up on that stand? Was this it? The final stage in his catharsis? Or had the prosecutor thwarted, by her line of questions, some other thing he'd been planning? I'll never know.

# 17

# F I S T S

THE JURY, AFTER CLOSING ARGUMENTS and the judge's instructions about the task before them, took less than an hour with their deliberations. They asked to review a single piece of evidence — Will's statement — and none of the court transcripts. Amid the hasty reassembly of order in the court — many had assumed it would take days and were on their way downstairs when they were called back — the foreman handed the slip of paper to the judge who, after taking a moment with it, handed it to the clerk to read the verdict:

*Guilty on all charges.*

It came out later, once jury members began speaking to the press, that most thought Will's account was thoroughly credible and had been looking for some testimony to change that opinion but found most irrelevant, mine unconvincing, and Arthur's, ultimately, damning.

At sentencing, Arthur was given three years in prison. There was a public outcry over this, but the prosecution didn't press for more, and the judge thought it fair in the scheme of similar cases. Not long after the trial was over, ADA Joanna Brady resigned. In an interview she revealed her misgivings about the case. As Benji's law school volunteers had surmised, there had been conflicts. But not with Penelope — with Brady's superior. Will's story had become, with time, inconsistent. She had wanted to drop the case but had been pressured to see it through. She had been shaken by Arthur's testimony and seemed to understand what he was trying to do — atone for past transgressions by calling down on his head his own conviction — and grieved at the verdict condemning an innocent man.

Penelope convinced her father to drop the civil suit, and Arthur convinced Benji to withdraw the appeal and let him serve out his time. He turned down an offer to return home to put his affairs in order. "Everything is settled," he said. On January 16, 2000, he was transferred to Groveland Correctional Facility in Livingston County, New York.

In prison, Arthur learns fear — the battery-acid tingle in the gums, the muscles' blind surrender. He pisses himself twice that first day, enduring hours of chafing cold between his legs. He has never known fear like this. Animal, aboriginal fear. The emotion he thought he knew wasn't fear at all, it turns out — it was a neurotic tic, borne out of unlikely worst-case scenarios: a drowning, a plane crash, a nuclear holocaust. This new, raw emotion is borne out of the very real threats of the present moment. Violence, palpable and everywhere, coming for him.

He does not sleep. In the evening, after lights-out, there are brief periods of unconsciousness. Mostly it's a vigilant awareness of his roommate, who won't talk to him, won't even look at him, as though he does not exist — or rather no longer existed. This, he supposes, is the look one gives a man marked for death. Merely one in a string of doomed roommates. Why bother learning names? Or so go Arthur's thoughts in the night.

A blaring loudspeaker honk begins the day.

He'd read somewhere that he'd have a choice of work assignments and imagined choosing the prison library, where he'd find solace among books, the quietude, the soothing orderly stacks, inmates coming in to seek help he'd gladly offer, and in exchange the inmates would offer Arthur protection from harm.

Wishful thinking. He is escorted with several others to the cavernous kitchen, where they are given hairnets and aprons. The clanging of pans, the hissing of meat on the griddle, are especially jarring. He is entrusted with a dull paring knife, but the knife does not make him feel any less vulnerable; in fact, he feels more so with it in his hand among these beasts—inadvertently pointed in the wrong direction it might be misconstrued as a threat. Like he could threaten anyone! The number 5 is branded onto the small knife's hilt. A guard notes the number on a clipboard. Arthur watches an inmate, behind the guard's back, snap the tip off a food processor blade, then slip the broken-off piece into his mouth. Eyes on Arthur the whole time. *Shhhh,* finger to lips. Unlike his roommate, these other inmates never take their eyes off him. They track him in the manner of predators, grinning as though they, too, knew his fate.

It comes as he's toweling off after a shower. Sharp crack against the side of his head, zoomtilt of bathroom tile coming at him. The second crack against his cheek, someone's bare heel. Chips like eggshells on his tongue. He cries, *Help! Help!* There is a guard outside; he can see him watching through the small square window on the other side of the door. His mouth fills with salty warmth. The third crack he feels against his side, but this one isn't as bad as the other cracks. It's softer. Two men grinning above him. No: there's a third. They say nothing, save the grunts of their exertions and the sharp exhales as they kick and kick, each softer than the last, gentle taps through a thick protective blanket.

Numb, he rocks himself to sleep.

Arthur wakes in a sterile room with caged fluorescent lights. Smells of talc and iodine. The male nurse—a fat man with a beard—tends to Arthur angrily. Don't move, he says. You'll pop the sutures. In the mirror, the person who stares back at Arthur bears no resemblance to himself. The left half of his face is thick with plum-red welts. Hairy black stitches. Lips sphincter-swollen. Right eye squeezed shut by a heavy blood-sac eyelid.

Pain orbits his awareness like an impatient vulture.

On his way through the corridors, fewer people grin at him. They seem less interested, despite his freakish appearance. Even his roommate—a wiry black man named Kennedy—hazards a look in his direction when Arthur returns after his overnight in the prison hospital; he tosses a protein bar on Arthur's bunk.

Here, he says. The first words to come out of his mouth.

Arthur accepted visits from Doc and Cynthia who received—those first weeks of his incarceration—the brunt of Arthur's abject terror. We sat with them at the carriage house while Cynthia cried and Doc talked about their most recent visit.

Doc said, "He's harassed, they threaten his life, every day they threaten his life. He's in danger being in there. They've beaten him. I see the bruises."

"He doesn't understand the rules," Cynthia said. "There are so many rules. The official rules. The gang rules. The unspoken rules. And they contradict one another. How is he supposed to survive? And all that fencing, even in the open yard, fencing inside of fencing. I nearly fainted from the claustrophobia of it. After that first time up, I said never again. Doc, I said. Never again."

Doc said, "And then what happened?"

"I got his letter."

"Artie's never written to us before," Doc said. But he couldn't go on. He held out the letter, his eyes wide with trying not to cry, and I took the envelope addressed to *Mother and Father Morel* with the address of the carriage house. It bulged with several sheets, and when I went to remove them, Cynthia took it back.

"No, this one's for us. Just us." She smoothed the envelope down on her leg and said, "So now we visit every weekend. Every weekend until he's released."

"It's a promise," Doc said, finding his voice again.

The trial has done something to them. They seem more cautious, less brash with their opinions. She is sweet to him; he is gentle with her. They've taken to keeping the rolling front entrance closed at all times, entering and exiting out the back, and have left the vandalized door the way it is. Out of defiance? Or maybe as a reminder.

Our visit came later. The final leg of the bus ride up had us on a long lonely stretch of road, where the only other travelers appeared to be deliveries to and from the prison. The place, upon first approach, seemed to go on for miles. The tops of the high walls glittered magically with what turned out to be, upon closer inspection, razor wire. Guards with rifles in high towers. In the prison yard, heads turned to follow our passage. The bus deposited us at a massive steel door, itself dwarfed by a pair of fortress-sized doors next to it.

We were buzzed in, treated to impersonal courtesy by the guards as we signed forms, answered questions, stepped through metal detectors, and were wanded on our way to the visitation room, a large cafeteria without salad bars or steam counters, only long plastic tables with built in benches and prisoners waiting for company.

Arthur saw us first and waved us over. He offered a strong hug, the duration of a full breath. We sat. His head was shaved, along with his face. He wore a white T-shirt and green pants like hospital scrubs. His left eye was cupped with a bandage and, trailing from it, across the eyebrow, were parallel scratches that made me think *fork*.

"You're supposed to knock," he said. "When you get up from your meal, you knock. Not to do so is considered a disrespect to the other gentlemen at the table. I'm still getting the hang of it, as you can see." In this light self-deprecating manner, he revealed other areas of his body that bore the marks of lessons learned the hard way: a chipped incisor from using a "reserved" shower stall, an angry zipper of stitches at the back of his head from speaking directly to a man who turned out to be a high-ranking member of the Bloods, a hideous mottled green-and-blue mark on his abdomen from cutting in front of someone in line on Chicken Day. "That was a misunderstanding. I hadn't actually cut the line. But trying to explain that was the real mistake."

He said that in spite of all this, he felt fine—wonderful, in fact. "Not all the time, of course. But right now, sitting here with you?" He breathed deeply. "It feels nice to be able to breathe again." He had taken up meditating. He had started at the detention center during the trial and was making a daily practice of it in here. He was not alone. Many of his fellow prisoners meditated as well. The library was full of books on the subject. "I use the chapel. People think I'm atoning for my sins. I'm just trying to stay out of the way, watching my breath, listening to the song of the barbed wire when the wind blows through."

Arthur had changed since the trial, too, come out of himself—or maybe back into himself. Gone was the intellectualizing, the analyzing; he no longer seemed to be in need of figuring things out. It would be too glib to say he was content in such an environment, but he did seem that way. Relieved. Purged, perhaps, of those things that made him chase himself so relentlessly.

We talked about the documentary, our progress and plans for it, small talk mostly; he already knew these things from our regular phone conversations. Weeks ago we put in a request to shoot some footage in here, conduct an interview or two, but so far the request had gone ignored. Arthur gave us a name, someone who he thought might be able to help us—and then it was time to go.

Another hug, two breaths this time, stubbled chin pressed tight against my ear.

A last look through the small square window of the closed door frames Arthur alone at the table, smiling and waving.

Six months later and he was dead, having served out less than a third of his time. So it turned out that three years—outrageously lenient by the standards of some—was really a death sentence for Arthur. He was found by his cell mate sitting with the drawstring of his pants around his neck, tied to the top frame of their bunk, hand in pants. A murder made to look like autoerotic asphyxiation, as though he'd been done in by his own dangerous masturbatory urges. Indeed the report from the investigation lists his death as *accidental*.

Among his effects is a letter to me. It's a long letter. In it, he talks excitedly of a new book idea. It's not quite coherent, but it's clear he's inspired. An inmate, planning a prison break, ends up finding enlightenment from his cell mate, the Buddha — who convinces the man to abandon his escape and serve out his time. Arthur seems swept up in the spiritual texts he's been reading. There's a passage from the letter that I find particularly moving in light of the struggles in his life to find peace with himself — and the urgency with which he wants to impart this newfound wisdom to me:

*We get it in our heads, he writes, that the past is a real place. Which is supported of course by this culture of facsimile we're steeped in. Right now I'm looking at the postcard you sent me — I have it taped up in my cell — the forest landscape in winter, the tree boughs heavy with snow, the lake frozen over, the sun tiny and hard in the sky. Looking at it, I was struck. I thought: thousands of people look at this image every day. It's an Ansel Adams photograph. I looked it up — it belongs in more than two dozen public collections and appears, I am sure, in many books of Adams's work as well as any number of anthologies. On calendars and mugs and T-shirts. Thousands — millions — of copies out there. It's iconic. We look at that picture and think of the place as real. We've seen it so many times we feel we know it. And in a way, with the proliferation of copies, and each successive viewing, it becomes real — more than real, if such a thing were possible — burned into some cortex of the brain. It accumulates a kind of rhetorical power, convincing us of its truth, of its reality. But it's not real. It was a moment in time back in 1922. After Adams set up his camera and snapped the shutter, after he picked up his equipment and walked away, the landscape changed. The snow melted off the branches; the lake thawed. A brushfire came and leveled that entire stand of trees. A period of drought dried the lake. Where once there was a forest, there is now an open meadow that blooms with purple wildflowers in spring. Everything in life is like that. Constant change. Yet we walk around with a million images in our heads, like this Adams picture, stories of our past — remembered experience, anecdotes told to us about others, or about ourselves — the museum of our own lives. This is memory. And it's — all of it — false. Time has razed it. The first step in saving your life starts with accepting this, that all you can do is what you are doing right now, the only thing in your dominion. The past has already passed, and the future is fiction. Wake up! Look around you! The only honest thing in the universe is what is unfolding right now. Just this. Breathe in, breathe out. Can you see it? Hear it? Just what you can smell, what you can taste, what you can feel with the tips of your fingers. Right here. And then it's gone.*

Benji gets the call. He is listed as next of kin. He contacts Doc and Cynthia, and arrangements are made. A hearse comes for Arthur's body, and it is brought back to Fanelli Funeral Home on MacDougal Street, a fifteen-minute walk from the carriage house. Benji suggested having Arthur's body cremated and his ashes spread ceremonially—on his intake papers at the prison, Arthur had declared himself Buddhist—but Doc, lapsed Catholic, objects. I don't want him feeling that heat for all eternity. It's just not right.

Cynthia is impressed. I think that's the first time in thirty years I've seen you put your foot down.

When was the last time?

The time you insisted I go to a doctor when I was pregnant.

Arthur's body is embalmed, touched up, and set out in a casket, lid up, in a sitting room with green velvet walls. At the wake, a priest is on hand to hold a short mass, after which Doc again puts his foot down, convincing Cynthia—and the priest—to marry them in the eyes of God in the small, cluttered back office of the funeral home. Benji stands to one side, hands clasped in front, chin to chest, shaking his head. I'll never, as long as I live, understand the two of you.

Each of the four viewings is packed to overflowing with former students. Benji has brought Sarah and Dolores. Dolores tells Cynthia that she is sorry for her loss. They embrace. Cynthia and Sarah marvel at each other.

Look at us, Sarah says. Menopausal.

Old farts, Cynthia says, and they both laugh.

Doc says, Come to the burial tomorrow.

It's a small service at a cemetery in Scotch Plains, the Morel family plot. It has rained the night before, and this morning the sky is clear and still. The grass is shivering wet, and after a few steps everyone's shoes are soaked through. Cynthia, Doc, Benji, Dolores, Penelope, and Will. The priest who married them only days before sanctifies the burial, and Arthur's casket is laid in the ground. October 17, 2000, nearly a year to the day from the publication of *The Morels*. In the end it was almost like he got what he wanted, Benji says to Sarah as they consider the black-lacquered piano-lid top of the casket, rose strewn, dirt strewn, at the base of the pit. Eaten alive by his own creation.

I thought about Penelope a great deal after Arthur died. At the wake she was warm toward me, and for some months after I might have gotten it into my head to begin courting her. I passed by the bakery and had a cigarette with her on our bench. But I could immediately sense its wrongness, sitting there with her. It would have been unseemly, swooping in after Arthur's death like that, no matter how much time had passed, and no matter how I justified it. I would have been the tractor salesman Claudius in *Dead Hank's Boy*, who usurps the wife and throne of his junkyard-king brother. Which would have made Will Hamlet, I suppose.

Anyway, whatever had passed between us that fall, now, late summer, was gone. I asked after Will, made promises to visit. But never did.

Media coverage made up somewhat for our lack of footage at trial; we were able to splice in news segments and on-air debates, and by festival time that same year, we had a cut submitted that we were all very satisfied with. It made the final round at every one of the places we sent it to, jury selection at four, and first place at two others. A remarkable reversal from *Dead Hank's Boy*, which had been unanimously rejected. It made its debut at the Tribeca Film Festival, screened in the very same arthouse on Houston where I was still employed. Which would have made it a classic success story had it not happened on Friday, September 15, 2001.

A copy of the film, transferred from digital video to thirty-five-millimeter reversal—three hexagonal cans of spooled stock—limped its way around the circuit until a distributor finally took an interest and it was sold.

We waited for news of its release—theatrical or otherwise—placed weekly phone calls to our man at the company, who gave us no definitive answers. "Right now it's just not a movie anybody wants to see. Give it time, though. Tastes change."

We gave it time; tastes did change, but not for the flavor we had hoped. Even we had to admit, viewing it more than a year later, in the light of this new postapocalyptic dawn, it seemed morbid and naïve. Who had time to navel gaze anymore? There were more important things to worry about. For Christ's sake, Dan Rather had wept on *David Letterman*!

And so the film was swallowed up by that great oily shadow, along with everything else that year.

The Netflix-only release of *Who Is Arthur Morel?* in the spring of 2009 coincided with Will's twenty-first birthday, a day spent moping about his apartment in a hand cast. His roommates were out at a bar, no doubt failing miserably at their endeavor to pick up girls. They had better success, they said, on Craigslist, with the girls who actually wanted to have sex. Bars were a lark—picking up girls just an excuse to drown their sorrows at failing to pick up girls. Or something like that. On another day, Will might have joined them, but birthdays were for sitting dejectedly alone in one's room. His roommates did not know it was his birthday—Will had not told them. Will tells most people very little of himself, a habit that began ten years ago, during the scorched earth period of his life.

After the trial, the situation at school quickly grew untenable. His mother cupped his face with her cool hands as she dropped him off his first day back late January and told him to expect things to be rough for a little while, that he was kind of a celebrity now and that if other kids teased him it only meant that they were jealous—to ignore them, or beat the shit out of them, whatever worked best. But he was unprepared for just how different things would be. He *was* a celebrity. Every head turned as he walked the halls, trying in his nervousness not to slip and fall on the glassy high-polished linoleum; every head turned as he traveled the stairwells with their too-loud echoes; every head turned as he entered his classroom to take his seat. A celebrity—but not celebrated. It was whispering at first. He would turn to see who was whispering to find two or three or four heads together, eyes fixed on him. Then it was the anonymous shout. *Faggot!* That was a common one. *Cocksucka!* That was another. Or *Daddy's Dick!?* Shouted in the manner of a furious drill sergeant. Between classes or in the recess yard or at the large exit doors—a clarion call among the anonymous swell of the throng, a call that would focus attention on Will, sending through those crowded around him a shiver of malicious glee.

From anonymous shouting to out-and-out jeering. This took less than a week. Once the thrill of the tease was on, it was a tenacious pack of wild dogs, its sheer relentlessness making it difficult most days to breathe. There wasn't a moment when he wasn't being singled out or ridiculed. In the cafeteria, he'd pass row upon row of boys with bananas protruding from open flies. *Touch it!* They'd gleefully scream. Even the girls did this. At recess they made up terrible rhymes to punctuate their jumping and skipping and bouncing of balls. Even in class, pranks were waiting for him—great glistening wads of gum on his seat or some terrible phrase scrawled on his desk or in his textbooks slips of paper that contained terrible pictures just waiting for him to discover. He had to sit up front every day and stare directly at the teacher. Turn his head in any other direction, and there was someone waiting to mouth some terrible, frightening word.

This was the good school, the one his parents brought him to after they moved into the new apartment, the one where the kids were supposed to be kinder, more like himself. There was nobody like him here.

His first assault happened in a toilet stall. Two older boys, impossibly tall. *Take it,* said one, brandishing a ripe banana at crotch level. *Go on, you know you want it.* When Will refused, the boy yanked him by his shirt collar down to his knees while the other one tittered. *Gobble gobble!* He shoved the banana into Will's face, its slime smearing his cheeks and teeth and plugging up both nostrils. Other assaults followed. After a class that was filing out teacher first, Will brought up the rear to find several boys behind him. The one at Will's side shoulder-checked him into the open coat closet, where he was smothered with down jackets and piled upon by knees and elbows until he could no longer breathe and passed out. After that, Will kept to the thick of a crowd or near an adult, honing his avoidance instinct, but somehow, no matter how hard he tried, he'd end up cornered in a stairwell or behind a door or in a hallway's dead end. Not only the older ones but kids his own age, kids who before January he might have named among his friends.

So he fought back. He punched and kicked and clawed and bit down hard, putting the full force of his jaw into it, until he heard that sweet cry of agony, until he tasted blood. *Crazy fuck!* A boy in the stairwell, threatening Will with a stubby screwdriver: Will shoved the boy down the stairs, running after him, fists clenched. A trio outside school, encircling: Will throws himself full tilt at one, wrestles and straddles the surprised boy, and with a fistful of hair drives the boy's head into the sidewalk. There was no more Fox Mulder, no more Nintendo or Jerky Boys or comic books. Those days—only weeks in the past—were long gone now, the myths of a sweet and simple golden age. Now it was Twisted Metal and Grand Theft Auto. Games wherein he was invited to drag people out of their cars at gunpoint and barrel through crowded inter-sections. For fun, he lumbered through an open-air café. Patrons leaped out of the way; the vehicle bumped and lurched over the crunch of bodies. Bloody tire tracks ribboned outward in the rear-view. At the edge of a park, he got out of the car and walked pur-posely to the most peopled section he could find and, withdrawing his pistol—its beastly heft a little slippery in his palm—and fulfill-ing no particular goal, open-fired on as many innocent people as he could before the police surrounded him and shot him blissfully dead.

His father's death did nothing to abate the onslaught at school. Yet now Will welcomed the blows, encouraged them even. He had killed his father, and now he was paying the price. And yet he still hated his father. His father was as much to blame for all of this as he. So, as Will was absorbing the blows meant to atone for his father's death, Will was also striking out with his own fists against his attackers, and it was his father's nose, his father's lip, his father's teeth, Will's knuckles crunched against—his father's groin his knee connected with.

Will's mother packed them up and moved them down to Vir-ginia, enrolled him at Annandale Middle School, her own alma mater. She told him he wouldn't have to worry, nobody would know his father's name—down here, kids didn't read books. They played soccer and hung out behind strip-mall convenience stores to complain about how bored they were. But within months, they found him out, and Will was forced to endure a similar isolation. Less violent this time around, more insidious. While engaged in a class discussion, the teacher uttered the phrase *a father's love*, and from the back of the room someone said, "Willy knows about a father's love." Several students laughed. Then someone else, "Tell us what a father's love feels like, Willy." The teacher, not in on the joke, stood there perplexed. Or copies of his father's book would wind up in his backpack, or in his locker. *These kids didn't read.* Ha! The enemy here was unseen—nowhere and everywhere—people he thought were friends would turn on a dime in front of others to offer a cutting remark at his expense. They would provoke Will into using his fists (and elbows and teeth) to fight back and then turn things around so that Will was the one in trouble. He was a caged animal at Annandale Middle School, snarling and snapping at cruel, ceaselessly prodding fingers.

This time, when Will's mother packed up and moved them yet

again, back to New York City, she enrolled him under her maiden name. Will would be Wright now. Will Wright. He liked the ring, its double-barreledness, much better than Morel, an edible mold that flourished in dark places.

It was at this point, during his first year of high school, that Will learned the art of keeping his mouth shut. He sat at the back of the class and never — not once in four years — raised his hand. No shortage of fellow freshmen those first weeks of school, wanting to strike up friendships with Will Wright, were turned away. When kids asked Will about himself, he answered vaguely or not at all or made stuff up. He was from Virginia and would be heading back there as soon as his father returned from fighting the Taliban. He was an exchange student, originally from northern Quebec; his parents came from a long line of trappers and only spoke French. By the end of the following semester, kids stopped caring who he was or wasn't. And Will tried to keep it that way, permanent firewall turned on.

Yet his fists still couldn't seem to help themselves. They continued fighting a war that was over. An off-the-cuff remark, even in the most innocuous context, uttered sweetly even, were it to contain a certain key word — *jerkoff*, for instance, or *faggot* or sometimes the word *daddy* — and the fists would let fly. He was no longer in control of them. His body would leap out ahead of him to connect with that word, to beat it from existence. No matter the size or gender of the speaker. His fists were especially sensitive to the word *morel*, on whichever syllable the accent fell. All friendships in high school were tenuous, provisional — and as soon as they got a load of Will's fists, bonds were severed for good. By junior year he'd been labeled by most as certifiably loco and given a wide berth.

Teachers, however, adored Will. Whereas other students sleepwalked through assignments — scrawled onto a sheet of loose-leaf paper in the hallway ten minutes before class — and bloated their essays to bursting with filler phrases, letting platitudes and clichés do their thinking for them, a generation of texters uninterested in the distinction between *their* and *they're*, *its* and *it's*, *whose* and *who's*, Will was different. He was an earnest and thoughtful student. He was impressively well read — as a loner and an only child Will was an avid reader of books — and had a knack with words. Will's homework assignments were little jewels laser printed on high-quality paper stock — focused, packed with vivid examples, little jolts of unusual vocabulary, fresh turns of phrase, language well-mastered. Other students spent their time before and after class begging for extensions on late work or arguing over a grade. Will did neither. Always on the day it was due, never a word of complaint. Other students, after glancing at the circled grade at the top of the page, tossed the returned assignments into the trash bin as they exited class; Will pored over his graded papers at his desk, carefully considering each red mark, frowning and nodding, the last to leave the room.

Women teachers were especially fond of Will. It was the black hair, the black eyes, and the way those eyes burned when he was called on to speak. The rough hands that turned in and accepted back assignments, the boxer's broken nose, the broad shoulders hunched at his desk — a man already, at the age of sixteen. They knew who his father was, who he was. In break rooms, over burned coffee, they swooned over his furious soul, but to him they said nothing. They were the keepers of his talent. They shepherded him through the college application process, test preparations, and personal statements and transcripts and interviews. They celebrated those that accepted him and cursed those that didn't. They hugged him tearfully at graduation and sent him on his way.

He wasn't going far; in fact, he wasn't even leaving the island of Manhattan. Will emerged from the Downtown Lexington Avenue local on Sixty-Eighth Street, passing that hulking black trapezoid, to enter the North Building of Hunter College on August 28, 2007, for his first day of class. That year he lived at home, commuting from their one bedroom in Washington Heights. The bedroom was Will's; his mother had insisted on it. For the past four years she'd made hers the living room, sleeping on the foldout couch which she meticulously put away every morning before Will awoke, aware of his guilt at these sleeping arrangements. Sure that he'd have vacated to some midwestern state by now, she was thrilled to have him still here, at least for the time being, to have been granted a stay from the empty nest.

During his commutes, on the occasions when the subway's gentle rocking set him to thinking back, age eleven, age twelve, he thought of the phrase *scorched earth*. In high school he had learned the term while studying the Vietnam conflict. The US military deployed a *scorched earth* policy there, sprayed millions of acres of cropland during Operation Trail Dust, its herbicidal warfare program, a strategy designed to expose enemy hideouts and deny food and shelter to the Vietcong. Which it did, though it also poisoned friendlies on the ground as well as the ones doing the spraying. It was this way with his father, too, with the war he fought within himself and the methods he deployed to fight that war. He might have destroyed whatever demons he'd been fighting, but he also poisoned those who stood beside him and, in the end, himself. That year, the year of the millennium, had been the year of scorched earth.

The firewall remained on, into his new adulthood. Back then it had been necessary, but now it served no purpose. He liked people, despite appearances to the contrary, and made friends easily here. He found he could have friends and still give away nothing of himself, as most other kids his age preferred to talk about themselves anyway. In college, he developed the art of listening. His friends talked; he listened. He found it was still possible to develop intimacy this way. He didn't have to say a word. Girls for some reason enjoyed the way he demurred to their questions. They reveled in the vague answers he gave about his past. They itched to know more, to peel back the layers. But to girls, too, he gave nothing away.

His fists, for the most part, had given up the fight. He redirected their energy, putting them to work now defending friends at drunken bar brawls or getting himself out of the odd late-night scrape. He'd once even thwarted a rape-in-progress. The old triggers rarely sent them flying anymore. It had been during his senior year of high school when they last came out. For some reason, the turn of phrase *sucking daddy's dick* was in fashion that year — as in "I've been popping ollies a long time, bro — longer than you been *suckin' on your daddy's dick.*" It was meant to be humorous, a play on *mommy's tit*, but Will's fists hadn't found it funny. So, three years ago.

And then again last week.

Will had declared his major early, end of first year — history, with a minor in education. He spent most of those first two getting the tough pills down — broad surveys and pedagogical theory — but this semester, fall of the third year, he allowed himself an indulgence: Fundamentals of Imaginative Writing I. A clear cool lake of spring water in this desert of academia. They wrote poems and short prose pieces. His teacher was a man who seemed not much older than himself — energetic, filled with hope for all of them as future wordsmiths. He put up on the overhead a line, *She wished this day had never come,* and told them to take it from there. Or had them pair off on a sonnet, trading couplets. He passed around a photograph of a man looking pensively out a window and then pulled out a small ragged teddy bear and put it on the desk. "Connect these dots," he said, and set them to work. He praised Will's writing, often making an example of it, which delighted Will, but also embarrassed him. He gave Will a list of authors, none of whom had Will ever read: Auster, Banks, Johnson, Stone. Muscular names. He brought in handouts from his graduate seminar for Will and gave him the latest copy of the literary journal he edited, hot off the presses. They talked together long after class was dismissed, his teacher sitting on the corner of the desk, Will cradling his textbooks as he stood, until an evening instructor kicked them both out.

During one of these after-class sessions, his teacher pulled a book from his laptop bag. Will had done his best these many years to avoid this book, successfully, too, since coming back to New York after his time in Virginia. The hardcover edition of *The Morels*, because of its notoriety, had received that year several additional printings past its initial run of five thousand; and a major publisher had taken a gamble on its paperback rights. But by the time Will hit high school, *The Morels* had long since disappeared from the remainder bins. Just to be safe, though, when browsing for something to read, Will avoided the *M*'s entirely, and steered clear of used bookstores. Brandishing this book now, his teacher said, "You're Will Morel."

"No," Will said, looking down, avoiding his teacher's eye, holding his hand up as if to ward off the book, "You've got—I'm not him."

"It's okay," his teacher said, his voice reassuring, not at all picking up on the cues that Will did not want to talk about this or reminisce about his father, not seeing Will's eyes go black and his hands become fists, pushing on about what a life-changing book this was for him, one of those happy few, like *Naked Lunch* or Michaels's *Sylvia*, despite what some would say, it could almost be argued— and then he was on the floor cupping a blood-gushing nose.

At the hearing, the dean recommended expulsion, but interestingly his teacher—nostrils plugged with gauze, eye hollows purpled—pleaded for Will's future at the college. A deal was struck. Will was to be suspended from college for the remainder of the semester, receiving an incomplete in whatever courses he was currently taking. He would lose his scholarship, unfortunately, nothing could be done about that; and when he returned in the fall, he would do so on academic probation. In the meantime, he was to see a college-appointed social worker every week and accept the young writer-professor as his academic adviser.

Will accepted these terms with thanks.

Which is how he finds himself moping about in a hand splint on his twenty-first birthday, the day of his encounter with the Netflix exclusive *Who Is Arthur Morel?*

Ironically, this punch landed Will the first true friend of his adult life. Henry Owen Lawrence. When Will asked if he could call his teacher by his first name, he said, "I've got three. You can take your pick." Will apologized for breaking Henry's nose, which was when Henry told Will about the mythos of the pugilist scholar, dating back to Plato. He related the story of Rick Bass, who once politely declined to have his nose broken by George Plimpton, editor of the *Paris Review.* Plimpton explained his unusual offer. You see, he'd had his nose broken in a boxing ring by a writer who had *his* nose broken by Ernest Hemingway. "A prestigious line of broken noses," Will said. "I would have taken him up on it."

Henry came by Will's apartment with coffee most mornings. He lived nearby, and stopped over on his way to work. He was trying to encourage Will to take advantage of the daylight hours. Some theory involving the word *biofeedback* that Will did not care to understand. Will had always been a night owl and couldn't see himself changing anytime soon. But he was grateful for the company—and the coffee—so played along.

"Listen, Achilles," Henry said one day. "You've got to get ahold of that rage of yours. It will destroy you if you don't." (The social worker Will had been seeing, a wiry and tenacious older woman, was forcing Will to dredge up all sorts of muck, which darkened his thoughts and made him extremely irritable.) "And you know where that journey begins and ends, don't you?"

"Come on," Will said.

"I'm serious."

"I'll always hate him—for writing it, for making me the instrument of his death. I'm going to feel this way for the rest of my life."

"That's a choice you're making."

Will took a sip of scalding coffee and winced. "There's no way out of it."

"There is a way."

"How?"

"I'll tell you but you won't like it." Henry pulled a bagel out of the paper bag next him and tore it in half.

"I can't forgive him," Will said.

"And yourself."

"How do I do that? Tell me."

"You need to get to know him first."

"He's dead."

"So?"

"So how do I get to know a dead man?"

Henry, mouth full of bagel, said, "Use your imagination."

Had the documentary not been available to stream instantly, Will might never have seen it. In all likelihood, by the time it arrived in the mail Will would have changed his mind, and the disc would have foundered on top of the television until one of his roommates sent it back. But it is available, so with Henry's words fresh in his ears, Will is emboldened to hit PLAY.

His reaction is not what he would have expected. For the first half of the movie, the back of his throat constricts as though he needs to retch, and he keeps a bucket nearby just in case. But after the movie is over, he finds himself—what's the word? Excited? His hands are trembling. He touches his palm to his chest and feels the knocking. Or maybe nervous. His father, just like that, on his laptop, after ten long years: Adam's apple bobbing under razor-burned skin, enormous hands that he always seems trying to get rid of, that he hides under his armpits or behind his back. So ill at ease with himself. Strange. That's not how he remembered the man at all. In the documentary, playing over a voiceover inter-view, still images of his father in the courtroom pan by, with his orange jumpsuit and his full beard. So thin! He recognizes in those eyes a fellow caged animal.

The collar of Will's T-shirt is wet. He touches his cheeks, and they, too, are wet. Has he been crying?

He watches it twice, and a third time, invites Henry over, and they watch it together.

They IMDB the filmmakers. "I knew these guys," Will says. "They lived down the hall from us. Those two used to babysit me!"

Spring semester his first year, Will had taken a class called Research Methods. One of the assignments had been to craft a portrait of someone no longer living, putting to use the techniques they'd learned in the course. Examining relics, interviewing direct and indirect eyewitnesses, synthesizing primary and secondary sources, conducting statistical inference and arguments from analogy. Whatever it took to arrive at an accurate narrative account of some key part of the person's life and a fuller understanding of his or her daily routines. The best were invited to read theirs to the class. Will found particularly moving a young woman's account of her great-grandmother of Japanese descent who, under Executive Order 9066 by Franklin Roosevelt, had spent a formative part of her childhood at the Minidoka War Relocation Center in Jerome County, Idaho. The student had crafted the story of her great-grandmother's life on the compound in the first person, which breathed a kind of magical life into this otherwise dry assignment.

It is of this account Will thinks as he starts out on his project. A portrait of his father in the first person. What better way to get to know a man than to see through his eyes, walk in his shoes. He will dust off the old textbook — if he hasn't sold it off already — and get to work. Henry tells him, "You do this right and you'll have the catharsis it took your father a lifetime to achieve."

From his mother, relics. As they'd never formally divorced, she had inherited the bulk of her husband's effects. In the course of three major moves, she has divested herself of much of it, but what remains — in two large plastic bins — she unearths from the back of a closet. Clothing neatly folded. Random photographs: a woman passed out, a dog and a cat, a guy smiling with a crying kid, several lurid close-ups of bruises and busted lips. An old musical score. A stack of letters addressed to the prison with various return addresses. Old journals and manuscripts. Two books, one by Rushdie and a slim volume in French. He sits with his mother at the kitchen table in her apartment sorting through it all. She says, "Do you remember what you said on your first trip out to see him?"

Will hadn't wanted to go. He was terrified at what might happen. He wept on the ride up. His mother said he could stay in the car with his grandparents, but she said it in a way that made him ashamed of even considering the option, so he went in. He hardly recognized his father. He was bald, and his eye was full of blood. Will could barely look. But he had never in his life seen his father so happy to see him. He swept Will up in his arms and pressed him close, and he smelled like shaving cream. He sat and listened to his parents talk. His father told his mother about the people that he knew here, and his mother told him about her life, and they talked about Will, even though he was sitting right there. By the end of the visit, they were touching hands across the table. When they said good-bye he hugged his father and whispered in his ear, I'm sorry. His father whispered back, I'm sorry, too. Will wept, hard, heaving for breath, and wouldn't take his mother's hand. In the car he made a promise.

"I promised to visit him every weekend," Will says.

"I should have kept you to it."

"It wouldn't have made any difference. I was already at school, fighting for my life."

It occurs to Will that this project, playing the role of his own father, will require him to complete an Oedipal journey he's been on for the past ten years. To become his mother's husband, her lover. Setting the lid on the box now, he regards her across the table. She is still beautiful. Age has hollowed her out some, given her face a new angularity. Her hair is long, which she keeps braided most days in a single black satin rope down her back. In her late thirties, she is younger than the parents of many kids he grew up with. He introduced her to one of his roommates some weeks back who went flush at the meeting. "That's your *mother*?"

Will says, "You don't have to sacrifice your life, too, you know. You deserve to be happy."

"I am happy."

"When was the last time you were on a date?"

"Ugh, I thought we were talking about happiness."

"You should find someone."

"You should get this stuff out of my house. It'll finally free up enough space in that closet to hang my dresses."

From the documentary, eyewitnesses. He orders the DVD online; when it arrives, he does the painstaking work of transcribing his father's words, in a sense trying to learn his father through the very fingertips. He contacts the filmmakers. Two have moved out to Los Angeles. The third manages a movie theater in Soho. Will arranges the meeting. On the phone, the man seemed overjoyed to hear from him, eager for a reunion. And yet, standing in the large atrium of the movie theater, the man does not recognize Will, and Will has to wave him over.

They sit at one of the cast-iron café tables. "This place is going out of business," he says, "can you believe it? After twenty-one years, it's the end of an era. There just aren't enough of these kinds of movies made anymore to sustain a box office for them. At least not in the US. And what's an arthouse without art? For all of your father's talk, that was one thing he got right. We live in a post-art world. The promise that Susan Sontag saw in film—it's lost. We just don't have the attention span for cinematic art. Two hours squirming in your seat, struggling with something you don't understand? It's too much for most people."

They talk about their time together a decade ago. Halloween, Thanksgiving, the prank-call marathon. The man carefully sidesteps Will's lie—the confrontation in the court's bathroom, the man's own testimony during the trial—which Will is grateful for. Will explains his project. He pulls out a voice recorder and asks if it would be okay to record what they talk about, and with the man's consent Will presses RECORD. Will asks how he knew his father, and the man describes their first meeting in the library at Morningside Conservatory many years ago, the gangly teenager with floppy hair penciling in notes on a piece of staff paper. As it turns out this man and Will's father have much in common, both native Manhattanites born into the arts. He talks some about his own history—his own mother and father, his pursuits and dreams, his misadventures in love. He talks about the profound effect Will's father had on him.

"I was very impressed by your father, Will. I wanted his passion, his drive. This was a time in my life when I was looking for the Answer, capital *A*, and your father seemed to have it — or at the very least was in hot pursuit of it — and so I followed him to the end of his road. He found the answer, I think. Ironic that it turned out to be one I already had. In An, in Viktoria, in Penelope."

"My mother."

"I was very taken with your mother. In the end, that's all I was really looking for. As you know, being an only child can be a lonely business, and back then I thought I needed a packed movie theater of people, a national audience, to end the loneliness. But I didn't need an audience. I needed a wife. A son. A family." He had declined the invitation of his two friends to come out to Hollywood in search of fame and fortune. He no longer wanted that. What he wanted he'd lucked into some months after his promotion to manager seven years ago. She was his first hire. When the weekend manager quit, he pushed for her promotion just so that he could ask her out and not be in danger of workplace harassment. She now manages their sister theater on the Upper East Side. They were married in 2004, and she has borne him two beautiful children, a boy and a girl, age two and age five. He shows Will the pictures. His wife is now pregnant with their third.

Will asks about his father, for him to relate anything that might shed light on the kind of man he'd been. "I used to think it was shamelessness, with your father. And I mean that quite literally. You know those people, missing that part of their brain that allows them to sense pain? They only know that they've burned themselves after they smell flesh cooking on the stove coils. That your father literally didn't have the capacity for shame is what I mean. But that day up there on the stand I realized — he's humiliated! This man is nothing *but* shame. Has been this whole time, his whole life maybe. To know this and then to look back on those things he did publicly, that he made public. Shocking things, humiliating

THE MOREL

things. This took courage to do. Your father was brave, Will. And he loved you a great deal. You have to believe that. And as strange as this may sound, those shocking and humiliating things? He wrote those things to protect you. He was trying to protect you from himself, the only way he knew how."

At their parting, they hug. The man, Will's one-time babysitter, walks him down the front steps of the theater and wishes him luck with his project. They make plans to speak again.

From here, Will heads south, to the address he's been given. The man told Will that after Doc's passing two years ago, Cynthia had left to be with relatives back in New Jersey and the carriage house was sold, but Will wants to see for himself.

It is, unsurprisingly, a boutique clothing shop now, like every other shop in the neighborhood. Its exterior is meticulously restored and barely recognizable but for the distinctive proscenium arch. This is now fitted with a single piece of plate glass and serves as a window display. Faceless mannequins wearing red cotton dresses and black leggings assume poses of impatience: hand on hip, arms folded. The entrance is through the side door. Will steps inside. It's freezing. The place is gutted raw and dimly lit. The hip-hop beat suggests a fancy cocktail lounge. There isn't a single person working here who's a day older than Will. He doesn't bother to ask any questions; it's clear nobody here knows anything. He takes a few pictures with his phone and leaves.

He has enough to go on, or at least enough to start with. So at home, alone in his room, he begins:

*I was born on November 29, 1968, to Cynthia Bonjorni and Arthur "Doc" Morel Senior. I lived on Greene Street and West Broadway in New York City.* In this vein he writes several pages. A few hours later, though, he stops, frustrated. Even though the facts are right, none of the sentences feels authentic. The costume does not fit. This much is clear, and no amount of aping around in it will help him accomplish what he has set out to do. And besides, he can't see his father while he's walking around inside his suit. He needs to be able to see the man.

So. Forget the first-person father. He tries again, like this:

*The earliest memory I have of my father is from the age of four. He has me by the hand and we are heading up the front walk of our apartment building in Queens.* But soon enough, Will finds himself deep into the woods of his own life, his father lost somewhere along the trail.

On a blank index card, in felt pen, Will writes, *Who is Arthur Morel?* and tacks it onto the corkboard above his writing desk, next to the picture Henry brought over earlier that week: lush Vietnamese foliage, crowded village in the background. A recent photo, Henry explained, of a place that had been razed in the late sixties by Agent Orange. "Given time," Henry said, "even scorched earth recovers."

Will takes a step back. He spends the rest of the evening cleaning his room. He organizes his books on the small homemade bookshelf by his closet. With a notepad and pen at his side, he sits up in bed listening through earphones to the interview with his former babysitter, transcribing a few of the more salient moments. Then he turns off the light and goes to bed.

The next morning, with a fresh cup of coffee, he begins again. Henry is right. The mornings are much better for thinking. His head feels like a clear autumn day. He looks through his notes from the night before. Most of it is in shorthand, barely legible, but among the scrawl is a sentence that calls out to him:

*The editor I was to fire worked out of his one bedroom in Herald Square.* Promising, he thinks, more promising at least than last night's efforts.

Will fires up his laptop and types out the line into a blank document, and when he does this, a window opens. There is something about the point of view, through the eyes of the man whose life has run parallel to his father's, eliding at key moments. Who talked about his father with great admiration, the first man to ever describe his father to him in fatherly terms, as courageous, protective. This is who should tell the story: his father's only friend.

Maybe, just maybe, he can show Will the way.

# Acknowledgments

A heartfelt thanks to Bob Dolan, first and foremost, for penning *The Dead Guy's Son* and for the ensuing adventures in filmmaking that it inspired.

Thanks to Mark Doten, whose sharp eye and editorial telepathy transformed this manuscript into the novel I'd been hoping for.

And Bronwen Hruska, along with the rest of the Soho team for their outright enthusiasm, and for taking a chance on this book.

Thanks to Douglas Stewart, whose faith in my abilities is a bottomless well.

To John Bean, for helping me figure it all out.

Good friends Leigh Anderson, Zoe Finkel, Jason Grunebaum, and Melissa Kirsch: Thank you for your valuable feedback on a messy first draft. And thanks to other readers along the way for their time and kind words: Jami Attenberg, David Gordon, T Cooper, Margarita Shalina, Michael Seidenberg and Cale Hand.

Thank you to Columbia University mentors Victoria Redel

ing praise. Also to Sigrid Nunez, Thomas Beller, Sam Lipsyte, and Jessica Hagedorn, other mentors whose teaching has been invaluable.

To the Owen Summer Residence Fellowship, for providing me with an environment perfectly suited to writing a book.

And, of course, a round of thanks to the Tracys: Catherine, Arnold, Claudia, Sam, Dee, Peter, Alec, Alexandra, and Aunt Joan Carvo. I couldn't ask for a more supportive and encouraging group of in-laws.